Turn up the heat with
Julie Ann Walker's Black Knights Inc.

Praise for *USA Today* bestseller *Wild Ride*

"Thrilling suspense... Walker's fans will love this, as will readers of Maya Banks's KGI, Cindy Girard's Black Ops, Inc., and Laura Kaye's Hard Ink series."

—*Booklist* Starred Review

"This razor-sharp, sensual, and intriguing tale will get hearts pounding."

—*Publishers Weekly* Starred Review

"High-octane romantic suspense with heart-pounding intrigue and a heart-twisting love story."

—*Kirkus Reviews* Starred Review

"Black Knights fans, rejoice! After much anticipation, we finally get Ozzie's story, and it' worth the wait."

—*R_____* 5 Stars

"Sizzling suspense _____ _____ _____ Ann Walker's Black _____ _____ _____ _____ itching to get their hand _____ _____ new readers are sure to fall for him _____"

—*Bookish*

"Very entertaining...the next great story in the BKI series...the story we have been waiting for."

—*Fresh Fiction*

Also by Julie Ann Walker

Black Knights Inc.

Hell on Wheels

In Rides Trouble

Rev It Up

Thrill Ride

Born Wild

Hell for Leather

Full Throttle

Too Hard to Handle

Wild Ride

Fuel for Fire

Hot Pursuit

The Deep Six

Hell or High Water

Devil and the Deep

BUILT TO

A BLACK KNIGHTS INC. NOVEL

LAST

JULIE ANN
WALKER

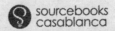
sourcebooks
casablanca

Published by Sourcebooks Casablanca, an imprint of Sourcebooks, Inc.
P.O. Box 4410, Naperville, Illinois 60567-4410
(630) 961-3900
Fax: (630) 961-2168
sourcebooks.com

Printed and bound in the United States of America.
OPM 10 9 8 7 6 5 4 3 2 1

To those who try to make the world a better place in small ways and large, this one's for you.

And to everyone at Sourcebooks who has worked to make BKI the best it can be…huzzah!

*Let us go forth with fear and courage
and rage to save the world.*

—Grace Paley

Prologue

Grafton Manor
St. Ives, England
Two weeks ago…

"Everyone calls me Angel."

The stranger's voice was raspy and deep. Quiet. But backed up by a sharp edge of steel.

When he spoke those four simple words, a feeling of doom slipped through Sonya Butler's veins. She'd just met him, and yet she could sense the menace surrounding him. It permeated the air in the library until her lungs burned with it. Mr. Tall, Dark, and Dangerous.

Jamin Agassi, a.k.a. "Angel," was not a man to mess with.

Which made the fact that he sat across from Lord Grafton, her boss and the undisputed king of the underworld, that much more terrifying.

"Angel, you say?" Grafton steepled his fingers under his goateed chin. His eyes were beady and black. Sonya sometimes thought they looked dead, but right then, they sparked with excitement.

Grafton had something on Angel.

Her feeling of doom increased tenfold.

Sitting forward in his leather chair, Grafton thumbed on the tablet lying atop his desk. He read the document glowing on the screen with deliberate intent, almost as if he were slow on the uptake. Sonya knew better. It was all a ruse.

Like a cat with a mouse, Grafton played a chilling game. He hadn't built and maintained the largest crime syndicate the planet had ever seen by missing any IQ points. In fact, in the six months she'd been his girl Friday, she'd come to realize he was quite possibly the most duplicitous man she'd ever known.

And definitely the most ruthless.

Case in point...

"But according to my sources"—Grafton eyed Angel—"your real name is Majid Abass." The spark in Grafton's eyes turned positively incandescent. Next would come the part he loved best. The *gotcha*. "Or maybe you're more accustomed to your nickname? Should I call you the Prince of Shadows?"

To contain her gasp, Sonya bit the inside of her cheek. Her eyes raked over the stranger in disbelief. The name Majid Abass hadn't rung any bells. Prince of Shadows set all of them clanging.

No, she thought. *He can't be. No one has seen or heard from the Prince of Shadows since the explosion in Tehran.*

Standing beside Grafton's desk like the good little lackey she was, she closely watched Angel's reaction. Or should she say *non*-reaction? He was so still he could have been a picture, betraying nothing of what he was thinking, what he was feeling.

"Everyone calls me Angel." His scratchy tone was unchanged. His eyes as black as pitch and...not dead-looking. Not like Grafton's. They were simply expressionless.

Grafton laughed at Angel's imitation of a broken record. It was a dry, snapping sound reminiscent of heavy boots stomping atop brittle bones.

"Come now," Grafton scolded. "You can drop the ruse. I know all about you." He swiped through documents on his tablet until he found the one he wanted. Holding the device up, he read in his urbane English accent, "Majid Abass, raised in Tehran. No brothers or sisters. Parents dead. You attended university on scholarship, where you studied nuclear engineering. It was there the Iranian government recruited you into their ranks. They wanted your help in their clandestine efforts to build a bomb. *The* bomb." Grafton set down the tablet. "Any of this sound familiar?"

For what seemed an eternity, Angel and Grafton had themselves an old-fashioned staring contest. Dead eyes drilling into inscrutable ones.

The strain in the air was palpable. It took every ounce of willpower Sonya possessed not to fidget. After fretting with the button on her blouse, adjusting it just so, she linked her hands behind her back. Squeezing her fingers together, she pushed the tension in her shoulders down into her palms where it could remain hidden.

Five seconds became fifteen. Fifteen stretched into thirty. She didn't dare breathe. Or scratch her nose — which, proving the universe was a twisted piece of *Scheisse*, had begun itching.

To her surprise, Grafton was the first to look away. He glanced at the tablet on his desk and continued to paraphrase the information on the screen. "But instead of helping your motherland become a nuclear power, you fell in with the Israeli Mossad, Iran's sworn enemy."

At mention of Israel's spy organization, she winced. Luckily, neither Grafton nor Angel noticed.

"And during your five years working as a double agent inside Iran"—Grafton continued, lifting a finger—"you infected the computers controlling their centrifuges with the perfidious Stuxnet virus, voiding the viability of their products." Up went a second finger. "You personally assassinated two Iranian scientists charged with miniaturizing warheads to fit on intercontinental ballistic missiles." A third finger joined the first two. "And you rigged an explosion at a secret missile base in Tehran, killing three dozen Revolutionary Guards and reducing Iran's stockpile of long-range Shahab rockets to a mound of twisted steel and rubble."

Grafton once again steepled his knobby-knuckled fingers under his chin. "But that time your cover was blown, yeah? Too many things added up for the Iranians, and all of them pointed to you. Now…" Grafton narrowed his eyes. The flames in the fireplace cast dancing shadows across his dark complexion. It was August, but the Cornish coast was cool and damp, and the best way to combat both in the drafty, old manor house was with a constantly crackling fire. "This is the bit where it gets *really* interesting. Somehow, the Mossad was able to spirit you out of Iran. You fled to Europe, where a talented plastic surgeon took *this* face…" Grafton swiped through documents until he stopped on a photograph. He lifted the tablet and angled it toward Angel. "And turned it into *that* face." He pointed a finger between Angel's hell-black eyes.

Still nothing from Angel. Not a twitch of his lips. Not a flick of his eyelashes. The stranger who had appeared at Grafton Manor like a puff of dark smoke, all intangible and foreboding, was either very, *very* good, or he wasn't who Grafton thought he was.

Sonya would be shocked if it was the latter. Grafton didn't make mistakes. At least he didn't make them often.

He hired me, didn't he? she thought, determined to make that the biggest mistake of his life.

When Grafton laid the tablet atop the desk, she glanced at the picture on the screen and nearly swallowed her tongue. She must have betrayed herself with a noise because Grafton glanced at her, brow furrowed.

"What?" He saw the direction of her stare and turned back to the photograph. "Haven't you seen a photo of the Prince of Shadows before? Surely you came across one during your previous career."

"No." She shook her head. "As the nickname suggests, his identity was always cloaked in darkness."

"Ah. Well, then, I'm fortunate to have this one, aren't I? Perhaps I should give Benton that raise he's been on about for the last few months." Grafton smiled when he referred to the young computer hacker he kept in his employ.

Sonya barely heard him. She was too engrossed in studying the picture on the tablet.

Grafton looked from her to the tablet and back again. "Still, you *do* seem to recognize him."

"No." She shook her head.

The subtle quirk of Grafton's right eyebrow said he wasn't satisfied with her monosyllabic answer.

Taking a deep breath, she tried not to choke on the smell of his woodsy cologne, which lingered in every room in the manor *including* her own. *Gag.* "But the man in the photo *does* look like someone I knew a long time ago," she admitted.

"Really?" Grafton was intrigued, and that would never do. What he already knew about her was too much for her liking.

"Someone who died," she clarified, hoping he'd consider the case closed. *Someone with the same slashing eyebrows and serious brow*, she continued silently. *Someone I loved*.

Although the man pictured had a smaller nose and a more prominent jawline, hell-black eyes instead of warm chocolate ones, there were enough similarities to have her mind swirling with a hundred beautiful memories. Her heart aching with a loss that even after ten years remained razor-sharp.

"Ah, Sonya..." Grafton's smile turned faintly sardonic. "You are unlucky in love, are you not? First a dead man and now an international criminal?"

She blinked, realizing some of what she felt was written across her face. Carefully schooling her features, she shrugged a shoulder and resisted the urge to punch Grafton straight in his smug, aristocratic nose.

He chuckled, knowing how much she disliked him and taking great delight in the power he had over her. If she squeezed her hands any tighter behind her back, her nails would break the skin.

After holding her gaze for a few seconds—both daring her to speak and simultaneously impressing upon her which of them was in charge—he turned back to Angel.

She breathed a sigh of relief.

Before being pressed into Grafton's service, she had known he was a bad man. But now? Well, now she knew he wasn't just a bad man; he was the *worst* of men.

She wondered if the devil himself had gotten tired of competing with Grafton in hell and had decided to dump him on earth. Which was to say that to be the object of Grafton's intense stare was to look upon the face of true evil. It always left her feeling a little corrupted. As if some of his depravity had wiggled in through her eye sockets and laid poisonous eggs inside her brain.

Grafton tapped the photo, glancing at Angel. As Sonya had hoped, he'd dropped the subject of her ill-fated love life and circled back around to his previous train of thought. "Compliments to your plastic surgeon. Not that you weren't an attractive man to begin with, but…" He let the sentence dangle, waiting for Angel to say something. Anything.

The only thing Angel allowed was the lifting of one dark eyebrow.

Sonya took the opportunity to study his face. Grafton was right. If, indeed, Angel *was* the man in the picture, then his plastic surgeon had been having an *extremely* good day when he or she carved Angel's new mug.

High cheekbones, broad forehead, solid slab of a jaw. His perfect profile begged to be minted on coins.

In fact, Angel was so gorgeous that Sonya's ovaries rejoiced. But when he turned his unblinking stare on her for the briefest of seconds, it threatened to shrink her uterus and throw her into early menopause.

Again, she was struck by the undeniable certainty that the man sitting across from Grafton was *not* someone to screw around with. Even though Grafton's home library was immense, filled with two-story bookshelves packed with first editions that delighted her and Sotheby's quality antique furniture that cost more than three years' wages, Angel's presence seemed to dwarf the space.

Could he be the Prince of Shadows? The man revered by Western intelligence agencies for single-handedly keeping the Iranians from becoming an atomic power? Not to mention, likely saving the world from nuclear war?

Grafton sighed, an indication he'd grown frustrated with Angel's reticence. As he swiped through the documents on his tablet again, Sonya knew he was poised to let loose with his coup de grâce. Hadn't it happened the same way with *her* when he'd summoned her to a meeting six months ago?

"Very well," he said. "I guess we'll do this the hard way. How clichéd." His top lip curled with distaste, but Sonya knew he loved every minute of this dangerous dance. Bringing people of quality, people of caliber, to their knees played to his ego and his continual search for power. Ever more power.

Sliding his tablet across his desk, Grafton turned the device around so Angel could see the single line of numbers glowing at the top of the screen.

"Am I supposed to know what that means?" Angel asked in his wrecked voice. If she wasn't mistaken, he'd had his vocal cords scoured. And the way he spoke was odd. Precise. If he was Iranian, it was impossible to tell. His syntax gave nothing away. And his accent? Some words sounded very American. Others had the harsh consonants common in Arabic. And a few had the soft, round vowels of the Romance languages.

"That's the number to the head of the Revolutionary Guard." Grafton once again donned his sardonic smile.

"I'm told they have ways of making men talk. Maybe *they* can get you to confess your true identity."

Angel's impenetrable mask slipped ever so slightly. A muscle in his jaw twitched as hatred blazed to life in his eyes.

"Who are you?" His tone was so low, so menacing, it sounded like a warning of swift and painful death.

No. Not a warning. A *promise*.

She rethought his earlier title and renamed him Mr. Tall, Dark, and *Deadly*.

"You know who I am. I'm Lord Asad Grafton, vice chairman of the Conservative Party and controlling owner of Land Stakes Corporation."

"No. Who are you *really*?"

Sonya was tempted to yell, *Spider! He's the infamous Spider! Run! Run away before he catches you in his sticky web!*

Grafton's smile turned positively poisonous. "I'm the man who holds your life in his hands."

For a few ticks of the clock, the stranger who insisted on being called Angel refused to speak. When he finally did, his gruff voice had gone guttural. "What do you want from me?"

"Ah." Grafton sat back, looking altogether pleased with himself. "That's easy. I want you to help me procure the fissile materials needed to build a nuclear weapon."

Sonya's jaw unhinged so quickly she was surprised it didn't hit the floor at her feet.

Chapter 1

Present day...

"*YOU WERE BORN WITH A DAGGER IN YOUR MOUTH AND A warrior's heart beating in your chest.*"

Those were the words the ramsad—the head of Mossad—had said to Angel the night he asked Angel to fake his own death and take over the identity of an Iranian university student. The night the ramsad had asked Angel to choose between the woman he loved and the stability of the world at large. The night the ramsad had explained to Angel that the mission to Iran would likely end with Angel dead, or if Angel *did* somehow survive, chances were good he would never see his homeland's glistening, sun-drenched shores again.

Looking out over the expansive back lawn of Grafton's home, ignoring the array of hulking guards Grafton had tasked with making sure he hadn't left the premises since that initial fateful meeting, Angel settled more snugly into the lush cushions of the deck chair. He took comfort in knowing friendly eyes were on him.

To show those friendly eyes he was A-okay, he lifted his face toward the weak English sun and studiously turned his thoughts away from the present, letting them drift back to a happier time. To a time when he wasn't Jamin "Angel" Agassi or Majid Abass, the Prince of Shadows. To a time when he was simply Mark Risa, a wet-behind-the-ears Mossad agent out to make his mark on the world and the spy community by hunting down a Palestinian terrorist responsible for bombing a synagogue in Jerusalem. To a time when an equally wet-behind-the-ears Interpol agent was assigned to help him...

"Excuse me. Are you Mark Risa?"

The voice that met his ears spoke delightfully accented Hebrew and was as smooth and as cultured as the chocolates they sold at Max Brenner back home. He turned his attention from the middle-aged woman walking her dog past the Café Constant on Rue Saint-Dominique and the man with the pencil-thin mustache who watched her from beneath hooded eyes, and looked up at the young woman standing beside his outdoor table. The sun was behind her, haloing her head. Even before he noticed her wide blue eyes, her strawberries-and-cream complexion, and her mischievous half smile, two words flitted through his brain.

Fairy princess.

She moved out of the sun, taking the seat across from him after a polite "May I?" It was then he realized she was anything but ethereal and sprightly. She was a flesh-and-blood woman. One good look at her had his libido sitting up and panting like a dog in the summer heat.

Down boy, *he silently admonished as she extended her hand to shake.* "I'm Sonya Butler."

Glancing at their clasped fingers, he noted two things. One, compared to his oversized man paw, her hand looked ridiculously delicate. And two, she wore hot-pink fingernail polish.

Hot-pink fingernail polish? What kind of Interpol agent does *that*?

Sonya Butler, apparently.

He decided to like her in that instant. She wasn't trying to prove how tough she was or how serious she was. Those hot-pink fingernails said, I can be young and vibrant and *still* catch the bad guys. Screw you if you don't believe me.

"Should we go somewhere to talk?" When she glanced around the busy café and the bustling Parisian sidewalk, he studied her graceful profile and the cascade of her honey-blond hair. She was, in a word, stunning. Not beautiful, per se. Her cheeks were a little too full, her nose a little too thin. But the twin sparks of intelligence and humor in her eyes, not to mention her lush mouth, were enough to stop a man in his tracks.

Turning back to him, she frowned and asked, still in Hebrew, "You are *Mark Risa, yes?"*

He realized he hadn't spoken a word since she'd arrived.

"Sorry." He popped his jaw, trying to relieve the tension in his face while simultaneously gathering his wayward thoughts into order. "Yes. I'm Mark Risa. It's a pleasure to meet you, Sonya."

Her half smile returned, and he felt it like a punch in the gut.

How unfortunate.

This was his chance to make the ramsad proud, to prove the man hadn't been wrong to recruit him straight out of the army and train him to be one of the world's most elite spies. He needed to focus on the mission, not the delicate line of Sonya's neck or the too-fast pulse beating next to the collar of her creamy blouse.

"We have a few things to talk about." She tapped the *file folder under her arm, her blue eyes crinkling at the corners as if she could read his thoughts.*

God, please don't let her read my thoughts.

"Right." He stood and motioned for her to follow *him to an alley arrowing around the side of the building. A set of exterior stairs showed the way to a second-floor flat—one of the many safe houses the Mossad kept around the world. He took the lead on the steps, not trusting himself with a view of her ass in those tight-fitting black trousers.*

"You have a lovely accent." He fumbled with the lock. *Her presence behind him on the narrow landing—not to the mention the smell of her, all fresh and sweet like freesia and apricot blossoms—made his heart pound. "Where did you learn Hebrew?"*

"My father was a diplomat in Jerusalem for two years, and languages have always come easily to me. Which made the jump from diplomat's kid to Interpol agent a no-brainer."

"How many languages do you speak?" When he *glanced over his shoulder, he dragged in a startled breath to find her close behind him. Close enough to touch if he wanted to.*

Oh, I want to!

He didn't believe in love at first sight. But she'd proven lust at first sight was a scientific certainty. Or at least a biological one.

"Five," she said.

"Pardon?"

"Five languages." Again, the corners of her blue eyes *crinkled. No. Not blue. Up close, he could see they were*

actually some color between blue and gray. A soft, gentle hue that contrasted starkly with those hot-pink fingernails.

"Five, huh?" He shook his head, silently laughing at himself for being such a cliché, for being the guy who couldn't hold a thought in his head for more than a second when an attractive woman waltzed into his sphere. *If my ramsad could see me now,* he'd blister my ears with curses... "That's one more than me."

"You speak four languages?" She canted her head. "Parlez-vous français?"

"No French. Only Hebrew, Arabic, English, and a little Yiddish."

"Three in common ain't bad." She'd switched to English, and the slang made him grin. "No chance we'll suffer a failure to communicate."

He spoke in English as well. "Don't tell me you speak Yiddish."

She laughed. It was a low, husky sound that had goose bumps rippling over his skin. "No Yiddish, unfortunately. But I do speak Arabic. I lived in Jordan for three years while my father did a stint at the embassy in Amman."

Pushing past him when he finally managed to unlock the door, she didn't hesitate to make herself at home. He liked that about her too. She pulled out a chair at the tiny bistro table fitted into the corner of the kitchen. The window was open, and the smell of the fresh herbs growing in a window box next door drifted around them.

When she set her purse and the file folder on the table, he caught a glimpse of the corner of a hardcover book peeking from the top flap of her handbag. What would a woman like her be reading? *he wondered. Then she* distracted him when she opened the folder and slid the top sheet of paper toward him. "Do you prefer English, Hebrew, or Arabic?" She was still speaking English.

"Dealer's choice."

"English it is." She beamed, looking right into his eyes. "Your accent is lovely too."

Before that sentence could sink in, she sobered and added, "This is all the information the Préfecture de police de Paris could find on your target. I'll continue to work with them to facilitate whatever you need from here on out, but for now, this is what you have to go on."

In fiction, Interpol was portrayed as U.N.C.L.E., sending in agents who had complete jurisdiction over local police in tracking down international criminals. But in reality, Interpol did no direct investigation or prosecution. It was an organization created to promote cooperation and communication between policing units from different countries.

When he'd come across information indicating his quarry had fled to Paris, and since he spoke no French, Mark had contacted Interpol, hoping they had an agent on hand who could coordinate his efforts with those of the local gendarmerie. He'd indicated he would be comfortable working with an agent who spoke English or Hebrew. They had sent him one who spoke both.

For two hours, he and Sonya sat and discussed what little information was in the file, and he passed along the questions he wanted her to pose to her contact inside the Paris police. It was only after the sun set and his stomach growled impatiently that he realized how much time had passed.

Looking at her across that bistro table in that tiny flat in Paris, he said the four words that would take him on a journey that would end in him losing his heart…and the last chance he had at living a normal life.

"Have dinner with me…"

"I see you rang up your source on the sat phone a bit ago. What did you discover?"

Grafton's highbrow English accent pulled Angel from his reverie. Or should he say *Spider's* highbrow English accent.

Oh yes. Angel knew exactly who he was dealing with.

To his cronies in the House of Lords, Asad was the well-respected Lord Grafton. But to those who lived in the mud and the muck, he was the almighty Spider. A weapons dealer. A human trafficker. A procurer of blood diamonds and financial supporter of piracy. A collector of assets. A destroyer of lives. The asshole of an asshole's asshole.

But he's finally met his match, Angel thought, hiding a secret smile.

"He has agreed to meet with me," he told Grafton, momentarily dismayed by the sound of his own voice after having spent so much time as his former self inside his head. Of all the metamorphoses he had gone through in the name of protecting Western civilization, the stuff done to his vocal cords was the most jarring. He sounded like a lifelong smoker when, in fact, he'd never taken a single puff. "But I have to go to him. He refuses to come to me," he added.

Grafton frowned. "Go to him where?"

"Moldova. He claims he is scared to leave. Too many

of his comrades have been seized by the authorities when they've tried to cross borders."

"Thanks in large part to *you*, no doubt."

Angel lifted a brow and shrugged, schooling his features into extreme unconcern because number one, he *wasn't* concerned. And number two, he knew his apathy would piss Grafton off. In the two weeks he'd been at the manor, he'd learned Lord Grafton—a man used to people falling all over themselves to do or say whatever he wanted—hated nothing worse.

"Oh, come now, Majid," Grafton scoffed, even though Angel could see his nostrils flare with frustration. "Surely you realize I know more about you than I revealed the night we met?"

"Everyone calls me Angel."

Grafton waved him off. Since their first meeting in the library, Grafton had refused to call him anything but Majid. As for Angel? Well, he refused to answer to anything but Angel. Just one of the many pissing contests they were currently engaged in.

"Given the task I've set for you," Grafton continued, "you must have come 'round to the notion that I've loads of information on what you've been on about since your escape from Iran."

"Have you?"

"Shall I prove it?"

"You do love to hear yourself talk."

A muscle ticked in Grafton's jaw, but then he took a deep breath and smiled. It was an oily smile. The smile of a man who thought he had something that would scare Angel to the depths of his soul.

"Under yet *another* false identity"—Grafton gestured

expansively—"you've been using your expertise in black-market fissile materials and your contacts within spy networks to help Western governments keep a group of thieves from selling their ill-gotten nuclear cache to unsavory buyers. And meanwhile, you've been getting closer and closer to finding out exactly *who* those thieves are and *where* they're hiding."

Once again, Angel had to work to contain a secret smile.

Facts were the hallmark of any decent false identity. It was much more difficult to *create* history than it was to tweak it. Plus, the most compelling and believable lies were always constructed almost entirely of the truth.

So, yes, everything Grafton knew about him was true.

What Grafton didn't know was that after leaving Iran, the Mossad had asked the United States government to hide Angel. The U.S. president at the time had decided the best place to keep Angel and his new face safe and out of the hands of the Iranians was to ferret him away inside the exalted ranks of Black Knights Inc., a covert government defense firm.

It was through the Black Knights—or, more precisely, it was with the full support of Boss, the head of BKI—that Angel had been afforded the freedom to do all the things Grafton had charged him with doing.

"So?" He made sure his face remained impassive. "Do you want me to set up the meeting with my source or not?"

Grafton narrowed his eyes, the slight curl of his upper lip broadcasting how irritated he was that Angel hadn't been taken aback by the breadth of his knowledge. A second later, he shuttered his expression. "You're sure this is the right bloke? For two bloody weeks you've been going on about how you couldn't be certain."

"For two weeks, he did not trust me enough to answer any of my questions. And without the answers to those questions, there was no way I could know if he was a legitimate seller or not."

"And now you know?"

Angel nodded.

"How?"

"He finally admitted where his material comes from."

"And where does it come from?"

"The same restricted Russian military installation where all the other samples I helped to remove from the black market originated."

Grafton's brow pinched. "So why didn't you capture this *source*"—Grafton made air quotes—"before now?"

"I only became aware of his identity sixteen hours before you summoned me here."

"It wasn't a summons. It was an invitation."

Angel indulged in a snort.

"Okay, so perhaps it *was* a summons." Grafton rubbed his hands together. "And how fortunate for me you'd just become aware of a legitimate seller of the very materials I need." Grafton glanced out over the lawn, eyes narrowed slightly as if something had caught his interest.

Had Angel had less confidence in his teammates, he might have worried Grafton had caught sight of them in the distance. As it was, he simply waited for Grafton to lose interest in whatever had snagged his attention and refocus on the conversation.

It didn't take long. There was determination on

Grafton's face when he turned back to Angel. "Moldova, you say?" At Angel's nod, he added, "Let me ring up a few folks, work out some details, then we'll get your contact back on the sat phone and give him a date and time. I'll pick the location."

Instead of answering, Angel simply stared, not attempting to hide his contempt.

Grafton chuckled. "The quicker you come to terms with your new situation, Majid—"

"Everyone calls me Angel."

"The better it will be."

"For whom?" Angel narrowed his eyes. "You or me?"

"*Both* of us."

"Go fuck yourself."

Grafton's grin became a sneer. "Careful, *Majid*. Right now I need you, so it behooves me to keep you alive and in one piece. That might not always be the case, so you should do your best to make me bloody well like you."

"Like I said"—Angel smiled—"go fuck yourself."

The muscle in Grafton's jaw gave another fitful tic before he turned and stomped into the house. Angel didn't swivel around in the deck chair to watch him go. Instead, he thought about all the ways he could kill the bastard with his bare hands.

It was a truly gratifying mental exercise.

"*Oh la vache*. You really shouldn't speak to him like that."

Angel closed his eyes at the sound of her voice. It was still smooth and cultured. It still reminded him of hot chocolate. *Oh la vache* was French for *holy cow*, or at least that's what she'd told him. That she cursed in languages other than the one she was speaking was a quirk that had made him smile. You know, way back when. Once upon a long, long time ago.

He wasn't smiling now, of course. He simply grunted in response.

"I'm serious," she insisted.

"What can he do?" He shrugged. "Sic the Iranians on me? Kill me himself?"

"Yes and yes."

Sonya stood beside the deck chair next to his. Today she wore her usual work uniform of tailored trousers and a form-fitting button-down blouse. Some things hadn't changed. Her wardrobe still managed to look both professional and yet ridiculously sexy, and there was the ever-present book clutched in her hand. She'd always loved the classics, and it wasn't unusual to find a copy of one of Austen's or Hemingway's or the Brontë sisters' novels in her purse.

Then again, some things *had* changed. Gone was the hot-pink fingernail polish. In its place were bare nails filed to a subdued length.

It was a stark reminder that the woman standing so close was not the same woman he'd met in Paris. *That* woman had glowed, so full of color and light that she had reminded him of a Lite-Brite. *That* woman had feared nothing, had laughed with him and loved with him and made him want to be a better man, the *ultimate* man. In the place of that woman now stood a traitor, a no-account bootlicker of one of the world's most vile men and—

Angel cut off his thoughts and stood.

He couldn't bear to breathe the same air she breathed

or smell her sweet perfume that still reminded him of freesia and apricot blossoms. The sad truth of the matter was, despite how far she'd fallen, despite what she'd become, there was a part of him that still loved her.

All of him still wanted her…

Chapter 2

"WHY DO YOU SCURRY AWAY LIKE A ROACH IN THE sunlight anytime you see me?"

Sonya posed the question to Angel's retreating back. When he stopped in his tracks, his shoulders snapping straight, she noted that it wasn't only his face that was pure perfection. His physique fell into that category too.

He had that quintessentially male V-shape. Wide shoulders tapered down to a slim waist, which gave way to a high, tight ass and long, muscular legs. His arms were roped with power. Veins stood out in sharp relief against the tan skin over his forearms and biceps.

To put it simply, he was a study in masculine architecture, and Mother Nature had injected him with more than his fair share of that most potent drug: testosterone.

Sonya had been suffering from a bad case of forbidden fruit syndrome since he'd walked into the manor. Which was absurd because…for one thing, she didn't know him from Adam—and what she *did* know about him had her shaking in her boots. For another thing, he'd agreed to work with Grafton, the scum of the earth, to acquire a bomb's worth of fissile materials, and that was just…*wrong*. If those two things weren't bad enough, she'd only felt instant attraction once before, a long time ago when she'd met a vastly different, but no less beautiful and mysterious man. She'd fallen for that man so

hard and so fast her head had spun. And the landing? It
had nearly killed her.

So yeah. She'd be smart to take all her unseemly
thoughts and bury them deep. Digging a fantasy twenty-
foot grave, she imagined tossing her ridiculous libido
inside and then throwing mounds of dirt atop it.

There. Done. She wiped imaginary hands and nodded
with satisfaction.

Slowly, Angel turned to face her, those hell-black
eyes narrowing as they went on a leisurely tour of her
body, taking rest stops at particularly interesting spots.

Her stupid, undead libido crawled out of its freshly
dug grave. *Ugh!* She mentally herded the silly thing
back toward the yawning maw of its final resting place.
This time she was determined to throw it in and cover
it with concrete.

"I did not realize I scurried away like a roach in the
sunlight," he said in that raspy, ruined voice, with that
odd formality and that ever-changing accent that made
it impossible to pinpoint where he was from.

No doubt that was his objective. He was making
certain that, along with the vocal cord scouring, no
voice-recognition software could identify him. If he
truly *was* the Prince of Shadows—and in the two weeks
he'd been at the manor house, she'd become convinced
he was—then the Iranians were searching the planet
for him. A fatwā, pronounced by the ranking ayatollah,
had been issued against him, demanding his head in the
name of Allah.

"Well, you do," she assured him.

"Why do you care?"

Merde. He had her there. Why *did* she care?

She opened her mouth. Closed it. Then opened it again. Nothing came out. Not a single word.

The man should be crowned the high king of shutting down conversations.

"Take a breath," he instructed after watching her fish-out-of-water routine for a few seconds. "It will help you relax."

"Who says I'm not relaxed?"

"Me."

"And how would you know whether or not I'm relaxed?"

"Your shoulders aligning themselves with your earlobes was my first clue."

Busted.

Blowing out a windy breath, she forced her shoulders down. "I care because I don't want to see a good man die," she told him truthfully.

"Are you sure I *am* a good man?"

"If you are who Grafton says you are, then your reputation precedes you."

He was quiet after that. Too quiet. With no conversation to use as a distraction, she was forced to focus on nothing but his intense stare. It was enough to make her shift from foot to foot.

When she couldn't stand it a second more, she added, "And besides, I'm pretty good at reading people."

"Don't give yourself too much credit."

Wow. Okay. So… "You don't like me much, do you?"

"I don't know you."

She chuckled, but there was no humor in it. "That's true. But it doesn't change the fact that you don't like me."

Angel neither agreed nor disagreed. As always, his

expression gave nothing away. Funny, since she got the impression that beneath his cold, calculating facade roiled a fiery cauldron of emotion.

"Do you mind if I ask why?" she asked.

"Why what?"

"Why you don't like me."

"What is there to like?"

She wasn't sure what she'd expected him to say, but it wasn't *that.* "Excuse me?"

"I said, what is there to like?"

"Yeah." She pursed her lips. "I heard you the first time. What I should have said was, *was zur Hölle*, dude*?* And in case you don't speak German, that means *what the hell.*"

"You work for him." Angel hooked a thumb over his shoulder, and her attention snagged on his hand.

He had gorgeous hands, all broad-palmed and long-fingered. Once upon a time, hands as strong and beautiful as his had moved over her body, giving her pleasure unlike anything she had experienced before or since. Seriously, those hands should have been registered as national treasures.

"So do *you*," she pointed out. "Work for him, that is."

"Under duress and protest."

She snorted. "And what on God's green earth makes you think I'm any different?"

"Are you?" He raised an eyebrow. For him that was the equivalent of full facial acrobatics.

"*No!*" She stomped over to face him, clutching Grafton's first edition of *A Tale of Two Cities* hard enough to crack the binding. She tried not to notice when the toe of her left ballet flat touched the leather tip of Angel's black tactical boot. Feet were not erogenous zones, were they? At least not fully clad feet? "I either work for him and do what he says, or he'll see me in jail."

Something sparked in Angel's eyes. Some sort of emotion. But damned if she could figure out which one it was.

"What does he have on you?" The guy did his best impression of a nightclub bouncer. All hulking shoulders and crossed arms and an I-like-to-kick-asses-so-don't-mess-with-me grimace.

She was startled by his question. Angel never offered up anything about himself—and *certainly* never expressed enough interest in anyone else to actually pose a personal question. Maybe her momentary shock was why she found herself spilling her guts.

"Before Lord Grafton, I used to work for Interpol. There was a man...a *good* man who got caught up in a bad situation. I helped him elude capture."

A butterfly chose that moment to flutter past them. It came to rest on one of the rosebushes planted in a neat line beside the large terrace. She had herself a real Forrest Gump and Jenny moment. Except that she didn't want to be a bird and fly far, far away. She wanted to be that butterfly. Beautiful and free and without a thought or care in the world.

For too long now, she'd had too many thoughts. Too many cares.

"I knew this man had only stolen a set of gemstones because he'd been forced to. Because he'd been stuck between a rock and a hard place," she explained. "And I knew he'd never do anything like that again, so yeah..." She shrugged.

"Where does Grafton fit in?"

Another question. It was a banner day.

"My superiors at Interpol suspected I'd helped the fugitive escape, but they couldn't prove it. *Grafton*, however, could. I mean, he *can*. Somehow he got his hands on phone records showing the communication between me and the thief. If I don't continue to work for him, he'll turn over the evidence to the authorities. I'll be locked up quicker than you can say 'traitor.' Interpol doesn't take kindly to rogue agents."

"Do you love him?"

Sonya's jaw slung open. Partly because that was three—*three*—whole questions. She heard Sesame Street's Count von Count's *bwa-ha-ha* echo through her head. But mostly because… Was the guy totally Nutso Bismol?

"Of course not." Glancing around, she lowered her voice. "Grafton is a dirt merchant. Worse than that. He's the single-celled organism growing on the dirt the dirt merchants sell. And no matter what he says or what he promises you or how long you work for him, don't think you can trust him for a second. He'll smile and shake your hand while driving a knife in your back."

"No. Not Grafton. The jewel thief."

The sun, which had been hidden behind a big, fluffy cloud, peeked out and shined brightly on Angel's swarthy face, into his eyes. She was startled to realize they weren't hell-black like she'd thought. Instead they were a deep, dark brown, reminding her of strong Turkish coffee.

For a couple of tense seconds, she considered telling him the truth. Oddly enough, in that moment she *wanted* to tell him the truth. But logic—and self-preservation— prevailed. "I do. I mean, I did," she lied.

Angel popped his jaw, a jerk of his chin to the side

and an accompanying *snap* of sound. It was quick. Over in a second. But it was enough to have her turning into a block of ice.

The wind whispering over the Cornish countryside was warm and inviting for the first time in months, but it might as well have been an arctic blast. Goose bumps erupted over her arms. Her scalp tingled. Dozens of memories crowded her brain.

She searched Angel's eyes, looking for a hint of something, *anything* familiar. "Do you speak Hebrew?" she asked him, having switched to that very language.

"Sorry. What?" He still spoke English.

She shook her head, laughing at herself for seeing ghosts. "Nothing. Sometimes I think the six months working for Grafton have made me cuckoo in the cranium. Know what I mean?"

"No."

"Ha!" He was so...*serious* with his answer. Without thinking, she placed her hand on his arm. "That was a rhetorical question."

Or at least that's what she *meant* to say.

She only got halfway through the sentence. The instant her fingers made contact with his forearm, she was struck mute by the lightning bolt of awareness that slammed through her. The back of her neck beneath her hair misted with sweat. His hot skin made her palm burn and itch.

She wanted him. Like...*wanted* him. The intensity of it shocked her into wide-eyed silence.

"You should be careful."

His raspy words had her eyes jumping from her hand, so pale against his arm, to his face. As always, his expression was unreadable, but there was no mistaking the flash of emotion in his eyes. Whether that emotion was anger or disgust or answering lust, she couldn't say.

"Careful of what?" she asked breathlessly as she pulled her hand back and curled her fingers around the heat his skin had left behind.

"Me."

That one word seemed to reverberate around the terrace and lawn. And inside *her*.

She was terrified…and a little turned on.

It's official. I'm losing my marbles.

"Are you going to do it?" she asked in a desperate attempt to get the conversation—and herself—back on track. She had to clear her throat because it sounded like someone had taken a Brillo Pad to her larynx.

"Do what?"

"Help Grafton get his hands on the materials he wants?"

"What choice do I have?"

She shrugged. "I don't know. I mean, you turned against your own country and sided with the enemy to keep a nuclear bomb out of unsavory hands. Makes me think you're not a man to put his own life above the greater good. You didn't do it then. Guess I'm wondering if you'd really do it now."

"Says the woman who used to work to bring down men like Grafton, and now here you are standing by his side." Sonya blushed at the censure she heard in his voice. "People change."

"Do they?" She studied him.

"All evidence points to yes."

"I'm not so sure."

He cocked his head. His black hair was cropped close to his scalp, but the tips had the slightest wave to them. She wondered if his hair would be curly if it was longer.

She loved curly hair on a man. Loved how the silky strands wrapped around her fingers when she speared them—

"I see you two are getting on." Grafton's voice had her jumping away from Angel. She realized then how much his blast-furnace body heat had wrapped around her. By contrast, the warm day felt startlingly cold.

"Yeah. We're one big, happy family." She didn't bother hiding the sarcasm in her voice.

Grafton leveled a warning stare at her. "A piece of advice, darling Sonya. Don't let him"—he pointed a finger at Angel—"rub off on you. You know I'm not keen on a mouthy bitch."

Two flags of heat burned in her cheeks. Her instinct was to fly at Grafton and scratch his eyes out of his criminal head. Luckily, good sense prevailed. "Sorry," she muttered. If she ground her jaw any harder, her teeth might explode. "It was a momentary slip."

"Make sure you don't have too many more of those."

Angel still watched her, but she couldn't make herself meet his gaze. She was too humiliated. Plus, she didn't want him *or* Grafton to see the rage burning in her eyes.

"We leave for Moldova tomorrow morning," Grafton continued after having satisfied himself she was back to being his meek and mild personal assistant. "Can your source meet us later in the day, Majid?"

"Everyone calls me Angel."

Grafton sighed. "Whatever. Can your source meet us tomorrow?"

"I think he can make that happen." Angel never took

his eyes off Sonya. She could feel his gaze like a physical touch, like a fist beneath her chin, forcing her to meet his unyielding stare. When she did, she didn't like what she saw in his face. Even his non-expression revealed disappointment…and pity.

Self-disgust burned like battery acid in her stomach, bubbling up into her esophagus. She swallowed it down and winced at the sticky noise her throat made. It was a weak sound. A *beaten* sound. She hated it even though she knew it was exactly how she *should* sound.

"But I need to use the phone to call my source," Angel added. "Just to make sure."

"Of course." Grafton swung his arm wide, indicating Angel should precede him into the house. Grafton didn't allow cellular phones on the premises. Any calls had to be made on his satellite phone, both for purposes of keeping the authorities from tracing those calls and to ensure Grafton knew *exactly* who his flunkies phoned.

He hadn't retained his Lord of the Damned status for as long as he had by being sloppy.

Angel didn't turn toward Grafton immediately, instead holding Sonya's gaze for a five-second count that left her fighting to fill her lungs with air. Then he spun on his heel and disappeared into the house.

"You'll be coming with us, of course." Grafton's statement pulled Sonya's eyes away from one of the most beautiful men she'd ever seen to one of the most disgusting.

Okay, if she was completely honest, Grafton wasn't a bad-looking guy. He carried his fifty-some-odd years well. Nary a gray hair or wrinkle in sight. His mixed heritage paired his dark skin with prominent features, making him fairly easy on the eyes. But his soul was black and decrepit, and it showed in his dead gaze and slimy smile.

"I don't know how I can help you in Moldova," she told him. "They speak Romanian. I don't."

"You'll provide *other* services." Grafton's self-satisfied smirk made her want to puke. "And besides, after that sarcastic little outburst a moment ago, I don't particularly trust you here alone. I thought you were finally coming to terms with your role. Now, I'm not so sure. So be a good little chit, and run along and pack your bags. We've an early flight tomorrow."

Sonya wanted to tell him to go take a flying leap—or more like she wanted to copycat Angel and tell Grafton to go fuck himself—but she forced a smile and sailed past him into the house.

It was only after she'd climbed the stairs, shut her bedroom door, and tossed the book onto her bed that she realized Angel hadn't answered her question about why he'd been willing to risk himself for the greater good before but wasn't now.

He said people changed. But something, some sixth sense or niggle of intuition, told her *he* hadn't changed at all.

Chapter 3

Midnight...

The witching hour.

Or, in Angel's case, the prearranged time for him to let all those friendly eyes watching the manor house in on the current plan.

Pushing aside the coverlet in the room Grafton had assigned him, he hopped from the large, four-poster bed and walked to the window to peek through the heavy curtains. One of Grafton's no-neck hulks trudged by below, his steps sluggish over the well-manicured lawns of the estate. No doubt the guy wasn't very hyped to have pulled third-shift perimeter duty.

Angel waited until No-Neck passed around the corner. Knowing he only had twenty seconds before the next guard appeared on the circuit—Grafton hadn't skimped when it came to strong-armed thugs—Angel took off his watch and turned its face toward the window. Depressing the button on the side, he watched the device light up.

Morse code was an old form of communication, but it was an incredibly effective one in situations like this. By the time the next guard appeared from around the corner, he had sent half his message.

He watched No-Neck Number-Two stroll past, thought about all the ways he could render the bastard unconscious, and lifted the watch to send the rest of the message as soon as the guard slipped around the side of the manor.

Then he waited. Waited as a third guard appeared and disappeared. Waited as a cloud passed over the moon, plunging the area into stygian darkness.

Keeping his gaze focused on the rolling countryside, he blew out a sigh of relief when flickers of light far in the distance told him his message had been received. Then, a brief summary of that message was relayed back to him. It ended with three long blinks followed by one long, one short, one long blink.

He responded in kind. The Morse code for *okay*. That easily, the plan was set.

Excellent, he thought, taking comfort that he was not alone in this. That the badass guys and gals of Black Knights Inc. had his back.

He considered returning to bed. The mattress was soft, the blankets plush and warm. But no matter how inviting it was, he couldn't fool himself into thinking the sandman would make an appearance. Probably because, with Sonya tucked in four doors down, the sandman had been ditching him for two weeks.

No. Wait.

In truth, it'd been months. Ever since the Black Knights had discovered that Spider, their ultimate quarry, was Lord Grafton and that the hot blond glued to his side was none other than Sonya Butler, the love of Angel's life.

"For fuck's sake," he grumbled into the quiet of his room.

He still had trouble wrapping his mind around it. How could the brave, high-spirited woman he'd known and loved be the same woman who hung her head and kowtowed to Grafton's imperious attitude and awful demands? *How?*

The only way he could fathom it was that there had to be more to the story. Besides the evidence Grafton had on her, did the slimeball also have something on the jewel thief? Like, perhaps, the man's location? Is that how Sonya justified herself? Was she sacrificing her own reputation, her own morals and ethics, to keep someone else safe?

While part of Angel desperately hoped that was true, another part of him let out a low, lethal growl at the thought. Because if he accepted that Sonya had done this, lowered herself to such a degree to save the jewel thief, he also had to accept she didn't just love the man, she was *in* love with him.

And that hurt.

Even though it shouldn't.

Hadn't he prayed she would move on? Hadn't he *wanted* that for her with all his heart?

I did. I do.

And yet, over the years he'd carefully avoided looking her up. In fact, he'd done everything short of shoving his head in the sand where she was concerned.

He popped his jaw, then winced.

His tell from all those years ago kept rearing its ugly head. Thinking back on how Sonya had zeroed in on his unconscious response and then immediately switched to Hebrew scared the living shit out of him. His entire mission hinged on him playing his part to a T, and that meant Sonya Butler could not—no way, no how—know who he truly was.

Blowing out a resigned breath, he pulled on a pair of jeans and a black, V-neck undershirt. Since he was screwed when it came to catching z's, he hoped a glass of water and a quick snack might provide clarity of thought.

"Next best thing to a night of restorative sleep, right?" he asked the empty room, then realized he was talking to himself.

Squaring his shoulders and blowing out a deep breath, he opened his bedroom door, determined to put everything but the mission from his mind. Peeking into the dark hallway, he wasn't surprised to find the manor house quiet. Sonya had turned in hours ago, along with Phelps, Grafton's loyal butler. Like a vampire, Grafton liked to spend his nights holed up in his library doing God only knew what. And the No-Necks who weren't on duty patrolling the grounds were bunked in a guesthouse at the back of the property.

Angel crept down the long hallway toward the stairs and studiously avoided looking at Sonya's door. Partly because he'd be tempted to knock and ask her to invite him in. But mostly because he was battling the urge to bust down the door, spirit her away into the night, and fuck Grafton, the mission, and everything else.

His footsteps on the treads were silent as he slipped downstairs, his way lit by the low-burning fire in the front room. After flicking a brief glance at the library's huge mahogany doors, he turned toward the kitchen.

The hallway leading to the back of the house was dark, but Angel made his way by feel and managed to keep from bumping into the long line of priceless Ming vases sitting atop cherrywood pedestals. When he reached the kitchen doorway, he paused.

He wasn't alone.

The life he'd lived, always looking over his shoulder, careful of every word, every gesture, had honed his senses. His eyesight was better than twenty-twenty and the BKI crew accused him of having the hearing of a bat. But the strongest of all was his sense of smell.

The sweet bouquet of freesia mixed with apricot blossoms tickled his nose.

No lights were on in the kitchen, but Sonya was in there.

His heart, which was always, *always* metronome steady, went haywire within his rib cage. He debated turning around and going back to his room, but the soft sound of a sniffle had him moving forward before he'd made the conscious decision to do so. Slinking into the kitchen unseen, he positioned himself inside the deep shadows beside the large walk-in pantry.

Scanning the cavernous kitchen with its industrial-size appliances, racks of pots and pans, and large center island topped by a soapstone countertop, his eyes finally alighted on Sonya. She stood in front of the farmhouse-style sink in a pair of silky sleep pants and a lavender T-shirt that looked soft to the touch. Almost as soft as her creamy skin. A glass of water was clutched in her hand, but her face was tilted toward the window above the sink.

Gentle moonlight bathed her cheeks in a silvery glow. But it wasn't her lovely profile or her pouty mouth—which he knew from experience loved kisses—that snagged his attention and had his hands curling into fists. It was the tears slipping from her eyes and the hard shudder that shook her narrow shoulders.

Sonya Butler was crying.

At that moment, it didn't matter who she'd become or who she worked for or why she'd done any of it. The sight of her tears was a sledgehammer blow to his heart, shattering the organ into a hundred sharp pieces.

Chapter 4

I DON'T KNOW WHAT'S WRONG WITH ME, SONYA THOUGHT AS she wiped away tears with the back of her hand, tasting their salty zing on her tongue. *Okay,* she admitted reluctantly, *so maybe I do.*

It was Angel. Angel and his popping jaw that was so much like Mark that for a moment she'd actually thought...

But no. Mark was dead.

Looking out at the starry night, she watched a dark cloud drift past the moon and was taken back ten years to the evening of their seventh date—although they'd never actually *called* them dates. Dates would have implied fraternization and unprofessionalism, and they'd been determined to play it cool.

Or at least he had. She'd mostly been determined to impress the hell out of him.

Instead of *dates*, they'd had *dinners*. Dinners that, yeah, involved a lot of talk about whatever new piece of Intel she'd gleaned from her sources inside the Paris police department or from her contacts inside the French intelligence agencies. But those dinners had *also* involved a lot of talk about themselves. About their favorite bands, favorite foods, favorite places to vacation, favorite pastimes.

She'd told him her favorite thing to do besides reading classic literature was watching old movies. Since she'd moved around a lot as a kid, she hadn't had a lot of friends growing up. Her parents had been her best buddies, her father in particular. And *he* had been a fan of the classics, both in print *and* in film. Instead of falling in love and going on adventures of her own, she'd read or watched fictional people do it from the safety of her living room with her folks munching popcorn beside her.

"Which movie is your favorite?" Mark asked. The candle in the center of the table flickered soft light over his features. He wasn't handsome so much as attractive. His nose was a little too big and listed slightly to the left. But he had beautiful, high cheekbones and the world's most tempting mouth. A big, wide mouth that didn't smile easily, but when it did... Holy be-zanna! She would swear her panties lit on fire.

"Casablanca," she told him.

"Aren't you a little young for that one?" And there it was. That elusive smile. If she looked down, would she see the edges of her underwear curling away like burned paper?

"Young for what? Watching a man make the noblest of sacrifices? Casablanca *is the preeminent love story," she insisted.*

"Of all time?"

"Yes, of all time."

"What about Titanic?*"*

She laughed. "You're joking, right?"

*"*Titanic *got great reviews, Leonardo DeCaprio makes the ultimate sacrifice, and the film isn't sixty years old. I'd say it is the preeminent love story. At least of our generation."*

"*Fine.*" *She waved a hand.* "*I'll admit it's a decent enough movie. But it doesn't hold a candle to* Casablanca. *Especially when it comes to quotable dialogue.*"

He spread his arms wide, revealing the mesmerizing breadth of his chest. "*I'm the king of the world!*"

"*My point exactly! It doesn't stack up to* Here's lookin' at you, kid. *Or* Of all the gin joints in all the towns in all the world, she walks into mine.*"

"*We'll always have Paris.*" *Despite his gorgeous Israeli accent with its drawn-out vowels, he'd donned a pretty spot-on Humphrey Bogart impersonation, wiggling his eyebrows as he leaned across the table. The look in his eyes was hot enough to melt the makeup off her face.*

"*Yes,*" *she said, her voice breathless.* "*We will.*"

For long moments, they didn't say a word, simply stared at each other. She wanted to memorialize his expression. Commission a master painter to capture it in oils so she could pass it down to future generations.

Cupping her chin in her hand, she asked him, "*So what's your favorite thing?*"

"*Spending the day at the beach,*" *he said, his TH sounds becoming D sounds so that to her ear it became,* Spending dey day at dey beach. "*Salty waves and sunshine,*" *he continued.* "*My feet in the warm sand. A cold drink in my hand.*" *He closed his eyes, and the candlelight made his eyelashes cast sooty shadows across his cheeks.* "*It's my idea of heaven.*"

Heaven… She was there now. Just looking at him. Just drinking him in.

"*You know,*" *he said, his voice deliciously low,* "*you never told me how old you were when you left the States.*"

"Four. I don't even remember living in Brooklyn."

"Have you been back since?"

"When my parents were alive, we would spend the Christmas holiday there with my aunt Louisa, my mom's sister. But other than that…no." She shrugged. "I guess you could say I'm a child of the world."

His face sobered. "How long ago did they die?"

She realized then that every time she'd spoken of her parents, she'd glossed over their passing. Maybe because it still hurt too badly. Maybe because she didn't want him feeling sorry for her. Or maybe because she still struggled with the reality herself.

"Three years ago." She barely recognized her own voice; it was so rusty-sounding. "It was a crash on the Autobahn. I'm told it was violent and instantaneous. They never knew what hit them."

He leaned across the table and took her hand. He wasn't tentative about it. There was nothing tentative about the man. But he was gentle. And his fingers were strong and warm. Rough compared to hers.

She hadn't realized how much she needed a comforting touch until he gave her one.

"I'm sorry," he said.

She'd heard those two words so many times since the crash. But never had they sounded more sincere. Mark Risa did nothing by half measures.

"I am too," she admitted around the catch in her throat. Then she batted away her sadness and sat up straighter. "That's enough of that. Tell me about your parents. Your father is a doctor, right?"

She remembered him mentioning something about his father's "patients" in one conversation.

"Was *a doctor*," he corrected. "He's dead now. He and my mother."

She deflated like a slashed tire and clutched his hand. "How?"

"They were attending a medical conference in Beersheba, in the south of Israel, when clashes with Gaza broke out. Their hotel was hit by a rocket. As with your parents, I was told they died instantly."

Sonya closed her eyes and released a shuddering breath. "Why does the world have to be so violent?"

He was quiet for a moment. Then, "I don't think it has to be. I think it can be better. As long as people like you and me continue to work for it."

She opened her eyes, saw the stubborn set of his jaw and the determination on his face, and knew he would spend the rest of his life working for it.

"*Voilà!*" The waiter appeared with a covered tray and lifted the lid with a flourish, effectively scattering the sad clouds hanging above their heads.

After a delicious meal of coq au vin, triple chocolate fudge cake—one could never have too much chocolate—and one too many bottles of French wine, they stumbled out of the restaurant into the soft Parisian night. The air was heavy with threatening rain. The city lights sparkled and danced as if they knew they resided in one of the world's most romantic cities.

And Mark? Oh, Mark looked good in his leather jacket and distressed jeans. His body was hot enough to fog an elderly nun's glasses, and he seemed much older than his mere twenty-four years. More than that, he was enigmatic and a touch dangerous.

Sonya knew that to protect the innocent, the Mossad sometimes did things that blurred or obliterated the lines of civilized behavior. What, exactly, had Mark done? What secrets did he keep locked away inside his razor-sharp mind? What dark deeds had those big, strong hands been tasked with?

The possibilities were endless, a little bit frightening, and a whole lot exciting.

"Can I walk you home tonight?" He glanced at her from beneath hooded lids. He had the prettiest eyes. So chocolaty brown. So inscrutable.

"Of course," she told him. Instead of heading toward the nearest subway stop, they turned down a narrow cobbled street that led to the Montmartre neighborhood where she lived.

For a while, they strolled in silence, each occupied with their own thoughts. Each intensely aware of the other. Then, he shocked her by asking, "Are you seeing anyone, Sonya?"

Her heart thrilled at the question.

Is this it? Is he finally going to drop his me-Mossad-you-Interpol, hands-off policy?

She'd done everything she could to give him all the right signals, to let him know she was interested. Well, everything short of flashing him her boobs. And honestly, she'd made up her mind if he didn't pick up what she was laying down soon, she might try that too.

"No." She smiled at him, intentionally catching the heel of one of her red-as-the-devil's-underpants pumps between two cobblestones so she'd have an excuse to stumble into him and grab hold of his arm.

Yes. She was shameless.

Don't judge me! *She shook an imaginary fist at the universe.*

"Why?" *he asked, placing his hand over hers.*

"Why what?" *She wrinkled her nose.* "Why am I not seeing anyone?"

"Yes."

He had the most beautiful voice, all deep and melodic. Even one tiny syllable was enough to have her imagining all the things she could do to his manly parts. With his manly parts.

"Frenchmen are notorious flirts," *he added.* "Surely you've had plenty of opportunities since you've been in Paris."

"I guess I haven't met anyone I wanted to… uh…s-see."

She hated the way she stuttered. It made her sound unsure of herself, and that's the last impression she wanted to give him. He always seemed so certain. So composed. So ridiculously confident!

Before she could stop herself, she added, "Until now."

He stopped in the middle of the street, turning to look down at her. She did so love a tall man. And a man who was still taller than she was even after she'd packed her five-foot-eight frame into a pair of sky-high, take-me-big-boy heels? Well, that was about the best thing ever.

She hoped to fake a brashness she didn't feel by pasting on a cheeky grin. "Was that too forward?"

"No." *His dark curls caught the light of the streetlamp on the corner, glowing with health.* "It was just forward enough."

Cupping her chin in his warm, callused palm, he bent toward her. Her lungs seized when his hot breath puffed against her eager, waiting lips.

Then the sky opened up...

Sonya shook her head at the memory of how they'd run to the nearest doorway and crowded inside in an attempt to escape the deluge. It had been too late. They'd both been soaked to the bone. Water had beaded on his inky eyelashes and dripped from the center of his delectable bottom lip.

She had shivered with the cold and he, being the consummate gentleman, had wrapped a strong arm around her shoulders. His body heat, and the hunger burning in his eyes, had chased away the chill while making everything inside her go liquid.

Even back then, at barely twenty-two, she hadn't been a virgin. And that, by no means, had been her first kiss. But she had been so nervous and shy that both things might as well have been true.

I'm going to kiss you now, Sonya, he had said, his voice rumbling through her chest like fireworks on the Fourth of July.

And then...oh, and then he—

Sonya shoved the memory away with a groan, palming her forehead as the pleasure of that long ago night was replaced by the pain of her loss.

"Who are you crying for?" A deep, raspy voice slid from the darkness.

She spun, her eyes darting around the unlit kitchen.

There. Over by the pantry door. He was a darker shadow in a pool of dark shadows.

"Come out where I can see you," she commanded, knowing she was spotlighted by the glow of the moonlight through the window above the sink and not liking the disadvantage it put her at. She hastily scrubbed the wetness from her cheeks.

Angel flowed into view as quietly as a ghost.

"Who are you crying for?" he asked again. "Your jewel thief?"

"No," she answered before she had time to consider whether or not the truth was the right thing to give him.

Why does he have that effect on me? Why do I look into his eyes and want to tell him everything? All my deepest, darkest secrets?

It was uncanny. And more than a little scary.

"I mean, not really," she quickly added. *Ugh. Talk about unconvincing, Sonya!*

"Is there more to the story?" he asked. The man was full of questions today. "Some other reason why you work for Grafton?"

"No," she blurted and saw his left eyebrow twitch.

Her training kicked in—*thank heavens!*—and she turned the tables on him. "Is there some reason besides his threat to hand you over to the Iranians that has *you* working for him?"

"No."

For long seconds, their eyes waged a war. Wait. It wasn't a war. It was a scouting mission. They were each searching for something in the other's gaze.

She got the impression neither of them found what they were looking for.

"Why does Grafton want the enriched uranium?" he asked.

The change in subject happened so fast that her thoughts suffered whiplash. Again, her mouth answered before her mind had time to consider her response. "How should I know?"

"I assumed he shared most things with you."

She snorted. "Hardly."

"Then why does he keep you so close to his side?"

That was the $64,000 question, wasn't it? The question that, over the last six months, she thought she had finally figured out the answer to.

"Four reasons," she told him. "Number one"—she lifted a finger on the hand not wrapped around the water glass—"he picks my brain and uses my knowledge of international police procedures to help him make sure his more nefarious businesses have a better chance of flying under the radar. Number two"—up went a second finger—"I can speak six languages, so he likes having me around to act as an interpreter."

Was it her imagination, or did the muscle beneath Angel's right eye twitch as if something she said had surprised him?

A third finger joined the first two until she formed a W in the air. "Number three, he's a sadistic *figlio di puttana* who loves to punish me on a daily basis by forcing me into situations that make my skin crawl."

"*Figlio di puttana?*"

"It's Italian for 'son of a bitch,'" she clarified, and now she held up four fingers. "And last but not least, I think he gets a kick out of having a younger woman on his arm. He likes to show me off to his fat, old friends in the House of Lords and pretend there's more going on between us than a sick and twisted business arrangement."

"Is there? More going on between you?"

Her gorge rose. "I'd rather set my vulva on fire."

Did one corner of Angel's mouth twitch? "I take it that as a no?"

"That is a *hell* no. I'll spend the rest of my life rotting away in an eight-by-ten before I touch so much as a hair on that man's…" Since Grafton didn't have any hair on his head, she finished with "chin."

Silence filled the kitchen after that little display of feeling. Then Angel took a step toward her.

She instinctively retreated. Angel projected an aura that said he knew one hundred different ways to kill a person with his bare hands.

He lifted those very hands in the air, palms out. "Are you afraid of me?"

"Yeah. *Duh*."

"I will not hurt you, Sonya."

She looked into his eyes and saw a million secrets. Secrets she would never uncover. But one thing he didn't try to hide was the truth of his words.

"Do you believe me?" he asked.

"Yes." Like before, her mouth answered without permission from her brain. "But I don't know why."

If it were possible for Angel's fiercely intelligent face to soften—which she wasn't sure it was—it would have happened then. Instead, the only thing that changed in his demeanor was the slight firming of his gorgeous mouth as he advanced on her again.

Even though she trusted him to remain true to his word, her inclination was still to run. Run from the spark of unnameable emotion in his eyes. Run from the way he made her feel. Run from the memories of

that other time and that other man his presence inexplicably evoked.

To her credit, she held her ground.

Or, rather, the kitchen sink held it for her. Its cold
porcelain lip pressed against her back.

"Wh-what are you doing?" She was dismayed by the
husky timbre of her voice.

He was directly in front of her now. Close enough to
reach out and touch. Close enough that she could smell
the spicy, masculine scent of his aftershave and see the
crinkly black chest hair peeking above the vee of his
T-shirt. His faded, worn jeans seemed to be in love with
his body—not that she could blame them. And she realized with a start that he was barefoot.

How odd.

A small vulnerability in a man who appeared, in all
other ways, impervious to everything around him.

When he lifted one broad-palmed hand toward her
face, her heart went crazy inside her chest. She couldn't
stop her sharply indrawn breath.

"You missed one," he said as he gently—so heart-
stoppingly *gently*—thumbed a tear from her cheek. It
was dizzying that a man as hard as he was...hard body,
hard face, hard *life*...could ever be so tender.

When he dropped his hand, Sonya was surprised to
find herself disappointed by the desertion. His touch had
been brief, but still she'd felt his warmth and the rough
scar on the pad of his thumb where his fingerprint had
been burned off in an attempt to further obliterate his
true identity.

The Prince of Shadows...

How much had he suffered and lost in the name of

saving the world? Would he save the world now? Would he really follow through and do what Grafton was asking?

"Who are you crying for?" he asked again. This time his sandpaper voice was barely a whisper.

"Why do you care?"

And yes, she'd used his earlier words against him. It was a ploy to cover up how much having him close affected her equilibrium, her ability to compose a rational thought or speak an intelligible word.

He lifted his hand again, this time cupping her cheek in his warm palm. The calluses were deliciously raspy against her skin. His pupils dilated the instant his eyes landed on her mouth, and her lips tingled as if his gaze were a physical touch. Her jaw slipped open the slightest bit.

An unconscious invitation.

Or maybe it was a conscious one. It was hard to tell with her blood pounding in her ears and her brain turning to mush.

"Call it professional curiosity." He glanced from her mouth to her eyes. "I find myself puzzled by what would make a fellow blackmailee cry into the kitchen sink."

"I don't think 'blackmailee' is a word."

"Sonya..." Her name was a deep, raspy purr. His tone said he knew she was stalling.

"I was crying for a man I once knew. The one you reminded me of when you were..._you_. When you were Majid Abass. Before all the plastic surgery."

"So...truly _not_ the jewel thief?"

"No." She swallowed.

"But you said you loved him."

"I'll never love any man the way I loved—"

There she went again, word vomiting the truth when she'd be better served with a lie.

Angel, who seemed to be the stillest man on the planet, grew stiller yet. Then, ever so slowly, his eyes slid back to her mouth.

"I am going to hug you now, Sonya."

Breath shuddered from her lungs. "What? Why?" That wasn't what she'd expected him to say, especially not after the way he'd been eyeballing her lips.

And, no, it hadn't escaped her notice that his words were incredibly similar to the ones Mark had spoken that rainy night while they'd been crowded into that dark Parisian doorway. How could two men be so different and yet so much alike?

"Because you need it."

And then...oh, and *then* he stepped forward and wrapped his big arms around her. It was like being hit with a live wire. A current blasted through her, burning her from the inside out.

She balled one hand into a fist so tight her knuckles cracked. The other squeezed her water glass so hard she was surprised it didn't shatter.

"Relax," he instructed.

"Why are you always telling me to do that?" She tried not to turn her head into his neck and snort in his spicy aftershave like an addict with a tempting line of cocaine. Memories of Mark tried to intrude, memories of how he'd eschewed cologne and aftershave in preference for lilac soap, but she shoved them away.

"You are strung as tight as a piano wire. It cannot be healthy."

Wow. Great. The almighty Prince of Shadows was

lecturing her on her health. All while hugging her. How bizarre was her life right now?

It wasn't one of those half-hearted hugs either. It was a full-on hip-to-hip, chest-to-chest hug, arms tight and big, wide hand splayed against the middle of her back. Angel might be all aloof and untouchable, but when it came to a hug, the man committed completely.

Her heart threatened to pop like a balloon. A hiccup of anguish slipped from her throat. She couldn't help herself; she melted against him. Soaked up his odd affection and let it fill all the cracks in her armor that had developed over the last six months.

She hadn't realized it, but Angel was right. She *needed* a hug. Needed to feel human connection to remind herself she wasn't alone in this.

Then she realized how self-indulgent she was being. How...*weak*.

Pulling back, she whispered, "Thank you. That's enough."

His brow pinched as he stepped away, breaking the connection of their bodies. She shivered as the room's cool air rushed in to replace his body heat.

The pity she saw in his eyes had her grumbling, "When you look at me like that, I want to go crawl into bed and throw the covers over my head."

"How do I look at you?" he asked.

"Like I'm pathetic. Like I'm a disappointment to you. But that's crazy because you don't even know me." Her insides, which a minute ago had been so soft and gooey, were now crawling with tension.

"Is that the *only* way I look at you?" He canted his head. It caused the moonlight to silver the short ends of his black hair. His laser-like focus made her feel like there were two red sniper dots on her face.

Those sniper dots moved down as he let his eyes travel past her mouth and shoulders, over her breasts, down to her hips, and finally back up again. He didn't try to hide the heat in his eyes. He let her see it for what it was.

Heaven help her, he wanted her like she wanted him. The difference between them was that he wasn't trying to hide it.

"No." She swallowed. "It's not the only way you look at me. There's *that* too." She pointed to his face.

"Damn right there is." His gravel-road voice had gone guttural, and she wondered what he'd sounded like before the vocal cord scouring. Had his voice been deep and smooth? Rich and resonant? It saddened her that she would never know. "And now I am going to kiss you, Sonya."

Her thighs quivered as heat coalesced between them. She should have told Angel to keep his gorgeous mouth to himself. She should have told him she had a headache… or head *lice*. But instead she heard herself ask, "Why?"

"Because you want me to."

Boy oh boy, did she ever. It'd been so *long* since she'd been kissed by a man. Longer still since she'd been kissed by one she wanted the way she wanted Angel. It was a bone-deep lust that confused her as much as it frightened her.

Why do I crave him so badly? Is it as simple as pheromones? One healthy animal responding to another? Or is it that he reminds me of Mark? If so, how twisted is that?

Oh, and speaking of twisted, there was a little

something she felt duty-bound to remind Angel of. "But you don't like me."

He snorted and it happened. It happened! His expression softened. It turned his beautiful face into something downright ethereal. She realized why he had assumed the name Angel, and she wouldn't have been surprised had a choir of heavenly hosts started singing *Ahhhhhh* in perfect harmony as a beam of holy light illuminated his face.

"I seem to be coming around," he rumbled. "But before you feel my lips on yours, before you know what it is to be kissed by me, I have to know one thing."

"What?"

"Something true."

She matched his stillness as a little alarm bell sounded shrilly inside her head. "What?"

"Do you *truly* love your jewel thief?"

She swallowed and, for once, considered her response before answering him. The company line said she should hold fast. But something in his eyes, something mysterious and intangible, told her the truth would serve her better.

"No." She shook her head. "I have only ever truly loved one man."

"Then why?" he demanded. "Why did you help the thief escape? Why do you let Grafton intimidate you, *keep* you?"

The whole story beckoned to be told. But she'd already given him all she dared. "You asked for something true. One thing. Now you have it. I won't give you more."

He did it again. He popped his jaw, and too many beautiful, painful memories tried to swarm her brain.

Closing her eyes, she wondered how her body could

want the man standing in front of her while her heart still hurt for...*longed* for...another. It made no sense.

When she blinked open her eyes, she found Angel's gaze once more on her lips. It was hot. It was hungry.

It was also a little perturbed.

She hadn't given him everything he wanted. In retaliation, would he deny her his kiss? If so, it would tell her a lot about who he truly was, if he was a man who would—

He bent his head and claimed her mouth.

She could have resisted him. She *could* have.

Until she got her first taste.

After that, she was dunzo. Gone. Lost in his flavor and his power, in the palpable peril and animal magnetism emanating from his every pore.

She didn't realize her water glass had slipped from her nerveless fingers until Angel broke the kiss and caught the glass before it could hit the tiles and shatter.

Holy moly, she'd never seen reflexes so fast. At least not outside special effects in movies.

"S-sorry," she stuttered. "I—"

That's all she managed before the Prince of Shadows set the glass in the sink, cupped her jaw in both hands, and once again laid on her a kiss that promised dark, unspeakable pleasures...

Chapter 5

WHAT WAS HE DOING? WHAT THE *HELL* WAS HE DOING?

Oh, right. With everything he had, he was kissing the woman he'd fallen in love with a decade earlier and, God help him, loved still. His mind and body had traveled down I-Want-Your-Sex Road so fast that he'd missed his exit to This-Is-a-Really-Bad-Idea Town.

A really *bad idea*, he warned himself and followed that up with, *It isn't fair to her*.

Of course, when she slipped her tongue between his teeth, tentatively exploring, it took everything he had not to fall to his knees. Her mouth tasted of love and loss, of a wonderful and terrible past and a murky, tormented future.

It's not fair, he silently reminded himself again. *She doesn't know who I am*.

And yet she wanted him.

It was there in her eyes when she looked at him. A familiar longing. A confused, punch-drunk hunger that defied logic and reason because it was instinctual, a product of their lizard brains recognizing in each other the perfect physical mate. All the plastic surgery in the world couldn't mask that.

"Mmm," he hummed when she sucked on his tongue. Just a little. Just a nibble. He angled her head so he could align their mouths more closely.

In all the years that had passed, he had tried to convince

himself their connection, their *passion*, had been a product of their youthful hearts. Two undisciplined lovers
hungry to experience the thrill of the fall. But now?
Oh, now, with her in his arms, with her mouth eager and
greedy on his, he realized it had been so much more.

He didn't believe in fated love or one-and-only's,
but neither could he discount the truth staring him in
the face. Or, rather, the truth gripping his shoulders and
trying to inhale him.

No woman had ever come close to touching his heart
the way Sonya had. And certainly no woman had ever
brought him the kind of pleasure she did.

And believe me, he thought as he nipped her plump
bottom lip, knowing it would make her gasp, *I let plenty
of them try*.

Since he'd left her, he hadn't exactly lived the life of
a monk. Looking back, he realized he'd been searching
for Sonya inside other women, looking for that same
connection, that same spark. But no matter how hard
he'd tried, no matter how many babes he'd bounced atop
countless beds, he'd always come up empty-handed.

Now, he realized that was because Sonya was it. The
one. The standard by which he'd judged women and
beauty and bravery and grace. He'd compared every
smile to her smile, every laugh to her laugh. To him, she
was everything a woman should be, her name branded
upon his heart.

Fool that he was, he took great delight in knowing
she felt the same, knowing she'd only ever loved one
man. *Him*.

Or, at least she loved me as I was back then, he
thought, stepping in to her until she was flush along his

front, loving the feminine heat rolling off her body and the way she didn't hesitate to rub herself against him.

That was the problem, wasn't it? Not that she rubbed herself against him; that was heaven on earth. But that she'd loved him as he was back then. Because—and this was God's honest truth—that man was dead in all the ways that counted. When Mark had become Majid who had, in turn, become Angel, he'd given up his home, his name, his *face*…and the woman he loved.

He'd done it in the name of Israel and freedom and the lives of innocent people everywhere, *including* hers. But he'd done it nonetheless. He'd left her.

Left her to miss him. Left her to mourn him. Left her to fend for herself in a treacherous and merciless world. And look what had happened. She'd fallen into the grasp of a man like Grafton.

How can she ever forgive me?

Anguish grabbed hold of his heart and shoved it into his throat at the same time she grabbed the back of his head and went up on tiptoe to press herself more firmly against him.

When guilt had threatened to swamp him over the years, he had always been able to justify things to himself and chase the insidious emotion away. Now, knowing what had become of her, knowing if he had stayed, she wouldn't be in this awful position, remorse wormed its way inside his gut and set up shop.

He'd wronged her for the right reasons. He'd made a decision that broke their hearts and quite possibly saved their lives. He'd wrecked their little world to make the larger one safer for everyone.

Yet…was it possible there might have been another

way? Could he have answered the call of his country and his ramsad *and* held on to the woman he loved? Ten years ago, he would have insisted that how things had happened was the only way any of it could have happened. Today? Well, today a seed of doubt had been planted.

For fuck's sake. It was all so complicated. *So confusing.*

There were only two things he knew for sure. First, he was determined to figure out *why* she allowed herself to work for Grafton, to discover precisely what the bastard had on her to keep her under his thumb if it wasn't her love and loyalty to the jewel thief. Second, along with bringing Grafton/Spider down, he was determined to save Sonya. She didn't deserve the circumstances she'd found for herself. He believed that with everything inside him.

His thoughts dissolved then because her starved and impatient kisses turned abandoned. She'd lost herself to passion, hungrily devouring his lips and tongue and running her hands over his shoulders, up into his short hair. His mind drifted back to a time when his thick, dark locks had been long enough to curl around her fingers. His cock responded to her wicked seduction by straining against the fly of his jeans, seeking the heat and the soft give of her belly.

She moaned with pleasure.

He moaned for more of her.

When she sucked his tongue into her mouth, laving it and loving it and flicking the tip, it startled him to realize she'd acquired new skills.

As soon as he had the thought, he firmly crushed it in an imaginary fist.

Since he'd been a far cry from a monk, he couldn't expect her to have lived like a nun. Sonya was too lusty for that, her sex drive too strong. Still, it was best if he didn't allow his mind to linger on the idea of her in another man's arms, or he might turn homicidal.

He repaid her for the pleasure she'd given him by sucking her sweet tongue into his mouth. With his tongue and his teeth and wet suction, he showed her how he would tend to her rose-colored nipples and that hot knot of nerves at the top of her sex…the one that grew hard and distended when she got truly warmed up.

"Angel," she whispered, coming up for air.

The way she said *Angel*, with such longing and desperation, was perfect. Except it wasn't his name. Not his *real* name, anyway. And the fool in him longed to throw caution to the wind and tell her the truth, if only to hear her call him Mark one last time.

Years of unquenched desire rode atop his shoulders. A decade of dirty words fell from his lips as he kissed his way back to her ear.

"Tell me you want me," he commanded, nipping her earlobe.

The way she groaned captured him. Trapped him. Except the truth was, she'd owned him since the moment she opened her mouth beside his table at that café in Paris and asked if he was Mark Risa in sweetly accented Hebrew. He was hers. Always had been. Always would be.

Instinct was his ruler now. Instinct and the memories of all the things she liked. All the things that made her yelp and purr and beg for more. Cupping her breast through the soft cotton of her T-shirt, he thumbed over her nipple, delighted to discover the peak already ruched tight with desire.

She was as responsive as he remembered. Possibly more so.

"Tell me you want me," he demanded again, needing to hear it. Needing her to admit it.

"I want you. God help me, I do."

If he'd only heard the desperation in her voice, he might have kept going. Except...overshadowing that desperation were hard notes of guilt.

Reality check.

He pulled back to discover her eyes were glassy with unshed tears. Everything inside him stilled—his heart, his lungs, his blood. Everything except his mind. It raced toward a conclusion he didn't want to face.

"Are you still crying for him?" he whispered. "This man from your past?"

"No." She shook her head. Then shrugged. "Maybe. I don't know. It's just that you remind me of him sometimes. The way you walk. The way you pop your jaw. The way you kiss, except..."

He wanted nothing more than to keep contact with her. But she had withdrawn from him emotionally, and the gentleman in him—a guy he rarely let out to play—demanded he withdraw from her physically. When he stepped back, breaking the connection of their bodies, it felt like everything that was important inside him stayed behind. Stayed with *her*.

"Except what?"

"Except you're better at it than he was. I didn't think that was possible," she was quick to add. "Because he was the best. The absolute *best*. And yet it *is* possible.

And I feel so…so…" She swallowed and searched his eyes. "*Guilty* for admitting it."

Angel shot a victorious fist in the air. Or, at least, he imagined he did.

Couple of things here… One, good to know that for her, and up until now, he'd been the best. And two, he *had* learned a thing or two since the tender age of twenty-four. He looked forward to demonstrating each and every new skill.

"Sonya, you are not wrong to want me. Your man is dead." The lie tasted sour in his mouth. "But *you* are still living. Still breathing. You have needs."

She frowned before ducking her chin and staring at her bare feet. He glanced down too and found, much to his delight, her toenails were painted a familiar hot pink.

So there is *some of the old Sonya left…*

"It feels wrong to want you." Her blond hair had fallen over her shoulders like the halves of a curtain. "I don't even know you."

He didn't mistake her words. They were essentially the ones he'd given her earlier. Except the difference was that in his case, he had *known* he was lying.

She lifted her chin, staring into his eyes. "Why? Why do I feel this connection with you? Is it because we're in the same boat? Because Grafton has us both by the nose?"

"I cannot say." Another lie. The pile was becoming unwieldy. "But I can tell you I feel it too."

He thought she would be happy to hear it, but she pressed the heel of her hand to her forehead and blew out a gusty sigh. "I'm tired. I should go to bed. We leave for Moldova in six hours."

Whoa. What? That was it? She was going to abandon the conversation when it was getting good?

"Good night, Angel," she said a little breathlessly.

Stay, he wanted to tell her.

No. Screw that. He didn't want her to stay. He wanted to toss her over his shoulder, cart her upstairs, and throw her on his bed and undress her. He wanted to kiss every inch of her naked body until she begged him to put himself inside her.

Instead, he took a step back and lifted a hand, wordlessly indicating she was free to go.

It took everything he had not to reach for her when she slid past him. Instead, he satisfied himself with watching her hips sway to the feminine rhythm of her body as she walked to the end of the kitchen island. She had filled out some over the years. Not that she'd ever been stick thin. God had smiled the day he made her and blessed her with curves. But what little angularity youth had given her was gone now. Her hips were fuller. Her breasts heavier. Everything about her screamed *woman*.

At the doorway, she swung around, a question in her eyes.

"Was there something else?" he asked.

"I know you think I'm broken." The misery in her voice hit him in the place where his shattered heart used to be.

Oh, Sonya. What happened to you?

He wanted so much to take her in his arms and remind her of what she once was. Of *who* she once was. But all he could give her was one simple truth. "The light only truly shines through people who have been broken."

Chapter 6

"IT'S ALL ARRANGED?" ASAD GRAFTON SPOKE QUIETLY into the phone. With the massive mahogany doors to the library closed and the fire crackling loudly behind the grate, there was no chance his conversation could be overhead. But still...

One can never be too careful.

"As per your instructions, the owner of the café has been properly paid off." Benton's thick Yorkshire accent sounded on the other end of the line. "He'll act as your server during the transaction. He knows what part to play. Also, your Al-Qaeda contact is on a plane to Moldova as we speak. He's been apprised of the plan and is ready and eager to go. As long as the Prince of Shadow's source comes through, everything should go off without a hitch."

"Good." Grafton nodded, running through possible scenarios to ensure they were ready for anything and everything. "Good," he said again when he was satisfied all was in place for the next day. "Oh, and by the by, he prefers to be called Angel."

Benton snorted. "For shit's sake, *why*? 'Prince of Shadows' is way cooler. Sounds dark. Sinister."

Grafton grimaced. "I think, even now, he's careful to protect his cover. You should hear the way he talks. Little slang. Very few contractions. His accent varies from word to word. It's impressive. And besides, if you'd ever met him, you'd understand it doesn't bloody well matter *what* he calls himself. The man *is* dark and sinister."

For a moment, there was silence on the other end of the line. Grafton used it as an opportunity to push away from his desk and walk over to the fireplace. When he added another log, sparks flew and were sucked up the chimney.

"You sound afraid of him," Benton finally said.

Grafton's hackles sprang upright. Partly because it would never do for one of his subordinates to speak to him with such familiarity. Partly because the almighty Spider was meant to fear no one. But mostly because Benton was right.

Angel didn't frighten him. Not exactly. But the man certainly made him…*wary*. The way Angel moved, that deadly knowledge that gleamed in his eyes anytime their gazes met all but screamed one word: *assassin*.

Given the chance, Angel would kill him. No questions. No second thoughts. No remorse. It was one of the reasons Grafton had doubled the number of guards patrolling the grounds, and why he was nervous that only *three* of those guards would be coming with him to Moldova.

Three trained security personnel against one man should be *more* than enough. In fact, he'd convinced himself they *would* be since that was as many as his private plane could safely seat. But still, there in the far, darkest corner of his mind glowed an ember of doubt.

I'll be glad once this whole bloody business is over and Majid or Angel or the Prince of Shadows or whatever the sodding shit he wants to call himself is out of my life, Grafton thought, walking back to his desk and taking a seat.

It was late. He should be tired. *Most* men were tired at this hour. But he got his best work done between 1:00 a.m. and 4:00 a.m.—when the world was quiet, and dark deeds could be hidden beneath dark skies.

He realized he'd been silent for too long when Benton's voice sounded in his ear, the young man's tone incredulous. "Jesus H, *are* you afraid of him?"

Grafton ground his teeth. "Of course not. And you'd best mind your tongue, boy. You've grown far too cheeky for my tastes."

"Please." Benton chuckled. "Don't pretend you don't love me. And honestly, if you sacked me, where would you find another keyboard jockey with a one-fifty IQ?"

"Same place I found *you*. Oxford is lousy with brainy little computer nerds."

"But none of them are as good as I am. And none of them would be your loyal lapdog."

"What a load of tosh," Grafton scoffed. "You're only loyal because I have proof you hacked the university's systems to raise your marks and the marks of all your friends."

"Don't forget I also *lowered* the marks of my enemies."

"A man after my own heart."

Besides being a dab hand at using the mysteries of the internet to worm his way inside various governments and navigate the dark web to gather Intel Grafton could use as blackmail, Benton was his own special brand of entertainment. The young man had become like a surrogate son to Grafton over the years.

That thought was enough to have him sobering. It was a stark reminder that his *real* son had been taken from him. Shot in the head in some seedy hotel in Chicago.

Strange, all Grafton's life he'd sought power for the

sake of power, collected assets to his side because with every new acquisition, his influence grew and his reach extended. Sure, there'd been setbacks over the years, people who had tried to turn on him or times when some government from this country or that had managed to take out one of the men or women who'd gotten themselves stuck in his extensive web. But he'd never taken any of it personally. It was business. The way the cookie crumbled. The way the game was played.

Until his son…

Even now, years after his Sharif's death, Grafton was shocked at how much that loss affected him. Not so much because he held any great affection for his progeny, but more because it *rankled* that anyone had the audacity to take something from him. And then, those bastards in Chicago had had the gall to actually try to—

"A man after your own heart, eh?" Benton interrupted his thoughts. "That's as close to an admission of love as I'll get, I suppose. And since you're in the mood to admit things, please tell me you don't *really* want to end the Prince of Shad…er…*Angel* after the handoff? I mean, with his connections and expertise, he could be a feather in your cap full of ne'er-do-wells. Or, if you *insist* he must die, then at least hand him over to the Revolutionary Guard. They've a ten million quid bounty on his head."

Grafton had himself a genuine laugh at that one.

He'd been born of the brief dalliance between a wealthy English lord and an affluent African princess. It was safe to say his inheritance alone was more than the GDPs of most third-world countries.

"You laugh," Benton said. "But let me remind you, while ten mil is nothing to you, it's quite a lot to most

people. And by *most* people, I mean your favorite computer hacker with the delightful Yorkshire inflections. I
scraped the dark web of the Prince of…bugger it all…
Angel's information before anyone else could set eyes
on it, but it would be a piece of cake for me to covertly
forward it along to the Iranians. With my bank account
information attached, naturally."

Once again, Grafton found himself fighting a smile.
"And what would *you* do with ten million pounds?"

"What *wouldn't* I do with ten million pounds?"

"You'd be surprised how little that actually buys. If
you've a mind to get yourself a yacht, then I hate to be
the one to tell you, but that won't—"

"No yachts," Benton cut in. "I get seasick. But I *do*
fancy the Rolls-Royce Sweptail. I mean, have you set
eyes on that car? She's bloody *gorgeous*."

"And bloody conspicuous," Grafton countered.

"Oh, I wouldn't drive her. I'd park her in my garage
and have my daily wank while looking at her."

Grafton shook his head. "In the parlance of your generation, that's TMI."

Benton's laugh echoed over the phone.

"No," Grafton continued. "We won't be handing
Angel over to the Revolutionary Guard. We'll deal with
him ourselves. It's the only way I can be certain the job
is done right."

Chapter 7

AS THE PRIVATE JET TAXIED TOWARD A SLIGHTLY dilapidated-looking hangar, Angel turned his attention from the drab scenery slipping past his window to Sonya. She sat on a plush leather sofa on the opposite side of the fuselage. It hadn't escaped his attention that she had carefully avoided making eye contact with him throughout the flight.

Last night had rattled her.

Good. He didn't want to be the only one suffering the aftereffects.

She glanced up from the copy of Hemingway's *A Farewell to Arms* she'd been pretending to read—yes, *pretending*; she hadn't turned a page in twenty minutes—to find him staring at her. Good manners dictated he look away.

Fuck good manners.

Holding her gaze, he let his eyes tell her all the things his mouth couldn't.

I still want you.

I still love you.

Please trust me.

But she wasn't a mind reader. Her confused frown

said as much. When he continued to stare, she swallowed and shifted uncomfortably.

What? she mouthed, her delicately arched eyebrows pinching.

Becky, the lead motorcycle designer at Black Knights Inc., had once told Angel he had the look of a predator. "*All piercing eyes and sharp focus.*" He hadn't told Becky at the time, but the truth was that he *was* a predator. The Mossad had trained him to be. Trained him to carry out vicious acts in the name of protecting innocents, his homeland, and all of Western civilization.

He tried to soften his gaze now, but apparently that didn't work. Sonya shifted again, and a blush spread down her throat, mottling her décolletage and drawing his eyes to the creamy slopes of her full breasts barely visible above the open neck of her turquoise blouse. The memory of the night before, when he'd palmed one of those delicious mounds—and a hundred memories of a decade ago when he'd tongued them and kissed them—swirled through his mind.

He was good at hiding his feelings. Better than good, he was *great*. But some of what he thought must have registered on his face. Sonya blew out a ragged breath, her pulse hammering heavily in her neck. *What?* she mouthed again, this time hardening her jaw.

He could have held his tongue. He probably *should* have held his tongue. But considering there were a million things he wanted to tell her and couldn't, this one truth seemed harmless.

And *necessary*.

He didn't want there to be any confusion that he

wanted her. That he meant to have her. That he *would* have her.

He mouthed, *Thinking about last night.*

She caught her bottom lip between her teeth and slid a tentative glance toward Grafton. The sack of shit was too busy making his way through the current issue of the London *Times* to pay them any mind.

When she looked back at Angel, she shook her head.

He didn't know if she was telling him not to think about last night or not to *mention* last night. He cocked his head, ready to mouth *why*, but the plane taxied into the hangar and the cabin's interior was thrown into shadow.

Grafton lowered his paper and blinked owlishly against the gloom before the pilot flipped on the interior lights. "Well, that was a ruddy fast flight," he muttered.

"Too fast," Sonya agreed, marking her spot in the book with a length of hot-pink ribbon that reminded Angel of her painted toenails. Then she unlatched her seat belt and reached beneath the sofa for her leather purse. Her jerky movements attested to her jitters as she stuffed the book inside her handbag.

Angel knew it was no longer *him* making her nervous. It was what they were poised to do here in Moldova.

When the plane came to a stop, the three hulking No-Necks who'd been seated at the back made their way down the aisle to the front. Combined, they smelled like a men's locker room. It was all BO and body spray, deodorant and old sneakers. They each carried a black nylon duffel filled with... Angel tilted his head and narrowed his eyes, taking in the smooth sides of the bags and the telltale sharp edges poking against their ends.

Filled with cash, he decided. He'd done plenty of

money drops over the years. He recognized the size and shape of a bag full of…as the Wu-Tang Clan and Ozzie, BKI's onsite computer whiz, would say…*dolla, dolla bills, y'all*.

Although, in this case it was probably euros or British pounds.

The pilot, a middle-aged man with a robust midsection that said he'd had a lifelong love affair with all things deep-fried, emerged from the cockpit and lowered the private plane's door. As soon as he did, the smell of jet fuel and damp concrete drifted into the fuselage.

Jet fuel would always remind Angel of the night he escaped Iran. And it would always make his stomach drop.

"You want to be ready to depart within a few hours, is that correct, sir?" the pilot asked, looking at Grafton. His expression said he was scared or timid or intimidated or…Angel narrowed his eyes…all three.

"That's right, Captain Wilfred," Grafton replied. "Thanks for the smooth ride on the way over. And sorry I couldn't give you more time to prepare for today's flight. I know Jenny is due to have some tests run this week."

At mention of Captain Wilfred's…*wife?…daughter?…sister?…mother?* the man blanched and swallowed so hard his Adam's apple bounced. Apparently, like most of Grafton's employees, Captain Wilfred was kept on the payroll and kept in line because Grafton had something on him. And if Angel wasn't mistaken, that something had to do with whoever this Jenny woman was.

"It's fine, sir." The pilot did everything but doff his hat. "I'll go back to the cockpit for a postflight check and to make sure things look good for our return trip."

Captain Wilfred left for the cockpit so fast Angel thought maybe he'd used teleportation.

After he'd gone, Grafton turned to one of the No-Necks. "Benton has already laid the groundwork," he told them.

Angel knew all about Benton Currothers. The kid was a menace, and Grafton might originally have pressed Benton into working for him because he had something he could hold over the little shitstain. But BKI had discovered Benton *stayed* on because he *liked* being employed by the almighty Spider. Nerdy little prick fancied himself a straight-up gangsta living the thug life, which might have made Angel particularly wary if he didn't have an ace in the hole. That ace's name was Ethan "Ozzie" Sykes, and he was the world's greatest cyber ninja.

Benton was good.

Ozzie was better.

And the proof was in the pudding.

When the Black Knights had decided to leak Angel's information onto the dark web in hopes of catching Benton's and therefore *Grafton's* attention, Ozzie had been there making sure no one but Grafton's computer prodigy had access to the Intel, keeping Angel's new identity and new face safe from the Iranians.

"All you have to do is hand off the cash," Grafton said to Lead No-Neck. "Do you remember the name of the man you're supposed to meet?"

No-Neck nodded. "Igor Grosu."

"Jolly good." Grafton slapped a hand down on the arm of his leather chair. "But remember, before you give him the bags, he must confirm where they're going."

"Right." The hulking security man nodded again. "The first one goes to the immigration official on duty. The second one goes to the air-traffic controllers. And the third goes to the ground crew here."

"Perfect." Grafton flicked his wrist. "Proceed."

The trio of security guards traipsed down the stairs, and Angel turned to eye Grafton. "Money talks, am I right?"

"In my experience." Grafton lifted the London *Times* from his lap and shook it open. "And it talks even louder in poor countries like this."

"I take it the cash in those bags is so this flight will never appear on any manifest or remain in anyone's memory?"

Behind his newspaper, Grafton smiled. "Precisely."

Not that Angel would have expected anything less from a man of Grafton's experience. Even if the exchange of the uranium went off without a hitch, it was still in Grafton's best interest to make sure he'd covered all his tracks. No one in their right mind wanted a black-market nuclear deal traced back to them.

On that topic…Angel asked the question that had been bothering him for two weeks. The only reason he'd waited until now was because he'd been sticking to his disinterested act, hoping that Grafton would offer the information on his own. But time had run out.

"Why do you want the uranium?"

Sonya's eyes widened and darted from Grafton to Angel to Grafton's driver who was still sitting at the rear of the plane and back again.

Since Grafton occupied the seat across the aisle from Angel, he was forced to turn slightly to look Angel dead in the eye. There was no mistaking Grafton's smugness, or his malice. Most men would have withered under his stare.

Angel wasn't most men.

Five seconds passed while neither of them so much as blinked.

Ten seconds passed.

Grafton's driver cleared his throat at the back of the plane. Sonya fiddled with the zipper on her purse as the air inside the aircraft grew heavy with expectation. Angel's heart was a steady thud against his rib cage, but his mind raced a mile a minute. He considered the possibility Grafton would refuse to answer. He wouldn't put it past the asshole to indulge in a little quid pro quo. But then Grafton's pride and audacity won out.

"I don't want it. Not really." Grafton made a show of carefully folding his newspaper and slipping it into the pocket on the side of his chair. "I've made it this far in life by refusing to dip my toe into the dangerous pool of bootleg nuclear materials. But when your information came across my desk, I realized if you could use your knowledge and contacts to get some uranium, then I could kill two birds with one stone."

"Which two birds would those be?"

Grafton's smile turned sinister. "Cementing a relationship with Al-Qaeda." At mention of the group that'd carried out so many attacks on Western soil, a cold chill stole up Angel's spine. From the corner of his eye, he saw Sonya suck in her cheeks in an effort to keep from saying anything. Or else she was simply trying not to scream in horror. "And getting revenge on the people who killed my son," Grafton added after giving his first mind-melting reason time to sink in.

Grafton enjoyed the dramatic.

"I didn't know you had a son." Sonya tried to make

her tone curious, but there was no mistaking the tremor in her voice.

Angel's day, which had started out as a carnival ride of fuckedupery, had suddenly gotten a whole lot worse. From the beginning, the stakes for his mission had been sky-high. Now, they reached all the way into the stratosphere. *Al-Qaeda? Seriously? Was Grafton insane?*

"Don't fret about it, my dear." Grafton smirked. "Nobody knew I had a son."

Angel and Sonya exchanged glances.

Grafton chuckled. "See? You two thought you had me figured out, didn't you? But let me assure you, just when you think you've peeled the last layer on this onion, you'll find there are infinite layers left."

God, the guy truly was the definition of a shitbag. His arrogance and smugness knew no bounds.

"That's why you're here," Sonya said.

"Pardon?"

"On this trip," she clarified. "You usually let your lackeys do things like this for you, always staying well away from the dirty work. But this is personal."

Grafton made a face. "You're quite right, dear Sonya. This *is* personal. Although, probably not for the reason you think."

"What do you mean?"

"I mean, I was never very close to my son. For the first five years of his life, I never set eyes on him. Then I rarely saw him except for the occasional holiday when he came home from boarding school. Even after he grew up, we chose to keep our familial ties to the bare minimum."

"Where was he for the first five years of his life?" Sonya asked.

"It's a long and sordid tale." Angel thought Grafton would leave it at that, so he was surprised when Grafton continued. "You see, like my father before me, I traveled to Africa as a young man." Grafton waved his hand expansively, seeming to relish their curiosity. Particularly *Angel's* curiosity since Angel had made it a point to remain studiously indifferent to anything and everything Grafton said. "I met a woman there. A Somali woman. She was so beautiful; I was instantly smitten. Alas, our romance didn't last."

"What happened?" Sonya asked.

"It's simple. The more I got to know her, the less I liked her, and the more her beauty faded in my eyes."

"What didn't you like about her?"

Angel didn't know if Sonya was truly interested in Grafton's torrid love life, or if she was stalling. With every passing second, they got closer to the time when they'd exit the plane and embark on a journey toward arming *Al-Qaeda* with a nuclear weapon!

"Like most beautiful women, she was arrogant. And mouthy. There's nothing more annoying than an arrogant, mouthy bitch. Wouldn't you agree, Majid?"

Angel didn't bother answering that ridiculous question. He made sure his expression projected his feelings that Grafton was misogynist prick who would better serve the world by pushing up daisies.

"Anyway…" Grafton waved a hand through the air again, batting away Angel's unspoken disgust. "Lo and behold, the conniving cunt turned up pregnant." A terrible look came over Grafton's face then. "I say 'conniving' because I don't think it was a happy accident. I think…" He shook his head. "No. I *know* she meant to entrap me, tie me down so I'd spend the rest of my life supporting her and her illegitimate brat."

Grafton's smile returned. This time it reminded Angel of a hyena's. It was full of malevolence, tinged with bloodlust. Over the years, Angel had met many men who smiled like that. Some of them were dead by his own hand, and the darkness inside him longed to put Lord Asad Grafton's name on that list.

"But she didn't know who she was bloody well dealing with." The pride in Grafton's voice turned Angel's stomach. "I left that impertinent bitch to fend for herself. Only once the child was five, old enough to go to school, did I offer to bring him to England for an education. Of course, my proposal stipulated she remain in Somalia."

"Impregnate and vacate." Angel curled his lip in contempt. "Is that your motto?"

"With her it was."

"Well, I guess you showed her, didn't you?" Sonya didn't bother hiding the derision on her face or the venom in her voice.

Angel fought a grin. He was ridiculously happy to see a hint of the fiery, plucky woman he knew and loved.

"Ah, ah." Grafton waggled a finger at her. "Remember what I said about arrogant, mouthy bitches?"

Sonya's eyes hardened right along with her jaw. She wanted to come back at Grafton, but bit her tongue. Angel was surprised he didn't see blood seeping from the corners of her mouth.

"The woman should have stayed in Somalia." Grafton continued with his tale. "But after a few years, she missed her son. At least that was the excuse she gave when she showed up at his boarding school. It didn't take me long to work out the real reason she'd travelled to England, however. She planned to blackmail me into providing her with a monthly stipend."

A snarl shaped his lips into something hideous. "She had the *gall* to threaten to go to the press with evidence she'd collected of some…uh…let's call it less-than-aboveboard business I'd done in Africa."

He paused, drawing out the suspense, snapping a glance first at Angel, then at Sonya. When he was satisfied they were on tenterhooks, he licked his lips. "I took her to a hotel, raped her, strangled her, and had her dead body tossed into the Thames."

Sonya winced so hard Angel was surprised she didn't strain a facial muscle.

The warning buzzer that had been sounding in his head since the first night he met Grafton turned into a high-pitched shriek of alarm. Why the hell was Grafton telling them this, *revealing* this? Did he want to impress upon Sonya what he did to women he called "arrogant" and "mouthy"? Was he trying to impress upon Angel how much of a true motherfucker he was?

Or is there another reason? What, exactly, is his angle?

"Oh." Grafton looked pleased with himself as he settled back in his chair. "And one more thing…I made my son watch the whole of it."

Sonya gasped. Angel's gorge rose.

"Why would you do that?" Sonya's voice was hoarse.

"Two reasons. First, because he needed to know how to handle women like his bitch of a mother. And two, he needed to know how to handle me. He needed to know what kind of man his father was."

As good as Angel was at hiding his emotions, that's

how *bad* Sonya was in that moment. Revulsion wallpapered her pretty face. If the muscles working in her jaw were any indication, she once again bit her tongue. Hard.

Grafton's eyes crinkled at the corners. He loved that he'd shocked them. Repulsed them. He thought he'd gained power from his abhorrent little tale. But the truth was, he'd only gotten one step closer to his ultimate downfall.

He doesn't know it yet, Angel thought with satisfaction, *but I'm about to burn his whole world to the ground.*

Chapter 8

"WHAT DO YOU SUPPOSE THE POPULATION OF THIS godforsaken country is?" Rusty asked.

Colby "Ace" Ventura turned his attention away from the alley and back door of the café where Angel said the drop was supposed to go down and glanced over at Rusty Parker. The redheaded behemoth was a former marine, former cod fisherman, and current honorary member of Black Knights Inc.—the latter due to a bizarre and complicated set of circumstances.

Oh, and Rusty was *also* a pain in Ace's ass.

"Who cares?" Ace asked him. "If everything goes right, we'll be out of here in a few hours."

Rusty gifted him with a scathing look. It was pretty much Rusty's go-to expression where Ace was concerned. Probably because Ace was vocal in his disapproval of Rusty's insistence on staying in the closet. Although, admittedly, lack of approval didn't translate into lack of desire. The chemistry that bubbled between them was as palpable now as it'd been the first time Ace met Rusty, when Rusty had sauntered toward him in fisherman's bibs and a ribbed sweater that emphasized the breadth of his shoulders and the powerful muscles in his arms and—

Son of a shit eater! Ace folded up the memory of that day and tidily packed it away in the mental lockbox where he kept all the *other* things he chose not to remember. Like the conversion therapy his father had sent him to before he'd gotten old enough to leave home, join the Navy, and never look back.

"I'm just making conversation." Rusty's expression broadcast how quickly Ace's irritable retort had pissed him off.

Good. Nowadays, Ace pretty much *lived* in Pissedoffville so he appreciated the company, even if that company happened to be the reason for his bad mood.

The truth was, Ace hated being led around by his dick, and anytime Rusty was within ten feet of him, the little head in his pants tried to take over for the big one sitting at the end of his neck. But mostly he hated *wanting* Rusty. Because wanting Rusty felt like "been there, done that."

The memory of Ace's dead husband appeared in his mind's eye. Glen Brogan, Air Force major and closeted homosexual, had been the love of Ace's life.

During the days of Don't Ask, Don't Tell, Glen had claimed keeping their relationship on the down low was a matter of keeping their jobs. But that hadn't explained why, in the end, when Glen had been lying in a hospital, dying from the wounds he'd sustained after being shot down, he hadn't told his family the truth. It hadn't explained why Glen had let Ace stand out in that hospital hallway like a *nobody* while he breathed his last because only "family" had been allowed in the room.

Once more turning his attention to the trash-strewn alley, Ace silently repeated the mantra he'd come up with when Rusty admitted he wasn't out. *Never again. Never again will I live in the dark.*

"I think it's about the size of Maryland," Ozzie piped

up from the back seat, reminding Ace that he and Rusty weren't alone.

Ace frowned in the rearview mirror at BKI's resident computer genius. Ethan "Ozzie" Sykes had Einstein-esque hair befitting the huge brain housed inside his skull. "What are you talking about?" he asked. "What's about the size of Maryland?"

"Moldova." Ozzie reminded Ace of what had started the exchange in the first place. "But I think its population is only about two-thirds of Maryland's so that'd make it...what? Four mil or so?"

Of course BKI's own brainiac would know the answer to Rusty's question.

"I think outside of Chişinău," Ozzie continued conversationally, "it's pretty much rolling fields and tiny villages."

"So you're saying I shouldn't judge the whole place by this little slice of heaven." Rusty waved out the window. "Can't understand what anyone sees in Soviet-era architecture."

Cranes dotted the skyline, proof that even more of the drab buildings Rusty found so unsavory were being erected as they spoke.

"Guess beauty is in the eye of the beholder." Ozzie shrugged.

"These guys used to be Russian. They can claim artists like Kandinsky and Serov. Their former countrymen built St. Basil's Cathedral and the Winter Palace. Why the hell not try to copy *those* examples?"

Rusty liked to play the dumb-jock card, but the man had a textbook knowledge of art, architecture, and design. The one time Ace had pointed that out to him,

Rusty had donned a mulish expression and said, "Right. And how gay is *that*?" So Ace kept his mouth shut now.

Chişinău was a brazen and dusty place. The cars on the streets were a testament to its fast economic growth having only benefited a handful of its citizens. There were one or two BMWs and Lexuses among the hundreds of taxis and old streetcars. The sidewalks were lined with pensioners hawking cheap, astringent-smelling soap, shiny samovars, and packages of ladies' underwear that had likely "fallen off a truck."

Bleating horns competed with the voices of the vendors, and the air inside the parked car smelled of old exhaust, stale cigarettes, and Rusty's outdoorsy after-shave. Ace would be damned glad when this mission, the Black Knights' *last* mission, was over and done with. Then Rusty would be free to go back to his cod-fishing business in England, and Ace would be free to forget he'd ever met the man.

"They're here." Boss's deep, bass voice sounded in Ace's earpiece, snapping his mind away from the subject of Rusty Parker—*thank the Christ child*—and focusing it on the task at hand. "Looks like we've got a party of five," BKI's leader continued. "I'm seeing Angel, Miss Butler, and a guy I assume is Grafton. Hard to tell since the dude's wearing a wig, big sunglasses, and a hoodie over his head. There are also three beefy, bearded ass-holes who are definitely packing heat in shoulder holsters. They keep looking around like they expect a horde of assassins to pop up from the sidewalk."

Ace leaned over the steering wheel, searching the alley running behind the café. Activating his throat mic, he told the team keeping eyes on the front of the place,

"No sign of activity on our end. The supplier might decide to waltz in the front door. Do us a favor and keep your eyes peeled."

"Roger that, *mon frère*," Rock Babineaux's Cajun accent came over the line.

"What he said," Nate "Ghost" Weller added.

Ace smiled. If there were two men he could trust not to miss a beat, they were Ghost and Rock. Ghost had an eagle eye, and Rock had a ninja's instincts. If Victor Popov, Angel's contact and the man who was supposedly in possession of the enriched uranium, showed up anywhere near the front of the shop, Ghost and Rock would spot him.

"You're sure the only way in or out of that café is the front and back doors?" Ace glanced at Ozzie in the rearview mirror of the ancient VW they'd purchased just that morning. They'd chosen the Bug because the windows were deeply tinted, perfect for a stakeout, and man-oh-man had the car salesman's eyes lit up when he saw a fistful of good ol' American greenbacks in Ace's hand.

"So say the schematics I found online," Ozzie assured him.

"Okay then. We wait." Ace looked down at the photograph of Popov that Ozzie had managed to scrounge up. It was taped to the dashboard for easy reference.

"Yo, home slices," Ozzie blurted from the back seat. "Is that movement I see at the other end of the alley?"

Ace glanced up from the photo. He could just barely make out the figure winding his way past the overflowing dumpsters and shoddy-looking cars.

"Yeah," he told Ozzie, squinting his eyes, waiting to see if he could make a positive ID.

The man wore dark pants and a faded jean jacket. Moldova was located smack-dab between Romania and Ukraine. Its northern latitude meant the average highs for August usually stayed in the seventies. A cold front had moved through the area the night before, dropping the day's temp to ten degrees below that.

As the man moved closer, Ace could finally clearly see his face. The guy's cheeks were fuller than in the picture. He'd put on about thirty pounds since the photo was taken. But there was no way to mistake the thick, wiry eyebrows shading deep, cavernous eye sockets.

"It's Popov," Ace said with certainty.

"You gotta be kidding me," Rusty whispered. "You think he's carrying that shit in a grocery bag?"

Ace's attention snagged on the brown paper bag held tightly in Popov's right hand. "Were you expecting a metal suitcase attached to his wrist with handcuffs?"

"Well...yeah. Kinda." Rusty shifted his monster frame. "Is it me, or is anybody else freaked the fuck out by what's in that sack?"

Ace seized on the opportunity to remind Rusty, "You didn't have to come on this mission. You could have stayed back in Chicago."

Rusty turned his attention away from the alley and allowed it to fall on Ace. "Why do you gotta keep bringing that up?"

"Thought maybe the obvious needed stating."

"I know I ain't the brightest star in the sky," Rusty said. See? Dumb jock card, whipped out and flourished in front of Ace's face. "But give me some credit. I get what the score is here. Thanks to you guys, I'm up to my ass in this shit whether I want to be or not, so how about you stop busting my balls? Besides, unlike *some* people, once I start something, I finish it."

Ace's hackles sprung upright. "And what the hell is *that* supposed to mean?"

"Oh, I don't know." Rusty shrugged the shoulder closest to Ace. Ace swore he could feel the friction even though they weren't touching. The molecules in the air separating them shifted and grated. "You tell me."

"I only kissed you all those months ago to prove a point," he ground out. "Not to start something."

"Why don't I believe you?"

"Is this going to be like *Moonlighting* where all the feisty banter makes you two fall in love and start screwing?" Ozzie interrupted from the back seat.

Ace frowned at him in the rearview mirror. "I'm sorry. *Moonlighting?*"

"You know, that old show from the eighties with Bruce Willis and Cybill Shepherd?" When Ace gave him a blank stare, Ozzie said, "Fine. Then let me put it to you both straight. I wish the two of you would bone and get it over with because I'm sick and tired of it turning into the Red Wedding anytime you're together."

Ace reached up to scratch his eyebrow with his middle finger.

"Oh, real mature." Ozzie grinned.

"Says the guy wearing the T-shirt printed with *If you can read this, my cloaking device is broken.*"

"Don't harsh on my threads, man." Ozzie looked down at the maroon T-shirt visible beneath his field jacket. "This is some legitimately awesome shiznit."

"Hey, man." Rusty looked over his shoulder at Ozzie. "Don't blame any of this on me. I've been game from the start. Hollywood Hair over here"—he hooked a thumb toward Ace—"put the kibosh on things."

"You *know* why I did that, damnit!" Ace said. "And stop calling me Hollywood Hair!"

"For the love of Leonard Nimoy!" Ozzie hissed. "Keep your voice down."

Ace clamped his mouth shut, properly chagrined.

"Hey, check it out." Rusty pointed out the passenger-side window. "Popov's at the back door."

Ace watched Popov glance nervously up and down the alleyway before lifting a hand to knock. The door popped open, and a short, fat, bewhiskered man in an apron ushered him inside.

Activating his throat mic, Ace pushed everything but the mission from his mind and relayed the following: "Elvis is in the building. Stay frosty up there because from back here it looks like it's go-time."

Chapter 9

LOU COX, THE HEAD OF GRAFTON'S SECURITY DETAIL, pushed open the door to the café and ushered Sonya inside with a hand at the small of her back.

"Hands off," she warned as she stepped over the threshold. She could take a lot when it came to Grafton and his hulking thugs. But invading her personal space crossed a big, fat line she'd drawn in the sand.

Lou flashed her a gummy smile. "Now, here I thought we was friends. I saw you kept that bookmark I gave you."

"Because I was tired of creasing the pages of Grafton's first editions with a paper clip." One would think working for the planet's most powerful underworld crime boss would be nothing but thrills and chills. But the truth was, more often than not, Sonya was bored stiff. She'd spent the months in Grafton's employ diligently making her way through his library to combat the monotony. "And just because I accepted your gift, that doesn't make us friends. It *certainly* doesn't give you the right to touch me."

Lou lifted his meaty paws in the air in that quintessential *guy* way that said without words, *Backing away from the PMSing female*. In her experience, meatheads like him blamed PMS anytime a woman stood up for herself.

She allowed her eyes to adjust from being outside in the bright sunlight. As the interior of the café came into view, she took note of herself and realized she suffered from three physical maladies.

A mile a minute. That's how fast her heart pounded.

Dizzy. That's how her head felt.

Trembling. That's what her knees were doing.

Not that she'd expected to find a masked villain sitting at a table with an atomic bomb on a silver platter like in some low-budget B-rate movie. But on the drive from the airport to the city center, her imagination had run away with her. Just a little bit.

Or a lot.

It hadn't helped that Grafton had used the drive to explain her role in this little adventure. He might have insisted on being part of the exchange, but *she* was to be his mouthpiece. While he hid beneath his fake hair and hoodie and behind his huge sunglasses, she was going to be in charge of making the swap. Of. Nuclear. Material.

Of course, if there was one bright spot in this looming disaster of a day, it was that the café was simply that: a café. Not some spooky, deserted crossroads, like she'd imagined. Not some crumbling abandoned warehouse.

Okay, you can do this, she coached herself as a waiter with a bright smile and a stark, white apron beckoned them to come in with a wave of his ham hock of a hand.

The ambiance of the place was nicer than she would have expected, considering that the building's exterior was covered in colorful graffiti—hence its name, Graffiti Café. The tables were draped with white linen. The chairs were covered in cheery red velvet. And the crystal light fixtures overhead caught the sun shining in through the three floor-to-ceiling windows at the front of the empty establishment and cast rainbow prisms against the pale-pink walls.

The smell of freshly brewed coffee and warm bread

filled the air as she took another deep, calming breath and allowed the waiter to direct her toward a table at the back of the room. The man appeared to be as wide as he was tall—both dimensions falling somewhere around five and a half feet. When he pulled out her chair, she noticed he had close-set, rheumy brown eyes and a habit of tugging on his beard as if he needed to assure himself it was still stuck to his face.

"*Mulţumesc*," she said as he scooted her chair closer to the table. It was one of the only Romanian words she knew.

"You are welcome." His thickly accented English made the phrase sound more like *you arrr velcome*.

She lifted a brow, wondering how he knew they were English speakers. Had he heard her growl at Lou? Then she got distracted when Grafton didn't follow her to the table. Instead, he claimed a seat at the table directly behind her.

Talk about conspicuous, she thought with irritation. What was worse was that Grafton's three security guards took up positions against the back wall.

"Way to make it obvious," she muttered.

"What's that, Sonya my dear?" Grafton asked, settling himself into his chair and causing the legs to scrape across the tile floor.

The smart thing would be for her to keep her mouth shut and pretend she hadn't heard his question. But she couldn't help herself. You could take the woman away from her job at Interpol, but you couldn't take the Interpol agent out of the woman.

At least not entirely.

"You're drawing attention to us," she whispered from

the side of her mouth. "And even if you aren't, *they* are."
She flicked a hand toward his security detail.

"Don't worry your pretty little head about it. I've the
situation well in hand."

Grafton's words were polite enough—well, except
for that infuriatingly misogynistic *pretty little head* part.
But his tone was full of razor blades, warning her she'd
once again stepped over the line.

After six months of carefully pandering and grovel-
ing, she'd spent the last couple of weeks pushing her
luck with him. Why the hell was she doing that?

Oh, right. Because of Angel.

She hated seeing flickers of pity and disappointment
in his eyes when she allowed Grafton to ride roughshod
over her. For reasons she dared not explore, she wanted
to show him she *wasn't* the meek, cowardly woman he
thought she was.

Shifting her gaze in Angel's direction, she found his
remarkably dark eyes watching her with the same interest he'd shown last night in the kitchen.

For a moment, she allowed herself to compare him to
Mark. *Mark* had talked about their animal attraction. He
had admitted to feeling pulled to her in ways he couldn't
explain. But where Mark had been the consummate professional and an all-around gentleman—and had tried
for weeks to deny the attraction that burned between
them—Angel hadn't hesitated for even one second.

And she? Well, she'd been right there with him. Trying
to inhale him. Trying to eat him alive. Willing to lose herself in him if only he would keep on kissing her forever.

Once again she was hit with a wave of confusion and
guilt and…and…*confusion*.

Why did Angel make her feel this way? What was it about him? And what the hell was wrong with her?

She was sitting in a café in Chişinău, Moldova, waiting for some shady dude with enriched uranium to arrive, and she was thinking about her love life? She immediately filed her thoughts in a not-now-are-you-crazy folder.

I mean, for heaven's sake!

"Can I get you something to drink?" the waiter asked Grafton, still tugging away at his beard. His thick accent turned the word *something* into *sumding*.

It occurred to her that he hadn't batted an eye at the three hulking brutes holding up the back wall. Nor did he seem confused that Grafton had chosen not to sit with her and Angel.

Suddenly, Grafton's assurance that he had everything well in hand made a heaping helping of sense. He'd set the stage. The waiter, if that was indeed who the man in the apron truly was, had been expecting them.

"I'll have a bottle of Perrier with a wedge of lime," Grafton said, accepting the menu the waiter handed him.

"And for you, miss?" *Meess.* The waiter turned from Grafton to look at Sonya expectantly.

"Nothing for me," she told him.

"Have something, Sonya." Grafton's voice slipped over her shoulder, brooking no argument.

"Fine," she gritted out. "I'll have hot tea with lemon." She too accepted a menu, although there was no chance on God's green earth she'd be able to stomach food.

"Nothing for me," Angel rasped, waving away the menu shoved in front of him.

"Like I told Sonya, have something." Grafton's tone dared Angel to naysay him.

Angel accepted that dare. "And like I keep saying, go fuck yourself."

Sonya briefly screwed her eyes shut. *Why* did Angel insist on goading Grafton? Did he have a death wish or something?

The waiter, sensing the rising tension at the tables, asked Sonya, "Would you like a hook for your satchel, miss?"

"Huh?" She glanced at him sharply.

"A hook for…" He pulled a small plastic holder from the pocket of his apron and attached it to the side of the table, indicating with hand gestures how she could hang her purse from it.

"Oh." Her hands automatically tightened on the handbag in her lap. "No. I'm fine."

She realized, once again, she'd answered too quickly, not taking the time to think about how her knee-jerk response might be perceived. Thankfully, Grafton didn't seem to notice. He told the waiter, "Give us a few minutes to look over these menus, would you?"

"Of course." The waiter shifted from foot to foot. The motion made his black leather shoes squeak. Then he gave them a little bow and disappeared through a door in the back wall, ostensibly off to fill their drink order.

"You never asked me how my son died or who was responsible for his death," Grafton said conversationally. When Sonya glanced over her shoulder, she found him casually perusing the menu.

Not that she gave a shovel full of *Scheisse* about him *or* his dead son, but for right now, and especially given her newfound penchant for back talk, she figured she'd better keep up pretenses.

"How did he die?" she asked dutifully. "Who is responsible for his death?"

Grafton set aside the menu and adjusted his hoodie so his face was completely shadowed. "He died from a bullet to the brain in a run-down motel on the bad side of Chicago. And those responsible for his death are known as Black Knights Inc."

The way he said the name made Sonya think she should recognize who he was talking about. She didn't.

Grafton glanced at her over his shoulder. She got the impression he studied her from behind the opaque lenses of his glasses. Eventually, he shrugged. "I thought, given your position within Interpol, you might have heard of them."

"No." She shook her head, then looked over at Angel.

He hadn't moved, hadn't spoken. His face was as impassive as always. But there was something about his stillness. It was punctuated by a weird energy.

Had *he* heard of Black Knights Inc.?

Before she could analyze him further, Grafton said, "Ah, well...they *do* run a good game. A good *shadow* game. When I first learned of them, when they killed my son, I thought they were nothing more than what they were purported to be. A group of leather-clad, beer-guzzling, custom bike builders whom my boy had the bad luck of running afoul of. But I've since learned they are much more than that."

"What do you mean?"

"I mean, they're government agents."

She raised both eyebrows, turning back to Grafton, but he was no longer looking at her. He was once more studying his menu. "How do you know that?" she asked.

"I had Benton do some digging on them after I found out they had captured Luke Winterfield."

Now *that* name Sonya knew. "That rogue CIA agent? He's one of yours?"

"*Was*," Grafton allowed. "Before he turned against me. But that's neither here nor there. The point is, the Black Knights captured the sonofabitch, and he must have given them something on me, because they bloody well started trying to suss out my identity. I'd already determined that I would go after them for the death of my son. Even though I wasn't close to Sharif, that doesn't mean I could condone anyone taking him from me. No one takes what's Spider's and lives to tell of it. But, like they say, revenge is a dish best served cold. So I was waiting. Biding my time. But after Winterfield, the Black Knights starting sticking their noses into my business and it shortened the timeline on my vengeance. Which is why we find ourselves here now."

And there it was. For the first time, someone had dared to take something from the almighty Lord Asad Grafton, and more than that, tried to bring him down. He was determined to *personally* make them pay for the presumptions.

"Spider?" Angel spoke up for the first time.

Grafton turned away from the menu to pin Angel with a look from behind his sunglasses. "My diabolical underworld nickname."

Sonya knew Grafton was careful about who he let in on the secret that he was the Mustache Pete of the world's largest crime syndicate. That, combined with the fact that he'd already spewed his guts about his son—and what he'd done to his son's mother—sent a chill up her spine.

No way was he airing his dirty laundry without some fiendish motivation. Absolutely *no* way. So what the heck was he thinking? Was he trying to impress the Prince of Shadows? Or was there something else going on?

Apprehension had pretty much been her sidekick all day long. Now full-blown alarm joined the gang. She thought she was beginning to understand Grafton's grand plan. "You're giving the…" She glanced around the empty café and lowered her voice. "The *stuff* to Al-Qaeda on the condition they use it against these Black Knights people, aren't you?"

"Let no one ever accuse you of being dim-witted, Sonya my dear. It's a win-win all 'round. Even though Daesh has suffered many defeats, they continue to occupy the attention of most Western Intelligence agencies. Which means Al-Qaeda has had the time and space to regroup and rebuild. They are making a comeback, grooming Hamza bin Laden to take up the reins from his dead father, and he's made it clear he wants to announce Al-Qaeda's continued threat to the world in a big way. When his group blows up the Black Knights' compound in Chicago, they'll prove they're able to hit America's heartland, and *I* will rain fire on the men who killed my son and who had the audacity to lock horns with me."

Sonya's voice was thready, her heart all skip-a-beaty when she said, "You'll kill millions of innocents."

"Thousands," Grafton objected. "Angel here"—he nodded to Angel—"was only able to get his source to agree to a small amount of the material. Enough to take out roughly ten city blocks."

"But the fallout…"

"True." Grafton shrugged. "More will die from that. Still, I doubt the death toll will reach six figures."

It took everything Sonya had to stay in her seat. And even though she had a contingency plan lined up, that didn't lessen the urge to stop this thing right here, right now. Before it had a chance to get off the ground. She glanced at the silverware arranged neatly on the table in front of her. Her hand itched to grab the fork and stab it into Grafton's carotid.

Maybe Angel was a mind reader. When she glanced at him, she would swear he gave her an almost imperceptible shake of his head.

"It's an ugly term," Grafton continued, blithely unaware of her homicidal thoughts. "Collateral damage. But sometimes it's necessary and—"

He cut himself off when the waiter appeared with a tray holding their drinks. After setting Sonya's tea in front of her, the bearded doughnut served Grafton, pouring from the giant bottle of Perrier. His voice was quiet when he leaned close to Grafton's hooded ear. "The first man is here." Only it sounded more like *De feerst man ees here.* "You want I should show him in?"

"Yes. Of course." Grafton nodded, nonchalantly squeezing his lime into his fancy water.

Sonya's adrenaline spiked again as the waiter disappeared through the door at the back. A second later, a man with a set of eyebrows that seemed to traipse across his face like woolly mammoths appeared in his place. A brown paper grocery bag was clasped in his right hand.

He didn't look around the café, barely spared Grafton a glance. Instead, he zeroed in on Angel and traipsed over to their table. Taking the seat to Sonya's left, he set the paper bag by his feet.

Showtime.

She opened her mouth to play the part Grafton had devised for her, but try as she might, she couldn't get a single word past the dump-truck-size lump in her throat.

Angel took one look at her and asked his source, "You have the product?"

She envied him his poise. Mr. Cool, Calm, and Collected. Knowing there was enriched uranium beneath the table had her pulling her legs under her chair and battling the urge to bolt.

"Is here," Eyebrows said in a Russian accent so thick his rolled *R* seemed to go on for an eternity. He tapped the top of the table with one finger. "Now, you pay me."

"Mind if we check the goods?" Angel asked.

Eyebrows swung his attention over to Sonya, sparing her a quick glance. "Of course."

Angel dug the bag from beneath the table and glanced inside.

"Looks good," he told his source. "Has the correct markings. But let me check."

He locked eyes with Sonya, nodding his head and motioning with two fingers in a *gimme* gesture. For a split second, she didn't have a clue what he wanted. Then she remembered the digital radiation monitor Grafton had given her in the car on the way to the café. It was a much more precise device than a Geiger counter, which couldn't tell the difference between enriched uranium and the small amounts of radiation given off by, say, a bag of cat litter or a sack of Brazil nuts.

Reaching inside her purse, she handed over the

gadget and watched curiously as Angel stuffed it inside the bag. His face registered nothing, but after a couple of seconds he nodded, set the bag on the chair to Sonya's right, and looked over her shoulder at Grafton. "You can transfer the money now."

Grafton didn't say a word, simply pulled his cell phone from the breast pocket of his puffy down coat. After punching in a number, he held the device to his ear and modulated his voice so it was unrecognizable when he said, "Make the transfer now."

He listened for what felt like forever as Sonya's heart did its best impression of a cat on a hot tin roof. She made sure to face Eyebrows, her fingers fumbling nervously with the button on her blouse until she'd satisfied herself she had everything she needed.

Grafton finished with "Very good" and thumbed off his phone before replacing it in his breast pocket. "It's done," he whispered in a purposefully scratchy voice, never turning toward the trio at the table behind him.

A muscle ticked in Eyebrow's cheek. He stared at the back of Grafton's hooded head before pulling his cell phone from his hip pocket. Glancing down at the glowing screen, his deep-set eyes crinkled at the corners before he grinned, revealing teeth so yellow there was no doubt in Sonya's mind his cigarette habit encompassed a minimum of two packs a day.

"*Spasiba*," he said before pushing away from the table and disappearing out the back.

Just like that, Grafton had bought himself a canister full of atomic material.

Sonya looked across the table at Angel, her gut twisting into a twenty-pound knot. She took a sip of tea, hoping the heat would help loosen it, but all it managed to do was make her want to puke.

She hadn't expected Angel to go through with the exchange. Not really. Not the man who had hugged her so sweetly last night. Not the one who had kissed her so passionately. Not the infamous and much-revered Prince of Shadows...

Chapter 10

RUSTY PARKER LOOKED OVER AT ACE AND FROWNED. Their mark had been inside the café for five minutes, and for five minutes the two of them had done nothing but argue.

Wait. That ain't right, he thought. *For* months *all we've done is argue*.

Which, on the one hand, was sort of fun. Trading insults with Ace always felt a bit like verbal foreplay. On the other hand? Well, it reminded Rusty that the only man he'd ever been interested in for more than a one-night stand didn't want a single thing to do with him.

"The trouble with a fact is it's true whether you believe it or not," Ace said, tapping an impatient finger on the steering wheel. The guy had beautiful hands. Broad-palmed and long-fingered. Rusty imagined what it would be like to—

Nope. Not gonna go there.

"It's not that I believe two people *can't* make a relationship work for twenty or thirty or forty years," Rusty insisted. "I'm saying when marriage was invented, people only *lived* twenty, or thirty, or forty years. The kids grew up, and then the couple croaked. We weren't supposed to be with one person for half a century. That's why the divorce rate is so high." Rusty turned in his seat to pin a *Help me out here, bro* stare on Ozzie. "You're a smart guy. Tell him I'm right."

"Don't drag me into this." Ozzie stared at the screen of the laptop sitting on the edge of his knees as if he was waiting on the winning Power Ball numbers.

"You're jaded because you're closeted," Ace said. "You don't think you'll ever find someone to spend a lifetime with."

"Wow." Rusty felt the muscles across his shoulders tense. "You forgot to switch on your turn signal for that little segue."

"It's not a segue. It's a logical observation, given the conversation."

"Somehow we *always* gotta come back to that, don't we?" The twin demons of irritation and indignation went to war inside Rusty's chest. Their battle nicked his heart and sharpened his tongue. "You should get that thing looked at by a doctor."

"What thing?"

Colby "Ace" Ventura was quintessentially So Cal—tan skin, beachy blond hair, eyes the color of the ocean on a clear spring morning. It was annoying.

"Your holier-than-thou gland," Rusty told him. "It's super swollen."

Ozzie snorted in the back seat, and Ace turned to glare at him.

"Sorry!" Ozzie tossed up his hands. "Pretend I'm not here."

Ace swung back to Rusty. "Okay. Let's take a look at your argument from the *other* side of the coin. If fifty percent of marriages end in divorce, that means fifty percent *don't*. Fifty percent of people stay together until *death does them part*. How does *that* prove your little evolutionary theory, huh?"

Rusty shrugged. "There are as many exceptions as there are rules."

Truthfully, at this point he was being bullheaded for the simple sake of bullheadedness. If Ace claimed something was white, he had the oddest urge to insist it was black.

The sigh Ace heaved was overly dramatic, but before he could come back with some pithy reply, Ozzie leaned forward and pointed through the windshield. "There's our guy."

"Shit." Rusty saw Popov heading back up the alley in the direction he'd come.

Opening the VW's door, wincing when the corroded hinges groaned, he stepped out into the cool Moldovan afternoon. He'd bugged out of the Marines a long time ago, but he liked to think he still had the chops. Unfortunately, had Ozzie not pointed out that Victor Popov had exited the café and was on the move, Rusty might have missed the man entirely.

Ace did that to him. Pulled him off his game.

"Hey!" Ace whispered before Rusty could shut the door and set off after Popov. "Don't forget to check in. These streets and alleyways can get confusing. I don't want to lose you."

Rusty placed his hand atop the car's doorframe and leaned down. "Ah, you say that like you care."

Ace's face fell, and something shadowed his ocean blues. "Just because I don't agree with every aspect of your life doesn't mean I don't care," he said softly.

That was the true rub, wasn't it? It would have been one thing if their constant bickering had been born of nothing but lust paired with dislike. But the truth of the matter was, except for the one salient fact they couldn't seem to agree on, they admired each other. *Respected* each other. And Ace? Well, he was infuriatingly *nice*. One of the nicest guys Rusty had ever met. And brave. And loyal. And—

What a train wreck.

"Will do." Rusty gave Ace a jaunty salute. Sometimes it was impossible to be around Ace's niceness without getting some of it on him.

After shutting the VW's door, he turned to tail Popov. Activating his throat mic, he reported to the group positioned in front of the café. "Elvis has left the building. I'm on his six."

Ace's voice sounded in his ear a second after the noise of the Volkswagen's engine sputtered to life. "VW Team is on the move."

"Roger that," Boss said at the same time Ghost replied, "Ten-four. We'll send Rock around back to take up your position by the alley in case the buyer comes or goes that way. Front Door Team over and out."

"Rusty..." Once again it was Ace's voice in Rusty's earpiece as he headed down the alleyway, dodging a suspicious-looking trash bag that seemed to be home to a rat, if the rustling sound inside was anything to go by. "I'll head south two blocks and wait for your instructions."

The baritone swirling in Rusty's ear made the hairs on the back of his neck twang upright. He realized he hadn't answered when Ace said, "Rusty? You copy?"

Activating his throat mic, he replied. "Yeah. I got you."

Except he didn't have Ace. He *couldn't* have Ace.

As if on cue, his cell phone vibrated in his pocket. When he looked at the screen, he saw the word "Mom."

Below that was a photo of his mother in her favorite apron, the orange one with the yellow daffodils embroidered around the edges.

She was the reason he couldn't have Ace.

Ever since he'd gotten himself entangled in Black Knights Inc.'s most important mission, she'd been calling him every couple of days. Checking up on him. Not quite believing his story about taking some time off from the Dover cod-fishing business he'd inherited from his English grandfather to hang out in Chicago with some former military pals who happened to design badass custom choppers.

He couldn't talk to her right now anyway, but even if he could, he wasn't sure he would. The truth was, he was sick and tired of lying to her. Tucking his phone back into the hip pocket of his Levi's, he turned up the collar on his leather jacket and trudged after Popov, careful to look nonchalant. A guy using the alley as a shortcut to get where he was going, that's all.

He might not have much control over some aspects of his life but, by God, he could control his part in this mission.

Chapter 11

THE LOOK ON SONYA'S FACE REMINDED ANGEL OF A loyal family dog that'd been left on the side of the road. Confusion. Sadness. And *fear*.

She hadn't thought he'd actually go through with it, and her expression made him feel like he'd been stabbed in the gut. There was a hot pain low in his belly that spread down the length of his legs.

Add to that agonizing mix Grafton's little revelation about the Black Knights. Not only about knowing them—BKI's operators already suspected they were on the infamous Spider's radar—but also about wanting to vaporize an entire section of the city of Chicago to get vengeance on them? It was safe to say it wasn't only Angel's stomach and extremities suffering. His head felt like it was filled with fire too.

Sonya turned to Grafton, placing a hand on the sleeve of his jacket. Angel winced at the contact. He could barely stand to be in the same room with the World's Biggest Single-Celled Organism. He couldn't imagine what it must be like to actually touch the bastard.

Her delicate pat must have surprised Grafton too. His goateed chin jerked back. Turning, he focused on Sonya through the dark lenses of his sunglasses, one brow raised quizzically until it disappeared under his wig.

"Sir, please." Her voice was hoarse. "Even for you this crosses a line. Surely you see that."

With her free hand, she subtly motioned to the bag on the chair. Angel could see the outline of the cylinder inside. In the casual atmosphere of the café, that brown bag filled with death was the visual equivalent of a scream.

Grafton grinned. "Ah, Sonya my dear. Are you trying to appeal to my better nature? Don't you know I haven't one of those?"

Sonya withdrew her hand. Fear quivered her chin and paled her complexion.

Angel wasn't one for ten words when two would do, but he heard himself say, "Giving a nuclear weapon to Al-Qaeda is like pulling the pin on a grenade and shoving it up your own ass. They cannot be trusted. You realize that, right?"

"Oh, ye of little faith," Grafton scoffed. "They'll do what they've promised. This little exchange is a test for everyone involved. I prove I can get what Al-Qaeda wants, *anything* Al-Qaeda wants. And Al-Qaeda proves they can be trusted to follow through on what they say they'll do, which will assure me they are a worthy partner for all further transactions."

Angel's skin crawled like the time he'd found himself in a room with the two Iranian scientists working to miniaturize warheads. They'd known him as Majid Abass, and they'd shared the breakthrough they'd had that morning. The thought of raining death and destruction down on the United States and wiping Israel off the face of the map, the thought of killing millions of "infidels" had filled them with glee.

Without a qualm, Angel had destroyed all traces of their breakthrough that evening. After saying his Isha'a prayers at the local mosque—Isha'a was the last of the five obligatory prayers in a Muslim's day; although he'd always used that time to secretly recite the Jewish Aleinu—he had crept outside the head scientist's first-floor apartment and carefully sealed shut all the windows and doors with plastic and duct tape. While the two men celebrated over a dinner of *ghormeh sabzi* and *shirazi* salad, he'd pumped nitrogen gas into the small flat. Neither of them had known they were slowly suffocating until it was too late.

"You are so far up your own ass," he told Grafton now, "that I bet you can wave out of your mouth."

From the corner of his eye, he saw Sonya shift uncomfortably in her seat, her biteable chin pinging over her shoulder to catch Grafton's response.

But Grafton didn't say a word. Not for a full five-second count. Then, "Careful. Remember what I said yesterday about keeping you alive because I need you? Well…" He waved a hand toward the bag on the chair. "I no longer need you."

"Then why am I still alive?" Angel recognized the lay of the land. The reasons Grafton had spilled his guts about his son, BKI, and his intentions in Chicago were twofold. First, he wanted to impress upon Angel, the infamous Prince of Shadows, just how powerful and vicious he truly was. Second, he had no fear of Angel using the information against him.

After all, dead men tell no tales. Grafton meant to kill him.

The only question that remained was what did he plan to do with Sonya, now that he'd opened his metaphorical raincoat and exposed himself. The last handful of years spent outrunning the Iranians had inured Angel to the threat of his *own* imminent death, but when it came to a threat against *Sonya*? His steady heart skipped a beat.

"I'm beginning to ask myself that same bloody question," Grafton said. To prove his point, he glanced at Lead No-Neck. The dull-looking bastard pushed away from the wall and didn't pretend subtleness as he reached inside his jacket for his shoulder holster.

Adrenaline flooded Angel's system. His muscles quivered in readiness as his eyes pinged from Lead No-Neck to the other two bodyguards, who look bored and unconcerned. "You should be careful," he warned Grafton. His gravelly voice sounded more like the growl of an angry beast than any noise a man might make.

"Careful of what?"

"Me."

Angel realized those were the same words he'd spoken to Sonya the day before. The warning in them couldn't be more different, however.

Grafton's nostrils flared wide. "Are you bloody threatening me? You realize I have three men who will take off your sodding head the instant I give them the order, yeah?"

"Nothing about you or your no-necked goons scares me," Angel assured him. He set the radiation monitor atop the table and leaned forward. "Has it ever occurred to you exactly who I am? I single-handedly stopped the Iranians from getting the bomb. I have worked with the world's most elite counterterrorism and Intelligence agencies for years to stop the spread of black-market fissile materials. I have come up against men far worse than you, and most of them are either dead or wasting away in prison."

"For fuck's sake!" Grafton gritted his jaw so hard his words slithered between his clenched teeth like worms.

Angel sat back. He had to remain primed and ready for when the time came. And it *was* coming.

"You *are* threatening me!" Grafton raged.

"No. I'm making you a promise."

Whatever it took, and whether it meant death or a prison cell, he *would* end Grafton. He knew it as surely as he knew Sonya had a little heart-shaped mole above her right butt cheek.

Grafton's right temple twitched beneath his wig. He looked ready to call on Lead No-Neck to make his move, but the waiter appeared through the door at the rear of the café with a flourish. He had a slightly exuberant look on his face. Ambling toward the table, he leaned close to Grafton's hooded head, pulling nervously on his beard.

Despite his low whisper, Angel could make out the Michelin Man's heavily accented words. "The second gentleman is here."

"Send him in." Grafton waved an impatient hand, motioning for Lead No-Neck to resume his place alongside his coworkers. Then Grafton turned and curled his upper lip back to bare his teeth at Angel. Most men would shit their pants if the notorious Spider pinned a look of such hatred and vengeance on them. Angel didn't suffer so much as a gastrointestinal gurgle. He simply lifted a brow and satisfied himself with knowing how it would all end.

The waiter did everything but bow and click his heels before scurrying—if you could call a waddle a *scurry*— back through the connecting door.

Three seconds later, a beanpole in ripped jeans entered

the café by way of the kitchen. He gave the dining room a bored glance, lifted his chin in a "whaz up" gesture at Grafton's three goons, and smirked at Grafton's silly getup before sauntering over to the table where Sonya and Angel sat. Black hair, black eyes, and skin the color of dark-roast coffee contrasted starkly with the white AC/DC T-shirt stretched across his skinny shoulders. He'd used a single finger to hook his leather jacket over his shoulder.

Even had Angel not known the man was Al-Qaeda—the *kid*, honestly; if the asshat was older than twenty-two, Angel would eat his tactical boots—he *still* would have labeled him as the definition of a shitbag. He wore an air of superiority that spoke of a permissive upbringing. Angel could tell by the way he carried himself that he was drunk on what little power he had in this situation.

His cockney accent was as thick as the pistachio halvah Angel's mother used to make as he grabbed the empty seat and said, "Oy! Ain't never been outside of England, but if this place is what the rest of the world looks like, I ain't been missin' much, now have I?"

"You're English." The two words came out of Sonya's mouth the way most people would say, *You drown kittens in barrels* or *You smother babies in their cribs*.

AC/Dickmunch smirked, revealing a set of big, crooked teeth. "East Ender born and raised, luv."

"But wh-why?" she sputtered. "Why would you…" She stopped there, shaking her head in confusion, obviously having trouble understanding how he could have grown up in a world of Western privilege and freedom only to side with a group of murderers, thieves, and sadists who'd embraced a nihilistic, almost medieval interpretation of Islam.

"Throw in my lot with those mad hatters named Al-Qaeda?" AC/Dickmunch finished for her. When she nodded, he said, "They're the future of the Muslim world." His eyes were those of a true believer.

No doubt the kid's extremism had been forged in the crucible of online propaganda and fostered by the radical teachings of some zealous imam. Angel knew so many young men like him, raised in Western societies but marginalized within those societies because of the color of their skin or their religious beliefs. It wasn't an excuse. It was a fact.

"Now"—the scrawny little bastard turned to Angel— "you got the goods or what?"

Angel was tempted to take out the canister of uranium and brain both Grafton *and* AC/Dickmunch. The world would be a much safer, much *saner* place without either of them in it. But cooler heads prevailed.

AC/Dickmunch glanced inside the bag after Angel handed it to him. "That's it, eh? That's the stuff?"

"That's the stuff," Angel assured him. Grafton had meant for Sonya to facilitate the exchange, but if the look on her face was anything to go by, it was taking everything she had not to jump up from the table and run screaming from the café. She fiddled nervously with the button on her blouse and stared wide-eyed at the kid.

"Don't look like much," he observed.

"Looks can be deceiving," Angel assured him.

"Ain't that the truth." AC/Dickmunch winked as he pushed away from the table and stood.

Before he could disappear through the back door,

Grafton elbowed Sonya. She cleared her throat. "Uh, when can we expect the…er…" She grimaced, and Angel could tell she didn't want to voice the question Grafton had insisted she ask. "The fireworks?"

"Seven days." The kid grinned around his big, crooked teeth. Then he shoved through the door and departed as quickly as he'd arrived.

Angel clenched his hands into fists. He'd spent too many years keeping that stuff *out* of the clutches of crazy-eyed little jackwads like AC/Dickmunch to feel comfortable handing it over without a fight. But he knew better than to do anything that would screw up the plan.

The roly-poly waiter appeared once more in the doorway. He tug-tug-tugged away at his beard and eyed Grafton. Grafton's nod was a subtle downward jerk of his chin, but that was all it took for the waiter to walk to the front door and turn the lock.

And so it begins…

Angel coiled in readiness, covertly scooting to the edge of his seat and lightly moving his tactical boots so they were on either side of his chair. The instant one of the bodyguards made a move, he'd spring up and disarm him. What happened after that would have to be played by ear.

"Sonya and I are going to exit out the back," Grafton said, standing and motioning for Sonya to do the same. "Angel, you and the others can follow us in ten minutes."

Sonya's expression was puzzled as she looked from Grafton to Angel and back again. "What? Why?"

"Because I want to make sure—"

"Let me stop you from squeezing a bullshit log out of that face anus you call a mouth," Angel interrupted. Just because he wasn't much for words didn't mean he didn't know how to employ a little artistic license when the occasion called for it. "You have no intention of letting me leave this café. You never did."

"What?" Sonya suddenly stood, clutching her purse tightly against her chest. *Lucky purse.*

Grafton's sneer said he'd like nothing better than to destroy the planet. Starting with Angel. "Come, Sonya." Grafton turned toward the back door at the same moment Lead No-Neck pushed away from the wall again.

A palpable menace emanated from the approaching man. Even from a distance of nearly ten feet, Angel could smell the brute's foul breath, see the murderous intention in his squinty eyes. In Angel's mind's ear *ticktocked* a clock. It counted down the seconds until it was go-time.

Three.

Two.

One!

Lead No-Neck reached for Angel and simultaneously removed his weapon from his shoulder holster. The second his sweaty paw landed on Angel's shoulder, Angel spun, grabbed No-Neck's thumb, and wrenched it backward, out of joint. No-Neck barely had time to yowl in pain before Angel yanked the weapon from his nerveless fingers. The barrel of the gun gently tapped against the bottom of the guy's jaw a split second before— *Boom!*—it removed the lower portion of his face.

The feel of warm blood splattered Angel's cheeks and forehead. He was momentarily deafened by the roar of the weapon in the relatively small space of the café, which was why he wasn't certain if the cry he heard had come from Sonya or Grafton.

Before No-Neck's dead body dropped to the floor, before either of the other two remaining men in Grafton's security detail could do more than gape and make a grab for their weapons, Angel darted around the table and snatched Grafton by the collar of his hoodie. He hauled the bastard in front of him and Sonya to act as a human shield and shoved the bloody barrel of the Glock against Grafton's temple. It had been a long time since anything had felt that satisfying.

Leaning close to Grafton's ear, he whispered, "Checkmate."

Chapter 12

THE SMELL OF SPENT GUNPOWDER PERFUMED THE AIR and lingered in Sonya's nose.

Not that she was complaining. The alternative was the scent of blood, since there was a huge pool of the stuff flowing from Lou's ruined face and gathering around the mountain of his crumpled body.

Nothing but a blur...

That's what Angel had been when he'd moved to disarm and dispatch the head of Grafton's security detail. One second, Lou had grabbed him. The next second, half of Lou's face was gone.

She couldn't quite wrap her brain around what had just happened. Okay, so probably not the best turn of phrase, given the shape of Lou's skull.

The waiter blinked owlishly, wringing his fat hands and looking from the dead man to Angel, then back to the dead man. Without a word, he sprinted across the café and burst through the kitchen door. A second later came the sound of the back door slamming shut behind him.

Had she not seen it with her own eyes, Sonya wouldn't have thought it was possible for a man of his girth to move that fast. A big part of her wanted to follow him straight out into the alleyway, but she doubted Charles Gibson and Gordy Mills, Grafton's last two bodyguards, would ignore her escape the way they'd ignored the waiter's.

Their weapons were pointed in Angel's direction,

their bodies angled in shooter stances. Charles, who was nearest the kitchen door, said, "Let him go." A muscle went to town beneath his left eye.

"Not a chance." Angel's ruined voice was barely above a whisper.

Sonya found herself the focus of his Turkish coffee eyes when he glanced over his shoulder at her. She gulped, realizing how right she'd been when she'd titled him Mr. Tall, Dark, and *Deadly*.

He hadn't hesitated, hadn't *flinched* before pulling the trigger and ending Lou's life. Then again, she supposed she shouldn't be surprised. After all, he'd been recruited and trained by the Mossad. They only employed people with unwavering constitutions. People who didn't dither, didn't ponder. People who *acted*.

A split second can make all the difference between life and death, between fanaticism overrunning democracy, she remembered Mark telling her when she'd asked him about the Mossad.

"You okay?" Angel asked her now.

Seriously? He was in the middle of a standoff, and he was asking *her* if *she* was okay?

No, she wasn't okay! There was a dead man lying at her feet! They'd given a canister of enriched uranium to some bucktoothed kid from the East End! And her entire plan of how to handle the situation was now completely shot! She was about as unokay as it got.

And, *yes*, she realized *unokay* wasn't a word. But, by God, it should be! She was determined to pop off an email to Merriam-Webster the minute she got out of this unholy mess.

If she got out of it.

"I'm fine," she managed, wondering why her eyes felt so dry. Then she realized it was because they'd been as wide as fried eggs since Lou had crumpled to the floor.

"I *told* you to let him go," Charles growled, sounding menacing enough to make Sonya's ass pucker.

"And I told *you* not a chance," Angel came back without a second's hesitation. Apparently he was immune to ass-puckering menace.

"I'm a bloody brilliant shot." Charles squinted one eye and took aim. A bead of sweat dripped from his brow, ran straight down the center of his short, wide nose, and dripped off the blunt tip.

"Are you now?" Angel cocked his head from behind Grafton, giving Charles a better target to aim at.

The room did a slow spin. Sonya's heart felt too big for her rib cage. "What are you doing?" she said or more like *croaked*. "Why are you—"

But that's all she managed before Charles pulled his trigger.

She screwed her eyes shut, expecting another ear-splitting bark of sound. But the only noise she heard was a telltale *snick*.

Doing a double take, she peeked around Angel's shoulder in time to catch his lips twitching. It was the closest thing to a smile she'd ever seen on his face.

"Know what that sound is called?" he asked Charles, shoving the barrel of the semi-auto harder against Grafton's head when Grafton tried to struggle. A bloody smear appeared on Grafton's temple. It matched the droplets running down Angel's face. "The dead-man's click," he continued. "The noise an empty weapon makes."

Charles squeezed the trigger three more times. Three

more times he ended up with a whole lot of nada.
Growling his frustration, he thumbed the clip release on
the side of his gun and pulled out the magazine.

"I emptied your mag when you went to take a piss on
the plane," Angel told him. His tone was as neutral as
it always was, but damned if she didn't detect the itty-
bittiest dose of satisfaction. "You were stupid enough
to leave your jacket and shoulder holster on the seat."

Charles glanced at Gordy.

"Don't blame him," Angel rasped. "He was asleep.
So was he." He tipped his blood-speckled chin toward
Lou's dead body. "And besides, any man worth his salt
would recognize the difference between the weight of a
fully loaded weapon and an empty one, so it is no one's
fault but your own. Then again, we all make mistakes.
Just ask your mother."

Sonya stared at his perfect profile in slack-jawed
fascination.

"Shoot him," Grafton growled at Gordy. "Shoot
him now!"

Like a venomous snake shifting its attention in
preparation of a strike, Angel turned his dark, cutting
gaze from Charles to Gordy. "Do *you* recognize the
difference in the weight of a fully loaded weapon and
an empty one? *You* went to the bathroom and left your
jacket and shoulder holster behind too."

Holy moly! Angel rocked some serious James
Bond. If her heart wasn't going ape crazy and there
wasn't a dead man lying at her feet, she might have
thought she was dreaming. Or else watching a good
action flick. Honestly, if a movie studio ever needed
a super-stud spy guy complete with fathomless eyes

and a mysterious aura, no doubt Central Casting would recommend Angel.

Gordy swallowed, his Adam's apple bouncing under his neck beard. He looked at his weapon as if he might have X-ray vision capable of seeing inside his magazine.

"Go ahead and pull the trigger." Angel's tone was as cool and somber as dirt over a fresh grave. "It will give me an excuse to pull mine. The difference being I will hear a bang and you will hear a click."

Gordy swallowed again. Unless Sonya's eyes deceived her, his hand shook as he steadied his bead on Angel. Everyone in the room held their breath. Sonya couldn't have blinked even if she'd wanted to. And she *wanted* to. Her eyes now felt like they were filled with fire ants.

Angel must've seen the muscles in Gordy's forearm twitch a second sooner than she did. Before she could open her mouth to scream, Angel swung the Glock away from Grafton's head, took aim, and—*Boom!*—drilled Gordy right between the eyes.

Gordy was dead by the time he squeezed his trigger, his muscles working off the last synapse sent before his brain was liquefied. *Crash!* His shot whizzed by Sonya's head, the round embedding itself in the wall behind them.

Oh God. Angel *hadn't* emptied Gordy's Glock. He'd been bluffing!

"You sodding sonofabitch!" Grafton roared, clamping his mouth shut when Angel not-so-gently reapplied the barrel of the weapon to his temple. Grafton hissed like the gun was hot. Sonya suspected it was, but Angel showed no mercy.

"Words hurt," Angel told him. "But not nearly as bad as lead flying into your brainpan at 375 meters per second."

"What are you waiting for?" Grafton snarled. "Just do it. Bloody do it! Kill me!"

Angel snorted. "You are poison. The plague. And I might have to put a bullet into that sick, twisted heart of yours someday. Unfortunately, someday isn't today."

Grafton went statue still. "What? Why would you let me live?"

"Because death is too good for you."

"Y-you plan to turn me over to the authorities." It was the first time Sonya had heard drop-dead fear in Grafton's tone.

"Yes," Angel responded. One word, spoken with unwavering clarity.

She wanted to shoot a victorious fist in the air. She wanted to scream her joy. She hadn't been wrong about him after all! He was one of the good guys and—

That's as far as she got because a knock sounded at the front door. All four of them turned to see a man in a sweater vest cupping his hands around his eyes and pressing this face to the window, trying to see inside.

Charles used Angel's distraction to lunge for the loaded weapon Gordy had dropped after Angel plugged him. Grafton, seeing Charles' intention, lifted his arm and elbowed Angel under his chin. The *crack* of Angel's teeth crashing together was loud enough to make *Sonya's* jaw ache.

What happened next was strange. She felt as though she was watching a film with frames missing. Everything was jerky and disjointed.

Angel, his bell sufficiently rung, lost hold of Grafton

who leapt across the room. Charles got his hands on Gordy's dropped Glock and aimed it at Angel's head. Having shaken off Grafton's blow, Angel upended the table they'd been standing beside and ducked behind it before... *Boom! Boom! BOOM!* Charles got off three shots. They all embedded themselves in the wood of the table.

Sonya was in a trance, standing there like an idiot until Angel grabbed her ankle—his hand was big enough to completely encircle it—and jerked her down onto the cold tile floor. She yelped, and the fall knocked her purse out of her arms. Panic grabbed hold of her before she found the leather satchel and hugged it to her chest. She didn't protest when Angel reeled her in and covered her body with his own as another round slammed into the table. The lead splintered the wood and made Sonya screw her eyes closed.

When she opened them again, she saw Angel scrambling off her. "Fuck!" he hissed, folding himself into a low crouch. "Fuck, fuck, *fuck!*"

Okay, so now she knew what he looked like when he displayed an emotion other than neutrality. And honestly? It was a little terrifying. His handsome face was pulled into a frown so fierce that instinct had her pushing up from the tile to crouch beside him. As far away from him as she could get and still be behind the table.

"Throw out your weapon!" Grafton's voice sounded from somewhere on the other side of the room. It was slightly muffled, telling her he'd taken cover behind something.

"Go fuck yourself!" Angel yelled back. That seemed to be his favorite retort.

His gaze flew around the room until he finally found

something of interest. Sonya glanced over her shoulder, following his line of sight down to the Perrier bottle. Miraculously, it had survived the fall from the upended table. Angel snagged it and held it by the neck in his free hand.

Now what was he planning to do with *that*?

"You might not care about your own sorry hide! But you care about Sonya's! A man with your moral conviction wouldn't want the death of an innocent on your hands!"

Angel shot her a quick look and popped his jaw. Despite the situation, her mind was thrust back a decade into the past to the second time she'd seen Mark pop *his* jaw. It was two days after they'd met, and he'd been arguing with the head of the Paris police department over a piece of Intel. After the kerfuffle was over, she'd asked him about the jaw popping.

"It's a tell my ramsad says I need to work on," he'd explained. *"I unconsciously do it when I'm angry or…"*

"Or what?" She'd blinked innocently.

"Never mind," he'd said, but she'd soon learned he did it when he was angry or *horny*.

"She is *not* innocent!" Angel yelled at Grafton, yanking Sonya from the past back to the present. "She works for you!"

Okay, that stung.

"I'll give you five seconds to toss your bloody weapon out from behind that bloody table before I have my man riddle it with bullets! It'll be like those old commercials. How many licks does it take to get to the center of a Tootsie Pop? Only, in this case, it'll be how many bullets will it take to bust through that table and get to our fine, fair Sonya?"

"I have two full clips in my pocket!" Charles called. Plenty of lead to make Grafton's warning ring true.

Sonya gulped. Not that it helped. Her throat was a desert.

"Fuck." This time Angel's ragged voice barely raised the word above a whisper. He turned to her. "I have to get you out of here."

She pursed her lips. "But I work for Grafton, remember?" Was her tone a little snippy?

"Forget that," he whispered. "That was a bluff."

She frowned. "You're good at that."

Pinning her with his bottomless eyes, his words were so quiet she barely heard them. "Do you trust me?"

Heaven help her. "Yes."

"Grab on to my back belt loop."

What-the-huh? Of course she didn't voice her confusion aloud, simply did as she was told.

"When I say run, you stand up and run with me. Got it?"

She was back to the whole eyes-as-wide-as-fried-eggs thing. What was that strange roaring in her ears? Oh yeah. It was the blood rushing through her veins at light speed.

"Five!" Grafton called, beginning his countdown. "Four!"

Angel reared back and chucked the bottle of Perrier at one of the three front windows in a move that would've made a major leaguer proud. It smashed against the glass, creating a spiderweb of cracks in the solid pane.

Sonya realized there was a crowd gathering across the street. The vendors had stopped hawking their wares. The guy in the sweater vest waved his arms dramatically, no doubt telling everyone who'd listen about what

he saw inside the café. Passersby stopped in their tracks
to see what the commotion was about.

"Ha!" Grafton's laugh echoed around the empty café.
"What were you hoping? To break the glass and yell for
help? Three! Two!"

"Run!" Angel roared, springing upright while wres-
tling one leg of the table onto his shoulder so it rose
with him and created a cumbersome, rectangular shield.
Sonya was right on his heels as he charged across the
café, headed for the spiderwebbed window.

Another round slammed into the table. The *boom* of the
weapon and the *crack* of wood seemed to happen simultaneously. And then *crash!* The corner of the table hit the
cracked glass and shattered it. Shards rained down around
Sonya's head and shoulders. Angel yelled, "Jump!"

She didn't need to be told twice. After hopping with
him over the foot-high windowsill, the two of them
stood on the glass-strewn sidewalk, half of Chişinău
gathered on the other side of the street, eyeing them in
open-mouthed surprise. If she wasn't mistaken, a few
cell phones were aimed in their direction.

"Run!" Angel bellowed again before Charles could
move into position to fire another round at their backs.
Since her fingers were still securely wrapped around
Angel's belt loop, she didn't have much choice. She
was jerked into a sprint behind him as he took off down
the sidewalk.

The man was fast. No doubt about it. By the time they
rounded the end of the block and ducked into an alleyway, the muscles in her legs burned and her lungs felt
like the colony of fire ants had moved from her eyeballs
into her bronchioles.

"What now?" she gasped, shoving her hands on her knees and bending at the waist, fighting for air. Fragments of glass fell from her hair to land on the dirty pavement. If she'd known she would be running for her life, she might have rethought her footwear. Kitten heels were not meant for speedy getaways. She could already feel the beginnings of a blister on her left heel.

"We need a car." He pointed to a dilapidated four-door that was minted sometime in the 1970s. It was more rust than metal, and one window was missing. A black garbage bag was taped over the hole.

"That thing looks like a fart," she told him, still blowing like a winded racehorse.

"A fart?"

She glanced up to see a smile spread across his face. Holy *Scheisse*! She nearly fell to her knees. The sound that slipped from her open mouth was a cross between a humorless laugh and a half sob.

"What?" He looked concerned.

"Oh, nothing. Just that smile. I mean, I don't want to piss on your bliss, but you should only whip it out when our lives are on the line. It's a deadly weapon."

His eyebrow arched before he jogged over to the... Sonya wasn't going to call it a car. The rust bucket was too pathetic to deserve that title. Trying the driver's side door, he found it unlocked. Sonya wasn't surprised. With the missing window, what would be the point?

"Get in." He motioned for her to climb into the passenger seat.

Since the hunk of junk was parked close to the alley wall, she had to clamber in through the driver's side and gracelessly make her way over the gearshift. She knew she gave him an eyeful of ass, but if he noticed, he didn't show it as he plopped down behind the wheel and ripped the plastic away from the steering column.

"Think it'll start?" She wrinkled her nose at the smell of spilled oil, mildew, and something that reminded her of moldy cheese.

Glancing around the interior of the vehicle, she discovered it was as bad as the exterior. The back seat was slashed to ribbons. Foam and springs poked up through vinyl that might have been blue once upon a time, but had since faded to a sad, dirty-looking gray. The floorboard beneath her feet had rusted through. She could see the trash-strewn pavement of the alleyway below.

Wonderful. If it *didn't* start, she could push her legs through the hole and Flintstone them to wherever they needed to go.

"I have big balls, but unfortunately neither of them is crystal," Angel said.

Sonya stopped her survey of the jalopy to gape at him. "Did you just make a joke?"

There was that smile again. It landed in her chest and detonated like a bomb.

"What did I tell you?" She pointed at his face. "Only in life-and-death situations."

Crash!

The back windshield exploded. She ducked the flying glass, then glanced over her shoulder to see Grafton and Charles barreling down the alleyway toward them.

"Like now!" she yelled.

Angel didn't say a word, simply gritted his teeth and sparked together the two wires he'd managed to strip with the edge of his thumbnail. The jalopy's engine huffed and sputtered, but miraculously turned over on the second try. It wasn't a healthy sound by any means, but Sonya wasn't complaining.

Thunk!

Another round hit the body of the rust bucket at the same time Angel worked the clutch and shoved the vehicle into gear. Stomping on the gas, he left twin strips of rubber on the alleyway as he peeled out. A visual *fuck you* to Grafton and Charles.

Had Sonya been standing, she would have indulged in a little end-zone victory dance complete with finger guns and high kicks. As it was, she was consigned to simply waving buh-bye to Grafton and Charles with her middle finger.

As Angel swerved out of the alley and onto the street, headed who knew where, she reached for the third button on her blouse, slipping it through the buttonhole and unsnapping it from the fabric.

"Uh…" Angel kept one eye on the road. The other was on her.

"Don't worry, I'm not about to do a striptease as thanks for saving my life. I need to download the pictures from the café onto my phone so I can transmit them to my boss. He'll contact the Moldovan authorities and have the guy who sold us the uranium and the one who took possession of it arrested before they can leave the city."

Digging in the lining of her purse, she took out the razor-thin smart phone she'd managed to smuggle into Grafton's home. Inserting the little button into the side, she thumbed on the device and waited while the tiny camera inside the button downloaded the pictures she'd taken while sitting at the table. It would be a bit. The little button camera used most of its available digital capabilities for fast picture-taking, and that came at the expense of quick download speed.

"Sorry…" Sonya wasn't sure it was possible for Angel's voice to sound hoarse, since sounding hoarse was its regular MO. But there was an additional graveliness to his tone. And no, *graveliness* wasn't a word either, but it should be. *Suck it, Merriam-Webster!* "Your boss?"

"Zhao Longwei, the president of Interpol. I work for Interpol."

It'd been months since she'd said that out loud. She'd forgotten how *good* it sounded. She tried silently singing it like Beyoncé. Even better. How about rapping it like Jay-Z? Better still!

When Angel gaped at her in astonishment, she decided she liked that much more than the pity and disappointment she was used to seeing in his eyes.

Winking, she said, "You aren't the only one who's good at bluffing."

Chapter 13

"BLOODY FUCKING *HELL*!" GRAFTON ROARED, HIS VOICE bouncing off the grimy walls of the alley. He slammed a fist into the side of a blue dumpster and immediately regretted it when pain exploded in his knuckles.

He couldn't remember the last time he'd been this infuriated and...and...what was that other feeling crawling around inside his chest like an army of centipedes? Oh yes. Fear. *Fear!*

He wouldn't abide it!

"Ring up Richie," he said to Charles, inhaling a deep breath and then immediately regretting that too. The alleyway smelled of old sneakers, rotting food, and the fetid aroma of stale urine. "Tell him to drive the car 'round to the alley."

"Right-oh." Charles scratched his whiskered chin. "But, uh, the crowds out front of the café might prove to be a problem. What are we going to do about them?"

"What?" Grafton scowled at his sole remaining security man. He should have listened to his instincts. Three strong-armed thugs *were* too few when going up against the likes of the mighty and mysterious Prince of Shadows. Damnit! Sodding shitting *hell!*

"They saw what happened inside the café."

"No." Grafton waved a dismissive hand. "They never saw *us*. The people on the street only saw Sonya and Majid...or Angel...or whatever he wants to call himself. My concern right now, my *priority*, is finding them."

"Of course. You're right." The bodyguard bobbed his big, brutish chin and palmed his mobile from the inside pocket of his coat, holding the device to his ear.

Grafton did the same with his mobile, flexing the fingers on his free hand to relieve the ache in his knuckles. His call clicked a couple of times, a testament to it being encrypted on the other end, then Benton picked up. By way of salutation, the computer whiz said, "Please tell me you've changed your fool mind and have come 'round to my way of thinking? I'm all set to turn over the Prince of Shadows to the Iranians and collect that ten million quid so I can buy—"

Grafton cut him off. "Shut up and listen. We've a problem." He outlined what had happened inside the café, hopping into the rented black sedan when it rounded the alleyway's corner and pulled up beside him.

The interior smelled of fine leather and cedar air freshener. The plush surroundings, much more to Grafton's taste than that disgusting alleyway, brought him a measure of comfort as he ripped off his wig and sunglasses. His blood pressure, which had been at a rapid boil, settled into a simmer.

Work the problem. All he had to do was work the sodding problem.

"I want all hands on deck," he told Benton. "Call every source and asset we have. Hack into all those lovely floating satellites that record every keystroke, every phone call, and—"

"It might be easier than you think." Benton's voice sounded excited.

Grafton's ears pricked up at that. "How so?"

"I had Lou plant a tracking device on Miss Butler a couple of weeks ago."

Grafton's eyebrows slammed into a scowl. "What? Why? And why the bloody hell didn't you tell me? You've no right to—"

"I worried you were so caught up in making sure the Prince of Shadows was secure inside the manor house that you might not have your eye on Sonya. She's never come 'round to our way of thinking, you know. She gets a petulant, conniving expression on her face when she looks at you sometimes. I thought she might use your distraction to make an escape or try to set up a meeting with her former cronies at Interpol or—"

"How would *you* know what sort of look Sonya gets on her face?" Few of Spider's assets had ever met him face-to-face. Benton included. "Did you plant sodding cameras in my h—"

"No!" Benton cut him off. "Sir, I would never be so foolish."

Grafton relaxed. Marginally.

"Lou told me about Sonya," Benton explained. "He said she acted twitchy. Said he didn't trust her."

Considering she hadn't hesitated to flee with the Prince of Shadows, Lou's mistrust wasn't misplaced. Not that Grafton had fooled himself into thinking Sonya had ever *willingly* stayed with him. But he'd thought her too cowed and cowardly to make a move against him.

At the proof he'd read her wrong, his blood pressure threatened to ratchet up to a boil again. The only thing that succored him was the sound of Benton's fingers racing against his keyboard. If anyone could help him through this mess, it was Benton Currothers.

"I didn't tell you because I didn't want to add Lou's suspicions to your already full plate," Benton continued. "I'd hoped we wouldn't need to use it."

"How does it work? Can you see her? Where is she?"

More keyboard clacking. Benton muttered something under his breath, then finally said. "She's still within the city limits, but that's all I can tell by satellite. She's carrying a simple signal emitter. It's a filament I had Lou put in the ribbon bookmark he gave her." Grafton's mind briefly conjured up the hot-pink ribbon he'd seen Sonya using to keep her place in her books recently. "It's small and completely unnoticeable to anything but the most trained eye. Good for remaining hidden. Bad for emitting a strong signal. The most I can do from here is tell you which general twenty-square-mile area to search. If you want to home in on her, you're going to need the handheld receiver."

"And where's that, pray tell? *What's* that?"

"It's a little plastic case about the size of a garage door opener. It runs on a regular nine-volt battery. Once it gets within a mile of the filament, it will begin beeping. The closer the receiver gets to the filament, the faster it will beep. Lou has it with him…er…*had* it with him." The distaste in Benton's voice was clear. Grafton hadn't pulled his punches when he'd described what had been done to Lou's face and head. "It must still be on his body."

Grafton looked over at Charles. "Go back to the café. Look through Lou's pockets. He carried a receiver." He explained what the device was supposed to look like. "We need it."

"Tell him to torch the place while he's in there," Benton added. "Burn away any evidence left behind."

Right. Good ol' Benton. Always quick thinking. Grafton gave Charles this last set of instructions and watched as the hulking man dashed back inside the café.

"After I get off with you," Benton continued. "I'll ring up the owner of the café and offer him a hefty sum for the place and for keeping quiet about what he saw today."

"Yes." Grafton nodded. "Do that. And then send in a man to kill him. This has gotten too far out of hand. I can't afford to leave any witnesses behind now."

"Of course," Benton said. "And if you find the Prince of Shadows—"

"*When*," Grafton corrected. "*When* I find him."

"Yes. *When* you find him, you're going to need help."

"Exactly. Like I was saying earlier, I want you to reach out to every one of my contacts with any sort of training in this type of thing. Book them passage to Chişinău." Grafton hadn't gotten this far in life only to let a conniving bitch from Interpol and a bona fide Iranian traitor bring him down. The *bee-doo-bee-doo* of sirens echoed in the distance just as Charles burst from the back door of the café. Smoke billowed out behind him, and Grafton saw orange flames licking inside the kitchen. They matched the hellfire in his heart. His tone was venomous when he added, "I want both of those motherfuckers dead before first light tomorrow morning."

Chapter 14

TRIPLE CHOCOLATE ICE CREAM WAS INVENTED FOR DAYS LIKE this…

Days when everything seemed to be coming up Rusty. Days when he was tasked with something of substance, something that *mattered*. Days when he could hold his head high because he'd come through with flying colors.

I love it when a plan comes together. He pumped an imaginary fist and then figured…*what the hell*…and gave himself an imaginary pat on the back too.

Activating his throat mic, he said, "VW Team, the device is attached, and Elvis has taken flight."

"Copy that." Ace's warm baritone swirled inside Rusty's ear, causing his stomach to swoop and drop like he was on a carnival ride. "Give us your location, and we'll swing around to pick you up."

Rusty squinted up at the street signs. They were written in both the Cyrillic and Latin alphabets—except that there were a bunch of weird accent marks used with the latter. But even given the familiar letters, he had a tough time pronouncing the Russian-sounding names. He did his best and then figured he'd better spell them out so Ozzie could plug them into the GPS on his handy-dandy laptop.

"Got it," Ozzie's voice sounded in his earpiece. Rusty could hear the *clickety-clack* of Ozzie's fingers across the keyboard. "We're five blocks west of you. Stay put, and we'll be there in a jiff."

"Like I got some place better to be?" Rusty quipped, smiling at the granny in orthotic shoes and a head scarf who scowled at him like he was crazy.

She mall-walked by him, her shoes squeaking in her rush. Considering it looked like he was standing on the corner of a not-so-nice neighborhood talking to himself, he couldn't blame her for the frown *or* the quick retreat.

Shoving his hands in his jacket pockets, he leaned against a lamppost sporting what looked to be no fewer than fifty coats of paint. Craning his head toward the west, he kept a weather eye out for the beat-up VW Bug.

Triple chocolate ice cream for sure. Too bad he would likely have to wait until he got back to Chicago before indulging.

He'd followed Popov for nearly thirty minutes down winding streets and narrow alleys. Always staying far behind the man, ducking into doorways and slipping behind dumpsters when Popov turned to glance behind him.

The circuitous route spoke of Popov's cunning. He'd attempted to make sure no one tailed him after the drop. Unfortunately for him, he wasn't slick enough to outfox, or outrun, a former marine. Especially one whose teammates used to teasingly call him Bloodhound because he had a nose for tracking.

According to Angel, the Russian thieves he'd been chasing were in possession of twenty-six canisters of enriched uranium. Over the years, Angel had helped to take fifteen of those off the black market. Today's canister was number sixteen. That meant ten canisters from the original heist were still out there. Still a threat to all good and civilized people, and it was Angel's hope that Popov would lead them back to—

Rusty's thoughts cut off when the Bug idled to a stop at the curb beside him. Ozzie, crammed into the back seat, reached forward and swung open the passenger door. "For the love of Jean-Luc Picard, man! Why are you standing there twiddling your dick? We got ourselves a bona fide hot pursuit! Get your ass moving!"

Rusty snorted and folded his six-and-a-half-foot frame into the passenger seat. No easy task, but somehow he managed. "Asshole" was his comeback to Ozzie, because they all knew that so far on this mission *he'd* done the lion's share of the legwork. Literally.

Behind the wheel, Ace made a buzzer sound like the ones on *Jeopardy*. "Oh, I know this one. Who is Rusty Parker?"

Rusty scowled over at the former Navy pilot, using what he hoped was telepathy to send a sarcastic retort since he couldn't seem to come up with one to say out loud. He must not have been successful because Ace smiled and wiggled his eyebrows.

"Any trouble attaching the tracking device?" Ace asked as he shoved the VW into gear.

"Just one," Rusty admitted. "First shot I took, I missed. Had to reload, and by that time, Popov's car was almost out of range. Nearly caked my pants." From his jacket pocket, he took out the short-barreled "gun" that shot tiny, magnetic tracking devices. He scowled down at the weird-looking thing in accusation.

"Didn't realize the tracking device would have that kind of arc once it left the barrel." He shuddered at the memory of how adrenaline had soured his stomach when his first shot missed its mark. "Had to aim the thing more like an archer shooting an arrow than a marksman shooting a bullet. Should've taken some practice shots before we left this morning. Almost screwed up everything."

"But you didn't," Ace told him, his voice softening.

"But I *nearly* did."

"Learn how to take a compliment, will you?" Ace ground the gears on the VW before he found the one he needed.

"Tall order since you so rarely send any my way. Can you blame me for not recognizing one when you finally do?"

"Aannnd they're at it again," Ozzie grumbled. When Rusty turned to glare at him, Ozzie tossed his hands in the air. "Sorry! Just pointing out—you know, in case neither of you is aware—that shitty attitudes are starting to become the rule, as opposed to the exception, with you two."

Rusty decided a change in topic was in order. "How's the signal? Everything copacetic?"

"For now, yes." Ozzie studied his screen. "But the range on that device is only about fifteen miles. Ace, my man, you need to hang a left up here at this next intersection and punch it. Looks like Popov is headed for the highway. We could lose him if we're not hot on his tail by the time he makes it there."

"Right." Ace hung a left at the crossroads and shifted through the gears. The transition from second to third sounded like he was giving the ancient little car a colonoscopy without any anesthetic. "The clutch on this thing is about as useful as a one-inch dick," he complained.

"And you'd know, wouldn't you?" Ozzie grinned at Ace in the rearview mirror.

Rusty felt his lips twitch. During the last few months living and working with the operators at BKI, he'd learned the guys were always looking for opportunities to malign one another's manly parts.

"Please," Ace scoffed. "You wish you had a fifth of what I'm packing. I feel so sorry for Samantha." He made an Oscar-worthy face of sympathy when talking about Ozzie's fiancée. "Just how *do* the two of you compensate for your woeful lack of man meat? Toys? Strap-ons? Inquiring minds want to know."

"They say deflection is the best way to tell if you've struck a nerve." Ozzie continued to stare at his laptop.

"More like you struck *out*," Ace said. "But if it's proof you need, I'll happily whip it out. Although…" He made a face. "This is a pretty small car. I'm not sure it'll be able to accommodate the anaconda once he's unwound."

Rusty couldn't resist a snort. The entire conversation had veered hard toward the absurd.

As Ace pulled the Volkswagen onto the highway, the Soviet-era-style buildings of Chişinău gave way to a landscape littered with run-down factories. Those soon moved aside for a little town that looked like it'd been largely left to ruin. And then, in a snap, they were in the countryside.

Goat-speckled grasslands stretched as far as the eye could see across Moldova's small hills. Horse-drawn hay carts rattled along on access roads, and Rusty couldn't shake the feeling they'd been transported back in time, pre–Industrial Revolution.

He switched on the Bug's radio and fumbled with the old-fashioned dial. Skimming past a station playing music that sounded vaguely like the stuff he'd heard at the one-and-only bar mitzvah he'd ever attended, past another where some Romanian-speaking guy angrily shouted at his listeners, he finally settled on a station playing the closing notes of an old Bee Gees' tune. As quickly as that song ended, another started.

He recognized the driving beat immediately and chuckled. Ozzie glanced up from his laptop, a huge grin spreading across his face. And Ace looked over at Rusty, shaking his head, but not trying to fight his smile.

The second the Village People started singing, Ace, Ozzie, and Rusty joined in. *"Young man, there's no need to feel down!"*

For the next four-and-a-half minutes, two covert special operators and one former-marine-turned-cod-fisherman-turned-honorary-member-of-BKI sang "YMCA" at the top of their lungs while chugging down a winding ribbon of highway in bumfuck Moldova.

Life was bizarre. And awesome.

It made Rusty sad to think of the time when this mission would be over, when Black Knights Inc. stopped being Black Knights Inc. When he was left with no recourse but to go back to being a cod fisherman in Dover, England.

He would *miss* the Black Knights so much.

He would miss Ace…

Chapter 15

"Don't send those photos, Sonya."

It had taken nearly fifteen minutes for the little button camera to finally download all the pictures she'd taken onto her phone. But finally, there on the screen was a grid of photos showing the caterpillar-eyebrowed uranium dealer and the scrawny, buck-toothed Al-Qaeda operative. She lifted a triumphant fist and whooped her victory, but Angel's request had the cry dying in her throat, her hand falling limply back into her lap.

He maneuvered the rust bucket through the streets of Chişinău like a race-car driver. Trucks roared past and motorcycles darted around them, but Angel managed to make dealing with the traffic look as easy as a Sunday morning drive down a country lane.

"I'm sorry. What?" she asked him warily.

"Don't send those photos."

A shard of ice sliced down her spine. There he was again. Mr. Tall, Dark, and *Dangerous*. Menace oozed from his pores as surely as the bead of sweat slipping between her breasts.

It wasn't a request. It was a demand. The dead-set look in his eyes left no doubt.

She glanced at the semi-auto between his legs. He'd shoved it there while hot-wiring their ride. It hadn't occurred to her then that it probably would've been more prudent for him to hand her the gun. That way she could have protected their six while he was otherwise occupied.

Why hadn't he handed it to her?

When he saw the direction of her gaze, his brow pinched. "Sonya, I told you before, I will never hurt you."

"Y-yes." She nodded. Apprehension had begun as a niggle behind her breastbone. She wasn't used to second-guessing herself, but…

"You believed me then. Why doubt me now?" he demanded.

"I don't know, I…" Her eyes traveled over his blood-spattered face. He'd wiped most of the stuff away, but there were still a couple of specks near his temple and one on his chin. Then her gaze dipped back to the Glock. Adrenaline left a sour taste on her tongue. "Why didn't you hand me the gun?"

He'd been keeping an eye on the traffic, but her question made him shoot her a quick glance. She wished he hadn't. His dark eyes sliced into her like diamond-tipped daggers. Something awful came over his face.

"Angel?" Those two syllables were a little too breathless for her liking. "You…you're scaring me."

His jaw hardened until it resembled a slab of stone. He grumbled something under his breath, and when he reached for the handgun, she flinched. She couldn't help it. The door handle was secured in her grip before she made the conscious decision to reach for it.

His ragged voice spit out his words like bullets when he snarled, "For fuck's sake, Sonya! Here!" He shoved the Glock at her. She had to release the door handle to accept it with shaking hands. "Take it."

The metal was warm from his body heat. The weight

of the weapon was not insubstantial, and given the abruptness of his move, she bobbled the gun before clutching it to her chest. Eyeing the Flintstone hole in the floorboard, she watched the roadway whiz by beneath her feet and realized if she'd dropped the Glock, she would have lost their only means of protection.

Now she didn't *want* the responsibility of the gun. She wanted to hand it back to him. But that would make her look foolish.

Tucking the Glock securely beneath her thigh for safekeeping, she whispered, "I'm sorry. When you asked me not to send the photos, I thought—"

"I asked you not to send the photos because I have everything under control," he said, switching on his turn signal and crossing two lanes of traffic. The rumble of the roadway echoed up from the rusted hole in the floorboard and in through the busted back windshield.

She frowned at him. "What do you mean?"

"If you truly work for Interpol, then—"

"*If?*" she interrupted him. Any apprehension she still felt morphed into indignation. "There's no *if* about it. I *do* work for Interpol. Have since I was twenty-two years old."

The look he sent her was pitying. She scowled at him because she'd thought they were finished with all that nonsense.

"I know all about you, Sonya," he told her. "I did my research before letting Spider catch me in his web."

He did research on her? Well, *that* sounded ominous. Except, hang on a minute…

"You *let* him catch you?"

"Yes." Angel hit her with his gaze. "I should not tell you what I am about to tell you. But I can see you need a reason to trust me. I had hoped..." He stopped, his jaw twitching from side to side like he wanted to pop it.

Hang on a *tick-tock*. Had her momentary crisis of faith actually...hurt his feelings?

What a mind-blowingly curious concept. She'd thought the Prince of Shadows didn't suffer feelings. At least not the way normal people did.

"Since leaving Iran, I have worked for an American defense firm funded, run, and overseen by President Thompson and his Joint Chiefs," he said, his ruined voice making each word sound as if it was filled with portent. "The goal of this defense firm was to handpick operators capable of completing missions too dangerous or too politically risky for traditional forces."

Okeydokey, then. That sounded...illegal. Of course, having worked with various governments and Intelligence communities, she'd come to realize *legality* was sort of like *beauty* when it came to international politics. It was in the eye of the beholder.

Truthfully, she wasn't all that surprised the Americans had gathered the Prince of Shadows into the bosom of their defense force. After all, they prided themselves on being the best of the best. And judging by what she'd seen of Angel so far, there was no one better.

"How can President Thompson oversee and run a defense firm when he left office in January?" She watched his reaction closely. She was good at spotting lies.

"He cannot. But before he left, he set up a trust to pay our salaries for one additional year and gave us one final mandate."

Color her intrigued. "Which is?"

"Destroy the man who goes by the name of Spider

and burn his criminal empire to the ground. Afterward, Black Knights Inc. will shutter its clandestine doors."

A hurricane of thoughts swirled and blustered inside her brain. She seized on one thing as it flew by her. "Black Knights Inc.? That's the group Grafton blames for the death of his son."

"Yes."

"And you *work* for them?"

"Yes."

An awful thought occurred. "Does *he* know you work for them? Did he bring you here because—"

"No." Angel shook his head. She squinted her eyes and tried to picture him with long hair like Mark's. It would suit him, she decided. Soften his harshly beautiful features. "I have never been listed on BKI's roster. Have never done any work for the civilian side of the business. President Thompson was careful never to mention me by code name in the internal documents he shared with his staff. Jamin "Angel" Agassi is a ghost, known only by whispered name to the Black Knights."

"But you've been working on this side of the pond, helping Western governments track down—"

"None of them know me as Angel. When working with them, I have always gone by an alias."

"Wow." She shook her head, flabbergasted by how complicated his life was. "How do you keep it all straight? Majid Abass became the Prince of Shadows when he turned double agent. The Prince of Shadows became Angel Agassi when he went to work for the American president. And then Angel Agassi became…" She cocked her head. "What's your *other* alias?"

"I could tell you, but then I would have to kill you."

She sucked in a startled breath. But then he looked over at her, his dark eyes twinkling.

"Oh, ha ha. Very funny." She punched him in the arm, immediately regretting it because one did *not* punch the Prince of Shadows. Thankfully, he didn't seem to mind. In fact, now *both* sides of his mouth twitched.

The storm in Sonya's head flung another piece of debris her way. "Grafton said the Black Knights were custom bike builders, didn't he?"

"Yes. The public face of BKI is a world-renowned custom chopper shop. Our lead designer, Becky, creates works of rolling art sought after by Hollywood stars, NFL players, musicians, or anyone else who can afford to lay down six figures on a motorcycle."

"I get it." She tapped her finger against her lips. "The whole custom-motorcycle-shop thing works well as a cover for a bunch of spec-ops guys because they're all big and burly. Probably covered in tattoos too. No one blinks an eye at them because everyone thinks they're bikers."

"Exactly."

"And your head designer is a woman?"

"A blond. About five feet tall."

Sonya chuckled at the notion.

"You laugh, but Becky is terrifying." He made a face. Angel actually *made a face*! Sonya was as awestruck as she was shocked. "She likes to play Mother Goose to all of us," he continued, "boss us around and tell us what to do."

"Huh." Sonya shook her head, trying to imagine a woman brave enough to take on the almighty Angel and…you know…actually *winning*. Then she latched on to another piece of information. "Was Grafton right? *Did* the Black Knights murder his son?"

"'Murder' is the wrong word." Angel shook his head. Yep. Long hair. Once the situation wasn't so dire, she'd advise him to let it grow. "Sharif Garane was working as a Somali pirate when he had a run-in with Becky." When Sonya lifted a brow, he shrugged. "Long story. Too long. In short, he followed Becky from the Arabian Sea back to Chicago. He kidnapped her, and she was forced to shoot him. It was self-defense. Not that Grafton cares much about the particulars, I suspect."

"Do the Black Knights know about the connection between Grafton and the dead pirate?"

"No. That will be a shock to them. It was a shock to me."

"It's a small world after all, huh?"

"Too small sometimes."

Angel flipped on his blinker and hooked a right, taking the vehicle up a short hill. They were on a small road that led to a simple-looking whitewashed church and an old, crumbling cemetery. Both were set in an overgrown and neglected parkland.

"Where are we going?" she asked curiously.

"Somewhere safe until this blows over."

As he pulled the hunk of junk off the road, carefully driving it into a stand of trees, she realized something. "You've been to Chişinău before."

"My hunt for the band of thieves who stole the Russian uranium has led me here a time or two."

The Russian uranium. Which reminded her...

"I need to get these photos to Interpol." A shot of adrenaline heated her blood. She'd been so caught up in Angel's revelations that she'd almost forgotten how much hot water they were in. "I have to stop that brainwashed Al-Qaeda kid from leaving the country with that canister. You know what's at stake if I—"

"Like I said, I have things under control. No doubt the Black Knights have caught AC/Dickmunch"—Sonya snorted. AC/Dickmunch? Angel Agassi had a sense of humor. Who'da thunk it?—"and are driving to Ukraine where they'll hand him and the uranium over to a NATO military instructor we know. As for the supplier," he continued, switching off the engine and turning his Turkish coffee eyes on her. Even in the shadowed canopy of the trees, intelligence and cunning glinted in his gaze. "A second BKI team is following him."

"They hope he'll lead them back to whatever is left of the cache of uranium," she guessed.

"Exactly."

"Good plan."

Again, one corner of his mouth twitched. "I thought so."

Ignoring the moldy cheese smell in the rust bucket, she took a deep breath and focused on the scent of Angel's spicy, masculine aftershave. It reminded her of the man himself. It was dark, mysterious, and it brought to mind hot nights spent on cool sheets in the arms of an enigmatic stranger. "How did you set all this up?"

"Easy." He lifted one big shoulder. She didn't notice how it stretched the leather of his jacket. Okay, so she noticed. Just a little. "I had Ozzie, BKI's computer genius, leak my identity as the Prince of Shadows onto the dark web knowing Grafton's keyboard jockey would ferret it out and—"

"No." She cut him off. She wasn't interested in how he'd managed to get himself on Grafton's radar—although it sounded similar to her own story. "I mean how did you set everything up for today? You had no idea Grafton would ask you to get fissile materials for him when you arrived in St. Ives. You had no idea we'd be in Moldova, so how could you possibly have arranged all this?" She waved a hand through the air. "Grafton took your cell phone that first day, and you haven't been allowed to leave the manor house until this morning, so…"

She left the sentence hanging, waiting for him to pick it up.

His face spread into another bone-melting smile. May God have mercy on her panties because that smile certainly wouldn't.

"The thing about men like Grafton," he said, "is they are so used to worrying about how technology can bring them down that they don't consider simpler means of communication. The Black Knights have kept eyes on Grafton Manor these past two weeks. Every night, I used Morse code to update them on the situation."

"Wow." She shook her head in wonder. Angel really *was* a super-stud spy guy. "And Grafton? What did you plan to do with him?"

"Initially, I was going to gather all the Intel I could on him until I felt I had enough to bring him and his empire down. But that flew out the window when he asked me to procure the fissile material." He gripped the steering wheel, drawing her eyes to his long, strong fingers.

In a flash, she was pulled back to the night before. To how it'd felt to have those hands on her face, her breast and—

She mentally slapped herself across the face to get her mind back on track.

"Then my mission became more complex in some ways," he continued. "Simpler in others. Instead of bringing down *one* bad guy, the Black Knights needed to bring down three. But, at the same time, no need for me to gather much Intel on Grafton. My testimony and the proof I have of the exchange of nuclear material is enough to levy charges against him and bring him in. The hope is that, once he is in custody, he will give up some of his criminal compatriots for lighter sentencing."

A ball of warmth glowed in Sonya's chest. Red roses of happiness bloomed in her cheeks. "You might not need to compromise on his sentencing."

Angel's eyes narrowed ever so slightly. "What do you mean?"

"I mean, *I've* gathered enough evidence against him to dismantle his organization."

One perfect eyebrow slowly climbed up Angel's forehead. She saw the intrigue—and was that admiration?—glowing in his fathomless eyes. If she'd had a football handy, she would have spiked it into the ground and yelled, *Booyah! Score one for Agent Butler!*

Chapter 16

ANGEL EYED SONYA'S WIDE SMILE. IT WAS THE SAME one she'd worn the day they met in Paris. A little naughty. A little nice. Full of mischief.

His heart rejoiced at the sight. At the proof the woman he loved was still alive and well. He wanted to pull her into his arms and smother her in the kind of kisses he knew she liked. Deep, wet, soulful kisses that made her moan and arch against him. And yet…there were questions that needed answers.

"Interpol does no direct investigation," he asserted adamantly. "They don't send agents undercover."

"True." She shrugged one delicate shoulder, reminding him of how she used to gasp when he sank his teeth into the tender flesh there as they made love. "But that was before Spider."

"Explain."

She snorted and snapped him a sarcastic salute. "Aye, aye, Captain."

He worked to soften his expression. He'd been so hardened by the years he'd spent undercover that he'd basically become one big callus. Social niceties were no longer his forte.

Not that they ever really had been.

"Sorry." He shook his head. "What I should have said was, would you mind explaining?"

Humor danced in her eyes. "I suppose not. Turnabout

is fair play, after all. But where should I start?" She
tapped her upper lip. That plump pad that used to look
so soft and succulent when it was wrapped around his—

"I guess I should start with my boss, Zhao Longwei,"
she said, cutting into his thoughts. Thank God. Now was
not the time. And the cramped and disgusting condi-
tions of the stolen vehicle were *certainly* not the place.
"He started seeing a pattern in cases around the globe.
Cases that mentioned the code name Spider. He wrote
a memo detailing his findings and sent it out to every
policing and Intelligence organization Interpol has ties
with. According to him, no one was interested in his
theory that some shadowy character had his fingers in
various and sundry black-market pots. In some cases,
he butted up against so much skepticism he began to
suspect Spider had people on the *inside* of some of these
policing and Intelligence organizations."

"How did he discover Spider was Lord Asad Grafton?"

"By happy accident." She took a deep breath. She
always did that right before she launched into a long story.

It was crazy the stuff he remembered. Or maybe it
wasn't so crazy. After all, Sonya had etched herself into
his heart, so was it any wonder every little thing about
her was also etched into his brain?

"I liaised on an investigation between Scotland Yard
and the *Préfecture de police de Paris*." He loved how
she used the French pronunciation. Nothing was sexier
than Sonya speaking French. Unless, of course, it was
Sonya speaking Hebrew. "It was a case involving ille-
gal blood diamonds being smuggled across the English
Channel from Calais to Dover. When the French police
came across a connection between the shipments and

payments to an account in the Cayman Islands held by none other than Lord Asad Grafton, I expected Scotland Yard to jump on the information and arrest the *Dummkopf*." He hid a smile at the German word for dumbass. "But they didn't. They gave the French police some song and dance about bad Intel, and the matter was dropped."

"Which made you suspicious."

"Hell yeah, it did."

Again, he was hard-pressed not to drag her across the console and kiss the words right out of her mouth. Realizing nothing about her had truly changed made his heart so full it was a wonder it didn't burst through his rib cage.

"So, I went all the way to the top of Interpol, to the president himself, and I told him what had happened." She shook her head at herself. "I must've made clanking sounds when I walked." When his eyebrows puckered in confusion, she added, "You know, because of my big, brass balls? I mean, I was a lowly agent. What was I thinking?"

"You were thinking you needed to listen to your instincts. You were thinking something was wrong, and you were going to the one man who might be able to help set it right."

She chuckled, and the sound reminded him of fireflies. Short, sweet bursts in the dingy gloom created by the trees. It was a familiar sound. A magical sound. A sound he wanted to listen to for the rest of his life, except…he suddenly realized…that wasn't an option, was it?

He couldn't keep her without telling her who he truly was. And if he told her who he truly was, she'd never forgive him for leaving her and letting her think he was dead.

A hard seed of remorse planted itself at the bottom

of his stomach and immediately sent up thorn-covered vines to prick his heart.

"Well, my chutzpah paid off. Zhao told me his theories and then asked me if I'd be willing to lay my reputation, my career, and maybe even my life on the line to bring Grafton, a.k.a. Spider, down."

He had no doubt how she'd answered. "You didn't hesitate."

"Nope." She shook her head, her silky blond hair swishing across her shoulders. "As you probably know from looking into my background, my father was a diplomat. So I grew up a child of the world. Which means I've seen firsthand the destruction caused by a *manyak* like Grafton." She used the Hebrew slang for *bastard*. "I jumped at the chance to make him pay."

He nodded as Sonya's and Zhao's plan became clear in his mind's eye. "So you and Zhao came up with this cover story about your fall from grace in the hopes Grafton would latch on to the information and reel you into his organization."

She nodded. "He'd done some digging—Zhao, that is—on his own and had discovered Grafton employed a lot of former soldiers and government agents. A lot of *disgraced* former soldiers and government agents. So we concocted the story about me helping an international jewel thief, planted the tale in all the newspapers along with the bit about there not being enough evidence to bring me to trial, and then made it easy for Benton, Grafton's keyboard jockey as you call him, to get his hands on a set of phone records supposedly showing half a dozen calls between me and the thief."

"Then, armed with this information, Grafton called you to St. Ives."

"Bingo." There it was again. That firefly laugh that lit up his whole world. "As planned, I gave Grafton a sob story about having fallen in love with the thief, and he promised not to hand over the evidence he had against me as long as I worked for him. I've been gathering Intel on him ever since."

"How?"

"By snapping photos of him with his colleagues and lackeys, getting shots of his computer files and phone records and anything and everything he let me see because he thought I was too broken and cowardly ever to make a move against him."

"You were able to smuggle in the cell phone and the button camera?" Grafton's bodyguards had checked Angel for wires and stripped him of his electronics before letting him in the room with Grafton.

"Grafton's goons didn't think to check the lining of my purse, especially after they waved an RT signal detector over it and came up with nothing suspicious. I had the battery hidden in the steel heel of one of my shoes." She wiggled her eyebrows. "And they *certainly* didn't think to go investigating my buttons."

Angel smiled at the tiny cell phone. It was no bigger than a Post-it note and almost as thin. The top of the line in spy technology—Ozzie would be so jealous. Then he glanced at her missing button. "I saw you fiddling with that thing. I thought you had developed a nervous tick."

"Kinda like your jaw popping?"

He knew his face hardened again when she withdrew,

pressing herself closer to the passenger door. "Sorry," she said. "I didn't mean anything—"

"The jaw popping is a new thing." It wasn't a lie. At least not entirely. For ten years he'd managed to overcome his tell, but something about seeing Sonya, being around her, had the long-buried habit rearing its ugly head.

"Maybe it's me," she mused.

"You are thinking of your man? The one you loved?"

"Yes." She nodded, a sweet look of melancholy crossing her face. It was enough to have those vines around Angel's heart tightening. Then she shook herself. "So, tell me, now that we know where each other stands and that we're playing for the same team—"

"Which team would that be?"

"Justice League. Home of the Good Guys."

He smiled. Sonya always had seen the world in black and white. Right and wrong. It was one of the things he loved best about her. And one of the reasons he knew she'd never forgive him for the choice he'd made. A thorn lodged in his heart, making his chest burn and ache.

"Anyway," she continued, "now that the air is clear, what's the plan?"

"Before I get into that, I need to ask you for a favor."

"Will wonders never cease? The Prince of Shadows needs a favor from little ol' me?"

"I need to use your cell phone to call the Black Knights. Let them know what happened, and that we are not going with Grafton back to England the way I planned."

He was gratified when she didn't hesitate to hand over her phone. Balancing the paper-light phone in his palm, he shook his head. "Nice hardware."

She winked, tossing the button in her hand and

catching it. "Nobody ever said it's an easy job, but it has its perks."

A small gust of wind drifted in through the shattered back windshield, bringing with it the forest smells of damp foliage and moss, and tousling the ends of Sonya's honeyed hair. One look at her pretty, smiling face reminded Angel that they were far from in the clear. His number one priority now was to keep her safe and well away from Grafton's long reach. It was past time they beat feet to their destination.

"Just give me a second." He thumbed on the device.

"Wait." Sonya placed a hand on his arm. His blood bubbled up to greet her touch, heating his skin. He knew his eyes were predatory because she swallowed loudly and hastily withdrew her fingers. "I still don't understand why I can't send my information to Zhao. At the very least he can help facilitate AC/Dickmunch's handover to the NATO forces. I'm pretty partial to that nickname, by the way."

"Ever heard the phrase *too many cooks in the kitchen*?" Angel asked.

Her brow furrowed. "Of course, but—"

"Let the Black Knights do their jobs," he said, cutting off her argument. "We *trust* this NATO instructor, but we don't trust anyone else. Besides, like you said, Zhao believes Spider has contacts inside police forces and Intelligence agencies all over the world. So who would Zhao call to help that he could be one hundred percent sure was *not* on Spider's payroll?"

Sonya frowned and chewed her lip. "True."

"After the dust settles," Angel continued, "we can call in an evac, and *then* you and Zhao can take what you have on Spider and disseminate it worldwide. You can clear your name, save your reputation, and watch Grafton's evil empire come tumbling down. It's a win-win. Everyone will be happy."

She snorted. "The only way to make *everyone* happy is if you're chocolate cake."

One corner of his lips twitched. "I guess some things never change."

He realized his mistake the instant her gaze sharpened. "What do you mean?"

"Just that women and chocolate have been in a love affair since the beginning of time."

Her expression relaxed. "Or at least since the discovery of the cocoa bean and sugar cane."

"Right." He secretly blew out a breath. What the hell was wrong with him? He'd nearly blown his cover. Over *chocolate*!

The memory of one rainy Sunday lazing around her Paris flat tripped through his mind. She'd spent a good portion of the afternoon covering his favorite body parts in chocolate syrup. And then licking them clean.

"Mmm," he remembered her humming, chocolate syrup smeared around the edges of her lips and all over the head of his dick. *"My two favorite things in the world. Chocolate and your…"*

She hadn't finished. Had simply taken him into her mouth, letting her tongue and teeth and the suction of her cheeks complete the sentence for her.

He shook his head, trying to rattle his brain around enough that it focused on the here and now instead of the much sweeter past. "So, what do you say?" he asked. "Are you down with the game plan?"

The fire of purpose lit her blue-gray eyes. "Since it ends with me clearing my name and making sure Grafton rots in jail? Yeah, I'm down."

"Good." He smiled. Despite everything, being near Sonya made him happy.

"Ah, ah, ah." She pointed at his face. "You better put that thing away. I've been paddling the pink canoe all by myself for a long time now, and that smile is enough to make me jump across this car, hold the Glock to your head, and demand you become my rowing partner."

"Paddling the p-pink—" He sputtered before cutting himself off and shaking his head. And then something remarkable happened. He laughed. Not a snort or a chuckle, but a full-on belly laugh that shook his shoulders and brought tears to his eyes.

How long had it been since he'd laughed like that? Ten years?

Wiping a hand over his eyes, he leveled her with a look. "You cannot go around saying things like that to a man like me."

"And why not?" Her mischievous smile was back in full effect. "Because it messes with your head? Makes you forget your own name? Makes you want to—"

"Yes, yes, and *yes*." He cut her off before she could finish her sentence.

"Well, that's good. That's what your *smile* does to me. Now we're even."

Shaking his head, he dialed a number he knew by heart and waited while the international call was connected. Then Emily, BKI's office manager, picked up on the first ring. "Black Knights Inc." Her South Side accent sounded tough, but he pictured her sitting at her desk wearing some ratty Chicago White Sox sweatshirt, yoga pants, her hair up in a messy topknot, and knew she looked about as mean as a cherry tart. "We want to put a little piece of heaven between your legs."

He snorted. Becky had come up with that slogan, thinking it was the height of wit. "Emily? Angel here. Change of plans."

Glancing over at Sonya, he found her watching him from beneath hooded lids. He remembered that look. That was her I-want-you-I-need-you-give-it-to-me-big-boy look. Like she'd predicted, he forgot his own name.

Chapter 17

SONYA LISTENED TO ANGEL EXPLAINING THE SITUA-
tion to some woman named Emily. At first, she felt a
kick of pride when Angel described the part she'd been
playing for the last six months, that she was, in fact, still
Interpol, a mole sent in to sniff out the true scope of
Grafton's empire. Unfortunately, that kick of pride was
soon replaced by a spark of jealously because this Emily
chick got to talk to him, got to have his scratched-up
voice swirling around in her ear.

How crazy was that?

How crazy was it that the warmth in his voice and
the affection on his face as he shared an inside joke with
Emily made Sonya want to claw the faceless lady's eyes
out? *Hiss. Meow. Ffft-ffft.*

Beyond crazy, she decided.

Still, it was there. That spark of jealousy. Because…
and this was the truly cracked part…she felt a little like
he was *hers*. He was so familiar in so many ways. Even
his laugh. That big roar that filled him up until it blasted
out of him. He laughed with his whole body. With his
whole heart.

Just like Mark.

How she'd *missed* hearing laughter like that.

Her mind drifted back ten years to the day she'd
helped Mark steal a guest register from a run-down hotel
on the outskirts of Paris. He'd hit a roadblock in his

search for the synagogue bomber, but he'd gotten a tip
the man might be staying at the ramshackle sleep-cheap.
Of course, the guy who ran the joint had decided to be
about as useful as a condom machine at the Vatican...

*"If your asshole were on fire, I wouldn't waste a piss
to put it out. So why do you think I'll help you find who
you're looking for?"*

*The man behind the tiny hotel counter was skinny,
wearing a mustard-stained dress shirt that was thread-
bare at the elbows, and had a look like he might have
spent some time behind bars. It was obvious he didn't
like people sticking their noses into his business or that
of his customers.*

*If the way he lit up a smoke and turned back toward
the black-and-white television in the corner was anything to go by, he considered their conversation over.
Done. Finito.*

*"Uh..." Sonya traced one of the many scratches on
the old wooden countertop. Then she turned to Mark.
He'd brought her along to act as his translator since the
hotelier didn't speak a lick of English, but she wasn't
sure she wanted to repeat what she'd heard. In any language. "He says...um...well, he says..."*

*Mark waved her off. "I think I got the gist." Reaching
into his pocket, he pulled out a card identifying him as a
United Nations police officer.*

*Sonya's eyes bulged at the identification because first
of all, it looked official. And second of all, it wasn't official.
Beneath her breath she said, "Where did you get that?"*

*Ignoring her, Mark beat on the counter to get the
proprietor's attention. When the man deigned to look*

*his way with enough disdain to make a king proud, Mark
slapped down the ID and stabbed it with one finger.
Once again he held up the picture of the bomber.* "I'm
looking for this man. I have reason to believe he's staying here or has stayed here. Now, unless you want me to
drag your smelly ass downtown to UN headquarters, I
suggest you answer my questions here and now."

*Sonya cleared her throat before translating his little
speech into French, leaving out the more colorful phras-
ing. Mustard Shirt didn't strike her as someone who
dealt well with name-calling or overt threats. When she
was finished, the skinny hotelier glanced from Mark to
her, then back to Mark. He made a hand gesture that
didn't need any translating.*

"Okay," *Mark grumbled.* "I tried the carrot. Time
for the stick."

"What are you—"

*That's all she managed before Mark hopped over the
counter like an Olympic hurdler and in one ninja-quick
move secured Mustard Shirt in a headlock that left the
guy's arms and legs flailing helplessly.*

"Grab the guest register!" *Mark hissed at her.*

"Huh?" *She was too stunned to move. Mark hadn't said
anything about assaulting anyone when he asked her to—*

"The guest register!" *With a jerk of his chin, he
motioned beneath the countertop.* "Sonya, hurry! I don't
want to choke him out. He'll wake up with a terrible
headache if I do."

"Choke him out? Are you crazy? You can't go
around—"

"Sonya!"

"All right!" *Her heart was in her throat, strangling*

her. Her legs felt like rubber, but somehow she managed to pull herself onto the counter, bellying her way across until she could hang her head down the opposite side.

There it was. An old-fashioned leather-bound guest register sitting on a shelf. Apparently Mustard Shirt eschewed technology in deference to the tried and true. She grabbed the massive book, hauled it over the counter, and stood on the other side with her mouth hanging open.

What was she doing? She wasn't a spy! She wasn't a police officer! She had no jurisdiction, no right to question a witnesses or gather evidence or—

"Run!" Mark bellowed at her. The word was a cattle prod, shocking her into action.

In a flash she was out the door, the bell tinkling behind her. Once she was on the sidewalk, the sun beating down on her, the guest register clutched to her chest, she looked left and right, and she realized she hadn't a clue where to go and—

Mark had her by the elbow and jerked her into a fast gallop up the block. Cobblestones were not meant for wedge sandals. That was a fact. But somehow she managed to keep up with him as one block turned into two. Two became three, and then she stopped counting.

Secondhand stores, sex shops, and tattoo parlors whizzed by on either side of the street in the seedy neighborhood. She was about to tell Mark they needed to stop so she could kick out of her sandals before she broke an ankle, but then he tugged her into a narrow alleyway.

Clotheslines crisscrossed the small space overhead. A rusted fire escape zigzagged up the side of the apartment block on the right. And the building on the left had plywood nailed over the windows and municipal flyers

*warning passersby that the space was condemned and to
Keep Out! Despite that, the back door stood ajar.*

*Shoving the guest register into Mark's arms, she
slammed her hands onto her hips and glared as best as
she could while trying to catch her breath. The alleyway
smelled of wet concrete, fresh laundry, and ripe trash.
"You're a liar and a thief!" she accused.*

*His chocolaty eyes twinkled as he flashed her a
diabolical grin. "You lack an appreciation for the dis-
tinctions of bad behavior. I'm an embellisher and an
appropriator."*

*"Appropriate?" She pointed to the stolen guest reg-
ister. "Is that what the kids are calling it nowadays?"*

*His grin grew even more mischievous. "You betcha." It
was a phrase she'd used that he'd taken a liking to. He'd
been whipping it out whenever the occasion called for it.*

*"Great!" She tossed her hands in the air. "I'll
embroider that on a pillow for you.* Mark Risa, master
appropriator. *Holy* Scheisse! *I can't believe we did that!"*

*He chuckled and wound one arm around her waist,
dragging her against him. Like always, the second she
was in his arms, she turned into a big pile of mush.
There'd been many more kisses since that initial kiss
in the doorway during the rain shower. But so far Mark
had slammed the door on more.*

*He said he didn't want to complicate matters. He said
it wasn't professional to sleep with a coworker. He said
a lot of things she thought were total bologna.*

*With her adrenaline pumping and the excitement of
the theft and escape like a fire in her blood, she wound
her arms around his neck, twisted her fingers in the
softly curling hair at his nape. "Make love to me, Mark."*

The laughter died on his lips. His Adam's apple bobbed in his tan throat, and his warm breath smelled sweet as it brushed against her cheeks. "Sonya, you know why I—"

"I don't care about complications. I don't care if it's professional or not. I want you. I want you more than I've ever wanted another man."

Damn her pride. It hadn't gotten her anywhere with him, and her lips were so chapped from all the kissing that if she didn't lay it on the line and tell him what she wanted, she'd have to start buying stock in ChapStick.

"God, woman." *He screwed his beautiful eyes shut. Sunlight beamed into the alley from overhead. She was struck once again at the sooty thickness of his lashes.* "You have no idea how hard you're making this for me."

The devil had her biting her bottom lip and cupping the evidence of his desire. Where she'd gotten the guts to be so forward she had no idea. But the deed was done, so she figured she'd better follow it up with more brazenness.

"Au contraire, mon ami," *she whispered in French because she knew he loved it.* "I *know* exactly *how hard I'm making it.*"

Hard and hot and…huge. Sweet mother of Jesus, he was a handful.

Mark sucked in a ragged breath. "Sonya…"

"Mark…" *She went up on tiptoe and bit his bottom lip.* "Please."

He shivered, his big frame shaking as if an earthquake rolled through it. Then he kissed her. Kissed her with the kind of passion she'd come to expect from him, with the kind of expertise that curled her toes. But it was more than that. More than their bodies rubbing. More than their tongues and teeth teasing. More than wet suction and hungry heat.

His kiss made her feel like stardust. Shimmery and light. It was like they were transported out of their corporeal forms and sent zinging across the cosmos together.

When he finally released her, she was sad to come back to reality. She wanted to stay among the stars forever. Fly into his sun and be burned up by his passion. But then he smiled and said the four most beautiful words she'd ever heard. "Your place or mine?"

"Neither," she told him. When he quirked a brow, she grabbed his hand and pulled him through the open door of the condemned building. "Both are too far away."

"And the craziest part about all of this," Angel's raspy voice dragged Sonya from her reverie. She shifted uncomfortably because the passionate memory combined with having Angel beside her in an enclosed space—Angel, emitter of pheromones, destroyer of panties, and incredible filler-outer of Levi's—meant her pump was primed. If she was any more raring to go, she'd be in the midst of orgasm. "Is that Lord Asad Grafton and Sharif Garane, that nasty Somali pirate who snatched Becky years ago, are related. Grafton is Sharif's father."

Sonya could hear Emily's squawk of surprise through the phone, but whatever words she said after were too soft and tinny sounding to make out.

"Right." Angel nodded. "Pass along the information to the team. And call me at this number when everything is set and Sonya and I are safe for an evac."

Emily said something else, and then Angel signed off. He immediately turned to Sonya. "Time to go."

"Go where?" She looked around, seeing nothing but trees. The narrow strip of forest he'd driven into was dense and untouched. A thick blanket of last year's leaves littered the ground, fertilizing the saplings and low bushes that competed for what little light dappled down from the thick canopy overhead. She'd expected they'd remain here, hidden among the trees in the cheesy-smelling rust bucket until, as Angel put it, everything was set and it was safe for an evac.

"Some place secure," he said. "Some place hidden. Do you trust me?"

"You can stop asking me that."

"Good. Then come with me."

He exited the vehicle, and Sonya snapped her camera button back onto her turquoise blouse before slinging her purse over her shoulder. After palming the Glock, she exited and quietly closed the door. Angel was already in the process of pulling up saplings by their roots to cover their stolen...er...*appropriated* hunk of junk. After he finished, he held out a hand to her. "You ready?"

She glanced down at the pads of his scarred fingertips, at his wide, rough palm. Such tough hands. Hands that could end a life without a second's hesitation.

There was a part of her that was scared of those hands. She'd asked Mark once, after she'd found out his mission to bring the synagogue bomber to justice meant he could take the man alive *or* dead, what it was like to kill another human being. The look that'd come over his face was etched in her memory.

He'd grown impassive, as if he'd donned a mask much like the one Angel always wore. Then he'd said, *"The Mossad teaches us to put the good of the many before the good of the few."*

She'd taken that to mean he didn't lose sleep at night.

"Sonya?" Angel's eyes looked slightly wounded. "That right there is why I keep asking if you trust me." He pointed at her face. "That Little Red Riding Hood look says I am the Big Bad Wolf and you think I might eat you."

Alrighty then. Apparently she needed to take a page from Lady Gaga's book, because Angel had no trouble reading her p-p-p-poker face.

"I'm sorry, but you're scary," she told him.

His eyes went from bruised to flinty in two seconds flat. "Why am I scary?"

"Because you're Mossad. You're trained to operate in enemy territory with the daily threat of capture, torture, and death, and you can kill a man a hundred different ways with your bare hands. Then there's the whole Iranian thing."

His chin jerked back. "Excuse me?"

"You're Iranian by birth, right? That alone is enough to strike fear into the hearts of most Americans. Your motherland has made chanting *death to America* a national pastime. And then there's this." She made a sweeping motion with her hand, indicating his entire length.

He glanced down at himself, then back up at her. A small line appeared between his eyebrows. "What?"

"You're huge and packed with muscle. You present a physical threat simply by breathing."

"I told you I would never hurt—"

"I know. I know." She flicked dismissive fingers. "And I believe you. But that doesn't make you any less scary, and sometimes that scariness is going to get to me and I'm going to hesitate. Try not to take it personally. Now, take my hand." She firmed her shoulders, and this time it was *her* offering *him* a hand.

When he slid his fingers between hers, she marveled at the warmth of his palm, at the latent strength she could feel in the bones and tendons. Perhaps he saw her pupils dilate on contact. Maybe he heard her heart skip a beat. Whatever her tell, he homed in on it instantly.

Heat flared in his eyes a second before he raised his free hand and brushed one rough fingertip down her cheek. When he got to the plump pad of her lower lip, he pressed gently, just enough to open her mouth. His gaze zeroed in on her exposed teeth, on the tip of her tongue.

"Do you want me?" he rumbled all low and seductive.

Chills raced over her arms. Flames licked through her veins. "What?"

"Do you *want* me? Because I want you, Sonya. And I don't want you to mistake me. Once we get where we are going, I intend to have you unless you tell me otherwise."

Well, küss meinen Arsch, she thought dizzily. Apparently, the man had never been introduced to the phrase *beat around the bush*. "I don't want you to mistake me either," she told him, blood pounding in her ears. And other places. "In some ways, you're so much like him. Like the man I loved." The man she *still* loved. The man she would *always* love. "I don't know if this attraction I feel for you is actually for *you* or because I'm stuck in the past, projecting my feelings for him onto you."

For a second, he stood and watched her. Okay, maybe not *stood*. It was more like he *hulked above her* like a dark, dangerous angel of doom. As always, she couldn't read his implacable expression, but his words were clear. "Does it matter?"

Some of the tension drained from her. "I guess not. I mean, if you don't mind being used as a substitute for—"

"I don't mind." He cut her off before she could finish.

"Wow." She gaped at him. "Underneath all that plastic surgery and all those aliases and that super-secret spy stuff you really are just a *guy*, aren't you?"

He stepped in to her, letting her feel how much of a *guy* he truly was because he was. She sucked in a ragged breath. Her knees threatened to forget their function and let her slide onto the forest floor in a hot pile of need.

"I *am* a guy, Sonya, in every sense of the word." His ragged voice had gone guttural.

Had he kissed her, she would have let him take her right then and there. Right up against a tree or down in the damp dirt and leaves. She would have let him have her any way he wanted, and she would have loved every minute of it. But he didn't kiss her. Instead, he stepped away.

Without the support of his big body, she felt bereft. Like a part of her had fused to him and he'd taken it with him when he retreated.

Dare she hope the little tick in his jaw meant he felt the same? Dare she hope—

He opened his mouth and popped his jaw. The warmth in her blood competed with the cold chill of distant memories. Looking at him now, standing so straight and tall, watching her with the kind of hunger that liquefied her bones, she would almost swear she was looking at a ghost.

"Come." He tugged her on a snaking path through the dense trees and undergrowth.

She tried to unscramble the thoughts in her head, the feelings of familiarity that competed with her uneasiness that mixed with her lust that rubbed elbows with her misgivings. Jamin "Angel" Agassi was the definition of the phrase *riddle wrapped in a mystery inside an enigma.*

So *why* did she feel like she knew him?

Chapter 18

"YOU ARE UNCHARACTERISTICALLY QUIET," ANGEL said after they'd hiked for a while, avoiding fallen logs and the places where the ground dipped and held puddles of water.

The gentle buzz of insects drowned out the sound of the distant highway. The pungent, tobacco scent of wet leaves mixed with the more fecund aroma of fertile soil and brought to Sonya's mind the time Mark had picked her up in a rented car and driven her outside Paris's city limits to a secluded little patch of heaven. Next to a cool, clear stream, he'd taken his time undressing her, and after a mind-numbingly sensual skinny dip, he'd made slow, passionate love to her under a weeping willow. She remembered how the water on her skin had turned to sweat, how her body had heated in the dappled sunlight and under the unparalleled intensity of Mark's desire.

"What are you thinking about?" Angel asked.

She could have beaten around the bush, she supposed. But beating around the bush felt too much like lying, and now that she was no longer undercover, she was finished with deceit. "The past," she told him. "Being around you makes a lot of old memories rise to the surface."

He glanced at her, his eyes fierce enough to strip the stripes off a tiger. Would she ever get used to that piercing gaze? Would she ever not feel exposed when he looked at her? "Are they good memories?" he asked.

"In some ways, yes. In some ways, no."

"Why no?"

"Because no matter how sweet they are, they're still only memories. All I have left of a lost love and broken dreams."

He was quiet for a while, the only sound that of their shoes scuffling through the damp leaves. Finally he asked, "If your lost love were here right now, what would you do? What would you say to him?"

The thought had her heart aching. "You mean after I tackle-hugged him, kissed him until he was cross-eyed, and then beat him repeatedly about the head and shoulders for being stupid enough to agree to that awful bomber's invitation to meet up?"

She realized Angel didn't know what she was talking about when he lifted a black eyebrow. She didn't explain herself. Instead she said, "I guess I'd ask him what heaven is like. Because if there's such a place, then that's where he's been. He was good and true. Strong and brave. No one deserves eternal happiness more than Mark."

She realized she'd said his name aloud when Angel made a noise of surprise.

"I've told you everything else; I might as well tell you that too." She shrugged helplessly. "His name was Mark Risa." She peeked over at Angel, figuring if she was in for a penny, she might as well go in for a pound. "He worked for the Mossad like you. But unlike you, he was Israeli. We met in Paris. He was there chasing a synagogue bomber. Did you..." She had to clear her throat. "Did you ever meet him? Mark, I mean?"

Angel searched her eyes, a question she couldn't fathom shining in his. Eventually, he shook his head.

She smiled sadly. "I guess that would've been too much to hope for. That you knew him." She sighed. "You would've liked him, I think. Like I said, you two are a lot alike."

"We are Mossad."

The way he said it made it seem as if that explained everything. And maybe it did. Maybe everything else— the way he moved and popped his jaw, the way he looked at her—maybe all that was simply coincidence.

Her thoughts cut off when Angel stopped next to a tree trunk. She hadn't realized it, but he'd been guiding her closer to the edge of the forest. Now they stood just inside the tree line, looking out at a large courtyard with a circular building squatting in the middle of it.

It was an odd structure with V-shaped prow beams circling a steeply pitched dome. The whole thing resembled a massive cement crown. An *abandoned* crown. The grass growing up through the cracks in the courtyard and the trash littering the front steps stood testament to the building's deserted status.

Oxidized playground equipment sat in an area of sand and patchy grass in back of the building. The swing set looked like an old skeleton. Proof that life had once been part of this place, but no more.

"What is it?" she asked, struck by its sad beauty.

"The old Chişinău Circus."

"A circus?" She looked at the cheerless structure with a bit of wonder.

"Circuses were huge in the Soviet Union. There was even a state-run circus school in Moscow where they trained the performers. But no one comes here anymore. It should be safe."

She shook her head. Apparently it was her lot in life
to get busy with beautiful, dangerous men in dusty,
dilapidated buildings.

"What?" Angel eyed her curiously.

"Someone once said—some baseball guy, I think—
that it's like déjà vu all over again." When Angel frowned,
she waved a hand. "Never mind. How do we get in?"

"Quietly," he told her, scanning the area before tugging her from behind the tree.

Quietly. Duh.

Walking across the courtyard left her feeling oddly
exposed. A forlorn dog barked in the distance. A crow
sat on the branch of a tree at the edge of the clearing
and scolded them for intruding on its territory. The
wind blew a lone plastic bag across the clearing while
gently pushing the swings back and forth, their rusted
chains emitting a melancholy *squeak, squeak, squeak.*
It all combined to give Sonya a chill similar to the ones
she got any time Grafton turned his dead eyes her way.
Which reminded her...

"Do you think he'll try to find us? Grafton, I mean?"

"Of course. That's why we need to stay quiet and off
the grid until we know it's safe."

"How long do you think that'll take?"

Angel hitched a shoulder. "No way to know. Less
than twenty-four hours would be my guess."

That was a relief. Sonya was totally on board with
having Angel all to herself since he didn't seem to mind if
she used him as a substitute for Mark, and since she was
sick and tired of engaging in ménages à moi. But she didn't
much care for the idea of spending days on end inside
a creepy old circus with no electricity or running water.

Not that she was a diva or anything. But if she didn't wash her hair every day, it turned into an oil slick. And without the benefit of a little foundation and some lipstick, there were times she could scare away small children.

"Make sure no one comes up the boulevard," Angel instructed. They'd reached the front of the building, and Sonya wasn't surprised to find the entrance sealed shut with plywood. Hanging above their heads was a clay crest supporting two dancing clowns. One was missing a head, and when the shattered pieces of pottery crunched under the soles of her shoes, she got the oddest feeling that she was walking on the bones of Moldova's storied past, a more prosperous time when it was part of the mighty USSR.

She surveyed the wide road leading up to the circus and tried to imagine what it must have looked like packed with cars brimming with bright-eyed children looking forward to a night of spectacular feats of derring-do. Now the boulevard was much like the courtyard, full of cracks where tall weeds and tufts of grass lifted their leaves toward the sun.

The forlorn dog barked in the distance again. The crow answered back as a soft-sounding squeak had Sonya turning to see that Angel had managed to pull one side of the plywood away from the entrance. When he pushed on the front door, it opened with a soft *shush* of sound.

Angel looked surprised. Well, as surprised as an expressionless man could look. Which was to say one of his eyebrows twitched. "After you." He motioned for her to precede him inside.

Curious what the interior looked like, Sonya ducked

under Angel's arm and slipped through the front door. She stopped barely a foot from the entrance, her mouth hanging open in wonder and surprise.

Tall glass windows circled the structure, but they were covered in the grit and grime of neglect—not to mention a ton of red Coca-Cola stickers. Still, they let in enough of the fading afternoon light to show two grand staircases that circled upward toward a second story. Dust covered the beautiful marble floors. Elegant light fixtures hung from ornate ceilings that showcased Stalinist architecture at the height of its appeal. In front of her was a ticket counter, a procession of little glass windows set inside a wooden enclosure. Old posters hung above the windows featuring clowns and tigers, acrobats and elephants.

All in all, it was enchanting. In a gloomy and abandoned way. Like a dollhouse left to gather dust in an attic.

When Angel slipped past her, she heard the *whack* of the plywood slapping back over the door, followed by the *shush* of the door shutting behind him. Unlike her, he didn't waste time gawking at the surroundings. Instead, he strode purposefully around the place, opening doors, poking his head through one of the ticket windows, disappearing through the entrance to the ring only to return a few seconds later. He made one full circuit around the building before trotting up the stairs and slipping from view for what felt like forever. It *wasn't* forever, of course. But it was long enough that Sonja began to feel the true solitude of the place, the true *loneliness* of it.

She was about to go in search of him when he appeared at the top of the steps. "Looking for something in particular?" she asked. "Maybe I can help."

"Familiarizing myself with the surroundings." He bounded down the steps, moving in an easy way that highlighted his supreme coordination and fitness.

She probably should have done some familiarizing herself. But unlike him, she wasn't trained in the fine art of espionage or even simple escape and evasion. She was trained in languages and how to make people from different countries and cultures work well together. When she thought about it, she was more of a politician than any sort of operator.

Perish the thought.

"I was right," he said, walking back toward the ring and stopping in the doorway. "This place will work well for our purposes."

"Sure." She swallowed, suddenly nervous. Or maybe the truth was she was never *not* nervous around Angel. "Our purposes."

She wanted to ask him which purposes those were exactly. The stay-out-of-sight-and-out-of-trouble purposes? Or the strip-each-other-naked-and-get-down-and-dirty purposes?

If it was the latter, God's honest truth was…she was beginning to second-guess herself.

She'd only known Angel for two weeks, and even then it's not like she really *knew* him. How smart was it to fall into the sack with a total stranger? *Especially* one who reminded her in so many ways of the love of her life?

Not smart at all, Sonya, a little voice piped up from somewhere in the far reaches of her brain.

And yeah, okay, so they had chemistry. Big-time chemistry that bubbled and boiled anytime they touched. But did that mean they should act on it? Was chemistry enough reason to allow a man as diabolical and mysterious as the Prince of Shadows to see her at her most vulnerable, all naked and uninhibited?

No, it's not, Sonya, that little voice chimed.

And so what if she hadn't been laid in two years. That didn't mean she got a free pass to play pelvic pinochle with the first guy who showed any interest in her, did it? She wasn't into casual sex—at least she'd never been before—and given Angel's lifestyle, he was the definition of casual sex, wasn't he?

Yes, he is, Sonya.

She must've given herself away somehow, because Angel reached both arms above his head and casually gripped the molding above the doorway to the ring. He leaned forward into the grand foyer where she stood. "You want to tell me what has you spinning out over there?" As always, his messed-up voice with its weird non-accent carried easily through the stillness.

"No." She shook her head. "I mean, *yes*. I mean, I don't know. I just—"

With his arms above his head, his cotton shirt had pulled away from the waistband of his jeans, and she could see a half inch of his stomach. All she could think was… *Tan*. And *hard*. And *hair*.

"You just…*what*?" He cocked his gorgeous head. He was too handsome for his own good. For *anyone's* good.

She dragged in a breath, the dry smell of dust tickling her nose. "How did you escape from Iran?" she blurted.

Whoa. That was a conversational about-face if ever she'd heard one. Where had *that* come from?

His dark eyes flayed into her even from across the wide foyer. She could now say with certainty that if she lived to be one hundred years old, she would *never* get used to his piercing gaze. "Why do you want to know?"

Because I'm stalling. Because everything about you makes me nervous and excited. Because I don't want to make a mistake with you.

What if she slept with him, and he reminded her so much of Mark that she transferred some of those old feelings onto him? Or worse, what if she slept with him, and some of those old feelings began to fade only to be replaced by *new* feelings?

"Just curious, I guess." This time she was too chick-enhearted to give him the truth. Although, it was *sort* of the truth, wasn't it? She *had* been curious about his escape ever since learning he was the Prince of Shadows.

He lowered his arms. *Thank goodness.* She couldn't think straight with that half inch of stomach showing. "It is a long story."

She looked around and lifted her hands in a helpless gesture. "You have some other way to pass the time?"

The second the words were out of her mouth, she wanted to pull them back in.

His lips twitched, and the skin over his face seemed to tighten. A leisurely journey…that's what his eyes took down the length of her body before returning to her face. She could see his hunger, his *need*. Unlike her, he wasn't afraid of it. Wasn't hiding from it. "I can think of a few things." He walked toward her.

No. *Stalked* toward her.

She didn't realize she'd taken a step back until her ass bumped into the cool glass of the door. She thought maybe he would cage her in, put a hand on either side of her head and prevent her from escaping. Not that she *would* have escaped. Despite her misgivings, she knew the second he touched her, she'd be down for the count, all her second-guesses having liquefied in her brain and leaked out through her ears. But he stopped a good foot from her and simply held out his hand.

"Come with me, Sonya." His scratchy voice had turned into a purr.

Swallowing dryly, she placed her hand inside his much-larger one. His skin was so warm and rough. His grip so unyielding and sure. And yep. There they went. All her second-guesses.

Docilely, she let him pull her through the door and down the steps leading to the circus ring. The large, cathedral-like room was dark. The only light shined in from the entrances to the circular foyer outside, but it was enough to show her the stadium-style seats surrounding the place. They were covered in dust and looked cheerless and despairing without an audience.

Stepping into the ring was sort of like stepping onto a stage. Except that there wasn't hard wood beneath her kitten heels. There was sand. It made soft *hissing* sounds as they made their way toward the center of the ring where the acrobats had left behind a thick mat. The thing was as big as three king-size beds, as thick as a pillow-top mattress, and covered in a dusty tarp that Angel whipped away and dropped into a pile along one edge.

"Have a seat," he instructed, not waiting for her before plopping down. He leaned back on his hands and crossed his long legs at the ankles, looking totally at ease.

Gingerly, she sat on the edge of the mat a good two feet away from him. The leather—pleather?—fabric rustled against her black dress slacks. It wasn't a bed, but it was close enough. Her throat closed up. Her heart went all giddyap. And when Angel moved, she held her breath, thinking he was going to reach for her.

He didn't.

He lay back, putting his hands behind his head and stared up at the ceiling that was painted with colorful scenes of clowns juggling and spinning plates, of trained elephants rearing on their hind legs as the ringmaster doffed his top hat and smiled broadly. "After I set the explosion at the secret missile base in Tehran, my cover was officially blown. The Mossad had to act fast to get me out of the country," he said, making her blink rapidly.

Right. His escape from Iran. She *had* asked him about that, hadn't she?

What was that heavy feeling swirling around low in her belly? Was it fear?

She concentrated on it and realized no. It was disappointment. She'd thought for sure Angel would turn to her and set about seducing her. Now, the last thing she wanted to do was *talk*.

Chapter 19

ANGEL CATALOGED SONYA'S EVERY MOVE, HER EVERY gesture.

Even in the dim light of the circus ring, he could see her hands shake as she shrugged her purse from her shoulder and set it at her feet. He could hear her ragged breath as she carefully reclined next to him, folding her hands over her flat stomach. He could feel the tension vibrating from her like she was a piano wire, strung tight and recently struck.

She was having second thoughts.

Second thoughts about him. Second thoughts about *them*. Because, and this was the truly demoralizing part, he frightened her. *Scary*, that's what she'd called him even though she claimed to trust him.

Fucking hell, he didn't *want* her to be scared of him. He wanted her to take him as he was and revel in it, be excited by it, as she had before. Ten years ago.

But that was the crux of the problem, wasn't it? He wanted to have his cake and eat it too. He wanted to let her go on believing he was the Prince of Shadows, *and* he wanted her implicit faith and trust because he was the same man she'd fallen in love with in Paris.

Tell her… His conscience cajoled.

Screw you, he cursed the idiot. *If I told her, I'd lose her. She'd be devastated. She'd never forgive me.*

The only way forward with her would be to retain

his cover and never let her know Jamin "Angel" Agassi a.k.a. Majid Abass, "the Prince of Shadows" a.k.a. Mark Risa were all one and the same.

And that's your plan? his conscience pricked. *To move forward with her? To keep deceiving her forever?*

Yes! he silently fumed, then swallowed jerkily because it was the first time he'd truly admitted it to himself.

He loved Sonya—heart, body, and soul. He'd already spent ten long years without her, and he didn't want one more day to pass where she wasn't by his side. If it meant being Angel Agassi, the Iranian formerly known as the Prince of Shadows for the rest of his days, then so be it.

He'd lived most of his adult life under an alias anyway. Was used to being someone other than his true self. This newest role wouldn't be any different. And if it got him Sonya, it would be worth it.

You're a bastard even to consider it.

Okay, that was it. He imagined his conscience as a little version of himself sitting on his shoulder. Then he visualized flicking the fucker away.

If Angel Agassi could win Sonya's love the way Mark Risa had, if Angel Agassi could make her *happy* the way Mark Risa had, then what were a few lies in the grand scheme of things?

Nothing, he assured himself. *They're nothing.*

Since his conscience lay in a heap across the room, Angel didn't hear a peep of protest.

"*How* exactly?" she asked, her soft voice echoing in the cavernous space.

"How what?"

She turned and looked at him. Her full cheeks and

lush lips made her look younger than her thirty-two
years. In fact, in the dusky interior of the circus ring,
she looked exactly as she had ten years ago. Youthful.
Sprightly. Her strawberries-and-cream complexion
glowed with health. Her wide, bluish-gray eyes were
bright with intelligence and humor.

She'd caught his mind wandering, and she probably
thought he'd been thinking about getting her naked.
Which, in a roundabout way, he had been. He'd been
thinking of how he'd be getting her naked for the rest of
their lives if he played his cards right.

"How did the Mossad get you out of Iran? The
Intelligence community speculated about it for years.
I heard rumors there are tunnels dug through the desert
that you used to escape. There was gossip that maybe
you'd been spirited across the mountains by the nomadic
Qashqai people. But my favorite story involved you
being strapped to an unmanned drone and flown out of
the country."

He chuckled. "Nothing that exciting. My escape
started with a series of safe houses. I was moved every
three hours until I hopped aboard a commercial flight
under cover of darkness."

She turned onto her side, curling her legs and going
up on one elbow to cup her head in her hand. "No way.
A commercial flight? The Revolutionary Guards were
scouring the entire country for you!"

"Well, it might not have been as simple as that."

She scooted closer, her curiosity overpowering her
fear. He'd take it. When it came to her, he'd take anything. Everything.

The smell of freesia and apricot blossoms surrounded

her in a soft cloud. He let it fill his lungs. Wanted to bury his head between her breasts where he knew the aroma was the strongest and just stay there forever.

When she'd said the name Mark earlier, he'd nearly given himself away. It'd been years since he'd heard that name in reference to himself. Even longer since he'd heard it from her sweet lips. No one had ever said Mark the way she did. Wrapping her mouth around the *M*-sound like Jessica Rabbit. So sexy he wanted to eat her alive.

"The Mossad had a commercial pilot and copilot on their payroll," he explained, shifting slightly because being this close to her, breathing her in and remembering the way she'd loved him, the way she'd *made* love to him, had his dick straining against his fly. "That night, those pilots were crewing a late flight from Tehran to Dubai. I cut a hole in the perimeter fence around the airport, and while they were taxiing, I ran across the tarmac and climbed inside the wheel well."

Her chin jerked back. "People have died doing that."

"They die from the cold and lack of oxygen at high altitude. My pilots faked a pressurization problem in the cabin, which meant they made the whole trip at low altitude." He shivered in memory. "I had no trouble breathing, but it was still *freezing*. From Dubai, I caught a flight to Germany. The doctors there thought I might lose a couple of toes to frostbite. But after a few days they pinkened up and I managed to keep them."

"Good God and a half."

He smiled.

"Stop that." She pointed at his face. "I've told you it's not fair."

"Maybe I don't *want* to play fair."

The teasing light in her eyes died. He could see the pulse in her neck kick up. "Sonya, I know you are having second thoughts. I know I frighten you and—"

"That's not why I'm having second thoughts," she interrupted.

"No?"

"It's just that…" She stopped and cleared her throat. "I worry if I sleep with you, I'll start having feelings for you. I know I keep harping on it, but you're so like Mark." And there it was again. That name. *His* name. "I fell so hard for him," she went on, having no idea what the sound of his name on her lips did to him. "*So* hard. Which makes me wonder what would stop me from falling for you too."

Angel's heart stuttered to a stop inside his chest. "Would falling for me be a bad thing?"

"*Yes*. I mean…" She waved her hand to indicate his length. "You're you. This top-secret spy guy. I don't want to fall for you and then have you break my heart when you wave buh-bye and disappear on a mission to who knows where doing God knows what."

"I told you Black Knights Inc. is closing its doors now that President Thompson is no longer in office. Once we bring Lord Grafton down, we all go back to being civilians. No more missions."

"Even you?"

"Even me."

Her face softened. "How do you feel about that?"

"I have sacrificed *everything* for this job." Emotion swirled in his chest. "My homeland. My identity. My face." *My woman*, he almost added, but stopped himself in time. "I have done my duty. I have given up my wants and needs for long enough, lived for *others* for long enough. Now...my turn. My *time*."

Time he claimed what should've rightfully been his all along. Claimed *who* should've rightfully been his because there was no more fooling himself. Sonya Butler was his one and only. The one he'd let get away because he'd been young and dumb and full of grand ideas about duty and sacrifice and saving the world.

God, that sounded so made-for-television Lifetime Movie–worthy.

Her throat worked over a swallow. "Angel, I'm not sure I—"

"Stop it, Sonya." He couldn't lose her. Not again. Which meant he had to stop playing the calm, cool, collected man of mystery. It meant he needed to rip open his chest and expose his heart. "If you don't want me, tell me. Stop coming up with excuses."

She flopped back onto the mat, blowing out a gusty breath. "Just because you're giving up your spy-guy persona doesn't mean you can't still hurt me. Right now you're all hyped on hormones and this chemistry we have, but what happens after we scratch our itch? You don't know me. You don't know I leave my wet towels on the bathroom floor. You don't know I eat peanut butter straight out of the jar, double-dipping my spoon with disgusting abandon. You don't know all the little things about me that'll end up driving you crazy."

But he did know all those things.

He went up on his elbow, cupping his chin and looking down at her. The way her blond hair spread out over the mat, the way she searched his eyes reminded him of a long-ago night when the moonlight had streamed

in through the window of her Montmartre flat. They'd
been in bed, lovers by then, and he'd seen the affection
and fear in her gaze. Her feelings for him had grown
beyond mere friendship and lust, and it had terrified her.

She was terrified again. Terrified she might begin to
feel for "Angel" what she'd once felt for "Mark." And
could he blame her considering how everything had
turned out for her the first time?

"You know, you could say all the same things about
me." He spoke quietly. "What if I fall for you, and you
walk away from me because of all the weird and irritat-
ing things *I* do."

"Like what?" she prompted.

He opened his mouth, then stopped himself. He
couldn't list his idiosyncrasies because they were
Mark's idiosyncrasies.

"Ugh." She made a mew of disgust. "You can't come
up with anything, can you? You don't clip your toenails
in bed or forget to clean the coffeepot until it's grown
brown scum around the edges. Admit it, you're perfect."

"Far from it."

She made a face. "I'm not convinced."

"You say you are scared of me. But Sonya…" He
reached forward, brushing a strand of hair behind her
ear before fisting his hand against his chest. "I am absolutely terrified of you."

She blinked. "Me? But…*why?*"

"The way you make me feel is different than any
other woman."

"But—"

He held up a hand, cutting off her argument because
he already knew what it would be. "And I know you

probably think that is ridiculous since we just met. But I have lived long enough, been with enough women, to know that what we have—not only this physical pull but this emotional pull too—is…something special."

She bit her lip and looked away.

"I want to explore this thing between us," he whispered because this was important, intimate, a truth only for her. "Explore everything about it. And maybe what you say is right. Maybe once we get to know each other, things will go south." There was a part of him that was afraid that's how it might be for her. After all, he *had* changed in the years since she'd known him. And not all of those changes were for the better. "But…" He gently caught her chin between his thumb and forefinger and forced her to look his way. "I think we owe it to ourselves at least to give it a chance. Don't you?"

She blew out an unsteady breath and searched his face. Looking for what? Reassurance? Sincerity? Something familiar? Whatever it was, he wasn't sure she found it because she squeezed her eyes shut.

In that moment, her name was the only thing in his head. The only thing in the world that meant anything to him. "Sonya…"

Her gorgeous eyes popped open. Emotion had darkened them. "There are only two things I want from you."

He sucked in a wary breath. "Okay?"

"The first is the truth. I want you to tell me the truth always, even if it will hurt me."

His heart plummeted into his stomach where acid went to work on it. "And the second?" His hoarse voice had turned to grit and gravel.

She grinned that seductive grin of hers and let his

mind fill in the blank. Then she grabbed his face, pulled him to her, and kissed all the thoughts right out of his head. Kissed him until the breath in his lungs was the breath she fed him. Kissed him until his heart returned to his chest and then matched the rhythm of hers. Kissed him until his misgivings disappeared and all he could think about was stripping her naked and feeling her silky thighs close over his hips, close over his *face*.

Soft...that's what she was. Soft skin, soft mouth, soft moans.

Warm too. Warm hands in his hair, warm breath on his lips, warm tongue dancing against his in a tangle of silken wetness and promise.

He wanted to go slow, but Sonya had something else in mind. Her mouth was greedy. Greedier even than his, and his was damned greedy. She hooked a heel behind his ass and pulled him on top of her. Chest to chest. Pelvis to pelvis.

She hissed her pleasure at finding him hot and hard and straining against her. And even though he was a big man, he knew he wouldn't crush her. She wasn't a tiny, fragile thing. She was solid. Solid and soft and warm and *all woman*.

Dear God, how he'd missed her. Missed *this*!

His heart ached with happiness for the present, with fear for the future, and all he wanted to do was—

"Take off your clothes." She shoved at the sides of his leather jacket.

He didn't hesitate, shrugging it off his shoulders and tossing it on top of the tarp.

"Shirt too." She pulled at the bottom hem of his long-sleeved Henley.

He reached behind his head and ripped off his shirt, sending it flying toward his jacket. The warm air inside the circus ring traveled over his newly exposed skin as sweetly as Sonya's eyes. The desire he saw in her face made his chest swell with pride.

Not that he was vain, or even particularly proud of the body his way of life had honed into a machine made for swift movement and tensile strength. But he was happy that looking at it brought her pleasure.

Reaching for the button on his jeans, she caught her bottom lip between her teeth. "And now for the pièce de résistance."

An icy chill rocketed up his spine, dousing the fire in his blood. "Wait." He stilled her busy fingers. "Slow down. I want…"

He stopped himself from saying, *I want to let it get darker outside and in here so you won't see the scar on my right hip where my birthmark used to be*.

His plastic surgeon had promised no identifying marks, and he'd meant it. The nip-and-tucker had carved out the crescent moon–shaped birthmark, leaving a large, ugly, puckered scar in its place.

It was supposed to look like a burn. Anytime one of Angel's lovers had asked him about it, that's the story he'd told them, that he'd been pushed into a campfire as a child. But he didn't want Sonya to ask about it. Not yet. He wanted to experience the unblemished, glorious truth of making love to her before he began the life of lies he was determined to live. Then again, was it *really* a lie? Everything that was Mark, everything that was *him*, had died. Everything but his love for her.

"You want what?" She tilted her head against the

mat. Her cheeks were already pinkened by passion. Her pupils had widened to consume her irises.

"Not to rush this." He took her wrists and pinned them above her head. "I want to go slow. So slow. I want to explore every inch of you. Taste every inch of you. Tell me you want that too."

Her voice was husky when she said the four sweetest words he could have wished for. "I want that too."

Chapter 20

ANGEL WAS A FINE SPECIMEN OF A MAN. NO DOUBT about it.

At twenty-four, Mark had been big boned and tall, but coltish. Beautifully lean. By contrast, Angel was just big. Heavy muscles roped his large frame. Sonya got an unencumbered view of them when he pushed up to kneel on the edge of the mat so he could slip her shoes from her feet.

The first word that came to mind when she took in the wonder of him was *built*. Not that he was overgrown like a bodybuilder or anything, but there wasn't an ounce of fat anywhere on him. He was simply bone and sinew and tendon and hard-packed muscle.

The second word that swirled in her brain was *smooth*. Given what a tough man he was, that was a strange adjective. But his skin was tan and silky. Not a freckle or mole marred its tawny perfection, only the occasional scar that stood witness to the dangerous life he'd led.

The third word that described him was…*man*. He epitomized the concept. From the flare of his broad shoulders to the tapered tuck of his waist, from his heavy pectoral muscles topped with flat, brown nipples to the patch of dark, delicious hair that grew across his chest, he was all man.

Which made her remember how smooth Mark had

been. Nary a hair on his chest. Only a single line of baby-fine gossamer arrowing down from his belly button. Proof of how young they'd been.

So, so young...

And speaking of happy trails, Angel's took her eyes on a journey south as it extended down the centerline of his body and raced over the corrugated ridges of abdomen past those V-shaped lines that bracketed his hip bones and plunged beneath the waistband of his jeans. What were they called? Aphrodite's saddle? It was something like that, and Sonya got it. Seeing those lines on a man's body made a woman want to ride.

The fourth word that came to mind... Nope. It was gone. The word had slipped right out of her head because Angel, having finished with her shoes, ran a hand up her leg. Goose bumps followed the path of his fingers until he stopped at the button to her slacks.

"May I?"

"Now, how fair is that?" she teased him. "You want to leave your pants on, but you want to take mine off?"

"My top for your bottoms." He toyed with her button. "Seems perfectly fair to me."

She chuckled. Even to her own ears the sound was low and seductive. "Well, I guess I can't argue with that. Your logic is impeccable."

The smile flitting around his mouth was fleeting. And then? Oh, and then he undid the button, slowly pulled down the zipper, and grabbed her waistband with both hands.

She had to help him by lifting her hips. She had a rear bumper on her. Getting in and out of pants took some effort and a bit of wiggling. He seemed to have no trouble, however, because two seconds later he dragged her slacks off her legs and dropped them on the corner of the mat.

Sweet heavens! Why hadn't she thought to put on sexier underwear this morning?

Oh, yeah. Because when she'd boarded the plane to Moldova, the last thing she thought she'd be doing come evening was getting naked in front of the freaking Prince of Shadows!

Judging by his clenched jaw and flaring nostrils, Angel didn't seem to mind her simple cotton thong. Passion burned like black flames in his eyes as he slowly lifted his gaze to her face.

"You are so beautiful."

She blushed. She *wasn't* beautiful. Passably pretty, at best. But the way he looked at her...

Mark had looked at her that way. Had made her feel like the most gorgeous creature on earth.

Grabbing his wrist, she pulled him down beside her. His weight depressed the mat and had her rolling toward him until they were both on their sides, face to face.

"You're not so bad yourself." She tentatively ran a hand over his bare shoulder. His skin was so hot it almost hurt to touch, so firm she was tempted to dig in her fingernails to test its limits.

He shuddered as she feathered her hand through his chest hair, so crinkly and rough her nipples ached because they knew how delicious it would feel to have that hair rubbing against them. When she lightly brushed a fingertip over his left nipple, she watched in fascination as it furled tight, the areola wrinkling delightfully.

Mark had been the one to teach her that a man's nipples could be as sensitive as a woman's. And Angel proved him right when he sucked in a ragged breath and shuddered again.

She knew her power in that moment. She was Wonder Woman. She was She-Ra. She was Sonya Butler, Goddess of Sex because she could make a big, dangerous man, an otherwise *unshakable* man, like Angel Agassi tremble.

"Angel…" She whispered his name into the space between them, listening as it wafted up into the dry air and echoed around the circus ring. His name was a prayer, an appeal, an invocation all rolled into one.

He would have taken her mouth then, leaned in and closed the small distance that separated them, but she wasn't ready for that. The moment felt intensely emotional, *profound*. She wanted it to go on forever. She wanted to learn every part of him, imprint him in her mind so that if they *did* end up going their separate ways when this was all said and done, at least she'd have a detailed memory of him to take out and savor.

She lifted her hand and traced the outer edges of his face, staring at his forehead. Then the corner of his eye. Over the sharp curve of his right cheekbone. Finally landing at the soft crook on the side of his mouth.

He was stunning. Not that he'd been hard to look at before. The picture of him when he'd been Majid Abass, when he'd reminded her of Mark, was still clear in her mind's eye. No red-blooded woman on the planet would claim he hadn't been a handsome man.

But now? Oh, now he was more than handsome. *Beyond* handsome. So dazzling he took her breath away. And that would never do. She *needed* her breath, or she'd pass out and miss all the good stuff that came next.

As he'd done to her earlier, she pressed her finger against the plump pad of his bottom lip and watched his mouth open. He shocked her when he ducked his chin and sucked her finger between his lips. She couldn't help the hungry gasp that escaped her. "Angel…" There it was again. That prayer. That appeal. That invocation.

Her finger slid from his lips with a soft *pop*. "Come here." He pulled her flush against him.

It was odd. With her bottom half bare and his top half bare, they weren't skin to skin. And yet her naked legs brushing against the rough denim of his jeans, and his chest hair rasping over the silk of her shirt, felt ridiculously intimate.

Then he kissed her, sucking and nibbling and licking and loving. He kissed her like Mark had kissed her. Like kissing was the be-all and end-all. As though it was the journey that was important, not the destination, and she marveled at his patience, at his ability to suck the marrow from the moment, revel in it, and not press for more.

In her experience, most men treated kissing as a means to an end, barreling through the process until they could get to something more pleasurable. But not Mark back then. Not Angel now.

After a long, gloriously torturous interlude, he snaked a hand between them and slowly unbuttoned her blouse. She might have protested. Now she would be bare on bottom *and* top, but the truth was she *wanted* to be naked with him. Wanted to feel his hot skin against her. Wanted to know what it was to have nothing separating them but their breaths and moans and heartbeats.

Her shirt joined her slacks in a pile on the corner of

the mat and then, with a snap of his fingers, the front clasp of her bra released. Both sides fell open as if the garment said, *"Help yourself, sir."*

And he did. Not asking permission before cupping her.

She hissed at the heat of his palm, moaned when the calluses on his hand rasped against her tender nipple. He dark eyes homed in on her exposed breasts. "Beautiful," he whispered reverently. "You are so *achingly* beautiful."

But she wasn't. *He* was the one who was achingly beautiful, and yet...when she saw herself through his eyes, a woman given up to passion, pink and flushed and ready and willing, she thought maybe she understood what he meant. Perhaps to a man, there was nothing more glorious than a woman in need. Nothing more sublime that a woman who'd surrendered.

Closing her eyes, she collapsed limply against the mat, her arms flung out to her sides, her breasts pointing toward the ceiling like an offering she hoped he wouldn't refuse.

He didn't. He leaned forward and sucked one tender peak into the hot haven of his mouth.

Sensation exploded. Waves of pleasure centered under his talented lips and undulated through her again and again, keeping time with each suck, each flick of his expert tongue. He palmed her other breast, rasping his scarred, fingerprintless thumb over the tip before catching her nipple and pinching it lightly.

She speared her fingers into his short hair, loving the raspy feel of his beard stubble against her tender skin. Loving that for long minutes, too many to count in her fevered brain, he tended to her breasts. Not so much kissing them or sucking them or palming them, but *making love* to them until she was mindless with pleasure, her body arching and bowing, begging wordlessly.

A fine sheen of sweat misted her skin. Tiny muscles on the insides of her thighs quivered. She was swollen and yet empty. Overcome with so much pleasure and yet painfully tender.

"Angel…" Her voice was a rough parody of itself. "Please, I need you to touch me. I hurt."

"Shhh." Her nipple popped free of his mouth. When she opened her eyes, she saw it was red and swollen and glisteningly wet. His eyelids were lowered to half-mast, but they didn't hide the hunger in his eyes. "Do you trust me?" he asked for what felt like the billionth time.

"Yes. I trust you. Just…*please*."

"Be still."

"I can't." She knew her mouth was screwed into a pout. Her legs scissored together, trying to relieve the terrible ache he'd built. "I need—"

"I know what you need." He claimed her mouth in a devastating kiss that was as deep as it was quick. "But you have to be still."

"Angel, *please!*" She cried out, mindless to anything but her body's hunger.

He laid a wide, warm palm on her stomach, growling his satisfaction when he found her muscles quivering. "Shhh," he soothed again. "Quiet, my sweet Sonya. Be still. I want you to feel every caress. Every touch. I don't want you to miss a thing."

Well, when he put it that way…

Biting her bottom lip, she forced her legs to stop their needy movement and gripped his shoulders to anchor

herself. Her nails sank into the tough flesh there, but he
didn't seem to mind. In fact, the flair of his nostrils told
her he liked it. And then, once she'd gone completely
still, he gave her what she wanted. What she *needed*.

Skating his rough hand over her stomach, he briefly
circled the hollow of her belly button before cupping
her mound. She pumped her hips, searching for friction.

Again, he scolded her. "Be still." But this time he
added to his reprimand by lightly slapping her mound.

She cried out at the beautiful sting of friction, at the
sharp stab of sensation against her distended clitoris.
"Do that again," she begged.

"No punishment this first time," he murmured, nuz-
zling her neck, licking at her pulse point. "Only pleasure." And then, through her cotton panties, he began to
rub the distended bundle of nerves at the top of her sex
with the heel of his palm.

"Oh God!" she whimpered as delicious sensation
blasted through her like a shooting star. Her blood was
liquid flame. Her body an inferno.

The steady, rough friction stoked her arousal to a
fever pitch, and stillness was no longer an option. Her
hips pumped. Her heels dug into the mat for purchase.
The crotch of her panties grew slick with her desire, and
when she didn't think she could stand it a second longer,
he pulled the leg of her panties aside and gently probed.

"You are ready," he purred with satisfaction, one
rough-padded finger circling her entrance.

"Yes." She panted. Wanton. Completely abandoned.
She didn't care how she looked or how she sounded.
"Angel, yes. Please."

He plunged not one, but two fingers into her core.

She hissed as he stretched her tight. But it wasn't a hiss of pain. It was a hiss of pleasure.

Maybe she'd have her card-carrying feminist status revoked, but she loved it when he crooned, "Good girl. So hot and wet and tight for me."

Whimpering, she elevated her hips, needing him to move.

"Greedy too," he rasped, dipping his head and sucking her right nipple into his mouth at the same time he pumped his fingers.

And that's how it was for maybe ten glorious seconds. Because with his grinding palm and his fingers that felt so good, that's all it took for her to reach the brink.

"Come for me," he demanded. "I want to feel it."

Violent pleasure ripped through her as his words shoved her over the edge. She screamed his name as bursts of light exploded behind her screwed-tight eyelids.

Stardust… That's what she was now. Splintered into a million bright pieces of pleasure.

Chapter 21

WITH HER EYES SO DARK FROM PASSION AND HER SKIN so flushed from desire, Sonya was the sexiest, most glorious thing Angel had ever seen. He had the nickname, but she was the true angel. A magnificent, celestial being made flesh, panting and limp and completely wrung out by the power of her orgasm.

She whimpered when he carefully withdrew his fingers from her tight little body.

"Easy," he told her. Loving how she had slicked his palm and bathed his fingers.

He was exceptional at exactly two things. Hiding who he truly was and giving pleasure to a woman. He'd never been happier about that second thing until this moment, because Sonya's pleasure was the sweetest thing he'd ever known.

As her smell assaulted him, that tangy, clean scent of a woman recently sated, his mouth watered. He was determined to bring her to the breach again. This time with his lips and teeth and tongue. He needed to taste her. He *had* to taste her.

"I want to make you come again," he whispered, spreading her juices over the tip of her breast before bending to lick it clean.

"Too soon," she murmured, hissing when he tongued her nipple to the top of his mouth, rolling it against his palate.

"Your mouth says one thing," he told her. "But your body says another."

Before she could protest again, he claimed her mouth, kissing her with all the violence and fury and worship inside of him. Then, when she was sufficiently silenced, he straddled her hips so he could begin his journey south.

Her breasts were hard and swollen from passion, her nipples ripe and wet from his mouth, but he kissed and sucked and plumped them anyway, delighting in how it made her squirm and whimper beneath him.

He counted her ribs with his lips, loving the sweet taste of her skin as he scooted farther down her body. Dipping his tongue into her belly button had her threading her fingers through his short hair and sighing wistfully. Nibbling on the soft, womanly curve of her lower belly had her spreading her legs, silently telling him that, despite her words to the contrary, she was more than ready for what came next.

Hooking his thumbs into the waistband of her panties, he pulled them down the length of her silky legs and tossed them onto the pile of her clothes. Then, he bent her knees and spread her legs wide.

He couldn't have stopped the moan that escaped him if he'd tried. She was shaved except for a little landing strip of dark-blond hair. Pink and juicy, her swollen clitoris peeked impudently from between her folds. It begged for the attention of his mouth, and he didn't disappoint.

Gently, because he knew she was tender from his ministrations, he settled his shoulders between her legs and pressed his lips to her. She gasped and shuddered when he opened his mouth so he could lap carefully at the sweet button.

"Angel…" His name was a breathy moan, and he wished…oh, how he *wished*…she had called him Mark.

But she would never call him Mark. He had to forget about that. Forget about everything but her.

He knew how she liked it and he gave it to her, licking her gently and lovingly at first. Then working his way up to quickly and ferociously when she was ready. She gripped his hair in her hands, her nails biting deliciously into his scalp—a little pain for her pleasure. When she arched her back, pressing his face between her legs, he knew she was close, straining and striving for another release.

As for him? Well, he never wanted to move away from this place he occupied. He wanted to live and die right here. Listening to her keen his name. Tasting her sweet saltiness against his tongue. Knowing she was his in every way as she writhed and panted.

When she cried out in frustration, her orgasm so close but still tantalizingly out of reach, he thrust two fingers inside her. Her body welcomed the intrusion by gripping and sucking. Then he curled his fingers upward, found the patch of rough, swollen flesh, and rubbed it in rhythm to his teasing tongue.

She released his head, and he glanced up from between her legs to find she'd plumped her breasts high, running her thumbs over her stiffened nipples. She pleasured herself and reminded him of how incredibly luscious her tits were.

His dick throbbed. He could come right here, right now. From tasting her. From watching her fondle herself.

But then she pinched her nipples, and as he'd known she would, she once again flung herself over into the hot, pulsing abyss of physical pleasure. He reveled in her release the way he reveled in her screaming his name until it echoed around the circus ring, flying up to the ceiling and bouncing back again.

For long moments, he continued to lap at her, rub her from the inside, prolonging her pleasure. Then her tremors gentled and the harsh breaths rasping from her lungs settled to sweet, little pants.

When he was satisfied the last of her release had shuddered through her, he climbed up beside her and gathered her into his arms. As he kissed her sweaty forehead, he had to clench his jaw to keep from sliding down his zipper, releasing his heavy dick, and pulling her leg over his hip so he could sink into her soft, wet heat. Because, good God, she was even more uninhibited than he remembered, more spectacular in the way she owned her sexuality.

"That was way, *way* better than paddling the pink canoe all by myself." She sighed.

He chuckled, grabbing a handful of her luscious ass. Seriously, Sonya's backside was the answer to the question, *What is the meaning of life?*

When he slapped it playfully, she yelped and shoved him flat on his back, looming above him until her blond hair created a curtain of privacy in the expanse of the large room. It was only the two of them. Nothing existed outside this space they occupied.

"How long has it been?" he heard himself ask, then immediately wished he could withdrawal the question. Did he honestly want to hear about her sex life?

"Two years," she told him without a moment's hesitation.

And even though he wished she'd said *ten* years, he

was still surprised by two. Sonya was a lusty woman. Why had she gone two years without sex?

"A long time for a healthy woman in her sexual prime."

She rolled her eyes. "Tell me about it. Problem is, I'm not down with one-night stands, and for a while before I went undercover I was too busy for anything *other* than one-night stands. So…" She shrugged. "Here I am, sex-starved and willing to jump into bed…er…" She lifted her chin and looked around. "Jump into the circus ring with the first guy who comes calling." She turned wicked eyes on him. "Of course it helps that the first guy who came calling happens to look like the love child from a threesome between Oded Fehr, Adam Rayner, and Jeffrey Dean Morgan."

Again, she startled a chuckle out of him. "Thanks." He shook his head. "I think."

"That's definitely a compliment." She nibbled on his jaw. Her soft lips and warm breath had his toes curling inside his boots. "What about you?" She popped up, staring at him quizzically. The scent of freesia and apricot blossoms was a heady mix when combined with the smell of sex and warm, satisfied woman.

"What about me?"

"How long has it been for you?"

"Not two years."

She pursed her lips around a smile. "I figured. A guy like you probably has a woman in every port."

That was alarmingly close to the truth…until a few months ago. Because the instant the Black Knights discovered the notorious Spider and Lord Asad Grafton were one and the same, and Angel discovered Sonya worked as Grafton's personal assistant, he'd given up all other women.

Sheet-diving was for men who didn't know what they wanted. One look at her in a news reel with Grafton, and Angel had known what he wanted.

"I can't imagine why I was worried this would be just another slam-bam-thank-you-ma'am," she teased, shaking her head. But he could see the real dismay in her eyes.

"Like I told you." He made sure his tone and face expressed the solemnity of his words. "You are different." And then, in an attempt to lighten the mood, he added, "And if you must know, it has been four months. Four long, lonely"—he let a devilish twinkle enter his eyes—"aching months."

She grinned, tossing a leg over his thigh. He could feel the warmth of her sex through the denim of his jeans. "Well, let's remedy that, shall we?" The sexy sparkle in her eyes left no doubt she had plans for him.

His heart beat with a happy rhythm he hadn't experienced in a decade when she claimed his lips. He welcomed the impudent intrusion of her tongue with a growl of approval and let her have her way for long minutes. Let her show him all the things she'd learned. Let her be the leader in this new game of seduction.

When he'd had all he could stand and was poised to roll her onto her back, she straddled his hips and set about leaving a burning hot trail of kisses across his jaw and back to his ear. When she nipped his earlobe, he grabbed her ass with both hands. When she swirled her tongue into the hollow of his ear, he tilted up his pelvis and ground himself against her.

"Too rough?" he asked when she hissed.

"No," she breathed against his neck. "Just rough enough. But I've already had my two." She bit his collarbone. "It's only fair if you have one."

Dipping her chin, she sucked his left nipple into her mouth, tonguing the sensitive tip until he would swear he could feel the tug of her lips at the head of his dick and deep inside his balls.

"Sonya..." His hands moved into her hair, his hips pumping up at her, rubbing and seeking and yearning for more friction.

Now it was *her* turn to whisper, "Shhh. Be still. I want you to feel every caress. Every touch. I don't want you to miss a thing."

A smile curved his lips even as his cock pulsed so hard a warm drop of pre-ejaculate squeezed from the tip. "You stole my lines."

She gently sank her teeth into one of his ribs. "They're good lines."

By the time she'd swirled her tongue inside his belly button, nipped at the skin over his hip bones, and sucked on one of the veins that ran diagonally down his lower belly—the big ones that supplied the blood to his dick— the sun had sunk below the tops of the trees surrounding the circus. Only soft, subtle light shined into the ring from the tall windows in the circular foyer. Enough to see by, but not enough to make out details.

That was good. At that moment, he didn't want to worry about the scar on his hip or her recognizing his dick. All he could think about was unpacking his cock and shoving it into any dark, wet, hot place Sonya would let him.

Her hands eagerly worked the buttons on his fly.
Once she had that open, she wasted no time grabbing
the waistband of his jeans and his black boxer briefs
and hauling them both down over his hips. Giddy with
its release, his thick cock smacked against his stomach,
then throbbed and waggled itself at her. You know, just
saying hello.

Sonya—gloriously naked, sweetly pink, and still
shiny with sweat from two orgasms—sat back on her
heels and stared at him. "I feel like Gollum looking at
the ring." When he quirked a brow at her, she gifted him
with a sinful grin and rubbed her hands together. "You
know... *My precious*."

A bust of laughter exploded out of him, shaking his
shoulders and making tears form in his eyes.

God, this woman...

She was everything good and wonderful. She could
make him weep with need one minute and weep with
laughter the next. Of course, when she took his dick in
her soft hands, his humor died a quick death.

Catching his breath, he watched as she angled his
hugely swollen crest toward her mouth. And then? Oh,
and then the seductive little vixen licked her lips. She
licked them like her mouth watered in anticipation of a
sweet treat.

"Sonya..." Those two syllables growled from the
back of his throat.

Catching her bottom lip between her teeth, she
grinned up at him. The cat about to go after the cream.
Then, still holding his gaze, she opened her mouth and
swallowed his swollen head whole.

"Fuck me," he groaned, curling the fingers of one

hand into a fist while he placed the other hand on the side of her face, wanting to feel the muscles in her jaw work, wanting to feel her cheeks hollow when she sucked him. "You have the sweetest mouth," he whispered. She rewarded his praise by sucking him deeper, swirling her tongue around the sensitive ridge surrounding his crest. "So eager."

The muscles in his thighs and ass quivered with the need to thrust. He couldn't help but indulge himself. Just a little. Uncurling his fingers from a fist, he grabbed a handful of her hair and slowly flexed his hips until the tip of his dick hit the back of her throat.

She gagged a little, but didn't struggle against him, willing to let him do whatever he wanted. That was his Sonya, a sensual creature that didn't shy away from the raw, erotic power of sex.

Shuddering, he pulled out of her mouth. Her teeth and tongue and lips stroked him the entire way. He wondered if he'd ever been harder than he was now. Even in the dim light, he could see every vein. Feel the ridge around his flaring head where it met the steely column of his cock.

"I want to fuck you now, Sonya." Although, in his heart he knew it would be more than that. It would be making love.

Her smile was sultry. "Yes, please."

Those two words were all he needed to hear. He had her beneath him before she could finish yelping her surprise. She welcomed him between her legs, her thighs tightening around his hips, her ankles crossing beneath his ass, her wet, hot channel slicking his hungry dick.

He stole kisses *from* her rather than sharing them *with* her. He kneaded her breasts. Strummed her nipples. Caressed her willing body with abandon. He'd given her what she needed, what she wanted, and now he was taking. This was for him.

When she was mewling and moaning and begging beneath him, he pushed to his knees, searched through the back pocket of his Levi's, which were now down around his ankles, and located his wallet. He didn't keep much of anything in there besides money. No ID. No credit cards. But he'd been a member of the Israel Boy and Girl Scouts Federation as a kid, and he knew all about being prepared for anything. Which meant a condom was a must in a grown man's tool kit.

Except…

"Oh, for fuck's sake."

"What?" She pushed up on her elbows, her hair a wild mess around her shoulders, her cheeks and breasts pink with beard burn. "What is it?" she demanded when she saw his face. He knew he probably looked like a man facing a firing squad.

"No condom," he told her, letting his head fall back against his shoulders. "Goddamn Christian!" he growled his fury, his words bouncing around the ceiling of the circus ring.

"Who's Christian?"

"A coworker. A teammate. A thieving sonofabitch who stole the condom out of my wallet so he could—" He cut himself off, shaking his head. "Never mind. The point is…no condom."

Sonya smiled. It was a knowing smile. A naughty smile. Then she feigned thoughtfulness and tapped her lips with one finger. "If only there were *other* ways we could make each other come."

He leveled an intrigued look on her, his dick wagging back and forth in anticipation. "What do you have in mind?"

"Take off your boots and jeans, and I'll show you."

Chapter 22

THREE! THREE GLORIOUS ORGASMS!

Sonya's dry spell was officially over!

She would have pumped a fist in the air except her bones had turned into wet noodles and her muscles quivered and twitched like she'd run a race. Movement was impossible. Which was why she was sprawled atop Angel, his breaths lifting and lowering her in a soothing rhythm, like floating down a big, warm, lazy river.

Sixty-nine-ing, while fun, was a lot of work when it was girl-on-top. Still, she was happy with how they'd come together even as they'd both come apart. Happy with how their bodies had given pleasure and taken pleasure, pulsing like a shared heartbeat.

Sex was odd in that it was the only thing in the world that was simultaneously selfless *and* selfish.

Now, Angel's dick, that fantastically *large* column of flesh and blood and steely strength lay spent against his lower belly. She wished she could get a good look at it, but the dim light made it impossible to make out any details. Like most Iranian men, he was circumcised. That much was obvious. And she reveled in the feel of his thigh, warm and hard and crinkly with man hair, beneath her cheek.

She yelped when he slapped her ass, his breaths hot against the insides of her thighs. "Move off me, woman. Unless, of course, you want me to start kissing your sweet pu—"

"Can't move." She cut him off even as her sweet *ahem* gave a feeble little throb of interest. "Bones have melted. Muscles have atrophied. You've killed me with orgasms. I hope you're happy."

"*Extremely* happy." He chuckled like only a recently sucked-off man could.

With supreme effort, she lifted her head and glanced around. The sun had sunk below the horizon. What little light remained had a distinctly blue hue. Soon it would fade to black, and then she and Angel would be cocooned in darkness.

That might have freaked her out. You know, the whole foreign-country/spooky-abandoned-circus/deadliest-crime-boss-on-the-planet-out-to-get-her of it all. But being with Angel was pretty much the equivalent of having a watchdog, a ninja, and a trained Navy SEAL by her side. With him here with her, there was nothing to be afraid of. Unless, of course, you counted the man himself and—

"What happened to you?" She realized her voice sounded breathless when she saw Angel's hip.

A prickle of suspicion and incredulity skittered up her spine, and as easily as that, her muscles and bones were in fine working order. She scrambled off him, staring down at the puckered scar that was in the same exact spot where Mark's birthmark had been.

She was crazy to be thinking what she was thinking. And yet...

"Sonya?" He slid a hand behind his head, making his huge bicep bulge. "What is it?"

She looked at him, *really* looked at him, searching for something, *anything* recognizable in what little light remained. But…Angel was so much *larger* than Mark had been. Hairier. A decade older. It was impossible to tell if—

"Sonya?" He sat up, gently brushing a lock of hair behind her ear. "What's wrong?"

She pointed to his scar. "What happened?"

He looked down at his hip, then back up at her. "I was pushed into a campfire and burned when I was a little boy. Not exactly pretty, I know, but—"

She cracked a nervous laugh, the tension in her belly loosening. She *was* crazy. Completely, totally, utterly *nutso*.

Swallowing, she shook her head. "Of course. Sorry, I…" She blew out a steadying breath and willed her heart to stop hammering. Mark was dead. He wasn't coming back. Angel *wasn't* him. "I'm seeing ghosts again."

"What?"

"For a minute there, I thought maybe—" She stopped herself from saying the words aloud. They were too ridiculous. "Mark had a birthmark in that exact same spot." She pointed to his scar.

"And for a minute there, you thought what? That I was him?"

"It sounds even more insane when *you* say it." She pasted on a chagrined expression. "But you two are so much alike, and yet…" She smiled and traced his features with a feather-light fingertip. "It's not fair to keep comparing you. I'm sorry, Angel." She took a deep breath and searched his eyes in the darkening room. "Maybe this was a mistake. Maybe I was right about projecting my feelings. Maybe I shouldn't have—"

"Come here." He gathered her into his arms and

reclined back until they were side by side, him spooning her and pillowing her head on his arm. The air inside the circus ring was cooler now that the sun had set, but Angel was a human furnace at her back. "This is no mistake. We are *good* together, Sonya. Admit it."

"I do, but—"

"No buts." He cut her off. "And I don't mind that you compare me to Mark. After all, you loved him, so he must have been quite a man."

Only someone with as much confidence and self-assurance as Angel could be so understanding. There was a gracefulness about him. A completeness. He was comfortable enough in his own skin that he couldn't be made jealous or insecure by anything she could say. He proved it when he said, "I would like to hear about him."

She laughed. "For God's sake, why?"

"Maybe I can learn a thing or two."

"Believe me. You don't need help being any hotter or more mysterious or more intriguing than you already are. You've pretty much cornered the market on that whole tall, dark, and handsome thing."

"Still…" He smoothed her hair away from her shoulder so he could plant a hot, open-mouthed kiss there. Even though she was completely spent, it still caused her belly to trill with excitement. "I want to know. Tell me something true. Something special. Tell me…" He hesitated. "Tell me about the moment you realized you were in love with him."

Incredulity hit her hard. "Seriously?"

"Yes. I want to know you, Sonya. Every part of you. All your stories."

She debated her options. Then figured… *What the hell. He asked for it. Here goes nothing…*

Closing her eyes, she pictured her old Montmartre apartment. Her bedroom had been the size of a Triscuit, only big enough for a full-size bed and a chest of drawers. But she hadn't rented the place for its square footage. She'd rented it because through the bedroom window was a breathtaking view of the Sacré-Cœur, the mammoth white church that stood sentinel on the highest hill in Paris.

The night she'd realized she loved Mark was as clear in her mind's eye as if it'd happened only yesterday. They'd been in bed, the moonlight streaming through the open window. Sacré-Cœur had been there on its hill, beaming down at them like a benevolent spectator, and Mark had been tracing her lips with his fingertip.

Boom! Like an atomic blast it had struck her. She loved him. Not a crush. Not simple lust. Not even puppy love. But *love*.

She'd never been more terrified in her life.

"What is it?" Mark asked, cocking his head until the moonlight glinted off his curly locks and into his chocolaty eyes. He claimed to need a haircut, but she loved *how long his hair was.* Loved *him.*

Oh la vache!

With her heart in her throat, she asked him, "Where do you see this going?"

"This?" He delicately sketched the outline of her nipple, smiling when her areola pinched. "I see it going two or three more rounds before the night is over."

"No. This." She waved a hand between them. "Us. Where do you see us *going?"*

When he arched a brow, she pressed on. "What am I to you, Mark? What is this thing between us? Am I just a distraction while you're here in Paris? Is this relationship just a way to pass the time until you go back to Israel?"

"Sonya—"

"I need the truth." Her voice sounded awful. So unsure and frightened and yuck! But she couldn't help it! "I need you to tell me because I think I might be falling in love with you."

She didn't have the guts to confess it was already a done deal. When he got still, when he searched her eyes while carefully schooling his features, she thought she might up and die.

"Scheisse!" She cursed and covered her face with her hands, pressing the heels of her palms against her eyes, trying to push back the hot tears that pricked behind them. "I shouldn't have said that. I'm sorry I—"

"Sonya…" He gently lowered her hands, holding them prisoner in his much larger one. "I'm in love with you too."

She hiccupped on a startled cry. "You are?"

"Of course. And you aren't falling in love with me. You're in love with me."

She laughed, fighting tears. "How do you know?"

"Because I see it in your eyes. Everything you're thinking, everything you're feeling shines in them." He smiled at her. "You'd make a terrible spy."

Then he kissed her. Kissed her with so much love and passion and…love that her tender, young heart felt like it would burst.

"How will we ever make this work?" Trepidation and wariness and passion had lowered the timbre of her voice. "You work for the Mossad. You wage shadow wars against states that sponsor terror. How can you do that and still hope to build a life with me?"

Mark swallowed, a dark cloud passing over his handsome features. "Are you asking me to choose between you and my country? You and my duty?"

"No." She was quick to answer even though her heart cried yes! "The work you do is too important." She shook her head, overwhelmed by uncertainty, swamped by a million questions that had no easy answers.

"The work we do is too important," he insisted.

"Right."

He lay back beside her and tucked her against him until her head was pillowed on his chest. She could hear the solid thud of his heart.

"What do you believe in?" he asked after a while.

"What do you mean? Like, in terms of God?"

"No." She felt him shake his head. "In terms of duty and sacrifice and living not for yourself but for the greater good."

"Oh, those little things?" She expected a laugh. She didn't get one.

"I'm serious. What do you believe?"

She took a deep breath. "I guess I believe the things that people say are fleeting, but the things they do? Well, those things last forever. I believe in duty and sacrifice and living a life of service to others, like you said. But I suppose I also believe that love conquers all. So maybe...maybe we can have it all. Do you think?"

He hugged her close. "I hope."

"Who knew two little words could be so profound?" Sonya said to Angel. "Mark died three days later. I mean...he was *killed* three days later."

Angel placed another hot kiss on her shoulder, but

this time it was meant to soothe, not titillate. In a way, Sonya *was* soothed. Maybe because, for the first time, she was able to talk about the worst day of her life without breaking down into a heap of tears and snot and choking cries. Maybe because, for the first time, a future without Mark didn't seem so bleak and pointless.

There was a small ray of light at the end of her tunnel now. It had a name. *Angel*. And, like Mark, the way she felt could be summed up with two small yet profound words. *I hope…*

"The bomber found out Mark was hot on his trail," she explained. "The guy said he was scared if Mark caught up with him, he'd kill him. So he agreed to give himself up. He arranged with Mark a time and place to turn himself in." Her heart was a stone in her chest, heavy and sad with the memory. "But that was bologna. The bomber had no intention of turning himself in. When Mark met him down by the banks of the Seine on the outskirts of Paris, he shot Mark through the heart, then put a bullet through his own brain. His final act of terrorism." Squeezing her eyes closed, the awfulness of that long-ago day cut into her like the rusty teeth of a chain saw. "I saw it all."

Angel stiffened behind her. "What do you mean? You saw CCTV footage afterward?"

"No." She dragged in a deep breath, letting his spicy aftershave give her the courage to continue. "I followed Mark the morning he was supposed to meet with the bomber."

"Good God, Sonya. No."

"He was working alone. He didn't have any backup. I thought I should go in case…" She shook her head at her younger self. "But I was helpless to do anything. I was across the river when I saw the bomber pull his gun. All I could do was scream Mark's name before he was gone and falling into the water. His heart, that heart that loved me, had been blown to smithereens."

She thought she trembled with the devastation of the memory, but then she realized it wasn't her. It was Angel. *He* was the one shaking.

Alarmed, she turned to see his face contorted in a horrible grimace. His eyes were screwed shut. A muscle ticked frantically in his jaw.

"Angel?" Fear had her voice sounding small. "What is it?"

He shook his head, but after a couple of seconds, he focused those sniper eyes on her. His expression was fierce with some sort of emotion. She couldn't say which one. "He would *not* have wanted you to see that."

"I know." She snuggled closer to him, tucking her head under his chin, loving how strands of her hair got stuck in his thick beard stubble. "I shouldn't have gone. And yet..." She fiddled with his chest hair. "There's a part of me that's always been glad I was there. No matter how awful it was, no matter how many nightmares I've had, at least Mark wasn't alone in those last few minutes. I was with him, even if he didn't know it. There's some comfort in that."

Angel's beefy arms clamped down on her so hard she could barely breathe. And then she was flat on her back, his big body pinning her to the mat, his mouth hot and hungry as it ravaged hers.

His kiss felt a little like punishment, a little like penance. But whatever the emotion behind it, she'd take it.

No one kissed like Angel...

Chapter 23

ANGEL'S HEART WAS AN OPEN WOUND.

He'd never meant for Sonya to follow him that day. Never meant for her to witness the moment Mark Risa ceased to be.

The thought of it was awful. Too awful to fully contemplate. So he did the only thing he could. He poured his hurt and his guilt and his open wound of a heart into her with hard, hot kisses.

He loved her so much!

Always had. Always would.

It *killed* him to know how much he'd hurt her, and there was only one thing for it. He'd spend the rest of his days making it up to her, giving her nothing but love and joy and smoking-hot, sweaty bouts of mind-blowing sex and—

"Condom!" she gasped, ripping her mouth away. "I have a condom in my purse."

That had him stilling above her. "Why are you just now telling me this?"

"I just now *remembered*. It's in the back zippered compartment of my wallet." She pushed at his shoulder, a wordless command for him to get off her.

She scrambled over to the edge of the mat, bending down and giving him an unencumbered view or her sweet ass, her delicious pussy, and that heart-shaped mole above her right butt cheek. Thank God there was still a sliver of light coming in through the entrances to the circus ring. He wouldn't have wanted to miss this sight for anything.

A surge of blood to his dick had the thing straining and aching. He soothed it with a hand while avidly watching her scrounge through her purse.

She took out the Glock and set it aside. She followed that up with her book, the hot pink ribbon dangling from between the pages, and a package of tissues. Finally, she pulled out her wallet, unzipped the main compartment, then a secondary compartment, and came up with a foil wrapper that was wrinkled and looking a little worse for wear but blessedly whole.

"Bazinga!" she crowed. Then she shoved the condom in her mouth so she could use both hands to repack her purse.

Condom.

Mouth.

Naked woman.

Amazing tits.

Angel didn't realize he was jacking himself off until Sonya cocked a sexy eyebrow and took the condom out of her mouth so she could wave it at him. "You want to put this thing to work or would you rather finish what you're doing?" Her eyes sparked with wicked heat. "Honestly, I'm fine either way. As long as I can join you."

He nearly swallowed his tongue when she reached down to touch herself, sliding her fingers between her folds and pinching lightly at the swollen bud of nerves.

Although there was a part of him that would be fine fisting his own dick if he could lay there and watch her get herself off, there was a *larger* part of him that needed to have her beneath him. Needed show her how much he loved her with his body because he couldn't tell her with his words.

Not yet anyway.

"Come here." He caught her wrist and dragged her down next to him, pressing his thigh between her legs. He was gratified when she eagerly rubbed herself against him.

Then he set about seducing her. Not because she needed it, but because *he* needed it. This was how he would win her heart. He would love her so thoroughly she would have no choice but to give in and give them a chance.

Her breasts were weighed and plumped in his hands. Strummed with his fingers. Sucked in his mouth. Every inch of her skin was examined by his fingertips. Kissed by his lips. Nipped between his teeth. He explored her softly and completely until she squirmed and mewled and begged him between ragged breaths.

"Stop being so gentle with me." She pumped her hips against the fingers he'd softly feathered over her mound. "Why are you being so gentle?"

"Because I know you want me to be rough." He carefully rubbed his thumb over her clitoris.

"Sadist," she accused. "You like torturing me."

"No." He bent to suck on her nipple. "I like making you wild with pleasure. I like watching your body blush with passion. I like seeing you helpless and hungry for me."

"Angel." Her eyes were smoky. "Please. I need you in me."

He picked up the condom from where it had fallen from her nerveless fingers and held it in front of her face. "Tell me, Sonya," he said, unconsciously modulating his tone, his accent. That was second nature now. "Tell me you are willing to give us a chance. I am not giving you what you want until you agree."

She grabbed his head, staring deep into his eyes. "You're ruthless."

"You have no idea. When it comes to you, no one will ever be more ruthless."

"Then I agree," she told him. "Let's see where it goes." She claimed his mouth in a kiss that left them both moaning.

When he finally pulled away, he caught the corner of the condom wrapper in his teeth and ripped it open.

"Ahhh, a foil wrapper ripping…" She watched him from beneath hooded lids. Her strawberries-and-cream complexion was now mostly just strawberries. "What a magical sound."

His lips stretched into a wide smile as he rolled on the condom and positioned himself between her legs.

The wide head of his dick kissed her entrance. He didn't give her time to catch her breath. He penetrated her without preamble.

She cried out in pleasure. In pain. Her body rippling and squeezing, shocked by the sudden intrusion.

A witch's brew of physical bliss and nerve-racking restraint bubbled inside him as he held himself still, letting her get used to him. Letting her feel the pulse of his heart through his shaft. Letting her body relax and then wind itself up with an aching need for more.

More hardness.

More friction.

He moved slowly at first, every slick retreat and

warm advance strafing nerves he would swear only came alive when he was inside Sonya. She fit him like she was made for him. Every part of her enveloping and caressing and stroking every part of him.

As the tension built, their kisses turned abandoned and sloppy. She crossed her ankles above his ass and moved in counter rhythm to his pistoning hips. Ripping his mouth from hers, he gently sank his teeth into her shoulder, holding her in place, holding her *against* him, even as he staved off his own release. He wouldn't go until she did.

And he knew just how to send her careening over the edge.

His slow thrusts picked up speed until they were rutting and screwing and making love so hard and so completely he would swear they were no longer part of the real world. Instead, they'd gone someplace new.

Someplace bright and shimmering.

"Angel!" She screamed his name as her body tightened. The grip of her internal muscles, the pinch of her nails into the tough flesh of his back, had his balls drawing up, his orgasm burning inside them.

One final thrust, and he was coming. Hot, heavy spurts of pleasure blew him apart and put him back together only to blow him apart again.

Miraculous. Metaphysical. Heavenly…

There were no words in the English language—in *any* language—that came close to capturing what it was to make love to Sonya. But he planned to spend the rest of his life doing exactly that over and over and *over* again…

Chapter 24

Corjova, Moldova

"WELL, I'LL BE DIPPED IN SHIT," ACE SAID AFTER HE'D quietly closed the driver's side door on the little VW Bug. "They're here. They're all here."

He turned to Rusty in the passenger seat, only to find the man's pretty hazel eyes as wide and unblinking as Ace knew his had to be.

"They were sitting there on the table like friggin' Christmas dinner," Rusty whispered in disbelief.

"What?" Ozzie asked from the back seat. "The rest of the canisters? You guys found them?"

"All of 'em." Rusty shook his head. "They're all right here."

After following Victor Popov to a small farm outside the tiny village of Corjova, they'd parked the car behind a stand of trees next to the tumbling waters of the Dnister River. Once the sun had set and there was no chance of skylining themselves against the horizon, and while Ozzie had waited for them back in the car, Ace and Rusty had silently slunk across the property and up to the old farmhouse.

It was a ramshackle place, badly in need of paint. The porch sagged on the western edge, and some of the clapboard siding could use the help of a few additional nails. But once they'd peeked in through the window, they'd found the interior was fully furnished, as warm and homey as one would expect a farmhouse to be.

Popov and two other men had been gathered around the kitchen table. Ace had surmised from the animated hand gestures and big smiles that they were happy with a job well done. Then, Popov had indicated the ten remaining canisters of enriched uranium lying in the middle of the table before pointing to his glowing cell phone screen and counting out some numbers on his fingers. Ace suspected he was calculating how much richer they'd be once they sold the remaining cache.

Not if we have anything to say about it, he'd thought while slowly slinking away from the kitchen window and pressing his back against the sagging siding. When he turned to Rusty, it was to find the big redhead staring at him in wide-eyed wonder. Then, with the moon bathing his face in a silvery glow, Rusty had winked.

That wink had stabbed Ace right in his heart. He'd known then and there he was in deep shit where Rusty was concerned. Despite their constant bickering—and despite his big talk about never getting involved with another man who wasn't out—the truth was Rusty had already wormed his way under Ace's skin and straight into that ridiculous organ beating behind his breastbone.

So it was official. When it came to men, he was Brokeback flypaper.

"We need to call Angel's Moldovan contact." Ozzie pulled his cell phone from his hip pocket.

"Anyone else feel uneasy giving the Moldovans the uranium?" Rusty shifted restlessly in the cramped front seat of the Bug. "Can't help but think it'd be better if *we* grabbed the stuff and handed it over to *our* government. The devil you know and all that."

"Angel says this guy will make sure the canisters are destroyed and removed from the black market," Ozzie said. "I trust Angel to know his shit even if he *is* mysterious as fuck."

Ace and the rest of the BKI crew were still wrapping their minds around the truth that the man they knew as Jamin "Angel" Agassi was really an Israeli Mossad agent by the name of Mark Risa who'd taken over the identity of an Iranian scientist named Majid Abass and single-handedly stopped Iran from becoming a nuclear power.

For years they'd known Angel spent most of his time away from Black Knights Inc. headquarters in Chicago, out on missions doing God, the president of the United States, and it turned out, *Boss* only knew what. But it wasn't until they'd come up with the plan to leak his identity and activities onto the dark web to lure Spider into approaching him that they'd become privy to the true scope of his operations and the confusing labyrinth of his many false identities.

Ozzie tapped a number into his phone. After Angel's Moldovan contact picked up on the other end, he relayed the information on the whereabouts of the fissile material. There were a few "sures" and "okays" and "of courses," and then Ozzie signed off.

"He says he's on his way with a team." Ozzie pocketed his phone. "But it'll take him about half an hour to get here, so he asked if we'd stick around to make sure Popov and his jackwad buddies don't fly the coop beforehand. Guess we'd better get comfortable, gents."

Great. More time crammed into the VW beside Rusty was just what Ace needed. *Not.*

"Getting comfortable is impossible in this sardine can," Rusty complained, rummaging around in the backpack on the floorboard by his big, booted feet. When he sat back, he blew out a dejected breath. "Crap in my lap. I forgot to pack energy bars. Anybody have any grub on them? I'm starving."

"Ozzie," Ace said over his shoulder. "Hand me my backpack. I think Becky stuffed some Dum Dum lollipops in there before I left."

Rusty sent him a sidelong look. "A sucker? Sorry, my man, that ain't gonna cut it."

Ace smiled. *My man.* Oh, if only that were true. If only Rusty would see that a life lived in the dark was no life at all. If only Rusty would admit to himself—and, more importantly, to his parents—who he truly was, then maybe Ace actually *could* be his man.

"Shit," Ozzie hissed from the back seat. "Did you guys hear that?"

"What?" A chill raced over Ace's skin. Since the air inside the Bug was warm from the body heat of three grown men, he knew it had nothing to do with the temperature. "What did you hear?"

Ozzie's face, even in the darkness of the vehicle, was limned in alarm. "It sounded like a twig under a boot and—"

"*Fuck!*" Rusty yelled at the exact moment Ace's driver's side windshield exploded.

Ace barely had time to register the shatterproof glass that landed in his lap in a cobwebbed sheet before the cold barrel of a rifle touched his temple and he knew his day had gone from bad to *much* worse.

Chapter 25

Rusty wasn't sure he'd ever *truly* known fear until that moment.

As a marine, he'd been pinned down in enemy territory too many times to count. More than once, he'd felt the displaced air of a bullet that, had it been one inch to the right or left, would have left him six feet under and pushing up daisies. But nothing compared to seeing the rifle barrel kiss Ace's head and not knowing if the next second the brains of the man he loved, the only man he'd *ever* loved, would be splashing into his lap.

Yes. He loved Ace. Hell of a time to admit it to himself.

Before he made the conscious decision to move, his hand was on the butt of the Kimber Custom semiautomatic he'd shoved into his waistband before they exited the car to recon the farmhouse.

"Don't," Ace hissed beneath his breath. "Not yet. Play it cool."

The guy wielding the rifle yelled something in Russian and punched the barrel of his weapon into Ace's head hard enough to make Ace grunt. The pain contorting Ace's handsome face had Rusty's jaw clenching until he worried for the integrity of his teeth.

"I think he wants us to get out of the car," Ozzie said from the back seat, his hands lifted shoulder high. "And, uh, in case neither of you have noticed, we've got more company on our six."

Rusty flicked a glance into the rearview mirror. Sure enough. The moonlight shone down on Popov and one of his pals. They stood at the rear of the VW, rifles aimed through the back windshield.

The three douchewagons had somehow spotted them. But that was less head-scratching than knowing the trio had then managed to get the drop on them. Rusty wanted to chalk it up to the guys being locals and more familiar with the terrain, but he couldn't discount the possibility he'd been so distracted by having Ace a mere six inches away that he wasn't on top of his game. That he'd missed something back at the farmhouse or on their walk back to the Bug.

"Even-stevens. Three against three," he muttered, his voice barely audible inside the car and definitely *not* audible outside of it. The river giggled and laughed ten yards away. It drowned out all other sounds. "Ace, you still carrying?"

"Yep. Back waistband."

"Ozzie?" Rusty whispered.

"Nope. It's in my gear bag. And I don't think these assholes will take kindly to me going on a fishing expedition."

The man aiming for Ace's head yelled something again. He punctuated his command by jabbing Ace in the temple one more time. It took everything Rusty had not to grab the barrel of that rifle and drag the asshole forward until his head poked through the broken window. It would only take a split second to shove his nine mil under the dickswab's chin and blow the top of his head off.

If he'd been assured success, and if he'd known if Ozzie would be able to unpack his pistol and get the

drop on Popov and his partner before they were able
to open fire and fill the VW was rifle rounds, he might
have done just that.

"Time's up," Ozzie murmured. "How do you guys
want to play this?"

"Get out of the car." Ace reached for his own door
handle from beneath the sheet of shattered glass. "From
the tone of this guy's voice, it'll be our coffin if we don't."

Adrenaline left a sour taste on Rusty's tongue as
he calmly and deliberately opened the passenger-side
door. Before he stepped outside, he zipped the bottom
of his jacket, concealing the handgun in the waistband
of his jeans.

Standing beside the car, he noticed the wind had a
chill to it that it hadn't had earlier. Of course, that chill
was nothing compared to the frost in Popov's deeply
hooded eyes.

Rusty recognized that look. It was the one men wore
when they knew they'd be dealing in death. Without
opening his mouth, Rusty let his eyes do the talking for
him. *I know what's in your mind, motherfucker*.

Popov's smirking expression answered, *Oh, yeah?
And what do you plan to do about it?*

Funny how silent eye conversations didn't require the
participants to speak the same language.

"I think they want you over here with us," Ozzie said.

Rusty broke eye contact with Popov to see Ozzie
and Ace standing shoulder to shoulder. Both had rifles
aimed at their heads. Both appeared amazingly calm,
given the situation.

Maybe Rusty looked calm too. But he sure as shit
didn't feel it as he slowly rounded the hood of the VW,

deliberately bumping Ace's shoulder once he'd drawn even because he needed to feel Ace standing there. *Alive*.

Popov joined his compatriots beside the Bug, the three asswipes lined up man-to-man in front of the three Americans. Then he snarled a few words at them.

Ace shook his head and said something that sounded like *ahngleeskee*, which Rusty assumed was Russian for *English*.

Popov's chin jerked back, confusion contorting his face. Once again, Rusty read his expression. It said, *What are Americans doing here?* Then, Popov shook his head and spoke to his comrades. The slew of guttural sounding words were an assault on Rusty's ears. Finally, Popov jerked his rifle and barked an unintelligible order.

"I don't guess that needs any translation," Ozzie muttered. "Let's go."

As a group, they rounded the small clutch of trees that had hidden them from view of the farmhouse—or, at least, they'd *thought* it had hidden them. Then they made their way across a fallow field toward the neglected structure, Ozzie limping slightly due to the wound he'd previously sustained from an incendiary device.

The buzz of night insects filled the cool air and competed with the babble of the river. The smell of untilled soil tunneled up Rusty's nose.

It might have been a bucolic scene if not for the trio of gun-wielding, uranium-selling jagoffs. The threesome stayed a few yards behind Rusty and his teammates, playing it safe and keeping their weapons out of grabbing range.

When they started whispering in Russian, no doubt discussing how, when, and where they planned to dispose of the bodies, Rusty used their distraction to mumble, "They're gonna kill us."

"Seems likely," Ace agreed.

"We should make our moves now, before they get us into the farmhouse." Rusty's muscles quivered, ready for action.

"Have something in mind?" Ace asked from the side of his mouth.

"Ozzie fakes a stumble. When they've got eyes on him, you and I turn and fire."

"It'll be tight. Two against three."

"Semi-autos against hunting rifles. I'll take our odds any day."

Popov shouted something again. When Rusty glanced over his shoulder, he saw Popov drop his hand away from the trigger of his rifle, using it to cover his mouth in a gesture for them to shut the hell up.

It was their chance. "Now!" Rusty hissed.

Good, old, gimpy-legged Ozzie stubbed his toe on a clump of earth and grass and went down for the count. Before he kissed dirt, Rusty and Ace had whipped their weapons from their waistbands and turned and fired.

BOOM!

The sound of their simultaneous shots rang across the open field like the main gun on an Abrams tank. Ace's round hit his target in the face, the bullet entering below the dude's left eye and exploding out the back of his head. Rusty's shot wasn't as clean. *Damnit!* His round had slammed into his target's chest, but he must've missed the bastard's heart because even though the guy stumbled, he didn't fall. Rusty pulled his trigger again, leaving it to Ace to take out Popov.

Bam! Another round, and Rusty's guy was dunzo.

Even though barely two seconds had passed, it felt like time stood still. Rusty saw Popov swing his rifle from Ozzie, who was flat on the ground, toward Ace. But even though Ace's semi-auto was aimed at Popov, Ace hadn't fired.

Rusty saw why.

Ace's handgun had stovepiped—the fired case had pulled from the chamber but hadn't fully ejected, causing Ace's slide to lock partially open, jamming his weapon.

Rusty turned his nine mil toward Popov and aimed, but knew he would be too late. At the same time he squeezed the trigger, he dove in front of Ace and felt the slug from the rifle bury deep in his gut.

There wasn't any pain at first. Only the shock of the round entering his body and tearing through his organs. Popov was falling to the ground, but Rusty squeezed off another shot, blowing away the top of Popov's head. You know, just to be sure. Then...*fuuuuck!*

A wrecking ball of agony slammed into him, and he would swear the world turned red. Pain beat like a demon heart inside him...*cold*. Why the hell was he so cold? Then he realized it was because he lay on the ground and the dirt beneath him was as cool and hard as the blood gushing from his belly was hot and wet.

Jiminy Christmas. He dropped his weapon so he could put both hands over his wound. He'd seen enough carnage during his years as a marine to know he was in serious trouble.

"Oh Jesus!" Suddenly Ace knelt beside him. "Let me see, Rusty. Damnit! Move your hands!"

Rusty moaned when Ace wrenched his hands away.

Panting, trying to breathe through the pain even though the pain was too thick to breathe through, he watched Ace's face in the moonlight. The man took two seconds to assess his injury, turned white as a ghost, then shoved his hands over Rusty's wound, applying hard pressure that notched up Rusty's torture.

"Ozzie! Hurry!" Ace shouted, his voice cracking. "There's QuikClot and transfusion equipment in my gear bag! We need all of it! *Now!*"

Rusty didn't see Ozzie sprint across the field. He was too busy cataloging Ace's expression. There was horror. There was determination. There was…fear.

It was the last thing that told him he wasn't in serious trouble; he was body-bag bait.

Well, hell.

"Never th-thought I'd be *that* guy." His voice was rough with agony.

Ace blinked at him, those ocean-blue eyes bright in the moonlight. "Which guy?"

"The one who got tired of wearing his guts on the inside."

Ace's face contorted into an awful mask. "I can't believe you're joking at a time like this."

Rusty chuckled, then hissed as it caused his guts to twist viciously. His vision went wonky. He could feel the savage teeth of unconsciousness chewing at his brainstem.

"Better to die with a smile on my lips, doncha think?" he managed.

"You're not going to die."

Rusty didn't miss the uncertainty in Ace's voice. "Don't bullshit a bullshitter."

"You're *not* going to die!" Ace's face was that of a

man who was prepared to go into hand-to-hand combat with the Grim Reaper.

"Ace..." Rusty grabbed Ace's hands, which were covered in blood. *His* blood. "I wanna tell you something."

"Don't you dare start making deathbed confessions, you asshole." A lone tear trekked down Ace's face and that, more than anything, let Rusty know there was no hope.

The math for blood loss was real simple. The more you lost, the weaker you got. And that kind of arithmetic meant you had to act quickly.

Before he went, he wanted to say the words he'd never said to another man—the three most beautiful words in the English language. He wanted to die knowing that, in the end, he'd swallowed his pride, swallowed his fear, and taken the leap.

"I love you," he whispered and watched Ace's face crumple.

The sound of Ozzie's unsteady gait reached his ears a split second before Ozzie knelt beside him, ripping open packages of QuikClot with his teeth. The guy might be hobbled by a bum leg, but there was still plenty of giddyap and go left in him.

"Move your hands," Ozzie commanded.

Ace stopped applying pressure to Rusty's wound, and the small reprieve as the pain let up was short-lived. Ozzie poured the clotting agent directly into the gaping hole in his belly, and the fires of hell set up shop inside his gut.

His eyes rolled up inside his head, and he felt for sure he was about to go lights out. Then, Ace whipped off his jacket, managed to finagle it beneath Rusty's back, and used the arms to cinch a slapdash tourniquet around Rusty's waist. Ace wasn't gentle about it either. He showed no mercy, tying the thing so tight that torturous pain ripped Rusty back from the brink of unconsciousness.

"Help me get him up." Ace's voice was hoarse with emotion. "We need to get him into the farmhouse. There might be supplies in there to help us stop the bleeding. If not, I think we'll have to do a BBT."

"We need to call in an evac," Ozzie panted. "Maybe Angel's contact could send—"

"No time!" Ace bellowed. "If we don't stop his bleeding in the next five minutes, he's dead!"

Ozzie didn't argue, simply grabbed Rusty's right arm and slung it over his shoulder while Ace did the same thing with Rusty's left. Both men strained and groaned as they hauled Rusty to his feet.

"For the love of Captain Kirk, you're one heavy sonofabitch, you know that?" Ozzie tried to insert a little levity into the situation.

"Always chose needs over wants," Rusty said, or rather *slurred*. His tongue felt thick. He was pretty sure his eyes were open, but his vision had tunneled until all he could see were two pinpricks of light. "I mean, I *wanted* to look like a Calvin Klein underwear model. But I *needed* cheeseburgers."

"This guy takes a bullet to his gut," Ace muttered, "and suddenly he's a stand-up comedian."

When they took a step forward, Rusty knew he couldn't make it. The pain was too intense, and every second that he fought unconsciousness only prolonged his misery. Figuring he'd said all he needed to say, figuring he'd ended his life on a good note, he fell into the waiting arms of oblivion.

Chapter 26

"TURN 'ROUND! TAKE THAT SIDE ROAD!" GRAFTON SLAPPED the back of Richie's seat when the small receiver in his hand let out a weak, sick-sounding *beep*. He immediately regretted the move when pain shot up the length of his arm.

He was fairly certain he'd cracked a knuckle when he punched the dumpster in the alleyway. And then he'd made his situation worse by keeping his hand balled into a fist all evening long. It was either that, or punch something else again.

And who could blame him? Even though Benton had called every hour on the hour to assure him that, according to the satellite readings, Sonya was still smack-dab in the center of Chişinău, and even though Grafton and Charles had had Richie zigzagging all over the godforsaken city in a methodical grid search, until this moment they hadn't heard a single thing out of the receiver, and his rage and panic had been getting the better of him.

No…not panic. He never panicked. But in the elapsed time, his mind had conjured up a million things Angel and Sonya could be doing.

Had they found a way to ring up their old cronies inside the law enforcement or Intelligence communities to pass along what they knew about him? Had they been comparing notes so they could present their evidence as a united front?

Richie carefully pulled onto the shoulder of the road before engaging his hazard lights and slowly backing up. A lorry blew by, the driver laying on the horn and making Grafton's already frayed nerves shred a little more.

Neither Sonya nor Angel have mobiles, he assured himself, going over the same lines of logic he'd been mulling for too many hours now. *I took those from them. Of course, that doesn't mean they haven't purchased pre-paid burners or found a pay phone or an internet café…*

Still, it would be their word against his. And there was nothing, *nothing* to prove he'd ever been in Moldova. If he could find Angel and Sonya and do away with them, hide their bodies where they'd never be found, he could easily pay any number of people to swear he'd been in St. Ives this entire day and there'd be no one left alive who'd be willing to naysay him. Any evidence against him that Angel and Sonya might have passed along? Rubbish. Nothing but two disgraced people looking to bring a well-respected businessman to his knees because…

Because they were trying to extort money from me!

Yes! *That* was the piece of the puzzle he had been missing. That would be his explanation for anything Sonya or Angel said.

I can get out of this mess, he convinced himself. *I just need to find that backstabbing bitch and that murderous bastard and—*

Beep!

His thoughts cut off when the receiver in his hand came to life again. "Where does this road lead?" he asked Charles, who kept track of their search area by using a GPS app on his mobile.

"Here in a bit," Charles said, studying the glowing screen, "the road forks. If we go left, we'll end up at a church. Right and the road dead ends at some place called…" He scrunched up his face and sounded out the words like a primary school student first learning how to read. "Circul Arena Mica."

In the hours Grafton had spent with Charles, he'd learned the man was far more brawn than brains. Typical for a bodyguard type, he supposed. But annoying, nonetheless. If it weren't for Benton's hourly phone calls, he might have died from conversational tedium.

Richie, though an excellent driver and a man Grafton had kept on his payroll for nearly fifteen years, wasn't one for small talk. Probably due in no small part to Richie having worked for the Brindle crime family in London before coming to work for Grafton. The man knew the consequences of loose lips and, as such, appreciated the sound of silence.

"Take a left at the fork in the road," Grafton told Richie.

"Why left?" Charles asked.

"Because you said the church is to the left. Maybe Angel thinks he'll Quasimodo this thing." At Charles's stupefied expression, Grafton sighed. "Quasimodo was the Hunchback of Notre-Dame. He took sanctuary in a church to escape the townspeople who thought he was a monster."

Charles blinked, trying and failing to make the connection. How trying. "Angel might be hiding out in the church while waiting for a way to escape the country."

"Oh." Charles nodded dumbly.

"But he's a fool if he thinks a house of God will stop me."

"Sir," Richie spoke up from the driver's seat, "your tracking device hasn't beeped since I made the left."

Grafton glanced at the gadget. Richie was right. "Go another half mile. If we haven't any action on this thing, we'll turn 'round and try the other road."

Five minutes later, they were on the other road, winding their way up a small hill with trees crowding around the sedan. It was obvious the old boulevard was deserted and unused. The moonlight shone on the myriad cracks and potholes in its surface. Fallen limbs required Richie to do some creative driving. And the night insects seemed louder here, as if they'd traveled into another world where everything was dirtier, darker, wilder.

Grafton might have fallen victim to the creepiness of it all, but the steadily increasing *beep, beep, beep* of the receiver had his heart pounding with anticipation. This was it! They were closing in!

"Kill the headlights," he told Richie as the trees looked to give way to a clearing up ahead. "I don't want to alert that bastard to our presence."

Richie switched off the high beams a second before they broke through the canopy of trees. He slowed the sedan to a crawl as the three of them took in the huge courtyard and car park. At the back of it all was a circular structure that sat like a huge gray crown in the moonlight.

"Stop." The receiver's steady *beep-beep-beep* told Grafton everything he needed to know. "They're here. We've found them."

Chapter 27

Sonya dreamed of Mark...

Not about anything that had actually happened. That's not how her dreams of him worked. When she lay her head on the pillow at night, it seemed her subconscious liked to play out what their lives *might* have been like, what they *might* have done.

Had he lived.

In this dream she and Mark were married, living and working in Paris. It was a Sunday morning. Too early for the kids to be awake—yes, they had kids. Two, in fact. Two little girls who had his curly dark hair and big, brown eyes. Mark was behind her in their soft, comfy bed. He was warm and naked and aroused, prodding against her bottom and whispering dirty words in her ear as morning's first tender light peeked through the filmy curtains, bathing them both in soft shades of pale pink and warm gold.

Even after all their years together, through the ups and the downs, the good and the bad, he could still light her fire with barely a touch.

"We have to hurry," she whispered, then moaned when he plumped her breast, his callused thumb twanging her nipple into rigid attention. "The kids will be up soon, and they'll be wanting your world-famous French toast and—"

She lost her train of thought when he pinched her nipple.

"That can wait until I give their mother my world-famous cock," he rumbled naughtily, making her laugh.

"Careful, Husband. Your arrogance is showing again."

"Don't pretend you don't love it."

"Mmm," she hummed when he slipped his hand down her belly to cup her. *"I love it."* She wiggled against him, lifting her leg to give him better access, silently begging for more.

He gave it to her by touching the spot guaranteed to have her panting. When he found her wet, he chuckled. *"Always so greedy."*

"Don't pretend you don't love it." She gave his words back to him.

"I love it." He parroted her, because apparently that was the game. Then he added, *"I love you."*

"Always have to one-up me, don't you?"

"And here I thought you liked two up you." Before she could respond, he plunged two fingers deep into her body, hitting that patch of tender flesh inside her.

He was lazy in his morning need, content to arouse them both slowly, playing with her gently and deliberately. She reached back to fist him and grinned when he moaned in her ear, grinned wider when he pumped his hips in earnest while at the same time increasing the rhythm and pressure of his fingers.

Sonya came awake to the feel of her body on the precipice. Angel, behind her, had no idea she'd been dreaming, caught in the twilight between fantasy and reality. After all, she'd been fully participating.

Guilt tried to overwhelm her. She was a horrible person for being with him while dreaming of another.

And yet, it was impossible to feel anything besides the pleasure he pressed on, *into,* her.

"I'm going to come if you keep that up," she gasped, her body tightening and aching, loving the retreat of his fingers, but loving their advance even more.

"I want you to come," he whispered. "I want you to show me how good this feels." Then he sank his teeth into her shoulder, a mighty beast holding his mate in place, and that's all it took.

"Mark!" she cried out as she went flying over the edge into star-spangled bliss. She was the sun going supernova, and he was right there with her, his huge cock in her hand pulsing with climax.

It was raunchy. It was raw. It was real. And it was...*Angel.*

Oh shit!

Had she called him Mark? He'd bitten her shoulder just like Mark used to do, and the dream had felt so close and she'd been out of her mind with pleasure and—

Her heart beat fast as Angel shifted from behind her. "Let me get the tissues from your purse." The mat dipped under his weight when he scooted toward the edge. Five seconds later, he set about cleaning the evidence of his desire from her bottom.

She pretended to keep her back to him to aid in his endeavor. Truth was, she was a coward. She didn't want to roll over and see the hurt or censure or...*whatever* in his eyes if she had, in fact, cried out Mark's name.

Eventually, though, she had to face the music. When Angel crawled back beside her, spooning against her, she managed to ask in a bullfrog croak of a whisper,

"Did I…um…did I happen to scream…" She swallowed, unable to go on.

Angel did it for her. "Mark's name?"

"Oh God." She buried her face in her hands. "I'm so sorry. That's awful. I'm awful. I was dreaming about him before you woke me up and—" She cut herself off. "Nope. Sorry. That's an even *worse* thing to say."

Angel kissed her shoulder. "Stop it, Sonya. You don't have to apologize for anything."

She glanced back, trying to search his eyes but it was too dark. The night had descended on them in all its stygian glory. "How can you say that?"

Before Angel could answer, a soft buzzing sound echoed from somewhere nearby. Suddenly, the room around them felt *huge*. And hollow. It occurred to her how vulnerable they were within its expanse, and a chill raced down her spine as her mind conjured up all sorts of terrible things…

What if someone had entered the building and watched them through night-vision goggles? Or what if someone lived here, like an ax murderer on the lam who'd waited for night to fall before making Sonya and Angel his next two victims? Or what if a circus performer had died a violent death here, and his ghost was bent on revenge? Not that Sonya believed in ghosts, but she could—

Buzzzzzzzzz.

"There it is again." She sat up, clutching her arms around herself. "What *is* that?"

"Relax. Just your phone."

"My phone?"

"I turned it off silent mode. BKI is probably calling with an update."

Blowing out a deep breath, she indulged in a weak laugh, chiding herself for letting her imagination run away with her.

"You okay?" he asked.

"Fine. Just jumpy, I guess."

"You are safe, Sonya. You are with me."

From any other man, that would have been the height of arrogance. From Angel, it was a simple truth.

Before scooting away from her and going in search of his jeans to retrieve her phone, he kissed her shoulder directly over the tender spot where he'd bitten her. He'd done the same thing when they'd had sex. Right before he came, he had sunk his teeth into her, marking her as his, *claiming* her as his.

That prickle of suspicion and incredulity from earlier was back, skittering up her spine. Okay, so maybe she *did* believe in ghosts because there were times, like now, when she would swear Angel and Mark were—

"Agassi here," he said after thumbing on the phone. "Hey, Emily. What do you know?"

The screen lit up the side of his face, that gorgeous face that'd come courtesy of a skilled surgeon wielding a sharp knife. Thinking back on the photo she'd seen of him before all the plastic surgery, she compared it to her memory of Mark.

They *had* resembled each other once upon a time. And yet…Majid's eyes, *Angel's* eyes, were not Mark's. They were too dark. Not hell-black like she'd originally thought, but definitely not Mark's warm, chocolaty brown.

Shaking her head, she realized she'd once again attempted to build sand castles in the sky. To make Angel

something he wasn't, *someone* he wasn't, because…
Okay, she was finally ready to admit the truth to herself.
After ten years she hadn't let go of her lost love.

Was she doing penance for not being able to do more
the day he was murdered? Was she treating her memories
like a memorial, constantly and lovingly tending them
because it was the only way she knew to commemorate
his amazing life? Or was it something more straightfor-
ward? Was she simply scared to let go? Was she holding
on to Mark so tightly because she was terrified of opening her heart to the possibility of something new?

Maybe it was all of the above, and for the first time
she asked herself one fundamental question: *Where has
it gotten me?*

The answer was obvious. *Nowhere.*

She was thirty-two years old, unmarried, no kids, a
workaholic who hadn't met a man she was interested
in sleeping with in over two years. And then there
was Angel…

Strong, brave, loyal Angel.

For whatever reason, he wanted *her*. Saw something
in her despite her disgraceful habit of comparing him
to… No, not comparing. When she'd yelled out Mark's
name, she'd gone *beyond* comparing them. She'd actually interchanged them, consolidated them.

She cringed at the thought, then squared her shoulders and thought, *Well, no more. It stops right here.
Right now.*

Angel wanted her to give them a chance, and by God,
she would. It was time she threw off the shackles of the
past and allowed herself to take another head-spinning
plunge into the future and—

"For fuck's sake." Angel raked a hand through his hair.

Her chin jerked back at the anguish she heard in his voice. At the anguish she saw on his face in the glow of the cell phone's screen. His impassive mask hadn't just slipped; it was completely gone. What was in its place shook her to her core.

Something awful had happened.

She wasted no time gathering her clothes, listening as Angel said a lot of "copy thats" and "okays." Then, she heard him ask, "And his prognosis? What do the doctors say?"

Bile gathered at the back of her throat.

Something awful had happened *to someone*.

She had to assume it was one of his teammates at Black Knights Inc., and her heart broke for him. Even though he had been careful to modulate his tone, hadn't told her all that much about them, she had still picked up on how much he respected and cared for his adopted brothers-in-arms.

She was dressed and buttoning her blouse when Angel said, "Thanks. Oh, and, Emily? How did Boss take the news about Lord Grafton being Sharif Garane's father?" A second passed as he listened to Emily's answer. Then he made a rough sound, something between a snort and a grunt. "I agree. Time to put an end to this asshole once and for all. Okay. Talk soon." Angel thumbed off the phone, and they were once again plunged into inky darkness.

"What happened?" she whispered.

He was a darker shadow against a backdrop of dark shadows. But she could see enough to make out his hulking form on the edge of his mat, his elbows on his knees, his head in his hands. She scooted next to him, putting a tentative arm around his broad shoulders, feeling the tightness of his hot, naked skin.

"One of my teammates..." He shook his head. "No. He is a civilian who got dragged into this mess, but—" He stopped again. "Not the point. The point is he was part of the team that followed the uranium supplier, hoping to be led to the remaining cache of missing canisters. But there was a shoot-out and my...whatever you want to call him."

"Friend?" she supplied carefully.

"Yeah." He blew out a weary breath. "Yeah, I guess maybe he *is* my friend. Anyway, he was wounded. *Badly.*"

"Oh God." She tightened her arm around him. "I'm so sorry."

"They got him to the hospital here in Chişinău, but the doctors are worried about his strength after so much blood loss and... *Fuck!*"

He fisted his hands in his hair.

"Should we go to the hospital? He shouldn't be alone and—"

"No." Angel shook his head. "Rusty isn't alone. Ace and Ozzie are with him, and I don't want to risk leaving here while Grafton is searching for us. The other team gets back from Ukraine soon. Once they do, we will figure out a new plan." He activated the a little light on his big, black watch, checking the time. Sonya was amazed to discover it was already two o'clock in the morning. The stress of the day, not to mention vigorous, sweaty, *mind-altering* sex had apparently put her in a small coma earlier.

"What's their ETA?"

"Ninety minutes or so."

An hour and a half is a long time when someone you care about is knocking on death's door, she thought.

She wished there was something she could do for him. Something she could say to make it better. But she knew from experience that nothing anyone said or did could make a dent in another person's remorse and regret and that awful feeling known as helplessness. But maybe if she kept him talking...

"You said there was a shoot-out. Was Rusty the only casualty or—"

"No. Three Russians are dead. Popov, the uranium supplier you met in the café, and two others."

"And the remaining canisters? Did Rusty and his team find them?"

"Yes."

She blew out a breath. "That's good. At least I *hope* it's good. I mean, with the shoot-out and everything, were they still able to secure them? Were they—"

"The canisters are fine," he assured her. "I have a contact here in Moldova who works for the SIS. He has the canisters and will make sure they are taken care of."

"He works for the *who*?"

"The Security and Intelligence Service," he explained. "The Moldovan equivalent of the CIA. Rusty and the BKI team called him once they located the uranium. Good thing too. He was already on his way to their position in a chopper when they phoned again after Rusty had been shot. If not for him, no way Rusty would have made it to the hospital in time." At the mention of Rusty and the hospital, the anguish was back in Angel's voice.

"I *knew* this plan had too many moving parts." He grimaced. "If only I had—"

"What about the Ukraine team?" She cut him off because he'd started in on the "what-ifs" and that was a death spiral. "Did they hand over that skinny Al-Qaeda kid to your NATO contact?"

"Him along with the canister of uranium he carried."

"That's good news." She breathed a sigh of relief.

For a while they sat in silence, both lost in their own thoughts. Then Angel abruptly jumped to his feet.

"Wha—"

That's all she managed before he slapped a palm over her mouth. "Shhh. Quiet."

She couldn't see the tension rippling through him. It was too dark. But she could feel it in the air, like when an electrical storm was close. A prickly feeling skittered over her skin. The hairs on her arms lifted.

Crazy person with night-vision goggles!

Ax murderer!

Ghost!

He dropped his hand and immediately grabbed his boxer briefs and jeans. She *badly* wanted to ask him what was going on, what he'd heard, but she didn't dare open her mouth. By the time he'd pulled his Henley over his head and sat so he could lace up his boots, she was having herself a mini panic attack. Her heart beat with a wild, erratic rhythm. She could hear her own ragged breaths in the silent, wide-open expanse of the circus ring. If she tensed her shoulders any harder, her scapulae might shatter.

Finally he spoke.

Afterward, she wanted to punch the delete key in her brain and erase his words. Oh, how she *missed* that time, just a few seconds ago, when he'd been blessedly silent.

"We have company…"

Chapter 28

"I AM BECOME DEATH, THE DESTROYER OF WORLDS," Grafton whispered and leaned back against the bonnet of the luxury sedan.

Insects buzzed loudly. The air was crisp, humid, and heavy with the fecund smells of damp foliage and decaying flesh. A carcass was somewhere nearby. A dead deer or a bloated squirrel or a missing pet that'd run into traffic on the nearby motorway and been hit by a speeding lorry before crawling up here to expire.

Seemed appropriate that the smell of death should hang in the air, for death was Grafton's goal. *Two* deaths, in fact.

Beside him, Richie mirrored his stance. Arms folded. Legs crossed at the ankles. Eyes watching the team of men Benton had managed to pull together and fly to Chișinău on a moment's notice.

Good ol' Benton. Maybe Grafton *should* give the rascally little prat a raise.

Around the time Grafton, Richie, and Charles had homed in on Sonya's tracking device, a private jet with five of the more capable men in Grafton's employ had landed at Chișinău International Airport. There were a couple of former RAF boys whom Grafton had drafted into his network when he discovered evidence they were part of a child pornography ring, one Royal Marine who'd killed a buddy in an incident of not-so-friendly

fire, and two Army Reservists who'd found themselves
on the wrong side of the law when they were accused—
but never convicted because Grafton held the evidence
against them—of sexually assaulting a female soldier.

Grafton *loved* it when Mother England spent the
time, money, and resources training people he could
then catch in his sticky web.

He watched as the quintet of disgraced military men
fanned out around the old circus building. Along with
Charles, they encircled Grafton's prey, cutting off all
avenues of escape. The *beep, beep, beep* of the receiver
that Grafton had handed over to Harold Ellis, the team
leader, grew quicker as the man climbed the steps
toward the front door.

The night might be growing long in the tooth, but
they still had time before morning's first light to finish
off that traitorous bitch and that murderous asshole
who'd dared to defy him. And bonus! Angel and Sonya
had picked a spot so far off the beaten path that Grafton
needn't worry about stealth or secrecy.

"That's spooky," Richie whispered.

Grafton blinked in confusion. "What is?"

"What you said about death."

"Ah." He nodded. "Well, I can't take credit for it.
It was Oppenheimer who said it. Although, if memory
serves, he was quoting some sacred Hindu text."

"Who's Oppenheimer?"

"J. Robert Oppenheimer?" At Richie's blank stare, he
added. "The father of the atomic bomb?"

Speaking of atomic bombs…he looked forward to
the devastation in Chicago that would show the world
and, more importantly, his Al-Qaeda business partners

that there was nothing on the planet Spider couldn't procure and—

"I think they're going inside now," Richie cut into his thoughts.

Grafton rubbed his hands together. He couldn't stop the smile on his lips or the anticipatory beat of his heart when he repeated, "I am become death, the destroyer of worlds."

While Oppenheimer had eventually come to regret his role in the mass murder of so many, Grafton had never suffered any such misgivings. Death was a part of life. If he happened to help someone to an early grave, what did it matter in the grand scheme of things?

In fact, he kind of relished it. Maybe he had a God complex.

He chuckled at the thought, causing Richie to shoot him a wary glance.

Chapter 29

SONYA'S HEART WAS IN HER THROAT WHEN ANGEL RAN from the front door back to where he'd stationed her by the entrance to the circus ring. It was lighter here in the foyer. The moonlight was bright enough to cut through the dingy windows and Coca-Cola signs and show the dark shadows moving around outside the building.

"You have a tracking device on you," he accused.

"What?" She blinked at him. "No, I don't. I—"

"Shhh." He lifted a finger, cocking his head. "Listen."

She heard a muffled *beep-beep-beep*. The sound seemed to be speeding up.

"Did Grafton give you something? Did he ever have access to your purse or—"

"No!" she hissed. "Nothing like that. I never—" She stopped and swallowed. Surely not. *Surely not!*

"What?" Angel demanded. "Sonya, hurry! What is it?"

"The bookmark Lou gave me."

"The pink ribbon?"

She nodded. Since her heart was still in her throat, it made speaking difficult. Not to mention *breathing*.

"Give it to me," he ordered.

Her hands shook when she reached into her purse and pulled the ribbon from between the pages of the book. He wasted no time shoving the Glock he'd taken from her purse into his waistband and running his fingers down the length of hot pink satin. He stopped about halfway down to investigate something that caught his attention.

"Filament tracker," he murmured in his gravel road of a voice.

Her head swam sickly. "Oh my God, I've killed us."

"Not if I have anything to say about it."

He snagged her purse and dropped the ribbon inside. "Is there anything you need from in here?" he asked.

"No. Nothing that—"

That's all she got out before he reared back like he'd done with the Perrier bottle in the café.

"What are you doing?" she hissed.

"Buying us some time!"

He chucked her purse with all his might, sending it sailing into the dark circus ring. She couldn't see it hit one of the stadium seats, but she heard it and winced at the thought of the book inside. Treating a first edition with such disregard was a travesty. Then again, she'd douse the thing in gasoline and set it on fire if it meant staying alive.

"Come!" Angel grabbed her hand and jerked her into a run. "As quickly and quietly as you can."

Quick and quiet were a problem when it came to kitten heels. Why was she always wearing the wrong shoes? Stepping out of them, she shivered as the cold, dusty tiles kissed the bottoms of her feet.

Angel took them halfway around the circus before stopping. They were now opposite the front door. He hopped over a long counter set near the wall. The clothing racks and hangers spread out behind the counter told her this was the old coat check, the spot patrons had come to leave their jackets and scarves and gloves. Then he turned to her, holding out his arms as if to say *Jump over! I'll catch you!*

Seriously? His plan was to squirrel away beneath the counter? That felt a little too John Bender hiding under Claire's desk in *The Breakfast Club* for her taste. Only it wasn't vice principal Dick Vernon they needed to protect themselves from.

Still, she knew better than to question Angel. Hopping onto the counter, she didn't protest when he caught her under the arms and dragged her over. Her bare feet hit the floor on the other side as a soft squeak met her ears. Whoever was outside had pulled back the sheet of plywood over the front door.

They were definitely in the *Scheisse* now. Blood pounded in her brain. Heaven help her, but her breath sawed from her lungs so loudly she thought *for sure* she'd give away their position the second Grafton's goons made it inside. She tried holding her breath, but that made her vision tunnel.

Best not to pass out. That would only *compound* their problems.

Raking in a ragged breath through her nose, she watched Angel slide between two metal coatracks. He grabbed the handle on a narrow wooden door in the wall.

Huh. She hadn't noticed that before. *Wouldn't* have noticed it. Again, she thought how smart he'd been to spend time scouting their location before settling in. Maybe whatever sort of space was behind that door would be big enough to hide in until—

Until what? What was the plan, exactly? Wait for his friends to show up?

Angel pulled her cell phone from his back pocket,

hid it inside his jacket to limit the glow of the screen, and typed something. Then he pocketed the phone and opened the door.

The yawning maw that materialized smelled of dry dust and tangy metal. She could say without a doubt she did not find it the least little bit inviting.

Angel stepped inside and disappeared completely, swallowed up by the blackness. His hand shot out of the inky gloom, two fingers beckoning her to follow. Careful not to jostle the coatracks and hangers, she allowed him to pull her into the space. He closed the door as a *shush* of sound met her ears. The front door sliding open.

Grafton's thugs have entered the building, she thought a little hysterically.

Angel's hand closed over her mouth. His breath was hot and humid in her ear when he leaned close and whispered so low he might have been only mouthing the words, "There are stairs behind us. They lead down to the engine room. I will use the light on your phone to give you a quick glimpse. Then we go down in darkness. Nod if you understand."

Her nostrils flared. Her heart banged against her breastbone so loudly she was surprised he could talk over it. She nodded.

Slowly, with supreme care, he turned her around. Her bare feet told her she was no longer standing on tiles but on some sort of metal mesh. Dropping his hand from her mouth, he fished the phone from his pocket and thumbed on the screen to shine light into the darkness.

She had enough time to make out the metal staircase leading down to a large room housing a quartet of old, rusted turbines, a few broken stadium seats, and snakelike sections of disused ductwork. Then he clicked off the light source, and they were plunged back into inky blackness.

She had never been afraid of the dark. That said, she wasn't sure she'd ever experienced darkness this complete. It was disconcerting not being able to see the hand she held up in front of her face.

She was grateful for Angel's solid presence and his reassuring warmth as they carefully, quietly made their way down the steps. Once they'd reached the lower level, she gently probed the area in front of her with her feet before taking a step, careful to avoid the broken chairs and ductwork. Then, what felt like an eternity later, they made it to the far wall.

Without words, he made it clear his intention was to tuck them behind one of the giant turbines. Only after he got her where he wanted her did he lean in and press his lips to her ear.

"Sit down. Get comfortable."

Was he *crazy*?

First of all, it was freezing down here. The floor beneath her feet was a sheet of ice. Second of all, sitting on concrete was many things, but comfortable wasn't one of them. And last but not least, there was a group of men looking for them up above. And if those men found them, no doubt their orders were to add a few extra holes to their heads.

Comfortable? *Comfortable?*

She silently slid down the wall until her butt hit the floor. Wrapping her arms around her legs, she tried to preserve her body heat. In the darkness, she couldn't see Angel, but she could feel him settle in beside her. The subtle *clink* said he'd set the Glock on the floor, and then his arm was around her, chafing her shoulder in an attempt to keep her warm.

His voice was so low it barely reached her ears when he said, "Try to stay calm. Help should be here soon."

"What help?" she whispered and felt him shrug.

"I sent a Mayday text to the Black Knights."

"What did you say?"

"Position compromised. Trapped. Will hide and wait for help."

She nearly groaned. "What do you think they'll do? The Black Knights, I mean."

"Try to reach my contact in the SIS. Or bust ass to get to us."

"What about the local police?"

"The Knights won't trust the local police to know one group of foreigners from the next. Locals have a bad habit of turning these sorts of things into bloodbaths."

She wished she could argue with him, but she'd worked for Interpol long enough to see the wisdom in his statement. Local authorities were good at handling local issues, *not* so good at managing international intrigue. Those kinds of situations turned them into shoot-first-and-ask-questions-later sorts.

"Then there is the question of my cover," he continued in his raspy whisper. "The SIS will keep their damn mouths shut. The local five-o? Not so much. Plus, we have no idea what happened at the café. The crowd out front saw us. I think a few might have even recorded some video. No doubt the local police are looking for us in connection with those deaths."

How she'd forgotten about the café carnage, she'd never know.

"If I called Zhao Longwei," she whispered, "he might be able to put together some sort of rescue that wouldn't jeopardize your cover and could save us from having to answer questions we don't want to—"

She cut herself off when a flash of light illuminated the darkness before disappearing. Angel had briefly turned on the cell phone. "No service down here."

"That's why you sent the text before we came down," she realized.

"Exactly."

The man thought of everything. A master strategist. Explained how he'd managed to stay alive working as a double agent inside Iran for all those years.

Despite Angel's body heat beside her, the cold from the concrete floor seeped through her slacks, flash-freezing her flesh and nipping at her bones. She began to shiver uncontrollably.

"Come here." He tugged her into his lap, opening the front of his jacket and pulling her against his chest. He folded the halves of leather around them, creating a warm cocoon.

Maybe she should have insisted she was fine. This *was* the twenty-first century, after all. Equality of the sexes stipulated she look after her own ass. But…the room was so cold and he was so warm. And despite how desperate their situation was, being inside the protection of his strong arms, breathing in the spicy scent of his aftershave, brought her a small measure of comfort.

So, okay, screw equality of the sexes. Right then she was *happy* to let him be all chivalrous and gallant.

Happy to play the part of the fragile damsel seeking the solace of the hero's arms.

And he was a hero. The stuff of legends and romance novels and Academy Award–winning cinema. When she thought about it, Humphrey Bogart's Rick Blaine character from *Casablanca* had nothing on Angel.

"So what do we do now?" she whispered, blinking owlishly into the darkness.

Oh, how she wished she'd kept her mouth shut when his only answer was "We wait for our fate…"

Chapter 30

"WHAT THE DEVIL IS TAKING SO LONG?" GRAFTON demanded of Charles who'd come out to give him a situation report.

His men had been inside the building for over an hour and so far...nothing. It was beyond the pale. Unacceptable.

"It's a large space, sir. Very dark."

"That's why you're wearing night-vision goggles, yeah?"

"There's loads of nooks and crannies for the two of 'em to hide in," Charles continued, ignoring Grafton's jibe. "We gotta go slowly and methodically. The Prince of Shadows is armed."

"I'd think *six* men against one would be more than enough to get the job done." Then again, Grafton had thought three armed bodyguards against one *un*armed Angel would be enough too. Look how that had turned out.

"We did find this." Charles handed Grafton the ribbon bookmark Benton had been brilliant enough to have Lou give to Sonya. Grafton really *must* see about getting Benton that raise.

"And this." Charles lifted Sonya's purse. The top zipper was undone, and Grafton could see his copy of Hemingway's *A Farewell to Arms* inside.

Usually he was thankful for the sorry turn of events that brought people into his employ, but he'd begun

to rue the day Benton had come across that information on Sonya Butler. And he hadn't *begun* to rue the
day Benton had come across the information on Angel
Agassi a.k.a. the Prince of Shadows; he'd *been* ruing it
since about three o'clock that afternoon.

"We found her shoes too." Charles had to raise his
voice above the chorus of night insects.

"But you haven't found *her*." Grafton was unable to
keep the impatience from his tone. "Is it possible they've
escaped? Slipped by you?"

"No. There are only two doors in and outta the place.
They're in there. We just haven't found 'em. *Yet*."

"Well, carry on then." Grafton shooed Charles back
toward the abandoned circus building.

After the man turned on his heel, Richie spoke up
from beside him. "You want me to go help, sir? Smack
'em 'round a bit and get their arses in gear?"

Good ol' Richie. Gangster to the core. Unfortunately,
in this case Grafton didn't need a gangster. He needed
exactly what he had, a group of highly trained military
men. "No, Richie. I think it's best you stay with me."

Richie nodded, then asked curiously, "Why do you
think they chose this spot? So far off the beaten path?"

"I suppose Angel assumed I'd have Benton keep an
eye on the train stations, airports, and rental car agencies, not to mention the border crossings. Probably
thought to lay low for a bit, maybe wait for someone to
come to their rescue. Plus, this is as good a place as any
to hide from the local authorities."

In the hours since the bloodbath and fire at the Graffiti
Café, the Chişinău police had been scouring the city in
search of the blond woman and the tall, black-haired gent

a couple of bystanders had managed to catch on cell-phone video. The manhunt was all over the airwaves.

"That smell is getting worse." Richie waved a hand in front of his face.

Wherever the carcass was, its decomposition had hastened. The sickly sweet aroma of rot was stronger now.

"'The dead body of an enemy always smells sweet,'" Grafton said, thinking...*hoping*...that his men would soon be planting Angel and Sonya's carcasses in a deep, dark hole somewhere in the surrounding woods.

"More Oppenheimer?"

"Vespasian. A Roman emperor."

"Ah." Richie nodded. "*Et tu, Brute?*"

Grafton chuckled. "Something like that."

"You know, I've always thought *you* were a bit like a Roman emperor."

"Me?" Grafton turned to Richie. "How so?"

"You're powerful and ruthless, and you're always looking to expand your empire."

Grafton was charmed. "That might be the nicest thing anyone has ever said to me." Not a god but an emperor. Yes. He liked the sound of that very much.

Richie shrugged, then narrowed his eyes and frowned in the direction of the circus. Grafton turned to see what had snagged his attention. He pushed away from the vehicle's bonnet when he saw Charles jogging toward him, the man's craggy face wreathed in smiles.

"What is it?" he demanded.

"We think we've found 'em."

Grafton's heart skipped a happy beat. "Then what the bloody hell are you doing out here? Go back in and make sure you finish them!"

Chapter 31

"I DON'T THINK YOUR SIS FRIEND IS COMING," SONYA whispered into the darkness.

She didn't know how long they'd been hiding in the freezing engine room, but it felt like forever. Her teeth, which she was amazed weren't already shattered from having been set on edge for so long, threatened to chatter despite the warmth of Angel's body and jacket. If help didn't arrive soon, they wouldn't need to wait for Grafton's goons to end them. Hypothermia would do the job all by itself.

"You are probably right." Angel's scratched-up voice was barely a sliver of sound.

Well, suck it. Not that she'd expected him to placate her with fallacies of their rescue, but still…

"Just FYI, if ever there was a time to disagree with me, this is it," she told him.

"When did you learn to speak Italian?"

Caught off guard by his conversational about-face, she blinked against the darkness. "What? Why are you asking me this now?"

"Just curious."

Narrowing her eyes, she wished she could turn and search his face. "Curious? Or trying to distract me because any second now we might take permanent vacations from our oxygen habits?"

"Both."

She swallowed a snort. "Honest to a fault, aren't you?"

"When did you learn Italian?"

Stubborn to a fault, too. "Five years ago. For a while Interpol was thinking of moving me to their offices in Rome. Guess you missed that in all your research on me, huh?"

She waited for him to add something, but he never did. Something felt off. *Odd*. But before she could figure out what it was, he shifted slightly, and she realized his legs had to be falling asleep.

When she moved off him, he whispered in her ear. "Where are you going?"

"Your legs have to be killing you."

"Straddle me."

She felt her mouth curl into a grin. Men. Always up for a little sumpin'-sumpin'.

"I'm all for distraction," she told him, "but that might be a little *too* distracting."

"Straddle me," he said again. It no longer sounded like a request.

Shifting around, she planted her knees against the cold concrete and wound her arms around his neck. When his hot, sweet breath brushed her cheeks, she sighed. Then she tensed at a series of *thumps* and *bangs* that sounded overhead and held her breath, listening.

"If you could be anywhere in the world right now, where would you be?"

His ploy wasn't the least bit subtle, but she welcomed it anyway.

"I don't know," she whispered, realizing that weeks ago her answer would have been Paris, a decade in the past and lying in bed with Mark as they watched the moon rise over the Sacré-Cœur. But things had changed. *She* had changed the moment Angel appeared at Grafton Manor. "Where would *you* be?"

"Too easy," he rasped. "The beach. Sand and sun and surf and an Arak Attack in hand."

She shuddered. "Yuck. Arak is that stuff that tastes like black licorice, right?"

"Anise," he corrected.

"My dad used to drink it when he was stationed in Jerusalem."

"Jerusalem is where you learned to speak Hebrew," he said. Not asked. *Said.*

She pushed up to look at him, forgetting she couldn't see two inches in front of her face. "How do you know that?"

"An educated guess. Am I right?"

"Yes, but—"

"So come on. Think." He cut her off. "Where would you like to be right now?"

"I guess I'd like to join you on that beach," she whispered. "But no Arak Attack. Maybe a mojito. Or a mai tai."

He rumbled his approval, pulling her so close their mouths nearly touched. "Good answer," he whispered.

She wanted to kiss him. He wanted to kiss her too. Straddling him made his interest obvious. But the second their lips touched, they'd be oblivious to anything else. And that would never do.

To divert *both* their attentions, she murmured softly, "I think you should let your hair grow out." She pulled a strand gently. "It's curly, isn't it? When it's long, I mean?"

He was silent for a moment. When he answered, his voice was somehow lower and quieter than before. "Yes."

"You'd look good with long hair. Devilish." She smiled when she thought about it. "Every angel needs a little devil in him, am I right?"

He didn't answer. Simply cupped her head and pulled her down until her cheek rested against his shoulder and his warm neck brushed against her lips. She relaxed against him. Or at least she tried to, but there was something...

Then it hit her.

She'd said he could choose any place on the planet, and he'd chosen the beach. Just like Mark.

Coincidence, she quickly admonished herself. *It's just another coinci—*

She didn't finish her thought. A loud *thump* sounded behind the door at the top of the stairs, and her blood ran cold.

The enemy was at the gate...

Chapter 32

ANGEL WOULD HAVE LOVED TO SPEND THE REST OF THE night—no, the rest of his *life*—with Sonya straddling him, her breath hot against his neck. Unfortunately, their time had run out.

One arm around her, his free hand clutching the grip of the Glock, he shoved to his feet. Finding her wrist in the darkness, he pulled her behind him and made sure to position them both directly between the big turbine and the cold concrete wall.

He didn't delude himself with thoughts that help had arrived. Had it been the Knights behind that door at the top of the stairs, they would have announced themselves or called his name. Same went for his SIS contact.

Adjusting his grip on the semi-auto, he tallied up how many rounds he had left. He'd used two on Grafton's goons in the café. *So…fifteen*. He needed to make each shot count.

When he felt Sonya curl trembling fingers into his waistband, he reached back and gave her hand a squeeze. It wasn't much in the way of reassurance, but it was all he could offer.

Time to dance.

The door burst open and banged against the inner wall. His keen sense of hearing told him a heavy boot hit the metal mesh of the landing. Using the mental image he had of the room, he lifted the Glock, peeked out from behind the giant turbine, and took aim at what he hoped was the right spot.

When he squeezed his trigger twice in quick succession, the back-to-back bark of the weapon was obscenely loud in the enclosed space. Still he didn't miss hearing the accompanying yelp of pain.

Gotcha! He thought a split second before the room exploded with weapon fire. The *thunk* and *screech* of hot rounds burying themselves in hard metal was an acoustic assault.

So much noise and chaos was designed to rattle the mind, rev up the lizard portion of the mind into fight-or-flight mode. But Angel was no ordinary man. Instead of cowering in the corner, he gritted his teeth and ducked back behind the turbine.

Adrenaline singed his blood as he listened closely to the cadence of the bullets.

Two shooters.

Both aiming precisely for the turbine and hitting it.

A less experienced operator might chalk that up to the enemy having seen the muzzle flash of his Glock, but the precision and placement of the shots told him the gunners weren't firing randomly. Which meant they wore night-vision goggles.

A slow smile curved his lips.

Sonya, dear, brave woman, was still standing tall behind him. He wanted to turn and hug her and tell her how proud he was to know her, but time was of the essence. Grabbing her hand, he gave her fingers another squeeze and leaned close to whisper in her ear, hoping his words carried over the racket of the assault.

"You have to let go of me for a bit."

Palming her cell phone from his hip pocket, he thumbed on the screen. It took him less than a second to locate the flashlight function on the device. Then he turkey-peeked from behind the big turbine and aimed the flashlight at the door at the same time he aimed the Glock.

He got a brief glimpse of the two shooters in night-vision goggles while they were momentarily blinded by the light. Luckily, a moment was all he needed. Four more squeezes of the trigger and the Glock spat up death.

His first shot hit the man on the left, entering under the asshole's chin and exploding out the back of his neck. In the yellow glow of the flashlight, the gushing blood looked as black as tar.

Angel's second shot arced wide—*damnit!*—burying itself in the wooden doorframe. Luck, or more like good training, ensured his third and fourth shots flew true. The second shooter took a round to the chest that knocked him back a step. The final slug exploded his right cheekbone.

Angel ducked behind the turbine, switching off the phone's flashlight. One man injured—he didn't bother speculating how badly. Two men dead. And who knew how many more were waiting to come through that door? He could hear at least three, maybe four distinct voices shouting from somewhere outside the room.

Three or four men and only nine rounds left. Would that be enough?

He could feel Sonya's presence beside him, hear her ragged breaths. *Wait for our fate*, he'd said. But surely, after everything he'd sacrificed, everything he'd *suffered*, surely fate wouldn't be fickle enough to end him now, just when he'd found the love of his life again. Just when he'd determined to start *living* again.

Closing his eyes, he concentrated on the voices coming from outside. Only two men were speaking now, and their words were hushed. Even so, he caught snippets of conversation.

"*Car...*"

"*Combat gear...*"

"*Frag grenade...*"

The last two words stopped the breath in his lungs.

He would fire every last one of his bullets, fight each and every man out there hand-to-hand if that's what it took. But one thing he could *not* combat was the destructive power of a fragmenting grenade.

Gritting his teeth, he quickly ran through his options...

He could run up those steps, gun blazing, and hope he could take out the rest of Grafton's men. Of course, if he didn't have enough ammo, or if one of the goons happened to slip into the engine room behind him, then Sonya would be—

He didn't finish the thought, simply moved on to option two. He could throw himself on top of the grenade when it hit the floor. He'd be blown to smithereens, but Sonya would be saved, except... Then no one would be left to defend her.

No. Nope. So that left option three. Maybe he could use the grenade against the men. Of all the scenarios, this one was the trickiest. He'd need to hit the flashlight on the phone at the perfect moment, track the trajectory of the grenade, snag it before it landed, and then send it back to its source before it went off. Plus, he'd need

Sonya to lay down covering fire so he didn't get shot. Timing would be everything.

And luck.

He was going to need a shit-ton of luck.

Not that he'd never doubted himself before. He had. Plenty of times. But this time… This time it wasn't only his neck on the line. It was Sonya's too. Sonya…

The only woman he'd ever loved.

The need to tell her was suddenly an overwhelming pressure on his heart. If this was to be their end, he wanted her to know how much she meant to him. How much she'd *always* meant to him.

Of course, telling her meant coming clean about his true identity. It was the only way she'd believe him since the man she knew as Angel Agassi had only known her for two weeks.

"Sonya?" He found her hand in the darkness.

Funny. While there'd been bullets flying at his head, his heart had remained steady as the old grandfather clock his mother had kept in the hall of their home in Tel Aviv. But now that he was ready to confess everything? The silly organ went buck wild.

She turned and flung her arms around his neck, pulling him close. "It's okay. I'm okay. Don't worry about me." He hated the anguish in her voice.

"Sonya, I…" He had to stop and clear his throat. "I want to tell you—"

That's all he managed before a fresh barrage of hot lead slammed into the old turbine.

Chapter 33

THE MUFFLED *POP* OF GUNFIRE COMING FROM INSIDE the building was music to Grafton's ears.

Until he saw two of his men slip from behind the plywood covering the front door, that is. They set off running in his direction, and he couldn't miss the determination wrinkling the team leader's brow. Deadly intent shone in Harold's dark eyes. He looked like a man on a mission.

Charles on the other hand?

Well, poor Charles was a little worse for wear. He held onto a wound on his arm, and slick, wet blood seeped between his thick fingers.

Apparently Angel was still alive and kicking.

Bloody hell!

"What are you two doing out here?" he demanded, no longer amused by the gunfire. Although he *did* thank his lucky stars that the spot was so far removed from the main thoroughfares and set well away from the nearest neighborhood, because at least he didn't have to worry that the ruckus would bring the authorities running.

"We've lost two of 'em," Charles panted, but Grafton wasn't sure if it was because of the pain in his arm or because he'd run the distance of the large courtyard and car park. Charles was a smidge thick around the middle, no doubt better at brute force than winning endurance races.

"Two of *whom*? What are you on about?"

"Two of the men."

"Two of *your* men?" Grafton turned to gape at Harold. The man resembled a squirrel. Beady eyes. Bushy hair that was prematurely gray except for a few streaks of brown. He was whip-thin. A stark contrast when standing next to Charles.

"*Your* men." Harold had the cheek to correct him. "But we've a plan. Agassi and the woman are holed up in a dark engine room. No way to escape."

"Unfortunately, not being able to escape hasn't precluded Angel's ability to do damage." Grafton motioned to Charles's dripping arm, not liking that only two men remained inside the circus to cover Angel. Two against one. Two against a *dangerous* and *well-trained* one. A sick sensation settled like a stone at the bottom of his stomach.

"The asshole is using the torch function on a mobile," Harold explained. "When we try to enter the room, he blinds our night-vision goggles and gets off a shot."

"Then what, pray tell, is your brilliant scheme to deal with him?"

"Frag grenades. I've two in my rucksack in the car."

Grafton turned toward the rental Benton had had ready for the team when they landed at the airport. Good ol' Benton. He seemed to be the only one Grafton could rely on to do his bloody job. "Then why are you messing about chatting me up? Go! Go!"

He shooed Harold and Charles toward the rental, but the men had only taken a few steps before two loud *cracks* echoed into the night. At the start of the gunfight inside the circus, the nocturnal insects had lowered the volume on their pulsing chorus, as if they knew dark deeds were afoot and awaited the outcome. These two

new sounds startled them into silence. It was eerie. Like
a switch had been flipped. Grafton could hear the wind
rattling the leaves of the trees, the subtle drone of the
cars on the motorway in the distance, and the *squeak,
squeak, squeak* of the sad little swings at the back of the
building as they were pushed by the breeze.

To his astonishment, he watched as Charles and
Harold toppled backward almost simultaneously, landing on the cracked concrete, neat holes through the
centers of their foreheads. Blood pooled behind them,
creating macabre halos that were shiny and dark, reflect-
ing the moonlight.

Before he could understand what he was seeing, a trio
of men oozed from the far tree line like deadly specters.
Richie reached inside his suit jacket for the weapon he
kept in a shoulder holster, but... *Crack!* Another shot
rang out, and Richie was dead before he'd cleared leather.

With his heart thudding somewhere in the vicinity of
his throat, Grafton watched Richie slide off the bonnet
of the car. Like the other two, a dark hole was centered
between his dead, sightless eyes.

Instinct had Grafton reaching for the weapon still
tucked into Richie's holster, but before he could do
more than get a hand on the butt of the pistol, a slow,
lazy drawl called out to him. "You pull that heater clear,
and you'd best be prepared for my friend here to get
inhospitable!"

Grafton slowly straightened, careful to keep his hands
where the trio could see them. The man who'd shouted
at him was tall and slim. Even from a distance, Grafton
could see he wore faded jeans, a green baseball cap, and
what appeared to be cowboy boots, of all things.

The "friend" he'd referred to was on his right, a tall, dark-haired bloke who aimed a sniper rifle in Grafton's direction like he knew how to use it. Judging by the bull's-eye head shots, he *did*.

Acid burned the back of Grafton's esophagus as he watched the trio approach. Who the hell *were* they? What the hell were they doing here? And more importantly, why had they left him alive when they'd had no compunction about killing those with him?

He hoped beyond hope it was because, whoever they were, they knew who he truly was. If they knew who he truly was, then they also knew what he could offer them. He'd yet to meet a man who couldn't be purchased. Everyone had a price. He simply needed to figure out what—or how much—these fellows wanted.

They stopped a good distance away, too far for him to make out their features. But it was impossible to miss the size of the third man in the group. He was a behemoth.

"Hello, Lord Grafton," he said in a rumbling bass voice. "Or should I call you Spider?"

"And you are?" He donned his most lord-like tone.

"We'll get to that in a moment." The behemoth turned to the two men with him. "Gentlemen? Mind going and helping our friend?" He cocked his head toward the intermittent gunfire still sounding faintly from within the circular building. "Sounds like he could use it."

"With pleasure, *mon ami*." The guy in the cowboy boots was already turning on his heel and trotting across the car park before he'd finished speaking.

The marksman holding the sniper rifle on Grafton— Grafton noticed it had a suppressor attached—didn't say a word. He didn't need to. Even from a distance, his flashing black eyes said without speaking that he'd like nothing more than to finish what he started and send a piece of lead through the center of Grafton's skull.

Luckily for Grafton, the marksman refrained from acting on impulse and, instead, nodded at the behemoth before setting off after Cowboy Boots.

After they'd gone, the behemoth started forward. Grafton watched him warily, taking in his massive shoulders and his huge thighs encased in a pair of jeans. His giant combat boots made *crunch-crunch* noises atop the cracked concrete. But the one thing that stood out the most in Grafton's mind?

He's unarmed!

Except for what looked to be a knife secured in a sheath on his belt, the behemoth wasn't carrying any weapons. Grafton couldn't believe his good luck. Likely, the brute wasn't used to people thinking they could best him. No doubt he figured Grafton wouldn't have the wherewithal or the bollocks to actually go for Richie's gun again.

Without telegraphing his intent, Grafton bent, snagged Richie's weapon, and—

OhmydearsweetJesus!

A snake jumped up and bit him. Or at least that's what it felt like. The pain that sliced into his shoulder was white hot. He cried out. He couldn't help himself.

Leaning heavily on the bonnet of the car, he looked down and was astonished to see the hilt of a knife protruding from the meaty part of his shoulder. Before he could do more than blink, a massive, scarred hand grabbed the hilt and yanked the blade free.

Grafton had never before heard the sound that issued

from his throat. It was a high-pitched squeal like a pig at slaughter. The agony... Oh, the agony!

It was enough to make his world tilt. Head swimming, he looked up to see a face like a train wreck staring back at him. A thick scar sliced through the line of the behemoth's eyebrow and another arced up from the corner of his mouth.

Fear wasn't an emotion Grafton was familiar with, but he recognized its sharp teeth when they sank into him. He *knew* that train wreck of a face. Had studied it plenty of times when he'd been trying to learn more about the mysterious group in Chicago.

Frank "Boss" Knight. Head of Black Knights Inc.

"You..." he croaked, hot blood seeping between his fingers as he held his wounded shoulder.

That scarred eyebrow twitched. "Glad we can skip the introductions."

Then it occurred to him what Boss had said to the others. *Mind going and helping our friend?* Friend!

"Angel is..." Grafton's voice trailed off. For the first time in his life, he thought it was possible he wouldn't be able to use money or his myriad contacts to finagle his way out of a bad situation.

"A member of Black Knights Inc.?" Boss nodded, the moonlight glinting off his shaggy brown hair. "You betcha."

Grafton's gorge rose. The pain in his shoulder was all but forgotten as he realized the sheer magnitude of the shit pile he was standing in. "He was a plant," he panted, his mind racing through the last two weeks. "You planted him inside my home."

"Yep." Boss dipped his chin, and Grafton wanted to

slap the smug smile off the man's sodding face. "Good thing too," Boss continued. "How else would we have found out you planned to give flippin' *Al-Qaeda* the means to construct a nuclear weapon and blow up our shop? Chaps my ass when I think about it."

"You murdered my son," Grafton gritted from between clenched teeth. Fear combined with dread to leave a harsh, ashy taste on his tongue.

"Your son was a filthy pirate bent on revenge. What happened to him wasn't murder, it was self-defense. But since you're a fuckwit of epic proportions, I wouldn't expect you to know the difference."

The insult slammed into Grafton's ears and made his blood pressure scream to a boil. It'd been years since anyone had dared insult him.

"And besides," Boss continued, "the way I hear it, you didn't give a shit about your son. The only thing you've ever cared about is yourself. You concocted this plan because you're prideful and arrogant and couldn't stomach us having the audacity to come after you." Boss's crooked smile widened. "And since we're on the subject, let me assure you we caught that skinny shit-stain you gave the fissile material to. He, along with the enriched uranium, are in good hands. Your whole scheme is dead in the water."

Grafton couldn't believe it. His world, the world he'd been so careful to construct, began to crumble before his eyes, and he had one man to thank. One man to *blame*.

Jamin "Angel" Agassi…

"Motherfucker!" He tilted back his head and roared his fury into the night sky.

Chapter 34

DISTRACTION...

That was the name of the game. The shooters firing into the engine room weren't actually trying to *hit* Angel. They were only keeping him occupied, pinned down so their buddies could run and fetch a frag grenade.

Frag grenade.

Never had two words sounded more abhorrent. Angel wasn't sure his snatch-and-toss maneuver would work. No. Scratch that. He was pretty sure it *wouldn't* work, but it was the only chance they had. The only chance *Sonya* had and—

His thoughts cut off when a loud *crack* sounded between rounds slamming into the turbine. It was immediately followed by another *crack* and then...silence. Angel closed his eyes, so overcome with gratitude he nearly fell to his knees. A penitent. A repentant. A man who knew salvation.

He recognized the bark of Sierra's report. Sierra was Nate "Ghost" Weller's prize sniper rifle. The deadly weapon had been fitted with a suppressor and shot subsonic rounds to further dampen the noise from each discharge, but still...

It was Sierra! *The Black Knights have entered the building!*

"What's happening?" Sonya's lips found his ear in

the darkness. Bringing her hand to his mouth, he kissed the tips of her icy fingers.

They were going to make it. They were actually going to make it!

"The cavalry has arrived," he whispered, so much joy in his heart he couldn't stop himself from pulling her into his arms. Burying his nose in her hair, he breathed deeply, drawing the sweet scent of her into his lungs and holding it there. Savoring it.

The sound of Rock's syrupy southern drawl slid into the room. "Stop twiddlin' your dick in there, *mon frère*! We got a plane waitin' to fly us outta this shit hole, and I don't know about you, but I'm ready!"

Angel pulled Sonya's cell phone from his hip pocket and thumbed on the flashlight. With an arm around her, he stepped from behind the turbine and aimed the light toward the door. It bathed his two teammates in a soft, golden glow, highlighting the harshness of their features as they stood over the lifeless bodies of Grafton's men as if standing over nothing more than fallen logs.

Something Angel had learned early on about the Black Knights was that, like the Mossad, they valued life, *innocent* life more than they valued the breath in their own lungs. But they had no compunction about taking the lives of the unvirtuous if and when the occasion called for it. Tough men. Brave men. Men ready and willing to rise to every challenge or make the ultimate sacrifice…those were the operators at Black Knights Inc.

He thanked God he could count them as friends, quickly reciting the *Sh'ma* in reverence. The Jewish prayer was meant to be spoken twice daily. Once upon waking and once before going to sleep, but Angel figured now was as good a time as any to offer praise where praise was due.

Of course, he said none of what he was thinking. Instead, he went with "Took you guys long enough."

He shuffled Sonya forward through the debris of broken chairs and used ductwork. He was surprised at how well she was handling their near-death experience. No tremors. No shock. Just a look of utter relief on her pretty face.

It was possible the shock and the tremors would come later, after her adrenaline let down, but he bet not. He'd always known that Sonya was tough. This day had taught him her fortitude was deeper and wider and stronger than he'd ever imagined.

If he hadn't already loved her with every inch of his heart, he would have fallen for her all over again then and there.

Adjusting his green John Deere baseball cap, Rock drawled, "We had to stop for ice cream. You know I can't resist a double scoop."

Angel snorted at the ridiculousness of the idea, especially since the Black Knights had probably broken land speed records trying to reach him.

"I don't feel the least bit bad about our delay either," Rock continued, flicking his fingers toward the mound of dead men as Angel escorted Sonya up the stairs. "Looks like you had the situation under control."

Once they reached the landing, Rock grabbed Sonya's hand from Angel's. "*Ma cherie*. It's a pleasure to meet you finally. I'm Richard Babineaux, but everyone calls me Rock."

Rock, the consummate gentleman, was likely trying
to put Sonya at ease, to lighten the strain of the situation—a heap of dead men lying in puddles of blood
tended to tinge the atmosphere with tension. Still, when
Rock bent to kiss Sonya's fingers, jealousy burned a
path through Angel's veins. It wasn't a sensation he'd
felt before. He couldn't say he particularly enjoyed it.

Five. Four. Three. Two...

"Enough of that." He pulled Sonya's hand from
Rock's when it became apparent Rock was in no hurry to
let go of her fingers. "Don't fall victim to this lothario's
smooth manners and Cajun drawl," he grumbled. "He
has a woman back home." Leveling Rock with a narrow-
eyed stare, he asked, "Tell me, Rock, have you made an
honest woman of Vanessa yet?"

Rock splayed his hand over his heart. "I ask her to
marry me every day, and every day she tells me to ask
her tomorrow. But never fear, *mon ami*, one of these
days she'll give in, *n'est-ce pas?* No one can resist me
forever. Right, *ma belle*?" Rock reached for Sonya's
hand again, and Angel would swear green edged into
his vision.

When Sonya tittered—yes, *tittered!*—he found himself dragging her hand from Rock's. *Again.* Deciding
a distraction was in order, he directed her attention to
Ghost. The sniper had leaned Sierra against his shoulder.

"This is Nate Weller," he told Sonya. "But you can
call him Ghost."

"Miss Butler." Ghost politely took Sonya's hand. The
green in Angel's vision expanded when, from the corner
of his eye, he saw Sonya blink up at Ghost in awe. Ghost
was a handsome devil, no doubt about it. His Native

American ancestry was evident in his flashing black eyes and shiny black hair.

Okay, it was official. Angel didn't like *any* man touching Sonya.

"Ghost has a wife, a daughter, and a baby on the way in what? Four months?" he informed her.

Her mouth twisted as she slid him a knowing glance. Then she turned back to Ghost. "Congratulations."

"Thank you, Miss Butler." Ghost dipped his chin.

"Please, call me Sonya."

Ghost gifted Sonya with one of his rare smiles and Sonya gasped—yes, *gasped!*

Angel began to rethink his stance on thanking God he could count the Black Knights as friends, and he began to wonder if maybe he might prefer it if Sonya were a little less stalwart. If she was busy dealing with shock and the revulsion of standing over dead men, she wouldn't have time to be charmed by his asshole teammates. "Now that the pleasantries are over," he grumbled, "what should we do with these assholes?" He kicked one of the dead men's booted feet.

"Leave 'em," Rock said, all jokes and flirting aside. Now, he was all business. "Your SIS buddy says he'll take care of 'em after we skedaddle."

"Speaking of my SIS buddy…" Angel let the sentence dangle.

"*Oui.*" Rock scratched his chin and made a face. "He wanted to come, man. He truly did. But the Chişinău police are after you two. Videos of y'all hoppin' out the front window of that café are all over the Moldovan TV channels. The local radio stations are broadcasting alerts every fifteen minutes tellin' folks to "be on the lookout." Your SIS guy's been busy alterin' CCTV footage and feedin' the police disinformation. Plus, he's been workin' the situation at the hospital."

At mention of the hospital, a pit formed in Angel's stomach. Sonya, dear, sweet Sonya, instinctively reached for his hand, giving it a squeeze.

Now that's where her hand belongs, he thought. *Not inside Rock's or Ghost's, but firmly inside* mine.

"How *is* Rusty?" he asked.

Rock's expression turned pained. "Alive. The doctors stabilized him, but he needs surgery. The bullet shredded a part of his lower bowel, nicked one kidney, and nearly severed his celiac artery. Thankfully, Chelsea was able to call in some favors from a few of her CIA pals." Chelsea was BKI's liaison to the CIA—a firecracker packaged inside a soft, curvy woman who barely stood taller than five feet.

"That private plane I mentioned earlier?" Rock continued. "She arranged it for us. Rusty, Ace, and Ozzie will be transferred to it once we're there and ready to take off. A team of CIA doctors are onboard. Their job will be to keep Rusty alive until we reach Ramstein Air Base in Germany. Rusty will undergo surgery there. Once he's strong enough, he'll be transferred to Northwestern Hospital in Chicago."

Angel wasn't sure he was ready for the answer, but he still needed to ask the question. "What are his chances?"

Rock doffed his baseball cap and ran a hand through his sweat-dampened hair. "Not as good as we'd like." Beside him, Ghost blew out a weary breath.

Angel closed his eyes. This had been *his* mission, *his* show to run. Knowing a teammate might die on his watch filled him with sorrow and regret.

God, he had so *many* regrets.

Barely two minutes later, they pushed through the plywood covering the circus's front door and stepped into the night. The breeze was cool and moist, but blessedly welcome compared to the stale air inside the engine room. Still, Sonya shivered as the cold and damp seeped into her. Angel took off his jacket, wrapping it around her shoulders.

"Thank you," she whispered, the moonlight shining on her blond hair, making it glow. "And not just for the jacket. Thank you for…" She swallowed and shook her head. "For saving my butt today."

"It was my pleasure. That thing is world class, you know?"

She blushed. "Is the incomparable Prince of Shadows actually flirting with me?" She placed a hand over her chest. "Be still my heart."

When he winked and smiled, she scowled and pointed at his face. "Give that thing a rest, will ya? I can only bear it for a few seconds at time before my…" Something flickered behind her eyes.

"What is it?" he asked.

"I just remembered… Were you about to tell me something before Grafton's men starting shooting at us again?"

His heart hopped into his throat. Now that they'd made it out alive, giving her the truth no longer seemed prudent. "It was nothing important."

She narrowed her eyes, her skepticism clear. Then Boss called out to them from the end of the parking lot. "For fuck's sake! Hurry up! We got a plane to catch!"

The man's timing was impeccable. Angel wasn't saved by the bell in this instance; he was saved by *the boss*.

"I think he wants us to run," Rock said with a sardonic twist of his lips as he glanced at Ghost.

"After all these years," Ghost told him, "you don't gotta teach me how to speak Boss. I'm fluent."

The two of them broke into a trot, Sierra still slung over Ghost's shoulder as if it were an extra appendage. Angel glanced down at Sonya's bare feet. Those hot-pink toenails winked at him from beneath the hem of her black slacks, and he chastised himself for not kissing and sucking each of them earlier. "I could carry you," he suggested.

She made a rude noise, grabbed his hand, and broke into a jog.

She truly is tough as nails, he thought, pride swelling his chest. *And she's going to be mine. I'm going to make her fall in love with me now just like I made her fall in love with me back then.*

He might have let his imagination run wild with plans for the future—a house, two little girls who would inherit their mother's bright, firefly laugh—if he wasn't suddenly face-to-face with the man of the hour.

Standing beside Boss, the infamous Spider didn't look very scary. His hands were bound behind his back with a bright orange zip tie and his mouth was covered with a length of gray duct tape. Blood dripped from his shoulder, and Angel caught the matching smear of crimson on Boss's jeans, testament to Boss having wiped off his Ka-Bar knife there before re-sheathing the blade in the holder clipped to his belt.

As good as Ghost was with a sniper rifle? That's how good Frank "Boss" Knight was with a blade.

"Lord Grafton," Angel said lazily, "may I say how splendid you look in handcuffs?"

Hatred—and he was happy to say more than a little fear—blazed from Grafton's black eyes when he snarled something that sounded like *fuck you* from behind the duct tape.

"I'm Frank Knight," Boss reached for Sonya's hand, ignoring Angel's exchange with Grafton. "If you want to call me Boss, that's fine. Everyone else does."

"Pleased to meet you." Sonya pumped Boss's big paw. "I'm Sonya. Plain old Sonya."

A crooked smile tugged at Boss's lips before he turned to Angel, his expression turning serious. "We won't fit in one vehicle." He frowned toward the tree line where Angel assumed they'd left their car. "You and Sonya are gonna need to steal Spider's ride and follow us to the private airstrip where our plane is waiting."

"You mean *appropriate* Grafton's ride." Rock grinned and winked at Angel. "Right, Angel?"

The Black Knights thought it was hilarious that he insisted on using the term *appropriate* instead of *steal* or *swipe* or *boost*. Little did they know it was because of a conversation he'd had with Sonya more than a decade earlier.

A loud buzz sounded in his ears as he looked her way, hoping she'd forgotten about the day they'd snatched a guest register out from under the nose of a greasy Parisian hotelier.

No such luck.

He watched the blood drain from her face. Saw her throat work over a hard swallow. She stared at him, her eyes moving over his altered features, looking for something that might answer the question he knew screamed through her head.

"*Appropriate*," she whispered. "That's the word Mark always used."

"Sonya—" He tried to grab her hand, but she yanked her fingers away, taking a hasty step backward. Her chest rose and fell in ragged breaths.

Shit. *Shit!* He could feel his web of deceit tearing away from its moorings. Filament by filament, all his lies were coming undone.

Turn back time, and stop this from happening! he demanded of the universe.

Like always, the universe ignored him.

"The way you crack your jaw..." Her voice was hoarse. "The way you walk and make love and..."

Boss cleared his throat, clearly uncomfortable. Both Ghost and Rock looked away, unable to watch while Angel's whole world imploded like a dying star.

"The scar on your hip where Mark's birthmark used to be," she continued. "I convinced myself all of it was coincidence, but this..." She shook her head. Then she firmed her jaw, looked him straight in the eye and demanded, "Who *are* you?"

Angel desperately racked his brain for a way to put the cat back in the bag. But the only solution he could come up with involved doubling down on his lies, convincing her she didn't know what she was talking about.

Convincing her she's crazy.

He looked over at his teammates, at men who worked in the dark but lived their lives in the light. Men who had dared to open the treasure chests of their hearts and show their women all the shining secrets inside. Each of them was an example of the kind of man he wanted to be. Each of their relationships was a gold standard to which he aspired, and he realized that not only was the jig up, but also that he was sort of relieved it was.

He was *tired* of deception. *Tired* of pretending he was someone he wasn't.

As much as the truth terrified him, he could finally admit that it was time. Time to step out of the shadows and into the sun. Time to stop hiding.

"Who *are* you?" she demanded again.

"I think you know who I am. I think, deep in your heart, you have known who I am from the beginning."

Her hand flew to her mouth. Tears filled her eyes.

"Sonya, please…" He softened his voice and reached for her again. Again, she wrenched her wrist from his grip. There were no words to describe how badly her rejection stung. It sliced him to the bone. Deeper. To his soul.

"M-Mark?"

He swallowed. How he'd yearned to hear her call him by his given name. Now it sounded obscene in her mouth. "Yes."

"No." She shook her head, her eyes wild as she tried to deny the truth. The truth that he'd lied to her. The truth that he'd left her. "No. You can't be."

"And yet I am." To convince her, to squash any chance she had at hiding from reality, he added, "And after all these years, I remember everything about us, about you. I remember how your lips tasted of wine and chocolate the first time we kissed in that doorway in the rain. I remember how pale your skin looked in the moonlight that shined in through the window of your bedroom in your Montmartre flat. I remember how terrified you were the night you told me you loved me. And I remember the joy that lit your gorgeous eyes when I told you that I loved you too. Sonya…" His voice cracked, but he had to get this last bit out. It was important. Perhaps it was the most important thing he'd ever done. Ever said. "I'm so sorry. If I could go back and—"

"But I saw you die!" she cried, cutting him off. "I saw that bomber shoot you through the heart!"

"You were never meant to be there that day."

She slapped her hands against the sides of her head as if she feared her brain might explode out of her ears. "What are you *talking* about?" Anguish had turned her voice into a harsh shriek that echoed shrilly across the open parking lot. "I don't understand any of this!"

"Angel." Boss's expression was pained. "We have to hurry. Rusty, he needs—"

"Right." Angel nodded, swallowing the lump in his throat. "You all go on. We'll be right behind you."

Rock and Ghost shot him commiserating looks— well, Rock did; Ghost was harder to read—before they grabbed Grafton's elbows and frog-marched him toward the far tree line. Grafton glanced over his shoulder, an evil light shining in his eyes. He was happy to see Angel in pain.

Boss slapped him upside the head, snarling, "Turn around, you sorry piece of shit." Then, Boss grumbled to Rock. "And you… Nice work, WikiLeaks."

"Damn," Rock whispered. "I had no idea. I thought…" His words trailed off as the quartet moved out of the range.

Slowly, Angel turned back to Sonya. The decimated look in her eyes was too much. He'd never been a coward before, but he was a coward then. Skirting past her, he bent and searched the pockets of Grafton's dead driver until he found a set of car keys.

Without looking at her—*unable* to look at her—he said, "We should go. A man's life is on the line and—"

She didn't let him finish, simply stepped over the corpse and opened the car's passenger door. He was left with no recourse but to follow suit. As they sat in silence inside the sedan, waiting to tail the BKI team to the private airstrip, he wondered if it might have been better had he never come back into her life.

Sure, she would still be mourning him. But perhaps his death was better, *easier* to deal with than the knowledge he'd abandoned and deceived her.

A charcoal four-door slipped from the edge of the forest, headlights flashing, telling him it was time to go. He responded in kind, and the engine on Grafton's rented sedan turned over with a well-tuned purr. They made their way down the cracked and crumbling boulevard, the trees crowding in on them like dark forest spirits peeking through the sunroof, curious about the clouds of outrage and suffering and heartache swirling inside.

Heartache…

Now, there was a word. Angel's heart actually *ached*.

"Amazing how much hurt the truth can cause between two people," he said more to himself than to her.

Her voice had lost its husky quality. It was sharp as a knife's edge when she blurted in Hebrew, "Tell me your favorite color. Tell me your real birthday. Tell me what my favorite movie is and who my favorite authors are."

Apparently, she required more proof.

Like her, he switched to Hebrew. The first word out of his mouth had her gasping. By the time he'd correctly answered all her questions, she was wide-eyed and gaping at him.

"How *could* you?" she demanded, having gone back to English. "I thought you loved me. I thought—"

He glanced over, hoping she could see the truth in his eyes. *Begging* her to see it. "I loved you then. I love you now. And I have loved you all the days in between."

"Shut up!" Her face caved in on itself. "Stop lying to me! Stop *lying!*"

Her grief overwhelmed her. It overwhelmed them both. He was helpless to do anything when she curled against the passenger door and buried her face in her hands. Her huge, gulping sobs made his own eyes well with tears. One rogue drop spilled onto his cheek.

"Sonya…" he said after a few agonizing minutes. "Please, you have to understand."

She lowered her hands and glared. "I *don't* understand! How could you do that to me? How could you do that to *us*? How could you—"

Her words cut off when she choked on another sob.

He wanted to curl up and die. He wanted to crack his chest open, take out his heart, and hand it to her. He wanted to go back in time and make different choices. He wanted…

Her.

She was the only thing he truly wanted, and she was slipping away from him.

"I thought I was doing the right thing." He flipped on his turn signal and merged onto the highway. It was mostly deserted now. A few delivery truck drivers were the only other souls on the road.

Seemed appropriate. The long, desolate stretch of

asphalt was an apt metaphor for what he suspected would be his long, desolate future. A future without Sonya or that house or those two little girls with their bright firefly laughs.

"How was leaving me the right thing?" she demanded.

How indeed? Looking back he wasn't convinced it was. *Damn hindsight! Why did it have to be twenty-twenty?*

"When my ramsad came to me, asking me to assume the identity of an Iranian nuclear science student because I already looked so much like him, when my ramsad told me I had the chance to stop Israel's greatest threat from becoming a nuclear power, I saw no way to say no."

"Why didn't you *tell* me? Why did you let me think you were dead, Mark?" Her brow furrowed. "Or Angel. Or Majid. Or…I don't even know what to call you!"

Call me your love, he wanted to beg her. *Call me anything you want, but don't call this thing between us over. Sonya, please!*

"My ramsad knew the training I would need would take a year. A year to school me in nuclear science so I could pass as Majid when I assumed his identity. A year to study his mannerisms and accent. A year to undergo the plastic surgery needed to make me his doppelganger. To take over Majid Abass's life, Mark Risa had to die. But, more than that, my ramsad didn't expect me to come through the mission alive. He convinced me it would be better for you, easier for you, *fairer* for you to let go of me then and there. So you could mourn and move on."

She choked on a wet laugh. "I *never* moved on!"

Yes, he knew that now. It made two of them.

"'She's young,' he told me. 'Don't let her spend these next years of her life worrying herself sick over you. If you die inside, don't let her always wonder what happened to you, because whether your mission is a success or a failure, we can never tell her the truth of it.'"

When he glanced at her, he found her staring at him in disbelief. "But Sonya, you *have* to know…" He wanted so badly to reach for her hand. "You were never meant to *be* there that day by the river. That show was put on for the CCTV cameras, proof that Mark Risa was dead so there would be no way anyone could ever question—"

"What happened to the bomber?"

The question had him shaking his head. "What?"

"The terrorist you were after when you came to Paris. What happened to him?"

"I captured him."

"When?" Her eyes had dried. He wasn't sure if that was a good sign or a bad one.

"Two days before my…uh…faked death."

"Then who was the guy with you on the riverbank?"

"Another Mossad agent."

"What happened to the *real* Majid Abass?"

This felt a bit like Twenty Questions, but he'd talk until he was blue in the face if that's what it took to make her understand. "The night I took over his identity, the Mossad killed him. He was injected with a deadly biological poison and buried in the desert. Majid was a loner. An orphan. It was easy to slip into his life."

"And easy to slip out of your own."

"No." He shook his head. "Never believe that. Leaving you was the hardest decision I ever made, but…" He watched the broken white lines on the highway race by.

How could he make her understand? He wasn't sure the right words existed to describe how the choice between honor and duty and the woman he loved had nearly broken him in two.

"But what?" she prompted.

"Do you remember what you told me about believing in duty and sacrifice and living a life of service to others?"

A muscle ticked under her puffy right eye. She nodded.

"I thought that's what I was doing. When my ramsad came to me, asking me to save the world, I was so young and naive that I thought I was doing what you would *want* me to do. I thought I was being the man you would *want* me to be, sacrificing myself for the greater good and—"

"Are you seriously sitting there trying to convince me you did all this for *me*?"

"No. Maybe I did it for myself. Maybe I wanted to leave my mark on the world. Maybe I wanted to be able to point at something and say, *See? I did that*. But if I could go back and do it all over again, I—"

"That's the rub, isn't it?" Her voice was quiet. "We *can't* go back."

He swallowed. "Sonya, I—"

"Can I have my phone back, please?"

He blinked, suffering from conversational whiplash. "Sure." He dug into his hip pocket and handed her the cell phone. "Why?"

"I need to call my boss. Bring him up to speed on my situation."

"Can it wait until—"

She dialed a number and held the phone to her ear. Okay, so apparently it *couldn't* wait.

He listened as she filled the president of Interpol in on what had happened over the last twenty-four hours. She was careful not to mention Black Knights Inc. by name when she told him about the group of Americans who had Lord Asad Grafton in custody. He was grateful for that. Grateful she understood the importance of keeping BKI in the shadows.

Then, his stomach belched up a load of acid so vile he nearly puked when she added, "They're evacuating me with them to Ramstein Air Base in Germany. Would it be possible to have a plane there waiting for me? I'm ready to come home. We have a lot of Intel to go over."

She listened for a while longer, then nodded. "Thank you, sir. I look forward to seeing you too."

When she clicked off the phone, he tried to talk to her, but all he managed was her name before she lifted a hand, cutting him off. "I really need you to be quiet. Will you do that for me?"

A muscle ticked in his jaw. After a brief hesitation, he said, "Yes. I will do anything for you."

Of all the truths he'd told her in the last fifteen minutes, that one was the most undeniable.

Chapter 35

28,500 feet
Four hours later...

THE INSIDE OF THE PRIVATE PLANE WAS BRIGHT AND cramped. It was also colder than Sonya cared for. She wished she hadn't given Angel—or Mark. *Gah!*—his jacket back. But after all the revelations, she hadn't been able to wear it. It held the scent of his aftershave and reminded her that the man she knew ten years ago, the one who'd eschewed cologne or aftershave for simple lilac soap, had chosen to leave her behind.

Bolted into the middle of the aisle was a hospital gurney. On top of that gurney was Rusty Parker, a giant redhead whom she thought looked more like a Zeus or an Atlas than a Rusty. He needed an epithet worthy of his colossal size. Between him and Boss, it was a wonder there was room for anyone else on the plane.

Of course, Rusty didn't look too mighty at the moment. Not with so many tubes and machines and drips hooked up to him. The only way she knew he was redheaded was because a tuft of hair had escaped his paper hospital cap to curl delicately against his beard-scruffy cheek.

A team of three doctors, who'd preferred not to introduce themselves—the CIA was funny that way—had been hovering around him the entire flight. Checking his vitals. Checking his lines. Checking his bandages. Luckily, there hadn't been an emergency. Rusty had remained unconscious and blessedly stable.

For their part, the Black Knights had tried to stay out of the way, cramming themselves into the small seats at the back of the plane but never taking their eyes off their wounded friend.

She'd been introduced to Ozzie before takeoff, a devastatingly handsome man with flashing blue eyes, flyaway hair, and a Star Trek T-shirt that might have made her smile under different circumstances. Then there was Ace…an equally attractive man who was so wan-looking she feared for his health. He had tried to be polite upon introduction, but he'd barely spared her a glance before turning his attention back to Rusty.

It was obvious the Black Knights were a tight-knit group. Just as obvious was that they weren't used to being helpless. For the entire flight, she'd watched emotions flicker across their faces. She saw fear for Rusty's life. Guilt that they couldn't do more to help him. And a bone-deep determination that he should live. They *willed* him to live. Ace more than any of them. The savage look in his eyes was sharp and bright, like a blade burned clean in a fire.

She was strapped into the jump seat attached to the wall behind the cockpit—the only free space on the plane and as good a place as any to remain out of the way. It had a nice view of the fuselage. As luck would have it, however, the gurney kept her from seeing Grafton and Angel—or Mark. *Gah!*—who were buckled into seats on the left side of the aircraft. Thankfully, Angel had done as she'd asked. He hadn't pushed. Hadn't prodded.

Hadn't actually said more than five words to her since she'd asked him for silence.

She still had trouble thinking of him as Mark. He didn't look like Mark. He didn't sound like Mark. But he *was* Mark, and so much of what had happened over the last day made sense. Like why he'd said "some things never change" when she'd made that quip about chocolate being the only thing capable of making everyone happy. He *knew* how much she loved chocolate. Also, it explained why he'd asked her about learning Italian. When he'd known her ten years ago, she hadn't spoken the language. And last but certainly not least, it was now clear why he hadn't gotten mad at her for calling Mark's name when she'd climaxed that last time. How could he get mad when he *was* Mark?

He's Mark. He's Mark *and yet—*

The pilot came over the intercom, informing them they had started their initial decent. "We'll be landing at Ramstein in approximately twenty minutes, folks," he said in that homespun drawl all pilots seemed to adopt.

The thought of the plane her boss had promised would be waiting for her, the thought that she would be leaving Angel/Mark behind very soon had her throat closing up. There was a sharp, searing pain in her chest, like her heart had stepped on a Lego and then tripped over the coffee table to smash its head against the wall.

On the one hand, she could maybe, sorta, kinda, *possibly* understand why he'd done what he'd done. Had the president of Interpol come to her ten years ago, at the impressionable age of twenty-two, and asked her to save to the world, she might have agreed to it. Selflessness and sacrifice had been big, bright concepts back then.

On the other hand, why hadn't he come to her *after*? Why had he let her go on without him all these years? All it would have taken was a quick Google search, and he could have seen she wasn't married, could have discovered she'd never moved on.

Then there was the not-so-small issue of all the lies he'd fed her since coming to Grafton Manor, all the times he'd let her think she was crazy when something he said or did reminded her of Mark. If Rock hadn't said that thing about appropriating Grafton's car, would Angel *still* be lying to her?

There'd been plenty of opportunities for him to come clean, and he never had. Not until the evidence was too overwhelming to deny. *That* wasn't like Mark. Backhanded trickery wasn't a part of the man she'd known. It wasn't the man she'd loved.

You need time and space, she told herself. *You need to get away from him to sort out your feelings and decide what to do*.

Right. She blew out a shaky breath. Okay, good. She had a plan. And now...

She'd had to pee for nearly two hours, but she'd forced herself to hold it for fear of actually having to walk by Angel—or Mark. *Gah!*—without first knowing what she'd say to him if he tried to stop her. Now that she had a plan, her screaming bladder told her in no uncertain terms that enough was enough.

Unbuckling her seat belt, she was careful to sidestep the doctors and the gurney, careful to keep her eyes steadfastly forward as she padded barefoot to the lavatory at the back of the private plane. After she'd relieved herself— imagining that her bladder sang her a rousing chorus of hallelujahs—she washed her hands in the little sink and took at hesitant peek at her reflection in the mirror.

She looked like an extra on *The Walking Dead*. She was so pale she was almost gray. All her makeup was gone, having been cried off or kissed off. And her hair was a rat's nest.

No. That was an insult to rats' nests. Her hair was the follicular equivalent of a preschool art class. It was chaos. It was anarchy. It was in serious need of a good shampooing.

Combing her fingers through the worst of the tangles, she studied her face, wondering if there was anything to be done there. She had no idea what had become of her purse after Angel hurled it into the circus arena, but she wished she'd at least had the wherewithal to take her compact powder out before he tossed it. The bags under her eyes were bigger than her carry-on luggage. Her nose was shiny but it didn't hold a candle to her forehead, which was doing its best impression of a grease factory. Grabbing some tissues, she blotted her face and glanced back at her reflection.

Deciding that was as good as it got, she slid the lock on the little bifold door. Before she could leave the lavatory, however, a huge bulk of humanity squeezed in with her.

"What in the world?" she hissed, crowding against the sink.

Angel towered over her. His big thighs bracketing hers. His wide-palmed hands flat on the bulkhead behind her head. His mouth...that gorgeous, *talented* mouth way too close.

"I know you asked me to keep quiet," he rasped. Of all the things he'd changed about himself, his voice was the one she lamented the most. It had been so smooth and deep and luxurious. Now, it was auditory sandpaper. "And I did my best for as long as I could. But, Sonya, we *have* to talk about this."

"I'm not ready to talk." She tried to make her tone stony and emotionless. She wasn't sure she succeeded.

He ducked his chin and held her gaze, his Turkish coffee eyes softening. "Sonya, I only want—"

"Why are your eyes so dark? Are you wearing contacts?"

The muscle in his jaw ticked. His expression said the last thing he wanted to talk about was his eyes, but he answered anyway. "My irises were injected with dye to darken them. But it didn't totally take. See?" He pointed to his left eye where, sure enough, a tiny sliver the shape of a pizza slice remained the same chocolaty brown color she'd grown to know and love ten years ago.

"And your accent? It's completely different."

"I had to work at that. First when I became Majid, and then when I became Angel. Voice-recognition software picks up more than tonal qualities. It also identifies syntax and diction. I have cultivated a more American way with phrases."

She shook her head, staring in wonder. "You're so different in every way."

"No." He placed his hand over his heart. "In here I am still the same."

Even though she'd told herself she wasn't going to talk to him about it, even though she wasn't *ready* to talk about it, she heard herself blurt, "But you're not. The man I loved would have *come* for me when it was safe." Her fingers curled so tightly around the lip of the sink her knuckles ached. "The man I loved wouldn't have lied to me and let me think I was going crazy when I started noticing similarities. The man I loved wouldn't have made love to me without first telling me the truth. You are *not* the man I loved!"

She realized she'd shouted this last bit. Reaching up, she pinched the bridge of her nose to keep her traitorous tears from falling. She'd shed so many for him over the years. She refused to shed any more.

"But I *am*, Sonya." He cupped her chin in his warm hand and forced her to look at him. He had such a beautiful face, but in that moment all she wanted was his *old* face. If he was saying these things with his *old* face, then maybe she could believe him. "Don't you see that I am?"

She had to ignore the pleading in his eyes, or it would be her undoing.

A recalcitrant tear blew past her defenses. It spilled over her bottom lid and streaked hot and salty down her cheek.

"Then why didn't you come for me? After you left Iran, why didn't you *find* me?" She hated that her voice sounded hoarse and small.

"I wanted to." He dropped his hand from her chin so he could grab her shoulders. "I swear to God I wanted to, but six years had passed. *Six years*. I thought for sure you had moved on."

Her insides had been quaking, but that made everything go still. "You were a coward then," she accused. "You are a coward now. If you weren't, you would have told me the truth the moment you knew I wasn't Grafton's lackey. You would have told me the truth all the times I said you reminded me of Mark. Of *you*!" Her volume had increased until she was shouting again. She didn't care. Let everyone hear. "I don't even know what to call you!"

His Adam's apple bobbed in his throat. "Call me Angel. I *am* Jamin 'Angel' Agassi now."

And there it was. The crux of the matter.

"Well, *Angel*, those years in Iran changed you into someone I don't know. Because the man I knew, *my* Mark, he…" She bit her lips when more treasonous tears threatened. "He would have come for me. My Mark would have told me the truth. My Mark would have—"

"Uh… Sorry to interrupt, *mes amis*." Rock's lazy Cajun accent sounded through the thin door. "The pilot says we need to take our seats in preparation for landin'."

"Fuck. Off," Angel growled.

"Okeydokey then. Pretend I was never here."

The *crank* and *thunk* of the landing gear sounded through the bottom of the aircraft.

"We need to sit down." Sonya breathed through her nose in the hope it would staunch the fire in her throat.

"No. We need to finish this conversation."

"We *are* finished."

"Don't say that, Sonya," he begged. Yes, *begged*. Maybe, after everything he'd done to her, to *them*, she should have felt vindicated by the surrender in his ragged voice, but all she felt was sad.

Sad at what had become of them.

"If I ask you something, will you promise to tell me the truth?" she whispered.

Wariness flashed in his eyes, but still he vowed, "No more lies, Sonya. I swear it. Never again."

"If Rock hadn't said that thing about appropriating Grafton's car, would you have told me who you really are?"

His expression remained unreadable—he was far too good at that—but after a couple of tense seconds he blew out a deep breath. "No."

She bit the inside of her cheek to keep from gaping. To hear him admit it was... There were no words.

"I knew how much the truth would hurt you, and I wanted to save you from that. From *this*." He made a motion back and forth between them.

Her teeth set. "Are you seriously trying to convince me you were going to lie to me for...maybe *forever*, and it was all for my own good?"

"No." He shook his head, and the move had her eyes snagging on his short hair. If he'd let his hair grow long, if she'd touched it and twined her fingers through his soft curls, would she have known he was Mark sooner? "That is *not* what I am saying."

"Then what *are* you saying?"

"After everything we sacrificed, I wanted only happiness for you, for *us*. I wanted you to fall in love with me again because of the man I am now, not the man I was ten years ago. I wanted nothing to stand in the way of what we can have together because I *love* you, Sonya."

She closed her eyes as her chin quivered, all her anger draining away as if he'd pulled the plug. *I love you*. They were such beautiful words. And yet...they were an assault on her ears. On her heart.

He'd given her his truth. Now it was her turn. "I don't know if I still love you. I don't know if I *can* love you. I don't know you anymore."

"Don't say that. Sonya, please." He pulled her into his arms.

She let him. Heaven help her, she let him because she was in agony and she needed the comfort he offered. Then she did something she swore she wouldn't do. She let the tears come.

But she wasn't crying for him. She was crying for *them*. For what could have been and what would never be.

The *whoosh* of the plane's flaps engaging sounded a second before the aircraft jolted and bounced as the wheels touched the ground. When the pilot applied the brakes, she tightened her arms around Angel's waist, wondering if this would be the last time she held him.

The private jet came to a stop, and the sound of activity from inside the fuselage drifted beneath the bifold door. She waited until a soft knock sounded before slipping from Angel's embrace. Opening the door, she saw Rock standing on the threshold. He had his John Deere baseball cap crumpled between his hands.

"Your...uh...your plane is here," he told her before flicking a tortured look Angel's way. "The pilots say they're ready to get goin' whenever you are."

She thanked him, and after she'd watched him walk down the aisle, she turned back to Angel. *Angel, Angel, Angel. He is Angel now. Mark Risa's heart might not have taken a bullet that day by the river, but he had died all the same*. Angel's dark eyes moved over her face, over her mouth. His impenetrable mask had slipped. She caught a quick glimpse at the anguish inside him and closed her eyes against it. She couldn't deal with his pain. She was having enough trouble dealing with her own.

"Thank you. Thank you for everything you did for me today," she told him. "Thank you for saving me from Grafton. Thank you for finally telling me the truth and—"

"Sonya, please don't go," he interrupted.

"No." She shook her head, opening her eyes so he could see the determination in them. "I have to go. I need time and space."

The muscle in his jaw went to town. She could tell he wanted to argue, but he held his tongue.

Before she turned to leave, she offered him a small smile. She tried to make her voice kind and forgiving when she said, "We'll always have Paris."

He sucked in a ragged breath. When a lone tear slipped from his right eye and slid down his beard-stubbled cheek, she couldn't take one more second of the torture. She left the lavatory, left the plane, and left behind the only man she'd ever loved.

Chapter 36

Northwestern Memorial Hospital
Chicago, Illinois
Three weeks later...

"YOUR WIFE'S HERE. SHE'S WITH MINE." BOSS'S LOW rumble nudged Rusty from the drug-induced sleep that was pretty much his life these days. "They're in the hall, and they look pissed. Go figure out what's going on."

"Me?" Ghost's quiet baritone pulled Rusty closer to full consciousness. "Why don't you do it?"

"Because I'm scared of my wife when she's pissed."

Incredulity laced Ghost's tone. "What makes you think I'm not scared of *mine*?"

"Did we forget something? Was there a meeting or—"

"Oh hell." Rusty heard a slapping sound that made him think Ghost smacked a hand to his forehead. "Was today the day we were supposed to go with them to register for the baby shower?"

"*Was* that today?" Boss sounded horrified. "Oh shit."

Rusty, high on drugs, found the doom in Boss's tone amusing.

"Why the hell do I have to be part of this again?" Boss demanded. "It's *your* baby."

"But *your* wife is the one throwing the shower."

"Right." Rusty could hear Boss's beard stubble rasp

against his callused palm when he dragged a hand over his face. "And she likes to torture me."

"That she does," Ghost concurred, a smile in his voice. "Or else she's softening you up for when it's *your* turn in the hot seat. Speaking of, when you gonna knock up Becky?"

"It's not like I'm not trying, man." There was a smug, self-satisfied quality to Boss's response. "I'm trying day and night. I try in the shower. I try on the back patio when everyone else has gone to bed. I try on top of—"

"Spare me the details. Let's go before we get in *worse* trouble."

"Right," Boss agreed. Then, "Well, Rusty, my man"—Rusty felt a heavy hand land on his shoulder, but he *still* couldn't manage to open his eyes—"we'll catch ya later. Keep on keepin' on."

The sound of booted feet clomping on the hospital's tiled floor met his ears. It was briefly interrupted by harsh female whispers. He caught the phrases *two hours late* and *lucky you're a smoke-show in the sack, or I'd smack you upside the head* before the voices drifted down the hallway outside.

With no distractions, oblivion threatened to close in on him again. Then, a sharp pain stabbed through his gut, and he was yanked from the soft arms of unconsciousness back to twilight. He patted around for the Button of Dreams—that's what he'd taken to calling the device that allowed him to self-administer his pain meds. Unfortunately, he couldn't find it.

"Damnit," he grumbled. Forcing open one eye was a herculean effort, and when he did, he ignored how his bandages made odd lumps beneath the hospital sheet.

He'd been told about his operation in Germany and then the flight to the U.S. once he was stable. But since he'd regained consciousness... What was it? Three days ago? Four? Time had gone all weird on him. He knew the Black Knights had been to see him. Remembered a few of their visits, thought maybe he'd dreamed others. One thing he *was* sure of was that his folks had been by his bedside around the clock. His folks and Ace...

He might have thought that was a bad combo considering his parents were so conservative and Ace was so...*gay*, but the few snippets of conversation he'd heard had let him rest easy. Ace wasn't about to out him, and his folks seemed to like Ace. In fact, just last night—or was it two nights ago?—he'd surfaced from his drug-induced haze to hear his dad and Ace speaking in low whispers.

"I sure wish you'd tell me what yinz were up to over in Moldova." Yinz. *His dear old pop was a Pittsburgher through and through. He actually used the colloquial expressions that graced souvenir T-shirts and bumper stickers. Things like* Tony's got it! *and* hygge. *"I promise I won't tell a soul," his father finished.*

"Wish I could, Mr. Parker," Ace said. "But just know that Rusty was a hero. He saved my bacon, and I'll never be able to thank him enough."

"First off, I thought I told you to call me Gary. Second, the way I hear it, you saved his bacon too. That tall dude, the one with the crazy hair who has a weird fascination with Captain Kirk?"

Ace laughed. "Ozzie."

"Yeah, well, Ozzie told me Rusty is still here 'cause

of you. Said you gave him your own blood during a BCT or a BTT or some such thing."

"BBT," Ace corrected him. "It's a buddy battlefield transfusion, and it sounds a lot more badass than it really is. I only had to donate a pint or two."

Rusty's father made a rude noise. "The way Ozzie tells it, you nearly bled out, you gave so much."

Rusty had feigned sleep, allowing the information to sink in and—

Aha!

He got distracted from his reverie when he found the Button of Dreams. Giving it three quick pumps, he settled more comfortably into his pillows and waited for the warm, floating sensation produced by high-powered narcotics. The first rush of drugs through his blood made his skin tingle. The second had his opened eye slamming shut.

"Now, Ace, sweetie, you didn't need to go to all this trouble." The sound of Rusty's mother's voice slipped into the room along with the soft *shush-shush* of her shoes against the tile. He fought the pull of unconsciousness. "I'd have been just fine with a salad down in the cafeteria."

"Those salads are more gray than green," Ace's soft baritone acted as a balm to Rusty's soul. Or maybe that was the drugs. It was hard to tell the difference. "And I know how much you like the chicken salad sandwich from Corner Bakery, so I stopped by before coming to the hospital. Where's Mr. Parker? I got him a roast beef and cheddar."

"I keep telling you to call us Sylvia and Gary. And he's downstairs in the lobby taking a phone call. Something happened back at the mill." What had Rusty said about his father being a yinzer through and through? The man actually worked at a steel mill. It didn't get any more Pittsburgh than that. "He's trying to sort things from here. Doesn't want to fly back home yet. Not 'til Rusty is better."

Rusty heard them settling into the chairs beside his bed and wanted to open his eyes to look at them, his favorite people on earth. Unfortunately, the painkillers were working their magic. Every muscle in his body was liquid.

The scent of mayonnaise and cooked meat drifted toward him, proving his nose was still in fine working order, but the thought of actually ingesting food made his stomach turn. When he was about to slip away to dreamland, his mother said, "Ace, I don't mean to pry, and you can totally tell me to mind my own business, but are you…" Her voice briefly trailed off. Her sandwich wrapper crackled. "Are you gay?"

A spurt of adrenaline shot through Rusty's bloodstream. It did its best to combat the drugs.

"Yes, ma'am. I am." Ace wasn't about to hide who he was. Rusty envied him that.

"Do you think Rusty is?"

Rusty's heart thundered. He tried to open his eyes, but they refused to obey. Why had his mother asked Ace that question? He'd never done anything or said anything to make her suspect. Hell, he'd moved half a world away so she wouldn't suspect and—

"Do you think Rusty is what?" Rusty's father's bass boomed into the room.

"Shush, Gary," his mother scolded. "Keep your voice down. For crying in the sink, Rusty's sleeping."

"He sleeps too much. Can't be good for him. Needs

to get up and get his body moving. That's the only way it'll heal."

"And you went to medical school and got your doctor's degree when?" his mother came back curtly.

"Mr. Parker, I picked up a beef and cheddar from Corner Bakery for you," Ace intervened before a round of bickering broke out. Rusty's parents loved each other to pieces, but that didn't stop them from arguing like…well, like a couple that'd been married for thirty-five years.

Rusty heard a *whack* and imagined his father had clapped a hand on Ace's shoulder. "Thought I told you to call me Gary, son."

"How did the call go?" his mother asked.

"Fine. Fine. I swear, them boys don't know their asses from holes in the ground, but I got 'em squared away. Now what's this you were talking about when I came in? Do you think Rusty is what?"

"Never mind," his mother said. "Eat your sandwich."

"Damnit, woman. You know I hate secrets. What's going on in here?"

His mother blew out a windy-sounding sigh. Or at least Rusty *thought* she did. Or maybe he was dreaming. Was he dreaming?

"I asked Ace if he was gay," his mother said. "He said he was."

For a while, Rusty's father said nothing. Then, "I reckon I sort of figured that one out on my own. He don't look at that pretty brunette nurse like a straight man should."

"And how should a straight man look at her?" His mother's voice held a warning edge.

If this was a dream, it was far too much like reality.

"Now don't get your tail feathers in a twist, Sylvia. She's young enough to be my daughter. And besides, I like a woman with a little meat on her bones." A loud smacking sound told Rusty his father had kissed his mother on the cheek. "But Ace here, he should be drooling. And he ain't. So...gay."

The low rumble of Ace's laughter reached Rusty's ears at the same time he felt himself sinking. Sinking. The meds, which had been lapping at his consciousness like steadily increasing waves on the beach, became a riptide and pulled him under.

Chapter 37

Ten days later...

ACE LEANED AGAINST THE WALL OUTSIDE RUSTY'S HOSPITAL room and took a long sip of his drink. The chai tea helped to mask the astringent smell of bleach left behind by the housekeeping staff after they'd mopped the floor.

"You want to clue me in?" Angel asked from beside him. Angel had barely had time to say *hello* to Rusty before the little brunette nurse Rusty's father thought was cute as a button had shooed them from the room.

Ace frowned over at him. "What do you mean? Rusty's getting a sponge bath, and the nurse—"

"No," Angel cut him off. "Not that. *This*." He waved a hand, indicating Ace's length.

Ace glanced down at his shirt and jeans, wondering if he'd spilled tea on himself. Nope. "Sorry." He shook his head. "You lost me."

"You realize if you were to look up the word 'melancholy' in the dictionary, you would find your sad sack of a mug next to it."

Angel's words made the tea sour in his mouth. He didn't want to talk about how these last few weeks, sitting beside Rusty's hospital bed and watching Rusty fight his way to health, had solidified his feelings for the guy. He didn't want to talk about how many times he'd compared *this* time in the hospital with *last* time in the hospital—here and now he was wanted; back then he hadn't been. He didn't want to talk about how much he'd come to adore Gary and Sylvia Parker. And he *certainly* didn't want to talk about Rusty's release at the end of the week, or that Gary and Sylvia planned to take Rusty home to Pittsburgh to convalesce, or that after Rusty was well, he intended to return to his cod-fishing business in Dover freakin' *England*. Half a freakin' world away.

"You're one to talk," he told Angel. "You've been walking around with a hangdog expression ever since we got back from Moldova. Have you heard from Sonya?"

Angel glared at him, his expression clearly saying he knew Ace's turn-the-tables game. Still he said, "She asked for space and time. I have been respecting her wishes."

"Mmm." Ace nodded. "I know all about respecting another person's wishes."

There were a couple of times when it would have been so easy to drop Rusty's parents a clue. But outing someone was a big no-no, even if keeping your mouth shut meant giving up any chance you had at being with them.

Ace took another sip of tea, hoping it would lubricate the lump that had inexplicably taken up residence in his throat. He mused aloud, "Have you ever heard the phrase *What starts in chaos ends in chaos*?"

Angel slid him a considering look. "No."

Ace shrugged. "I can't help but think that's how it is with Rusty and me. We met each other in the middle of a life-and-death situation."

Angel cocked his head. "So you think you two were doomed from the start?"

"Something like that."

"Bullshit."

Ace sighed, wanting to believe Angel but not quite getting there. "Then what about you and Sonya? You guys came together on a crazy mission to catch that synagogue bomber and look how *that* all turned out."

"Sonya and I are *far* from over." A muscle ticked in Angel's square jaw. The man was a handsome sonofa-gun, no doubt about it. If not for that whole straight thing—oh, yeah, and if Ace weren't head over heels for a certain redhead—Angel would've been just his type. Strong, brave, and stubborn.

Why do I always go for the stubborn ones?

"It's been over a month," he pointed out, "and you haven't called her or gone to see her or—"

"She needed time to shine. This was her victory."

Ace harrumphed. "You got a point there. Her and Zhao Longwei have been having a field day dissemi-nating the Intel she scored. Don't think I've ever seen so many arrests. And all the people inside government organizations? Holy demented shit! It's mind-boggling. No wonder Grafton was able to fly under the radar for so long. I think he had spies inside every Intelligence agency and policing community in the world."

"So the headlines would have us believe," Angel agreed.

"And Grafton? You heard anything about him?"

"Sucked down some CIA-rendition rabbit hole, no doubt."

Ace blew out a windy breath. "Wherever he is, I hope it's cold and dark."

"You and me both."

"It's weird. We were after him for so long, all our

efforts on finding him and bringing him down, and now that it's happened, it feels sort of…" He shrugged. "I don't know. Anticlimactic."

So many of the Knights already had plans in the works for how they'd spend the rest of their lives. Ghost and Ali were staying in Chi-Town—where they'd probably make a gazillion more babies. Ali loved her job as a kindergarten teacher at the Latin School of Chicago, and Ghost was considering a position with the Chicago Police Department as a weapons instructor and shooting specialist.

Boss and Becky had decided to keep running the custom bike business, of course. Becky wouldn't have it any other way. Honestly, neither would Boss. The man loved the shop and his ace mechanic of a wife so much that as long as she was happy, he was happy.

Snake and Michelle were *also* going to call the Windy City their permanent home, with Snake helping to build the hugely sought-after BKI bikes and Michelle keeping her job as a pharmaceutical rep while they raised their two adorable and rambunctious boys up in Lincoln Park.

Rock and Vanessa were in talks with the FBI, which always needed good interrogators (Rock) and good language specialists (Vanessa). And Vanessa, for the first time in history, had said *yes* when Rock got down on one knee and gave his daily spiel. They were planning a summer wedding. Rock insisted it be a blowout. "*A fais do-do for the ages!*" he'd announced only yesterday.

Wild Bill had landed a job with the Chicago Public Library, of all places. Although Ace wasn't all *that* surprised, considering ever since he'd known Wild Bill, the man had had his nose buried in a book. Eve had finally finished her doctoral thesis and was now the vice president of animal health at the world-renowned Shedd Aquarium. When the two of them weren't canoodling in a corner somewhere, they were out on their sailboat. Ace had a sneaking suspicion they liked getting it on with the help of the "motion of the ocean." Or, more precisely, the "motion of Lake Michigan."

Mac and Delilah had decided to split their time between Chicago and Texas. Their plan was to winter in Texas on Mac's family ranch and summer in Chicago so Delilah could keep an eye on her bar. BKI's favorite watering hole wasn't going to be the same without Delilah working the taps, but Ace supposed he'd have to get used to all the changes. He just wished everything wasn't happening so fast.

Steady had applied to Yale Medical School and received his acceptance letter three days ago. He intended to finish his medical degree and become a practicing physician. Abby, his botanist wife, was looking into a job at the Marsh Botanical Garden on the Yale campus to be close to him. Considering she was the ex-president's daughter, Ace didn't suspect she'd have any trouble snagging whichever position she wanted.

Dan and Penni were also content to make their home in Chicago. Dan planned to continue working at the shop, and Penni was going to be a stay-at-home mom to their adorable baby girl, Cora May. After Penni's harrowing job with the Secret Service, Ace was a little shocked at how quickly she'd settled into domestic life. According to Dan, Penni had taken up cooking and served successful—which Dan said meant marginally edible—dishes at least fifty percent of the time. Ace couldn't bear to think what she served the *other* fifty percent of the time.

Ozzie planned to stay in Chicago to help Becky come up with new designs to keep BKI on the cutting edge of custom bike building. The FBI was trying to convince him to do some consulting work for them—hacking jobs and such—but Ozzie seemed iffy about it. Ace suspected Ozzie's hesitation had more to do with not wanting to keep any secrets from his first-rate investigative reporter fiancée, Samantha, than any qualms about working for the feds.

Zoelner had accepted a position within the CIA. Considering that's where he'd started his career, Ace figured it was a bit like going home for him. Chelsea, his wife, was still working for the Company, so it had all worked out. Ace was happy they were happy, but he'd miss them. Even though they'd promised to fly back once a month for a visit, it wasn't going to be the same as seeing them day in and day out.

Christian and Emily were *also* going to be staying in Chicago. Emily planned to stay on as BKI's office manager. She might not have the title, but she was definitely the boss of Black Knights Inc. Christian was still trying to figure out what he wanted to do, which pretty much made him and Ace spirit animals since Ace had no freakin' *clue* how he planned to spend the rest of his life and—

"You know what conversational remorse is?"

Angel's question drew Ace from his thoughts. He blinked at the hubbub in the hospital hall, tuning in to the beeps and whistles of the machines and the soft, comforting voices of nurses and doctors as they interacted with patients.

"Sure," he said. "It's when you think of all the things you *should* have said."

"I hate it." Angel's brow furrowed. "Keeps me awake at night."

Ace took another sip of his tea. "I take it we're talking about Sonya here." Angel nodded. "You know, if you're convinced there's still something there to pursue, if you have things you need to say to her, then screw how busy she is. Screw the time and space she needs. Go and see her."

Angel glanced down the hallway, past the nurse's station. Ace couldn't be sure, but he thought he saw Angel's Adam's apple bob as if Angel's throat ached.

For so long, Angel had been the expressionless, seemingly *emotionless* enigma in their ranks. Seeing him struggling with heartache hit Ace particularly hard. He understood the agony of being in love with someone who had rejected him. He understood how bleak a future without that love seemed and how it could weigh a man down, heart and soul.

"I'm sorry, Angel. Don't listen to anything I say. I mean, seriously? I'm the *last* person to give you relationship advice."

Angel glanced his way. "Have you told him you love him?"

Ace laughed, but there was no humor in it. "What good would that do? He says he loves me but not enough to stop hiding. And since I *refuse* to go back into the closet, I don't see how telling him how I feel will help either of us. Besides, I don't—"

"Hello, boys!" Sylvia Parker called out as she sailed down the hallway toward them. She had a red

Tupperware dish in one hand and a Starbucks cup in the other. The quintessential *mom* type, her hair was cut in a bob, she wore the flowing blouse and not-too-tight jeans that hid what she wrongly assumed was a little extra weight, and her sneakers looked like they provided good arch support. She was pretty in a comfortable-in-her-own-skin way, and Ace hated that soon it'd be time to say goodbye to her.

"Since Rusty's appetite is back, I spent the whole morning in the kitchen cooking up his favorites." She lifted the Tupperware dish as proof. "Between you, me, and the wall, I hate the electric stove in that extended-stay hotel. You can't tell how high your heat is without a flame."

She stood in front of them now, her powdery-smelling perfume mixing with whatever was in the dish, something that had a lot of garlic and onions and butter. She gave them both a kiss on the cheek before straightening away. Then she frowned. "For crying in the sink, what are you two doing standing out here?"

"Rusty's getting a sponge bath," Ace explained.

"Oh." Without missing a beat, she grabbed the handle on the door and pushed inside.

"Mom! What the cob?" Rusty bellowed. "I'm gettin' bathed here. What if my dick had been out?"

"I helped you wash that thing for five years," Sylvia told him. "I don't think I'll faint at the sight of it now."

"Oh, for the love of—"

That's all Ace heard before Sylvia shut the door behind her.

He couldn't help but laugh. Of course, the next second he frowned again. He wished he could hate Rusty for choosing the closet over what they could have together. But the truth was…he got it. Rusty and his parents had such a *good* relationship. Easy. Having experienced the flip side of that coin, he couldn't say with one hundred percent certainty that he wouldn't do exactly the same thing if he were in Rusty's shoes.

"There it is again." Angel pointed at his face. "Melancholy."

"Go suck a nut, will you?"

"More your thing than mine, yeah?"

Ace's jaw dropped open. "Did you just make a joke?"

One corner of Angel's mouth twitched. Ever since Sonya had come back into his life, Angel's mask had cracked. Before he'd been an automaton. Mr. Poker Face. Now Ace caught fleeting glimpses of emotion. Today he'd seen both humor *and* pain on Angel's face. It was the latter that brought him back to what they'd been talking about before Sylvia's interruption.

"You know," he said, "I take back what I said earlier. You *should* take relationship advice from me. As someone who has loved and lost *twice* in his life, believe me when I say if there is anything, *anything* you can do to salvage a relationship, you should. *Go* to Sonya. Now. Today. *Talk* to her. At least then you won't be living in limbo and wondering what-if."

"Preaching to the choir." Angel glanced at the big, black watch on his wrist. "My plane leaves in three hours. I just stopped by to see Rusty before I go."

Ace smiled and nudged Angel. "Good for you, man."

"That remains to be seen." Angel sighed heavily. "But I have to give it another try. And probably another try after that if she sends me packing this time." He clapped a hand on Ace's shoulder. "And speaking of preaching to the choir, ever thought of taking your own advice?"

Ace shrugged. "I believe in happily-ever-afters. I really do. But I don't think everyone gets one."

"Not exactly sending me off with visions of white weddings in my head, are you?"

"Sorry." Ace made a face. "I wasn't talking about you."

"Hope not." For a minute it looked like Angel wanted to say something more on the matter. Then he sighed, saying, "Catch you on the B side," before turning and striding purposefully down the hallway. Off to try to win the heart of the woman he loved.

"Good luck!" Ace called to his back, crossing his fingers that somehow, someway Sonya could move beyond the pain and betrayal that kept them apart and—

His thoughts cut off when the door beside him swung open. The little brunette nurse stepped through, dragging behind her a plastic cart loaded with all the things needed to sponge down a patient.

"All finished," she told him cheerfully. "You can go back in now."

"Thank you, Marcy." He grinned down at her and knew it for a mistake when he saw her pupils dilate. All too often, the opposite sex confused his friendliness for romantic interest.

"You seem really nice," she told him, sidling close. "I mean, most guys wouldn't spend all day in a hospital for a friend." Her expression seesawed between shy and predatory.

Here it comes, he thought.

"I like nice guys." She'd lowered her voice so her

colleagues at the nurses' station couldn't hear. "Do you...uh...do you want to exchange numbers?"

He'd learned long ago not to prevaricate. A woman on the prowl could be willfully dense about such things, especially a woman as attractive at Marcy who was used to men falling at her feet. "If I swung that way, Marcy, I'd totally take you up on your offer."

"Oh." She blinked as realization dawned. Then she turned toward Rusty's door, which she'd left slightly ajar. "Oh!" she said again, this time drawing the word out. "Everything makes sense now."

Instantly Ace realized his screwup. "No. That's not..." He shook his head. "I mean, it's not what you think. Rusty isn't—"

"Gotcha." Marcy winked and pantomimed zipping her lips. "Your secret is safe with me."

She turned and sashayed down the hall. Only after she'd wheeled her cart into another room did Ace pinch the bridge of his nose and indulge in a round of cussing. His colorful self-recriminations came to a sudden halt, however, when a snippet of conversation from inside Rusty's room reached his ears.

"Mom." Rusty spoke softly. "I'm glad I have you alone. There's something I want to tell you." When Rusty's voice cracked, Ace leaned closer to the door. He shouldn't be spying, but...

"What is it, sweetheart?"

"I'm scared, Mom." Rusty's throat sounded thick with tears, and Ace's breath wheezed from his lungs. Surely Rusty wasn't about to out himself. *Was* he?

"Scared of what, baby?"

"Scared if I tell you, then you won't—"

"Oh, Rusty, stop right there." Ace peeked through the door to see Sylvia sitting on the edge of Rusty's bed. She looked tiny compared to her son. Tiny and *strong* as she put her arms around Rusty and pulled him close. "There's nothing you could say that would ever make me stop loving you. You realize that, right?"

Ace clutched a hand to his chest, remembering his own coming-out and how horrible it had been. His father, who'd promised to love him no matter what, had flown into a rage, quoting scripture and damning him to hell. He wanted to burst through the door and tell Rusty to stop, to keep his mouth shut and preserve his relationship with his parents.

"Don't wanna disappoint you." Rusty's voice was hoarse with emotion.

"Oh, sweetheart. You could never disappoint me. *Never*."

"You say that, but you don't know." Ace couldn't see Rusty's face because Rusty had tucked it into his mother's neck. But he knew Rusty was crying. A lone sympathetic tear streaked hot and slick down his cheek.

"Just say it, Rusty baby." Sylvia rocked her child gently, giving strength and comfort in the way only a mother could. "I might already know."

Rusty pulled back, his eyes puffy and bloodshot. "Once I say it, I can't take it back."

Sylvia used her thumbs to brush away Rusty's tears. "Oh, my sweet boy. Don't you know? The truth will set you free."

Ace winced at the scripture.

"Mom…" Rusty's big hands came up to clutch at his mother's slender shoulders. "I'm gay."

Ace held his breath as those last two words hung in the air, pulsing like a heartbeat. It was the moment of truth, and he ached, *ached* for Rusty, hoping and praying Sylvia would come through as all mothers should.

Sylvia's smile was small and sweet. "Of course you are, sweetheart. Of course you are."

"I'm s-sorry, Mom," Rusty sobbed, his big shoulders shaking. Ace could feel his own sobs stuck in the center of his chest, rumbling like an earthquake.

"Don't be sorry, you big goof," Sylvia soothed. "There isn't a thing to be sorry about."

"But I know you think it's wrong. I know you think the Bible says—"

"Hush now," Sylvia cut him off. "The Bible says lots of things, and some of them are contradictory. But the one thing I know is God don't make mistakes. He certainly didn't make one when He created you."

Ace bawled like a baby now. *This* was how it was supposed to go. *This* was how a parent was supposed to react.

Sylvia continued to rock Rusty for a while. Then she said, "You know what I've prayed for every night since the day you were born? I've prayed for you to be happy. For you to find love and build a family of your own. It don't matter to me what form that family takes."

"But Dad, he—"

"Shh. Shh." She patted his shoulder. "Don't you worry about your father. I'll bring him around. Not that I think it'll take much. Up 'til you started dating girls in high school, we both had our suspicions."

"You did?" Rusty scrubbed his hands down his cheeks. "Why didn't you *say* anything?"

"Wasn't our place. It was *your* place to tell us if and when you thought the time was right."

Rusty dropped his mother's loving gaze and picked at the hospital sheet crumpled around his waist. "What did Dad think back then when you both suspected?"

"Oh, I mean, he wished it wasn't so." Rusty's face caved in on itself. "Stop that." Sylvia grabbed his chin and forced him to look at her. "He didn't wish it wasn't so because he thought it was wrong or wicked or any such thing. He wished it wasn't so because he didn't want you to suffer. Not everybody is nice about these things, you know. Your dad didn't want folks to be mean to you or make you feel like you were less than you are."

"I once heard him say something once about a *fuckin' fairy*." Rusty's voice choked on the words. "Why would he say that if he didn't think being gay was wrong?"

Sylvia sighed. "Blame it on our generation. We weren't raised in a PC world. We were brought up using ugly words, and we didn't know how destructive they could be. But tell me, have you heard him use language like that lately?"

"Not since I was little."

"There you go." She smiled. "Proof an old dog *can* be taught new tricks."

Rusty's laugh was garbled by his tears, but his smile was made all the sweeter for them. He pulled his mother into a hug so hard Ace feared for the woman's ribs.

After they drew apart, Sylvia said tentatively, "So? You and Ace?"

Ace stopped breathing, his ears straining toward Rusty's answer.

"I love him, Mom. I do. He's a good man."

"You don't gotta convince me, sweetheart. I've spent weeks getting to know him. I think you've made an excellent choice."

Ace's heart swelled. Here, *finally*, was acceptance he'd always longed for. The acceptance he'd never received from his own family or even from his own husband. Before he could stop himself, he burst through the door and blurted, "I love you too!"

Sylvia clutched her heart. "Dear Jesus! You scared the life out of me."

Ace didn't pay her any attention. His entire focus was on Rusty.

"You do?" Rusty's expression was so sweet and hopeful that Ace nearly broke down.

Luckily, he kept his shit together. "Of *course* I do."

Sylvia, obviously the most perceptive woman in the world, quietly got up from Rusty's hospital bed, indicating Ace should take her place.

He didn't waste a moment and flew to Rusty's side.

His heart was so full, he thought it a wonder it didn't burst like a balloon. Before he considered whether or not displays of affection were something Rusty was ready for—especially in front of the folks—he grabbed Rusty's face between his hands and kissed the man of his dreams with all his too-full heart.

After a minute, Sylvia cleared her throat. "Oooh, I can't wait to help plan the wedding."

Reluctantly, Ace pulled back from the kiss, seeing love—pure, true love—shining in Rusty's hazel eyes. He turned to inform Sylvia, "Your son doesn't believe in marriage, Mrs. Parker. He says it's an antiquated institution destined to fail."

Sylvia walked over and whacked Rusty upside the head.

"Ow, Mom!" Rusty rubbed his noggin. "What the hell? How can you hit a wounded man?"

"What's this claptrap about you not believing in marriage?"

Rusty frowned. "I was only making a point that fifty percent of them fail, and it's probably because they weren't supposed to last forty or fifty years. But…" He turned to Ace. His roguish smile nearly had Ace melting into a puddle on the floor. "I do like the idea of us being the exception to the rule. Don't you?"

With all the joy and pride and amazement inside him, Ace said two words he hoped to be repeating *legally* very soon. "I do."

Chapter 38

Black Knights Inc. Headquarters…

ANGEL SNAPPED A SALUTE TO MANUS CONNELLY, ONE OF THE four brothers who'd been manning BKI's front gate since long before Angel joined the ranks. It was a cool September afternoon, and Manus wore a red flannel shirt that made his hair look orange by contrast. The smattering of freckles across Manus's face stood out in sharp relief when the sun shone in through the open window of the gatehouse.

"You got company!" he called to Angel before hitting the switch that opened the giant wrought-iron gates.

The Black Knights' compound took up a full city block and was surrounded by ten-foot-high brick walls. Inside those walls, standing over three stories, was the old menthol cigarette factory that housed the shop where beautiful custom motorcycles were built, where an entire floor of loft-style bedrooms had once housed all the BKI operators, and where…until recently…the clandestine offices of the Black Knights were located. Beside the factory building squatted a little foreman's cottage, and at the back of the property were various outbuildings, some—like the weapons shed—useless now that BKI had gone civilian.

Angel took it all in at a glance and yelled at Manus above the idling rumble of Divinity's engine, "What do you mean? Who?"

His affiliation with the Black Knights was still hush-hush. Who would know to come looking for him—

His thoughts cut off, realization dawning at the same time Manus yelled back, "A Miss Sonya Butler! Becky took her out back! She's been waiting for the last thirty minutes and... Never mind! There they are!"

Heart in his throat, Angel looked toward the old factory. Sure enough, Becky and Sonya had come from the back courtyard via the side gate. Even from a distance, he was dumbstruck by Sonya's beauty.

Her golden hair gleamed in the sunlight, and the slight nip in the air had pinkened her cheeks. She wore painted-on jeans, a suede jacket, and stacked-heel boots that made her legs look about a mile long. The muscles in his arms twitched with the need to close around her. To feel her lush, feminine curves, to hold on to her woman's heat.

He hadn't realized how long he'd sat there until the gates began to close automatically, forcing Manus to hit the button again.

"What are you waitin' on?" Manus yelled.

"Sorry!" Angel waved an apologetic hand and twisted his wrist, gunning Divinity's engine. The motorcycle growled her pleasure at the influx of fuel and all too soon ate up the distance to the front of the factory building.

Becky cocked her head when he rolled to a stop beside them. "You should turn down your idle screw!" she yelled above the noise of the bike. "It's set too high!"

Ignoring her, he killed the motorcycle's engine, booted out the kickstand, and dismounted. Pulling off his helmet, he watched Sonya's eyes widen. "You're letting your hair grow out," she said.

Her voice hit his ears like an acoustic grenade, rattling his brain and making his breaths come hard and fast. How he'd *missed* the sound of her. The look of her. The feel of her. *Her*.

"You said I should." He was surprised at how calm his scratchy voice sounded, considering his insides were bouncing around like they were filled with grasshoppers.

When he'd left the hospital, he'd been determined to go see her. To pour out his heart and tell her all the things he'd wished he'd had the wherewithal to say a month ago. But now she stood in front of him, and he couldn't shake the feeling that it wouldn't matter what he said.

Maybe it was the look in her eyes, half sad and half resigned, but he got the distinct impression she'd come to say her goodbyes. His heart plummeted into his boots. He wanted to squeeze his eyelids closed to escape that look.

"I...um...just remembered I have something..." Becky's voice trailed off after she glanced back and forth between them. "I'm gonna go inside now," she finished feebly, spinning on her heel and disappearing into the shop.

After the door slammed behind her, Angel hooked his helmet over Divinity's handlebars and leaned back against her leather seat. Crossing his arms over his chest, hoping he looked far calmer than he felt, he let his eyes roam across Sonya's face. He memorized every feature, every tiny detail of how she looked right now, in this moment, in case this was the last time he would see her.

"You look good," he said. "Dismantling the world's worst criminal empire suits you."

"I'm not doing much now," she admitted. "Once

Zhao and I distributed the Intel, the government agencies and police units took over. They get the credit for bringing down Spider and his cronies."

"Still…" He nodded. "Quite a feather in your cap."

Her expression was tinged with something he couldn't quite define. "Are we really doing this? Standing here talking like strangers?"

He glanced down at his booted feet and let the smell of warm bricks baked in the sun and the fishy aroma of the Chicago River running behind the back of the property fill his nose. They were ordinary smells. Everyday smells. And yet…with Sonya at BKI, it was *far* from an ordinary day.

He wanted to rage at her, tell her he'd been young and dumb and full of grandiose ideas. He wanted to beg her to forgive him and promise he would never deceive her, never *leave* her again. But he'd said all that already. And it wasn't what had been keeping him awake at night.

Glancing into her beloved face, he offered a small, sad smile. "You know, I didn't realize that after everything I had done, after everything that had been done *to* me, that there was so little life left in me. Not until I saw you again. Then, it was like your life force came rushing into me, filling me up."

"Angel—" She tried to interrupt, but he stopped her by raising a hand.

"No. Before you say whatever it is you came to say, let me finish."

She nodded. One lock of hair fell over her shoulder and curled over the upper curve of her breast. He was jealous of that lock of hair. Jealous that it got to touch her, got to warm her, got to *be* with her. And how ridiculous was that? To be jealous of *hair*?

"I will spend the rest of my life regretting the decision I made ten years ago," he told her. "And I understand why you don't forgive me for it. I understand why you blame me for being too cowardly to look you up after I left Iran. I understand your hurt that I continued to deceive you even after I realized who you really worked for. I understand, Sonya. All of it. And I want you to know you're right to feel the way you do."

He glanced back down at his boots, heartbreak a living thing that chewed at his insides. "If you came to tell my goodbye, and that all those things are too much to overcome, then I understand that too."

"Angel—"

When she tried to interrupt again, he talked over her. "I want you to know I can live without you because I will never *really* be without you. You are a part of me now. The way you smell. The way you move. That firefly laugh of yours…so quick and bright. That day with you in Moldova was a precious gift. It made me feel more alive than I have in years, and I don't tell you this so you feel burdened by it. I tell you this to set you free, to let you know that all the good in me comes from you and is enough. It is enough to sustain me, Sonya."

Her eyes had filled with tears. Now two giant drops streaked down her satiny cheeks. He longed to brush them away, but he curled his hands into fists and stayed where he was.

For a long time she said nothing, simply stared at him. Then, finally, "My dad once told me that smart people move on from hurt like it's an exception, not a rule."

A brief flicker of something sparked to life inside him. He thought perhaps it was hope. "What are you…" He had to swallow. "What are you saying?"

She briefly closed her eyes, squeezing two more fat tears from between her lids. They caught the sunlight and glittered like diamonds. "I'm saying I understand why you made the choices you did. I'm saying…"

When she trailed off, he realized he'd been holding his breath so long his vision had tunneled. There was only her. Only Sonya. Nothing else existed in his world. "What, Sonya?" he begged. "What are you saying?"

"I'm saying I love you. I'm saying I've always loved you and *will* always love you and—"

He didn't realize his knees had buckled until he felt them smack into the concrete. He'd spent most of his adult life hiding his emotions, keeping his feelings locked behind thick fortifications, but now the dam burst and all the pain and rage, all the love and fear, all the longing and guilt came pouring out of him.

He didn't recognize the sound at the back of his throat. It was something a dying animal might make. And the tears… They were endless. No matter how quickly he wiped them away, more came. And then? Oh, and then Sonya, his dear, sweet, beautiful Sonya knelt in front of him and put her arms around him.

Her soft lips kissed his wet cheeks as her warmth flowed into him. It was a benediction. A baptism. Her love and forgiveness combined with his tears to wash him clean, and still he couldn't stop crying.

"Shhh, my love," she crooned, running her fingers through his hair.

At the endearment, one he hadn't heard in ten years,

he crushed her to him. Held her to his heart. Tried to braid her into his soul.

They both sobbed now. Both clung. Both whispered words of love and regret and absolution.

How was it possible to break apart and be made whole at the same time?

Chapter 39

"Mmm," Sonya murmured, smiling at the feel of Angel's lips soothing over the bite mark on her shoulder.

She barely remembered him herding her upstairs to his loft-style bedroom—although she had a vague recollection of the smiles on the faces of his colleagues when the two of them had run past. But one thing she'd never forget was the way he'd made love to her. Fast and frantic at first, then slow and steady until neither of them could hang on and they'd both had to let go.

Her body was a thing of liquid warmth now, sated and soothed. Her heart was a thing of hope and happiness, hot and full. And her mind? Well, that was pretty much mush. A couple soul-shaking orgasms did that to a gal.

Reaching back, she ran a hand over Angel's hip, feeling the scar that covered what used to be a beautiful birthmark. So many changes. The way he looked. The way he spoke. Even his name. And yet...beneath it all, he was still the man she loved.

It had taken her a while to reconcile the choice he'd made ten years ago. But working with Zhao Longwei to bring down Grafton, knowing she had done something to make the world a better place, a *safer* place, had helped her understand Angel. It took courage to answer the call of duty. Courage to give up your hopes and dreams for the greater good.

Was there a small piece of her that wished things

could have been different? Of course there was. There
always would be. But love was about sacrifice and compromise. It was about generosity and forgiveness. And
the truth was, she respected him for all he'd suffered,
all he'd forfeited. He'd been utterly selfless—and who
wouldn't love a man like that?

Plus, he looked hot on a motorcycle.

She thought back to the bike, its white fuel tank
painted with pearlescent angel's wings. Where most
motorcycles were chromed out, Angel's bike was
fitted with shiny gold gadgets. She didn't know much
about choppers, but she knew the front forks had been
stretched, knew the fawn-colored leather seat had been
hand-tooled. It was more a work of rolling art than any
true mode of transportation. Like the man who rode it, it
was almost too pretty to look at.

"I like your motorcycle," she said lazily as the setting
sun sent shafts of warm light in through the leaded-glass
window. It bathed them in its golden glow, dappling
their skin with moving masses of shadow and light.

"Divinity," he said from behind her, softly tracing
the heart-shaped mole above her right butt cheek. He'd
always had an affinity for the thing. "All Becky's bikes
have names."

"I like Becky. She seems like the kind of woman
who's allergic to drama."

"Hit the nail on the head there."

Since he'd brought up Becky…and, by association,
the rest of the Black Knights, she asked, "So what are
your plans now that BKI is simply a chopper shop and
not a cover for clandestine activities? Will you stay
on?" She tried to make the question sound casual, but

her breath strangled in her lungs as she waited on his answer. They'd waited ten years to be together, and if choosing him meant choosing his life in Chicago, she'd do it. But it would be hard. She *loved* her job at Interpol.

He pushed up on one elbow, a dark curl falling over his brow.

Oh, how she loved his hair. When he'd pulled off his helmet and she'd seen his dark, curly locks, she'd wanted to run over to him and feather her fingers through them. His hair and the pie wedge of warm chocolate brown in his otherwise coffee-colored eyes were little pieces of proof that the man forevermore known as Angel was also Mark Risa. She cherished those pieces.

"I guess that all depends on you," he said.

She couldn't help the smile that pulled at her lips. "That's a good answer."

"I want to spend the rest of my life with you." His expression was serious now. "I want to marry you and have little girls with bright firefly laughs and their mother's weakness for pink, sparkly fingernail polish."

To prove his point, he lifted her hand and kissed each of her fingertips. Since pink, sparkly fingernail polish didn't match the persona of a woman mourning a jewel-thief lover and pressed into the service of a crime boss, she'd gone the au-naturel route while working for Grafton. But the instant she'd been back inside her Paris apartment, she'd donned her signature color.

Her voice was breathless when she said, "You want to *marry* me?"

"Undoubtedly." He smiled that devastating smile. "For, oh, about ten years now."

"And what if we have little boys instead of little girls? Ever think of that?"

"Guess we will just have to keep trying for the little girls. What do you say? Will you spend the rest of your life with me making up for the decade we lost because I was young and dumb and—"

She shoved a finger over his lips. "And selfless and courageous and wonderful," she finished for him. "Yes, you fool. Of *course* my answer is yes!"

He kissed her then, kissed her with so much love and heat that soon they were panting and aching and hurrying to join together. As before, what started as frenetic and hasty soon slowed to soft and savoring.

After they'd pulled apart, lying on crumpled sheets, she hesitantly mentioned, "I told my boss about you." He stiffened beside her, and she realized her mistake. "No. Not *all* about you. Only that you were a good agent. That you helped me with Grafton. And that you might be looking for a job soon. There's an opening in Interpol's Paris office…"

She let the sentence dangle. Even though he'd said his future depended on her, she didn't want to force him into anything.

"And Zhao Longwei would hire me? Just like that?"

"He says my vouching for you is all it'll take. Well…" She bit her lip and grinned at him. "That, and you'll have to learn French."

"I already know French."

"You do?"

"Sure. *Voulez-vous coucher avec moi ce soir?*"

She laughed. "Do you know any French *besides* what you learned from Lady Marmalade?"

He nuzzled her shoulder. "You will have to teach me."

"Is that a yes? You'll come with me to Paris?"

"From here on out, I promise to follow you anywhere. Besides, I like Paris. And this way...we'll *always* have Paris."

She hugged him close, loving the feel of his hard chest against her breasts, his crinkly man hair and his heat. *Mr. Tall, Dark, and Delicious,* she thought. *Mr. Tall, Dark, and* Mine.

"I like the way you say it," she told him. "Bogart's got nothing on you, babe."

"So true," he rumbled in that scratchy voice that would always remind her of all he'd suffered, all he'd sacrificed. Then, he caught her lips in a kiss that turned from sweet to hungry. When she felt him swell against her hip, she pulled back.

"Three times in one afternoon?"

"We have ten years to catch up on."

"So true." She parroted his words at the same time her stomach rumbled loudly.

He lifted an eyebrow. "Hungry?"

She made a face of regret. "I'm starving, but... Hey! Where are you going?"

He'd hopped out of bed and yanked on his jeans. She admired the hard curves of his naked ass before they disappeared under the denim. "Down to the kitchen." He winked at her and lowered his voice to a seductive growl. "To get the chocolate syrup."

Epilogue

Four months later...

"THAT MAN HAD A DEEP STREAK OF LONELY UNTIL YOU CAME along, *mon ami*."

Rusty turned to Rock, who'd sidled up beside him. Then he looked across the expanse of BKI's shop floor at his husband, who sipped a Goose Island IPA and laughed at something Becky said.

Yes, that's correct. *Husband*. Rusty was still getting used to that word.

I have a husband! I have a husband*!*

"You could say the same for me," he told Rock, taking a sip of his beer. It was the first time he'd had alcohol since being released from the hospital, and he felt its effects. Of course, if ever there was an occasion to get a little tipsy—or a *lot* tipsy?—it was at your own wedding.

The BKI crew had cleared the shop floor of equipment and motorcycles and festooned the huge space with bunting and balloons and paper lanterns in all the shades of the rainbow. Rusty had teased Ace and his mother, who'd conspired together to plan the wedding, about being a little too *on the nose* with the color scheme. Both of them had insisted it was the only way to go. Rusty was *out*, and it was a *celebration!*

Confetti littered the concrete floor. The folding chairs and wedding altar that had been used during the ceremony had since been shoved back against the walls. And the sugary smell of the decimated wedding cake competed with the familiar Black Knights Inc. aromas of grease guns and coffee.

Rusty thought it was perfect, and his heart glowed with so much happiness he was surprised light wasn't streaming out of his orifices.

"Thank you for playing and singing during the ceremony," he told Rock. "You have a beautiful voice, and I know it meant a lot to Ace."

"My pleasure," Rock drawled. "I'm just sorry this damn blizzard meant the party got cut short."

Rusty glanced at the huge leaded-glass windows on the north wall and saw the flurry of snowflakes battering themselves against the panes. He shrugged. "That's the risk you run when you plan a January wedding in Chicago. Besides, the party's still going." He motioned with his hand around the room.

Mac and Delilah cuddled on the old leather couch shoved beneath the base of the metal stairs. They shared a glass of champagne and whispered in each other's ears while their big, goofy yellow Lab—who sported a rainbow bow tie for the occasion—snored loudly at their feet. Zoelner and Chelsea stood over by the dessert table, feeding each other wedding cake between sweet, laughing kisses. And Wild Bill and Eve shared the dance floor with Ghost and Ali and Dan and Penni.

The three couples swayed slowly to the soft music coming from the small sound system Rusty had rented for the occasion—the only detail of the wedding Ace and his mother had allowed him to have a say in. A plastic baby monitor hung from a carabiner clipped to a belt loop on Dan's suit pants and a matching one hung from a string around Ghost's wrist. Ali had delivered a healthy baby girl two weeks ago, and they'd put her and her older sister to bed upstairs soon after the ceremony. Same for Dan and Penni and their little bundle of joy, Cora May, as well as Snake and Michelle's two sons.

When the blizzard had hit earlier, and after Rusty and Ace had called cabs for the rest of their guests, the Black Knights along with their children had decided to spend the night at the shop in their old rooms. They didn't want to stop celebrating with Ace and Rusty.

And what a celebration it was. So much dancing and singing and good-hearted ribbing and drinking and—

"Your folks make it to their hotel okay?" Rock asked.

Rusty patted the breast pocket on his suit jacket where his cell phone rested close to his heart. "Texted and said they're snug as bugs in a rug."

He smiled when he thought back on the look of sheer joy on his mother's face when he and Ace had said their *I do's*. His smile widened when he remembered the way his father had shaken Ace's hand afterward, dragging Ace close and threatening to cut off Ace's balls if Ace ever hurt Rusty.

"Rock, baby." Vanessa, Rock's fiancée, snagged Rock's arm and gifted him with a siren's smile. "Take me to bed, or lose me forever."

"Don't gotta ask me twice, *ma petite*. Lead the way."

"Beautiful ceremony, by the way," Vanessa told Rusty. He nodded and winked at her. "You're next."

"I know! And Rock's driving me crazy with wedding plans." She slid Rock a sidelong glance and leaned in to mock-whisper. "How did you stand Ace these last few months? I swear, Rock is a groomzilla!"

"A word of advice?"

"I'm all ears."

"Let him have his way." He gave her a conspiratorial wink. "He'll thank you for it in the most...*pleasurable* ways imaginable."

Rock grinned and pulled Vanessa toward the staircase. "Sound advice," he told her. "Sound advice indeed."

"Wait a minute!" Becky called when she saw the couple headed for the stairs. "You two can't go to bed yet. Frank and I haven't made our big announcement!"

After the guests had left, Becky had told the gathered group that she and Boss had something important to discuss with them later on. Rusty glanced down at his watch. It was 11:54 p.m. He supposed that qualified as "later on."

"Let me guess," Vanessa said. "You're finally pregnant?"

"Well, yes," Becky said impatiently. "But that's not our big announcement and—"

"What?" Boss thundered, his craggy face draining of color as he stared down at his tiny, blond-haired wife who, for once, wasn't wearing coveralls covered in grease. Quite the opposite, tonight Becky had on a royal-blue cocktail dress and six-inch stilettos that still only raised the top of her head to Boss's shoulder. "You're pregnant?"

Becky blushed and caught her bottom lip between her teeth. "I took the test this morning, and I was gonna surprise you with it tonight, but it just sorta slipped out and—"

That's all she managed before Boss whooped and

lifted her into the air, spinning her around. When Boss finally set her back on her feet, he laid a kiss on her that was so deep and passionate that more than one person in the room felt the need to clear their throat.

"Oh, for the love of Paul Konerko," Emily complained, looping her arm through Christian's. The Brit looked dapper, as always, in a tailored Hugo Boss suit. Emily looked pretty spiffy, too, in a red knee-length slip dress. She'd deigned to put away her yoga pants and ratty sweatshirts for the occasion. "You two keep that up for much longer, and I'm gonna need to bleach my eyeballs."

"Oh, let them have their fun, darling." Christian hugged her close. His English accent made the last word sound more like *dahling*. "It's not every day a bloke learns he's going to be a father." He looked meaningfully at Emily. Just last week *they* had announced they were expecting a bouncing baby boy sometime around the first of June.

"Knew you had it in you, partner." Mac had risen from the sofa to slap a hand against Boss's back.

Then everyone crowded around Becky and Boss to offer their congratulations. The dog, excited by the activity, raced around the group, barking happily, his tail whacking people on the backs of the knees and making them wince.

Rusty saw Sonya hold back from the celebrating group. As the newest member of BKI's tight-knit assemble, she still wasn't confident in her place. He wrapped an arm around her shoulders, understanding what it was to be the odd man out. He wanted to assure her that to love a Black Knight was to *become* a Black Knight. "I'm so glad you and Angel made the trip from Paris. It's a long flight, and I know how busy you both are."

"Angel wouldn't have missed this for the world." When she grinned up at him, Rusty understood why Angel was crazy about her. There was goodness in her eyes and sweetness in her smile. Both proved that beneath her tough Interpol agent exterior lay a heart of gold.

Of course, he would always think he and Ace had the most epic love story of all time. But he could admit that maybe Angel's and Sonya's came in a close second.

"Hey!" Ozzie yelled around the clamor of voices. "Quiet down everybody! I have it. Becky, if it's a boy, you two should name him Jedediah Isaac."

"What?" Becky wrinkled her nose, sharing a look of confusion with Boss. "Why?"

"Because then he'll be Jed I. Knight." Ozzie mimed a three-beat drum solo. "Bah-dum-tiss."

Everyone groaned as Steady Soto and his pretty wife, Abby, emerged from the hall leading to the kitchen. Given Steady's disheveled hair and Abby's kissed-off lipstick, there wasn't much question what they'd been up to. "What'd we miss?" Steady asked.

"Becky's pregnant!" Emily announced, doing a happy dance complete with finger guns. "*Finally!*"

Steady and Abby cheered, and the excited questions and raunchy jokes about Boss's aging pistol still having a few rounds left started up again. Then the alarm on Boss's watch went off. He glared down the thing as if it'd personally offended him.

"Well, shit." He raked a hand through his hair. "I'd hoped to run all this by you guys before they arrived, but

I didn't want to fuck up Ace and Rusty's big day. Then I was having so much fun that time slipped away."

"Maybe they won't come." Becky glanced out the windows at the swirling snow. "Maybe the blizzard kept them away."

"Hope so." Boss made a face. "Didn't realize everyone would be staying over when I extended the invitation. Where the hell are they gonna sleep?"

"We'll put them in the foreman's cottage," Becky patted his arm reassuringly. "There's the sofa and the blowup mattresses and—"

"Excuse me," Ozzie interrupted. "Run all *what* by us?"

Boss didn't answer. He simply stomped over to the far wall where Becky usually kept one of her rolling tool chests. After hitting the big red button affixed to the bricks, a beeping sound had everyone turning to the opposite wall.

"What in the world?" Sonya murmured from beside Rusty, her eyes wide as a section of the wall slowly slid open. Two seconds ago it had been a seamless brick expanse. Now, it revealed a growing black hole.

"It's the Bat Cave," Rusty told her.

"Bat cave?" She blinked in disbelief.

"I'll explain it to her." Angel appeared beside them. He disdainfully tossed Rusty's arm from around Sonya's shoulders, the look on his face saying *Get your own*.

Rusty chuckled and stepped aside. Angel was a smidge proprietary when it came to Sonya. Okay, so maybe more than a smidge.

Feeling a warm, familiar hand slide into his, Rusty smiled over at his husband. *Husband! I have a husband!*

"Any clue what's going on?" he whispered from the side of his mouth.

"Not one." Ace shook his head.

Together they watched as the wall continued to slide on hidden tracks, the black hole getting larger and larger until the smell of damp concrete filled the shop. For a while, there seemed to be a whole lot of nada in the Bat Cave. Then, squinting, Rusty was able to pick up movement. Within five seconds, six men appeared out of the gloom to stand in the opening. They all wore cargo pants and combat boots. Army green duffel bags hung from their hands and from around their shoulders.

Rusty recognized their hip-shot stances and the looks on their faces. Looks of intelligence mixed with the kind of toughness and stoicism that only came about after a person had danced with the devil too many times to count. To a man, they were military, certainly. Spec ops most likely.

Rusty looked over at Ace and raised a questioning brow. Ace shook his head.

"The president of the United States has realized there are certain things she needs accomplished that can't be done using traditional forces," Boss announced.

Ozzie snorted. "No shit, Sherlock. Only took her a year to figure that one out?"

"She contacted me yesterday to ask if BKI would act as the cover for the group of operators she's hand-picked." Boss ignored Ozzie. "Told her I couldn't make any promises. Said I needed to talk to you guys first. She agreed but also suggested we meet her men before making our decision. So here they are." Boss waved a hand toward the group still standing silently at the mouth of the tunnel.

In typical BKI fashion all hell broke loose. Everyone starting asking questions at once.

"Sorry!" Becky called to the newcomers as the sound system flipped from a slow dance to a much more upbeat Selena Gomez tune. "Family meeting! We'll be right with you!"

After a few minutes, it became clear that the question at the forefront of everyone's mind was what, exactly, the president expected of the original Black Knights.

"She says we don't have to play any role if we don't want to," Boss told them. "And even if we *do* want to, she wants us to limit ourselves to mission support. Make no mistake, ladies and gentleman, the torch has been passed. What we have to decide is do we want to provide the cover for that torch."

There was silence following that proclamation, but Rusty knew what the Knights' answer would be before any of them opened their mouths. They were patriots, one and all, and when their country needed them, they wouldn't ignore the call.

"Of course we'll help," Ozzie said.

A soft chorus of agreement ran through the group and then everyone turned toward the newcomers only to discover that Peanut, BKI's on-site mascot, a fat, ragged tomcat that wasn't good for anything but eating and mischief, sashayed toward the arrivals.

Apparently, the tom wasn't one for weddings. He'd been hiding since the Knights cleared out the shop and began decorating. Even the buffet table hadn't been enough to coax him out from beneath the sofa.

Now, however, in typical cat fashion, he wound his rotund self around and between the legs of the men still standing inside the mouth of the tunnel, smelling their shoes and bags. Once satisfied he'd thoroughly investigated them, he flopped down on the floor, lifted a leg over his head, and started gratuitously cleaning his balls.

Boss threw an arm around Becky's shoulders and laughed. "Welcome to Black Knights Inc., gentlemen!"

Acknowledgments

Living and writing in the Black Knights Inc. world for six years has been a dream come true. Not always unicorn farts, rainbows, and puppies, mind you. There have been challenges and setbacks and frustrations. But that's the nature of creation; triumph and tribulation go hand in hand. The truth is, I wouldn't change any of it, and I have so many people to thank for putting up with me along the way.

Without further ado...

Thank you to my husband. Sweetheart, I know you had no clue what you were in for when I came to you and said I wanted to be a writer. You didn't know about the late nights I'd be spending at my PC when deadlines loomed and copyedits were due. You didn't know about the weeks I'd be away from home at conferences, signings, and writing retreats. You didn't know about all the publicity that would interfere with dinner dates and movie nights and so much more. Never once have you complained. Your support throughout this process has been remarkable and unassailable. I *love* you. Period. End of sentence.

Thanks so much to the folks at Sourcebooks. From the first title to this last title, you've all worked so hard to make BKI the best it can be. I bless the day I made Sourcebooks my writing home and the folks there in Naperville my writing family. The future looks bright!

As always, a *huge shout-out* to my agent, the amazing Nicole Resciniti. Nic, you believed in this project when it was a just a couple of sample chapters and a grand plan percolating in my head. Then you made other people believe in it too. Couldn't have done it without you, babe. Cheers to you!

And last but certainly not least, hugs and kisses to all the fans for coming with me on these wild and crazy adventures. Thanks to all of you, the guys and gals of BKI will live on. And remember…twist your wrist, keep your knees in the breeze, and RIDE ON!

About the Author

Julie Ann Walker has saved the world. Or…at least the characters in her books have. In real life, Julie prefers vino over villains, baked goods over bullets, and massages over missions, so she gets her international intrigue fix by writing romantic suspense novels that have been described as "alpha, edgy, and downright hot." A *New York Times* and *USA Today* bestselling author, Julie enjoys riding her bicycle along Chicago's lakeshore, fishing with her father, and going to baseball games with her husband, a self-confessed diehard Cubs fan. To stay up-to-date with Julie's upcoming releases, sign up for her newsletter at julieannwalker.com.

BLACK KNIGHTS INC.

These elite ex-military operatives are as unique and tough as their custom-made Harleys

By Julie Ann Walker, *New York Times* and *USA Today* bestselling author

Wild Ride

Former Navy SEAL Ethan "Ozzie" Sykes is the hero everyone's been waiting for. When he's stuck distracting reporter Samantha Tate, he quickly loses his desire to keep her at bay…

Fuel for Fire

Spitfire CIA agent Chelsea Duvall has always had a thing for bossy, brooding covert operative Dagan Zoelner. It's just as well that he's never given her a second look, since she carries a combustible secret about his past that threatens to torch their lives…

Hot Pursuit

Former SAS officer and BKI operator Christian Watson has fought for his life before. Doing it with the beautiful, bossy former CIA operative Emily Scott in tow is another matter entirely.

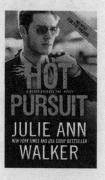

Built to Last

Jamin "Angel" Agassi is a spec-ops virtuoso whose cover can't be broken. That is, until he encounters Interpol agent Sonya Butler—the one woman who knows everything about him.

EVERY DEEP DESIRE

First in a sultry, swampy romantic suspense series
from author Sharon Wray

Rafe Montfort was a decorated Green Beret, the best of the
best, until a disastrous mission and an unforgivable betrayal
destroyed his life. Now, this deadly soldier has returned
to the sultry Georgia swamps to reunite with his Beret
brothers—as well as the love he left behind—and take back
all he lost. But Juliet must never know the truth behind
what he's done…or the dangerous secret that threatens to
take him from her forever.

For more Sharon Wray, visit:
sourcebooks.com

I AM JUSTICE

First in an action-packed, band of sisters romantic suspense series from award-winning debut author Diana Muñoz Stewart

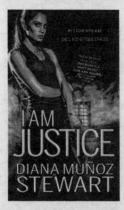

Justice Parish takes down bad guys. Rescued from a brutal childhood and adopted into the wealthy Parish family, Justice wants payback. She's targeted a sex-trafficking ring in the Middle East. She just needs a cover so she can get close enough to take them down…

Sandesh Ross left Special Forces to found a humanitarian group, but saving the world isn't cheap. Enter Parish Industries and limitless funding, with one catch—their hot, prickly "PR specialist," Justice.

"High-octane and sexy, this book is a must-read!"

—Julie Ann Walker, *New York Times* and *USA Today* bestselling author of the Black Knights Inc. series

For more Diana Muñoz Stewart, visit:
sourcebooks.com

SURVIVE THE NIGHT

Third in the thrilling Rocky Mountain K9 Unit series

K9 Officer Otto Gunnersen has always had a soft spot for anyone in need—but for all his big heart, he's never been in love. Until he meets Sarah Clifton.

All Sarah wants is to escape, but there's no outrunning her past. Her power-mad brother would hunt her to the ends of the earth...but he'd never expect her to fight back. With Otto by her side, Sarah's finally ready to face whatever comes her way.

"Vivid and charming."

—Charlaine Harris, #1 *New York Times* bestselling author

RUNNING THE RISK

Second in the pulse-pounding Endgame Ops series
by rising star Lea Griffith

Jude Dagan's life as he knew it ended a year ago. On a
mission gone wrong, he was forced to watch as Ella
Banning, the only woman he's ever loved, was killed. Or
so he thought...

Survival is crucial. Trust is optional.
Love is unstoppable.

"Immediately engaging... This is one terrific tale of
romantic suspense!"

**—*RT Book Reviews* for *Flash of Fury*, 4.5 Stars,
TOP PICK**

For more Lea Griffith, visit:
sourcebooks.com

Also by Julie Ann Walker

Black Knights Inc.

Hell on Wheels

In Rides Trouble

Rev It Up

Thrill Ride

Born Wild

Hell for Leather

Full Throttle

Too Hard to Handle

Wild Ride

Fuel for Fire

Hot Pursuit

The Deep Six

Hell or High Water

Devil and the Deep